La Vie, According to Rose

LAUREN PARVIZI

Published by Lake Union Publishing, Seattle

www.apub.com

ISBN-13: 9781662509858 (paperback)
ISBN-13: 9781662509865 (digital)

Cover design and illustration by Kimberly Glyder

Printed in the United States of America

For Matteo, you were born and so was this book.
Dreams do come true.

1

A flight to Paris from SFO at the end of July cost $1,300. High this year. I wrote down the number in my worn Moleskine notebook.

Recording fares felt like writing in code. A diary with nothing but numbers and dates spelling out my secret hope. The notebook had become sacred, a place to go when work and family and memories of Dad were both too much and too little, proof that escape was a plane ride away.

In the beginning, I'd tracked fares to all sorts of major cities—Istanbul, Dublin, Prague, Stockholm, Barcelona—but eventually I chose Paris. If I could have one trip, that's where I would go.

The City of Light.

What a cliché, right? Sad, single, unsatisfied woman goes to Paris and finds joy, passion, herself. But the cliché was kind of the point. Who didn't want a happy ending?

I tucked my Moleskine back into the wicker bookcase where I'd kept it since college and abandoned the cocoon of my living room for the kitchen. The rich scent of sautéed onions and garlic filled the space. The smell always made me think of Dad standing at the stove wearing his PERSIAN RICE, RICE BABY apron we'd gifted him for Christmas one year. Mom still had it hanging in her kitchen, the fabric stained with yellow splotches of saffron and tomato spatters faded pink.

I pulled off my own apron and peeked in the oven. I was ready. Or as ready as I could be.

Another sister-mom Sunday brunch was underway—the time of week when we all came together *no matter what*.

Iris called it "Brunch and Bitch." Lily called it "Brunch for Bitches." Either name made Mom cringe: "Do you need to throw around the B-word like that? Can you imagine what your father would say if he heard the way you all talk these days?"

Mom constantly conjured Dad's memory, reminding us how to live in his image. Except what else could we do but imagine? He'd been gone our entire adult lives. Pancreatic cancer out of nowhere. As fast as it was fierce. And somehow twelve years had passed. Which was how long it felt like I'd been trying—and failing—to get out of brunch.

I leaned against the counter and inhaled deeply, as if I could breathe him back to life, or at least savor my final moments of peace before my thoughts were smothered by the arrival of the other Zadeh women.

At the sound of the doorbell, I clicked on the coffeepot and hurried to greet them before they started banging down the door.

Mom entered like a blonde dervish, her polka-dot skirt whirling as she examined my apartment. She pointed to a recessed bulb in the kitchen. "You haven't fixed the light. It's like a cave in here."

"I need a ladder. I'm waiting to hear from the landlord."

"For the record, this is why I keep saying you should move in with me. No landlords. And you'd have your dear old mother for company." She pulled me in for a squeeze and a big peck on my cheek, and for a half second I let myself be held by her soft, comforting form.

"Us single ladies have to stick together," she said, and I pushed away from her, my blood beginning to simmer.

I hid my defensiveness with an indifferent shrug and fussed with a platter of fruit, tucking mint leaves beneath a mound of nuts and feta cheese. "I'm not lonely."

I *liked* living by myself. At least, most of the time.

This was the first place that had ever been mine alone, and I loved my old brocade chair, my overfilled bookshelves, my potted ficus I called FiFi, my print of Renoir's *Bal du moulin de la Galette* in a two-dollar flea market frame.

And if sometimes there wasn't enough air in the room, in all the apartment even, and I had to race from my chair to the window, press my mouth against the screen to gulp the bare evening breeze, that wasn't because I was lonely. In the middle of a sprawling suburbia like San Jose, even an oasis could be suffocating.

A minute later, Iris trailed Mom inside, lugging two cumbersome boxes and an armful of bulging canvas totes. She slipped off a pair of bright-white sneakers, and her shiny raisin-brown hair bounced against her fitted cardigan buttoned to the neck despite the heat. Iris taught kindergarten, but she carried herself like a flight attendant, calm and in control, never so much as a chipped nail. I couldn't say the same about myself. Sometimes I forgot to brush my hair. One time I drove all the way to work before I realized I was still wearing my slippers.

"Rose, can you please help?" Iris said.

I reached for one of the boxes and led the way into the living room, which was mercifully bright thanks to a ray of summer-morning sunlight.

Iris set the rest of her supplies on the floor and nodded. "This will work."

"You agree, right?" Mom said to Iris. "Moving in with me makes sense. Think of the moola she'd save."

"I'm not broke. I have a job. I have some savings." There was no way I was going to move in with Mom, not if I could help it. But the closer we got to Iris's wedding, the more often she brought up the topic. I made a mental note to brag about a raise once I finally got my promotion. Any day now—fingers crossed.

"She's only thirty-two," Iris said. "She's not ready to throw in the towel and live with her mother." To me, she mouthed *Sorry* and rolled her eyes in solidarity.

"Eventually, though. When her lease runs out."

"It's month to month," I said.

Mom sat down on the couch, tucked her feet beneath her skirt. "Is Lily here yet?"

Iris snorted in amusement. "Has she ever been on time? The girl is always late."

"No one is *always* anything."

Iris and I exchanged a look. Mom complained all the time about Lily's tardiness but prickled if we dared to agree. Which was so Mom, our walking contradiction. Part-time energy healer with fake nails and impeccable makeup. Raised in a conservative Christian family but married to an agnostic Iranian immigrant and self-described as "intensely spiritual." *I was born again, alright. The day I became Alice Zadeh,* she liked to say. A pink and fuzzy peach of a woman who raised three daughters with light brown skin and dark brown hair. In the sun, she roasted while we toasted to the color of dates. "Beautiful," she called us. She was also the first to point out when our eyebrows grew too close together, or our hair looked greasy, or our pants fit too tight.

Now she homed in on Iris. "Are you flushed? I hope you're not overdoing it for the wedding."

"I've never felt better," Iris said.

I flicked on the overhead fan. "It's warm in here."

"Hmm." Mom sounded unconvinced. "It's July. It's always hot in July. I know the difference between a heat flush and a fatigue flush."

"I'm pretty sure I know how to manage my health," Iris said. "I've been dealing with it my entire life."

Iris had been playing Whac-A-Mole with mysterious symptoms since forever. The doctors guessed an autoimmune issue, but she'd never been properly diagnosed, not since childhood, when she had her first health scare and the bottom dropped out of our family for the first time. The second time was when Dad died. We didn't talk about it, but we were all holding our breath for disaster number three and handling our uncertainty in different ways. That's probably why Iris was such a control freak—she had to be to stay functional. The thought slapped my heart awake and left a pain lodged between my ribs for my younger sister, sturdy as a hardback book despite repeated kicks to her spine.

"She's okay, Mom," I said. I looked at Iris. "You'd tell us if you weren't, right?"

She gave me a tight-jawed look, nonverbal sister-speak for *Don't egg her on*. I raised my hands in apology and fled to the kitchen.

"Hello?" I heard Lily's voice and found her in the entryway.

She wore slouchy sweatpants, a ragged, cropped T-shirt, and flip-flops, and somehow looked better than me on my best day. I would have killed for her long, wavy mane instead of mine, which never grew as long or dark and didn't so much curl but frizz like a sweater run through the dryer too many times. She was tall and slender, and even though everyone said we sisters all had the same oval eyes, hers lifted to the edges of her face while mine and Iris's sat too scrunched to our noses to be remarkable.

Lily's kind of beauty couldn't be made under, but plum-colored circles sat beneath her eyes like she hadn't slept. She chewed the inside of her lip.

"Are you feeling okay?"

She glowered at me. "Are we having mimosas?"

"No. Were we supposed to?"

"A girl can dream."

She was probably hungover.

From the living room, Mom called, "Are we eating? Or should I break out my CBD mints?"

Lily rolled her eyes. Her gaze landed on the dish in my hands. She grimaced. "Quiche."

"It's *kuku sabzi.*" I failed to add that I'd been laboring over it for two hours, chopping the herbs by hand like Dad had done, cooking it first on the stove, careful not to let it get too dark, before popping the whole pan in a low-temp oven so that it could heat through gently.

She raised a hand as if to say, *Whatever.* "So quiche with herbs, right? Yay," she said, and skulked into the living room.

"Yay," I mimicked. But my sarcasm needed work. I sounded like I meant it.

❦

Every week, I fantasized about putting my foot down. A Sunday to myself—to cook something entirely new, to drive into San Francisco and wander the latest exhibition at the Legion of Honor, to nestle among a stack of books in a creaky corner of Green Apple with a paperback—was that so much to ask? No judgy commentary about my dating life. No guilt trips from Mom. No family obligations, period. But there was always a reason why I couldn't skip brunch.

Backing out this week would have been impossible.

We usually met at Village Diner in Campbell, but Iris was getting married at the end of September, and we needed to work on wedding decor: colorful paper flowers and hundred-foot-long paper chains to drape above the tables. Iris and Ben shared a studio, Lily lived with her bro-fest boyfriend, Dev, and Mom pounced on any excuse to come over. That left hostess extraordinaire, yours truly.

"Breakfast is served." I set down a platter of fruit, sliced the *kuku* into wedges, and plated a piece for Mom. *"Nooshe jan!"*

Mom nibbled at a bite before popping the forkful into her mouth. She swallowed and went back for more. "Oh, Rose, it's delicious. Tastes just like Dad's. You've really nailed it."

"You think he'd like it?"

"He'd love it," she said, with her mouth full.

"What does that mean again?" Iris asked. "Noosh whatever?"

I frowned. None of us could speak Farsi, but I at least tried to remember the few phrases Dad liked to use. "Bon appétit," I said mostly to myself. Iris had already moved on to her artistic vision, describing the proper way to cut the flower petals, the exact length of each loop on the garland.

"I still can't believe you're getting married." Lily grabbed a pair of scissors and settled beside Iris. "P.S. I need your input. This girl at work is driving me nuts. It's a juice bar *on campus* and she acts like we're running a Michelin-starred restaurant. Hello, it's seven a.m., I can't even deal with your drama right now. I'm trying to finish my degree, not perfect my juicing skills, you know?"

I was four years older than Iris, but Lily went to her for advice, and me for help. Sometimes hanging out with my twentysomething sisters made me feel like I was an out-of-touch *Cosmo* article from a decade ago—amusing, maybe, but not very relevant.

I tuned out the conversation and reminded myself that soon they'd be gone, and with them the confetti bits of paper littering my floor, the constant chatter pecking at my ears. I would return to my regularly scheduled programming, which wasn't exactly the sophisticated affair I fantasized about but a standing date with my computer. I had at least three hours' worth of copy to write and revise before this week's brand relaunch. I'd work until my eyes bled if it finally got me the content lead position.

Mom grabbed my shoulder, startling me back to the room.

"I can't believe I almost forgot to tell you." Her eyes were quarter size. "A mouse! A live mouse in my kitchen last night. I kid you not, I nearly fainted. If I had, who would have helped me? I could have hit my head on the counter and died. Who would have found me?"

"Well, us, presumably," Lily said, unwilling to take the bait.

"And when might that have happened? I'll tell you when, after my corpse had gone cold."

"That's a little extreme." Iris twisted her glue stick like a tube of lipstick.

I could feel Mom's focus shift to me. I kept my eyes on my scissors, trimming the edges of a petal.

"Iris is getting married. Lily is next, and at some point, she'll finish her degree and get a real job, and she won't have time for me anymore. I want my daughters to thrive, I do . . ." Mom trailed off. "I guess I'll have Rose. You won't leave me."

A large stone settled in my throat and slunk its way down my windpipe. I took a shallow breath but couldn't speak. Bits of pale pink paper fell to my feet.

When I didn't respond, she added, "But you work all the time. Like your father. Work comes first."

"That's not true." I may have inherited Dad's mildly masochistic work ethic, but he always put family first, and so did I.

"Nothing is more important than family. We're all we have. That's what your father said, didn't he?"

"Yes." The stone was heavy on my lungs. Unless it wasn't a stone at all, but a heavy hand wringing out each lobe, one by one, like a sponge.

"You know one great thing about my condo?" she said, her mood shifting without warning. "Room for two!"

"Mom, I appreciate the offer, I do—"

"I know, I know, but I'm lonely without someone else around. All this time without your father, and I'm still not comfortable living alone. Humans are social creatures. I need people. My people."

Was *this* my future? I saw a Venn diagram of my life and Mom's, her circle slowly encroaching on mine until she consumed me like an insatiable Ms. Pac-Man.

She continued, "Can you at least help me find someone to take care of the pest problem? I'm terrible with that stuff."

"An exterminator?"

"Sure, but someone humane."

Lily cackled.

“No problem,” I lied.

“That reminds me,” Iris said. “Is it cool if I leave these here?” She gestured at the growing pile of decorations. “Our place is stuffed with wedding favors and vases and candles and whatever else. It’s out of control. I think Ben might call the whole thing off if I bring more home.”

I studied the living room, trying to imagine where they could possibly fit. I’d have to line up the boxes in the hallway. I’d be tripping over them for the next two months, but I couldn’t refuse a wedding request.

“Sure.”

Iris smiled and tipped her head toward mine, cupped her hand over her mouth. “I’d leave them with Mom, but you know she’d set something heavy on them or start using them to fill her vases.”

“I heard that,” Mom said, but she didn’t protest.

“Rose!” Iris wrenched the pink paper from my fingertips. “What happened?”

The petal had become a sliver, cut within an inch of its life.

2

The airy, industrial floor the Genomix content team occupied reeked of coffee and popcorn and something alarmingly savory. The combination raked the back of my throat. Dozens of open cubicles revealed empty chairs and an endless number of tchotchkes. A screen saver flashed a cartoon devil holding a sign that read CONTENT IS CORPORATE. The whoosh of cold air from the AC sent a shiver down my back.

As I neared my pod of desks, I could see Aidan hovering over my filing cabinet, typing into his phone with a lasered focus verging on maniacal. I threw back my shoulders and plastered on a docile smile.

"Morning, Aidan. Happy Monday." I proffered a plastic tub in his direction. "Cookie? There's chocolate chip or *nan-e berenji*. It's a rice flour cookie with rose water. But don't worry. It's not super floral." Sunday had ended with an anxiety baking marathon. *Nan-e berenji* was the only Persian cookie I could make edible. Aidan stopped pacing, peered into the bin, and wrinkled his nose, batting the morsels away like flies.

"Look at this." Settling on my desk, he shoved a sheath of papers into my hand. "A typo. A typo! In the lede of the press release."

"What did Kara say?"

"She said, and this is a quote, 'I'm going cross-eyed. What do you want from me?'"

"I can hear you." Kara, our copyeditor, popped up from her desk a dozen feet away. She was pint-size with bleached-blonde hair, her pale pink skin a perfect match for the peach Crayola color that never quite fit my own olive hue, a difference that in elementary school left me shy around other girls.

But Kara's natural looks belied her dark vibe. Two parts Daria and one part Eeyore, she dressed like a '90s goth chick going to a funeral. She was a nonconformist, and she wanted you to know it. In other words, we couldn't have been more different. That's why we worked so well together. I was the content editor, so technically, Kara was under me, but we'd always been equals. We saw what the other couldn't, and we always had each other's back, since her first day three years ago when she cornered me in the hallway and asked if we could get lunch. By then, I'd been at Genomix long enough to be friendly with everyone, but I hadn't befriended anyone. I didn't realize how much I needed Kara until I had her.

"I already feel bad enough," she said.

I gave her a supportive look. "Don't beat yourself up. It could have happened to any one of us."

Aidan tapped a manicured hand against his rigid slopes of gelled hair. The same level of care extended to his writing. A high-visibility typo was tantamount to stepping in dog crap, and the rebrand was a big deal.

"The first two sentences have changed twenty times." Kara came to stand beside me. "I'm trying to keep up. I'm fixing errors as fast as I catch them."

I cringed. "Sorry," I said. Those errors were probably mine. Normally, I triple-checked my work, but I'd been working double time to get everything done.

"Not good enough," Aidan hissed. He abandoned his phone to rub his temples, and I considered banging my head on my desk.

The launch was fraying my nerves. Aidan was head of marketing, so the campaign was technically his baby, but almost all the collateral—the press release, the website, the physical brochures, the copy on the packaging—was my writing. Even the new slogan was mine, born during one of our brainstorms to figure out how to convince people we were a genetic diagnostic company, not a data-gathering firm. *Genomix: Changing your life from the inside out.*

We'd built the entire campaign around my words. I wanted this to go well as much as he did.

"The release hasn't gone out yet. We have plenty of time to make the change."

"It's already done," Kara said.

"Plenty of time?" Aidan checked his watch. "Is nineteen hours and forty-two, make that forty-one, minutes enough to review every word? I'm talking with a fine-tooth comb. You said you wanted to own this project. Well, own it." He picked up his phone and began typing again, tossing me a sidelong glance. "You can work late tonight, right?"

"Sure." Not that the question was a request. "Of course."

Poof. Just like that, Aidan waved his magic wand and my evening plans vanished.

I'd tucked a bottle of champagne in the fridge before I left that morning, excited to get home and celebrate the launch with bubbles and a solo showing of *Roman Holiday.* I needed the thrill of vicarious adventure and the cathartic cry at the end. Despite having seen it a few dozen times, I never stopped hoping Princess Anne would abandon her responsibilities and run into Joe Bradley's arms.

"I'll get it done. It's not a problem."

He nodded his approval, pivoted, and zipped toward his glassed-in office.

As soon as his door closed, Kara turned to me. "He's officially the worst. All he cares about is his image. His whole 'I'm a real writer. I went to USC journalism school' schtick. Whoop-de-freaking-do. Like dude, you're shilling marketing copy. He's a shitty sellout like the rest of us."

I flinched at her delivery, grateful no one else was around to hear. "He's our boss."

"He's an ass."

"An ass who my livelihood depends on," I whispered.

"*Whom.* An ass *whom* your livelihood depends on. An ass *who* takes advantage of you."

"I need to work." I dropped the stack of papers on my desk, opened my laptop, and turned on my desktop monitor, but the sound of Kara's signature scoff pulled me back to our conversation.

She glanced toward Aidan's office. "You're only working late tonight so *he* can sleep better. You know we don't need to review everything again."

"It's for the launch, not Aidan."

"Rose"—she placed her small hands on my shoulders and stared up at me—"I don't know how to say this nicely, but you're kind of . . . what I mean is . . . people walk all over you."

"They do not."

"Oh really? How about the guy you went out with last week? You made out with him for an hour in the restaurant parking lot because you felt too guilty telling him you wanted to go home. Or the guy before him who talked you into buying dinner for the both of you in the name of feminism. And don't get me started on your mom and sisters."

I opened my mouth to defend myself, but she wasn't done.

"All I'm saying is sometimes it seems like you'd do anything to avoid disappointing or upsetting someone. You never push back on Aidan, even when you're totally in the right. And when you do get promoted, he's only going to make your life harder."

I placed one of my hands atop hers and gave a reassuring squeeze before prying her fingers from my shoulders. "I know. Trust me."

Aidan loved to make people squirm, and he seemed to find torturing me particularly satisfying. When I was promoted—*if* I was promoted—he'd find new ways to make me bend over backward. There'd be more work, more excuses to drag me into his office and demand more ideas. And even with a better title, Kara was right—I was never going to be able to stand up to his unreasonable demands. But he'd also admitted that creating the new content lead position was a testament to our thriving team. "It's time to grow," he'd told me. "Basically, we need more of you." I'd glommed on to those words for weeks.

I had a plan: first, I'd get promoted to content lead, then I'd get to hire my own content team. "I'm a manager," I imagined telling my dad. Sure, Dad had managed a massive team of engineers, not a few lowly writers, and sure, he could never wrap his mind around my interest in writing over math and science, but I'd still managed to use my only real skill to get a job in an industry usually reserved for scientists, data engineers, and sales reps. If I got the promotion, I could almost believe Dad would be proud of me. So what if my job eroded a little of my soul each day? It was income, stability.

"I just don't get it," Kara said. "You don't even love this job. And you're a great writer. Wouldn't you rather do something else? I don't know, write a romance novel or something?"

I gave her an incredulous stare. "Romance? Not exactly my genre."

"Okay, fine. How about a personal newsletter?"

"Who would care what I have to say?"

Her hand darted into the air. "Me. Me. Pick me."

"I sort of need a paycheck." I took a deep breath and dropped into my chair. As for what I did want to write, well, the specifics were blurry, but I sensed a shapeless spreading in my soul, like the way Dad used to bloom delicate strands of saffron in butter to stain a whole pot of rice yellow. I just wasn't sure what I needed to say. "Who needs to *love* their job anyway? It's good enough to have one." If I said it enough, maybe it would be true. Aidan would promote me to content lead, and I would stop wishing for something else, somewhere else.

I opened my email, and Kara settled back at her desk.

"Did you read *Gladys* yet? The letter is . . . relevant."

"Not yet."

"I'll send you the link."

Your Grrl, Gladys was an online advice column, definitely not work-related, that we read and dissected with glee. I'd written to Gladys a thousand times in my head, imagining what her response might be. Reading her answers was like putting on a pair of prescription glasses you didn't know you needed. In the moment, everything in front of you became clear and sharp, and you wondered how you'd ever managed without them.

The URL popped up in a message on my screen. I tried to turn my attention to the hours of work before me, but I couldn't ignore Gladys. I clicked on the link and the column appeared in front of me.

Dear Gladys,

I turned 50 years old last month. My life is hardly over, though I worry it might as well be.

I've had the same rote job for 20 years. I've never cared about my work, not in any deep, meaningful way, but it's always paid the bills and provided health insurance, which, for a long time, felt like more than enough. Even if I didn't.

In fact, the only times I felt like I was enough were the ones when I was too much. Too much for my family, my friends, the men who came into my life but never stayed long.

And all the times I wanted more made me feel so ashamed that I made myself as small as possible to compensate.

Mostly, I'm not lonely. I have coworkers I eat lunch with, some friends I talk to every other week. I'm a loving aunt to my three nieces. And, as of a couple of weeks ago, I moved back in with my aging parents under the guise of saving money. I'm there to look after them, though I'd guess they would say they're the ones taking care of me.

The problem is, I'm empty. Every day is the same, like I'm on a conveyor belt to the grave.

Once upon a time, my family and friends encouraged me to date or take advantage of my single status by traveling, leaning into work, exercising. As time passes, those things, too, seem a lost cause.

There are a couple of things that still bring me joy, so I guess I'm not totally dead inside yet. My Sunday baking projects, for one. I nurture my sourdough starter the way others do their dogs. And speaking of pets, I have Whiskers, my pet rat.

My sister gave him to me for my birthday. I've found myself talking to him a lot, as if he understands me and can respond. He's cleverer than you might think, but my care for him makes me sad. Is this all there is for me, Gladys? A rat named Whiskers? Is it too late for anything else? And, if it's not, how do I fill my empty tank? How do I forgive myself for all these wasted years?

Sincerely,
Crazy Rat Lady Aunt Rachel

Dear Crazy Rat Lady,

It's not too late. Full stop. I'll repeat that: It's. Not. Too. Late.

It's never too late. This is a fact—remember those?—which means you should ignore your family and friends if they tell you otherwise.

Okay. Now that the easiest question is out of the way, let's talk about that empty tank. You're missing your "why," Rat Lady, and despite how it might feel, it's not an uncommon problem. Some people find that their career answers their big "why," for others it's their kids, family, a love of the great outdoors, volunteering at a homeless shelter.

You're picking up what I'm putting down, right? Your "why" can be anything. There's no wrong answer. There's only your answer. What your parents expect for you won't do. What your friends want for you won't work either.

You say you bake. Maybe your "why" is making the best dang sourdough loaf anyone in your family's ever experienced. Or it's not. But like you do with dough, you need to give your "why" the right environment to rise.

We've all got passion within, but for some of us, it needs to double, quadruple in volume.

Give yourself permission to play, explore, make mistakes. Try everything that comes your way. Nothing coming your way? Put yourself in the way.

Find a pet rat club, because why not? Meet people who love their rats as much as you love Whiskers.

As for how you forgive yourself, you don't. Nothing requires your forgiveness. All these years haven't been wasted; they were just your inner fermentation process at work. (Embrace the bread metaphor the way you would a warm loaf, mmkay?) For some of us, it takes longer than others. I don't know why that is, but there's no shame in blooming late.

So if you still need permission: go—as slowly as you have to, but go.

Your Grrl,
Gladys

Reading the letter and Gladys's response left my heart slugging against my rib cage. I closed the browser window and sifted through the mass of papers Aidan had abandoned in my care. I tried to follow the words, but my brain kept seeing Gladys's column.

Was Kara implying that I was Crazy Rat Lady?

No, no way. Rat Lady wasn't like me at all. *I* didn't live with my parents, for one. Two, I had passion. I did. I was a writer, dammit! Was there a more passionate profession? Okay, so I wrote marketing copy, but still. And as for my "why," it was my family, obviously. At once, the thought made me blench. Because it wasn't true. Or it was, but I didn't want it to be.

My sweaty palms left creases on the papers, and I abandoned them to shove a cookie in my mouth, the bittersweet chocolate coating my palate in a sour tang.

Without my noticing, Kara had come to stand beside me. She grabbed a *nan-e berenji* and took a bite. "I think these are improving." She chewed, wiped her lips. "Are you sure they're supposed to be so dry?"

"They're an acquired texture." I yanked away the tub as she nabbed two chocolate chip cookies. "And they're for *everyone* to share. Morale booster."

"Look," Kara said, gentler with the cookie in her mouth. "We'll get it done. We always do, don't we?"

"We always get what done?"

She cocked her head and gestured at the papers scattered across my desk. "The work?"

"Oh. Right."

I shoved Gladys and Rat Lady out of my mind. I needed to focus on the rebrand. The promotion. Even if the new title didn't matter to anyone except me, and even if all it meant was a lot more work and a little more money, the hope kept me going, a carrot dangling at the end of the stick. I settled back into my chair and readied myself for a long day.

"You're right. I got this." I smiled at Kara and hoped she couldn't see the worry in my eyes.

So much for Gregory Peck. So much for champagne and stress-release tears.

❦

I walked in the door of my apartment at eleven o'clock, drooping with fatigue. My eyes burned from staring at my computer for the past fifteen hours. At least we were done. The new content was live. The press release would go out at 4:00 a.m. PDT, typo-free.

My worries about work dissolved the second I stepped inside. Something was off. The hallway light shone, but I hadn't left it on. My lungs clenched and blood stormed my limbs. Should I dial 911? Run out the door?

As I pulled my phone from my purse, I dared a peek into the kitchen and discovered my special-occasion champagne open and sweating on the counter, alongside an empty tub of hummus and a torn bag of pita chips.

I sighed and plopped my purse on the floor. I wasn't being robbed, unless you counted the stolen snacks. Tonight, of all nights. My legs wobbled from the scare and the endless day. I rubbed at my dry eyes and tried not to think about how late I would get to bed.

"Lily," I called. "What are you doing here?"

I found her in the living room draped across the couch watching *Friends*. Without rousing, she said, "You're home late."

I'd given her a key, in case of emergencies. She'd taken the gesture as an invitation to show up unannounced before. But never this late and never with suitcases in tow. Three rolling bags sat on the floor. My brocade chair had already become a dumping ground for her clothes. My chest sank, the air knocked out of me.

I shoved her feet aside to plunk down on the couch and poked her in the ribs. "What's wrong?"

"Ouch." She sat up, wiped the crumbs from her shirt. "Don't make it a thing, but Dev and I are taking a break."

"Oh. Wow. That is . . . Why?"

I could think of a million reasons not to date Dev, like how, even though Lily didn't have a car, he rarely let her use one of his two Teslas, or how he had, for real, a tattoo of YOLO across his left biceps. Or how he could never make it to any of our family gatherings but expected Lily to be available as arm candy for every last-minute client dinner and underground party he threw with his wannabe "high net worth" friends.

Lily, however, didn't mind Dev's shortcomings. In return, he funded her retail habit and let her live in his apartment rent free while she tried, for a third time, to finish her accounting degree.

They had a mutual attraction; I knew because Lily had shared every grimy detail since the one-night stand that kicked off their relationship. She'd floundered so long after Dad died—acting out in high school, dropping out of college after her first year and an alarming six weeks that followed when she shacked up with a forty-year-old and started referring to herself as a sugar baby, partying, shoplifting, racking up credit card debt, and who knew what else. If it was destructive, Lily gave it her best shot. Once she settled for Dev, at least she'd been safe, and I could finally fall asleep without wondering where she was. Even if the guy wasn't my favorite, even if I didn't get how looks alone could make a relationship, a break, out of nowhere, prickled my big-sister sense. I wanted to protect her. It was my job to protect her and had been since we were little and Iris got sick. But she made the prospect so impossible sometimes. Most of the time.

"I need some time alone," she said.

"Did you have a fight?"

She brushed aside the question with a shake of her head. "We've been together forever. I mean, more than five years, and that's basically a half a lifetime when you're only twenty-six. Sometimes you have to switch things up, ya know? Wait," she said, changing direction, "you probably don't. No offense. Anyway, it's not a big deal. A few days or a couple weeks. A month at most. Breathing room, that's all I need." She glanced at me; her eyelashes fluttered. "But, technically, it's Dev's place, so I was wondering . . ."

The sinking feeling transformed into a ripple of nausea sloshing against my hollow stomach. I regretted skipping dinner. Kicking my flats from my feet, I swallowed against the tide of discomfort rising in me.

I pictured Lily's stuff piling on top of Iris's wedding decorations, an avalanche crushing me on the way to the bathroom. I could tell her to go to Mom's, but she'd never sink that low. She'd just keep begging and begging, and she wouldn't leave until she got her way. And maybe she *did* need time to figure out she deserved better than douchey Dev. Without him, she might embrace her independence and transform back into the spunky girl she'd once been, instead of the beautiful but excessively stabby cactus she'd become after Dad died.

She'd be a terrible guest, no doubt, but if I could help . . .

My vision blurred, and I saw my bed in the other room, neatly made and ready for me. I could feel the cool pillow on my cheek, the pleasure of gravity weighing me down, the end of this endless day. I only had to say the word.

"Of course."

3

The next morning, I was shaky from an awful combination of exhaustion and too much coffee. After Lily's unexpected appearance, I couldn't sleep. The muffled sound of the TV she watched to drift off kept me awake, along with a sense of dread I couldn't shake, even when the sun rose and my room brightened.

I briefly considered calling in sick, until my conscience got the better of me. I'd put hours of precious life into the rebrand. I wasn't about to bail with the promotion on the line. That and the fact that, four years in, my perfect work attendance record remained. It wasn't like you won an award or anything, but I couldn't break my streak, not now.

I expected Aidan to be at my desk ready to pounce. But the office was quiet, eerily so, like it was any old Tuesday and not the official release of the rebrand we began ages ago. I dropped my bag at my desk, heaped with last night's red-lined drafts and email printouts detailing Aidan's required edits, and beelined to Kara's.

"Where is he?"

She gulped from a smudged stainless steel mug cluttered with stickers, her fingers gripping a rainbow Daft Punk decal. She nodded, and I followed her gaze to see Aidan striding past our pod of desks, his mouth drawn in a stark line.

"Morning," I called, hurrying to join him.

He scanned me up and down. "You look like hell."

"I didn't sleep much. How's the launch being received?"

"Beautifully," he said. I kept pace with him as we neared his office, waiting for something more, a crumb of positive feedback, a thank-you. He paused, rolled his shoulders, and looked down at me from the tip of his pointy nose. "Actually, since you're here, let's chat for a minute."

My mind spun from lack of sleep, but I swore I heard the crackle, bang, pop of fireworks. This was the moment. The conversation I'd been waiting for: *Rose, your work here has been exemplary. You've really been our senior content lead since you started four years ago, and now your title will match your role. Congrats! Also, here's a 10 percent raise.*

My whole body buzzed, and I lurched after him.

"Come in." He gestured through his office door. "Sit."

I did as told while he installed himself behind his desk and scanned something on his monitor. He didn't give the impression he was going to deliver good news, but he never did.

"I had a talk with HR this morning."

Hope lifted like a helium balloon. I clasped my hands together to keep calm.

He squinted, picked up a stack of papers, tapped them together, and then did something so truly out of character, this had to be the moment when all my effort, all the microsacrifices I made every day, clicked into place: his lips raised into a quarter smile, and he broke into a giggle.

Yes! Yay!

"I'm sorry, I'm laughing because—"

I was so distracted practicing my gracious acceptance speech, I almost missed what he said next. "Wait, what?"

"It's just so one thousand percent you that it amuses me. HR says you're maxed out on PTO. They claim you've never taken a vacation day and told me their records concerning Rose Zadeh must be amiss. I assured them their information is probably accurate."

"It is." I sat up straighter. "Do I get a perfect attendance merit badge? Ha ha."

"Afraid not. But you do get a mandated vacation. So congratulations, I guess?"

"What?"

"Here's how it works. Either you burn three weeks of earned paid time off. Or you can take three weeks off and get paid. Now, it's fine by me if you want to work yourself to death, but HR frowns upon it. They prefer you go away for a while, so that all those press releases we put out touting how stellar company culture is around here are, you know, somewhat accurate. But hey, it's your call."

"Is this some kind of punishment?"

Another breathy laugh. "You're killing me. But"—he pulled himself together—"logistically, whatever you're going to do needs to be decided before the next pay period."

"What about the content lead position?"

He closed his eyes. When they opened, all signs of amusement had fled his face.

"Let me tell you something. Despite my youthful appearance, I've been around the block a few times. Here's the big secret. You don't get what you want by being polite and tiptoeing. You have to know you deserve it. It has to be yours already. So I'll ask." His eyes bored into my face like a dare to blink. "Do you deserve Senior Content Lead? Like in your heart of hearts deserve it?"

What did he want me to say? Of course I deserved a promotion, but *he* was supposed to decide if I got it, not me. Was this a test of some kind? What more could I do to make myself worthy? A beat passed before I could summon a response.

"I've proven my dedication to the organization. I'm a strong writer," I said, an embarrassing shake in my voice. "The team likes me and . . .

and I . . . I've never missed a day of work." Even I recognized my lack of conviction. Hope had come and gone, leaving me a deflated shell. "I'll do whatever it takes, but I really need this—"

He waved a hand to shoo away my words. "I've always appreciated your resilience, Rose. You're not a whiner. You're a doer. And we're lucky to have you as a content writer. But I need a bold thinker—"

"I have ideas."

"—someone who speaks his mind. You know, a creative leader. It's a *lead* position after all. Fresh blood is better for all of us. We need to think of what's best for the team, the organization. I'm sure you can understand that."

"What am I supposed to do for three weeks?"

He stared at me, dumbfounded.

❦

Refusing to relent to the slow fall of evening, the summer heat fought against the whir of my Mazda's AC while I accelerated through one yellow light and the next, determined not to get stuck at an eight-stop intersection where the signals were long enough for you to panic you might be trapped forever.

Sometimes when I drove home from work, I challenged myself to notice the beauty in the suburban sprawl—the clusters of unexpected wildflowers growing at the broken edges of the sidewalk, the way the modern buildings' stark angles drew stripes across a bright blue sky. Tonight all I could see was the curtain of dust-brown smog hovering above the fast-food and supermarket signs, the foothills gone drab and yellow, the way they always did in high-drought July.

A Tesla cut me off and I raised my hand to honk, but my palm landed too softly to engage the horn. I couldn't even honk loud enough for anyone to hear.

Dear Gladys,

The job that I've worked so hard for is going to someone else less deserving (probably; male, definitely), my best friend thinks I'm a doormat, and the square box I call a life shrinks a little bit every Sunday. What should I do?

Sincerely,
Sickeningly Sorry for Herself in San Jose

I nudged up the AC to clear my head. The Tesla and I caught the next red light.

"Freaking hell."

God, I hated driving. Really, really hated it. San Jose, too, all of Silicon Valley, in fact. Sitting at the intersection, right hip cramping, hot flashes gave way to cold sweats. How could I not have gotten the promotion? I was the perfect candidate. No one knew the job better than me—*I* was the job! They needed a bold thinker. Well, I had creative ideas. I had things to say. *I* was the brains behind our entire rebrand, not that Aidan would ever admit it. Instead, he rewarded me with three weeks of forced vacation, a generous description given that I felt like I'd been suspended from school for something I didn't do.

Kara had a point, though. I didn't exactly stick up for myself. I didn't tell Aidan he was an idiot who should feel lucky to have me. So maybe he was right. I wasn't a born leader. But I was a good writer. Maybe the world needed more leaders like me. Nice leaders who cared about other people's opinions. I snorted at the ridiculous idea and gripped the steering wheel as if I could rip it apart.

What if I kept driving? What if I left it all behind and disappeared? Where would I go?

The answer occurred to me as if it made perfect sense. *Paris.*

Could I? No.

Even without work, I still had obligations. People relied on me. I needed to help with Iris's wedding and make sure Lily didn't burn down my apartment. Who would watch out for Mom?

But the word was a nagging voice inside my head. *Paris. Paris. Paris.*

What if this was it? Hadn't I wanted an excuse to leave? If I didn't take this chance, would I ever have another opportunity to go?

I had a passport, pristine and unstamped, tucked away in a folder "just in case," as if someone might unexpectedly sweep me away to a foreign country. As if the opportunity to go might fall right in my lap. And here it was.

Cobblestone streets. Cafés. The plastic wicker chairs where I could devour my *TBR* pile cover to cover while munching croissants and sipping coffee from a real cup and saucer. A park bench where I could spend an afternoon people-watching and collecting pithy observations about the day's adventures in a notebook. Time, nothing but time, to do as I pleased without regard for anyone else.

"Stop right now. What are you thinking?" My voice, but it was Dad I heard, his practicality. The loss of him was a sharp pebble in my shoe, impossible to ignore, and exhausting, too, his absence somehow larger than life.

My longing to escape would disappoint him. The question was only how much. Even the word "escape" would irk him, earn a well-worn tirade about where he'd come from, how privileged I was to be born in the United States, to live so near my family when he'd never seen his parents or brother after he left Tehran. Did I know his own mother never went to school? And I didn't even have student loans. I had everything. His dream had been to give his daughters every opportunity, but as far as I could tell, we weren't supposed to take them. We were supposed to build safe lives with stable jobs close to home.

As for travel, Dad didn't believe in it as a pastime. He could hardly stand the annual work trips he made to India to meet with his Bengaluru-based team of engineers. He complained about the hassle at the airport. He never made it through security without his bags being taken aside, rifled through. He'd been pulled into a small room and interrogated by customs officials more than once, nearly missing his connecting flights. "My name is like a red flag. And forget about a beard. Good thing Mom likes a close shave, eh?" he joked, rubbing his hand over his smooth brown cheeks.

But it was more than that, like he couldn't shake the feeling that any time he got on a plane or left California without his family he might never make it home again. The same fear seemed to extend to the rest of us. "We have to stick together," he told us. "We're all we have."

Even at the end of his life, he was most scared to leave us, to have to go on to whatever came next alone.

I shook away the recurring image of him slack on his deathbed, reaching for my hand, and trained my eyes on the brake lights ahead of me. The symbolism was hard to ignore: I wasn't going anywhere.

4

Village Diner was a crescent moon of Santorini-blue booths and wobbly tables surrounding a Formica-topped bar where plates of eggs and toast and crispy ribbons of bacon gathered awaiting their final destinations.

Mom stood from our regular square four-top near a sun-soaked window where she sat with Iris and waved when she saw me and Lily, her arm sweeping across the air like a windshield wiper on a semi.

The heads at nearby tables shifted to watch her, and she basked in their interest. Mom thrived on attention. Her clawlike acrylic nails, the bright-blonde hair she curled every day whether she left her house or not, her passion for bold prints. It was a package deal.

I cringed inside; Lily moaned. "Why does she have to be this way?"

"Be nice," I said, waving back.

"You two are late." She squeezed us each into a tight hug.

"Blame Rose," Lily said as we sat down. "She drove."

We picked up the plastic-sheathed menus even though we knew our orders by heart. We'd been coming here for years, sitting at the same table, at the same time, nearly every Sunday. The waitstaff knew us. Sometimes the owner, Vasilis, came by and kissed Mom's cheek, which flamed bright pink in response.

"How's the bride-to-be?" I asked Iris.

Her face lit into a grin. Before she could respond, Mom butted in.

"I've asked if Sylvia can come to the wedding, but Iris says it's too late. You know, it's not uncommon for parents to invite their friends, especially single parents."

"I didn't say it was too late. I said we don't really know her."

"Well, of course you do. I wouldn't invite a stranger to your wedding. The Darianos lived down the street from us for almost thirty years. Sylvia's still in the same house."

Iris mouthed *Help* across the table.

"You'll know plenty of people there," I said.

"A companion for the mother of the bride. Is that so unreasonable? And what about Sylvia?"

"What about her?" Iris said.

"It would make her month. Her year! She's had it rough, trust me." But before we could, she began to monologue. We all sank lower in our seats. "After their nasty divorce, Sal practically abandoned her and their sweet Marco. To think of a child left behind by his father. It makes me sick. Marco had to be sent away to boarding school. Can you imagine?" Mom was talking so fast, she paused to catch her breath. "It's a small miracle Sylvia's brother worked at that fancy East Coast prep school. Changed the trajectory of Marco's life, that's for sure. Now he's all grown up and quite accomplished apparently. He teaches art history at one of the American schools in Paris. *Très* chic."

All this sounded familiar. She'd probably done the poor Sylvia routine a time or two, but with this telling, memories of riding bicycles with Marco, a fuzzy-headed boy in stiff blue jeans, a paperback wedged in his pocket, popped into my head. We'd stopped spending time together around middle school, and he'd disappeared shortly thereafter. I hadn't thought about him in years. How had he wound up in Paris and I got stuck at brunch?

"Too many details, Mom," Lily said. Iris and I nodded in agreement.

Mom's gossiping was like a compulsion, except in true, hypocritical Mom fashion, the overshares only applied to other people. The juicy bits of her own life she withheld for vague, unsatisfying anecdotes or well-practiced one-liners. She wouldn't tell us anything about the parents she'd been estranged from for as long as we could remember. "We didn't see eye to eye anymore. There's nothing else to it," she said, if pushed. We'd long since given up trying to get anything meaningful out of her.

"Sylvia remarried, didn't she? And had another kid," Iris said, exasperated. "It's not like she has no one."

"Oh, sure, but her husband's as boring as watching paint dry. Trust me, she never gets out. You don't understand what it's like to be women our age. We might as well be invisible."

Cue collective sigh around the table at Mom's melodrama.

"Anyway," Mom went on, "her younger son's off at some out-of-state college now. I don't know how she bears having both her boys so far away. I would die."

Iris and Lily rolled their eyes to the ceiling. My whole body tensed, and I shrank into my seat. When Dad died, Mom had barely functioned for a year, leaving everything to twenty-year-old me, coming out of her stupor only when Lily was picked up by the cops for stuffing a Victoria's Secret PINK collection thong in her sweatshirt. She snapped back to her old self after that. Well, mostly. Becoming a widow sucked away some of her natural joie de vivre, the void filled with a devotion to maintain Dad's place in the family, the way you'd save a seat for someone who'd stepped away. They'd been a perfect example of how opposites attract, and when he was gone, it was like she'd lost her balance, either sinking or floating. I couldn't blame her for struggling. After she dragged herself out of bed to get Lily from the police station, it took me another five years to get brave enough to move out, and I hadn't gone far. I couldn't.

As if reading my mind, Mom added, "Thankfully, my girls aren't going anywhere."

I poured a splash of cream in my coffee to avoid her eyes, added a hefty lump of sugar even though I knew it would make her grimace.

Iris fondled a packet of sweetener with one hand and pinched the wide ridge of her nose with the other, the latter a childhood habit that flared whenever she was stressed. "We didn't really do plus-ones, Mom. You know that."

"You'd let Rose bring someone, if she had someone to bring, wouldn't you?"

"But she doesn't. And a significant other is different than a friend."

I stirred my coffee, willing the minutes to pass faster. Death by a thousand brunches. Nothing reminds you you're painfully alone like other people discussing how alone you are as if you aren't in the room.

Mom looked at me. "Don't you think she's being unfair?"

"They have a budget. They can't invite everyone."

Mom scowled and crossed her arms in a huff. "You always side with Iris."

It wasn't possible to exist in this family without upsetting someone. I searched for the right thing to say. "I mean, if someone else can't come, could Sylvia take their place?"

"Gee, thanks for the support," Iris said.

Mom's eyes brightened. "If Dev doesn't come—"

"It's a break. That means temporary," Lily said. "God."

Mom threw her hands into the air. "Then what's even the point?"

Lily was leaning so far back in her chair one push would send her tumbling. I stifled the impulse. *Temporary? Really?* In a week, she'd commandeered my apartment. Her stuff was everywhere. Stuff she didn't even need, like a UV nail dryer and a melon baller. I couldn't see the floor in the living room anymore. But I didn't say anything because hadn't I told her she could stay? It would take time for her to realize she was better off without Dev, and if I spoke up, she'd get all sensitive and miffed and run right back to him.

I wanted to hug the waitress when she appeared, smiling, asking after Mom's nail polish color. We recited our orders, sticking to the script. Veggie scramble for Mom with whole wheat toast; granola and plain coconut yogurt for Iris, hold the drizzle of honey; a half order of eggs Benedict, add avocado, for Lily; and a cheesy omelet for me. The server promised to return with more coffee.

"Speaking of significant others." Iris gave me a skittish once-over and my whole body tensed. "I've got a guy for you to meet. A friend of a friend of our neighbor, but before you say no, he sounds great."

"I'm not sure." The tongue-lashing from Kara about letting people take advantage of me flashed through my mind.

I'd been in one actual relationship in college over a decade ago. Bone-dry, emotions-are-toxic Rhys. Who dumped me the day of Dad's memorial because "tragedy brings clarity," and clearly, according to him, I had some "dark stuff to work through." The relationship worked best when I was as happy as a puppy, and as eager to please.

To be fair, I'd found eagerness to please appealed to most men. Earnestness, not so much. Given my bleak dating history, I may not have been equipped for love at all. Which was just as well. I'd never liked dating, only its potential for romance, its promise of a life-altering meet-cute that had never come to pass. Anyway, I had bigger problems to solve, like what I was going to do about my job.

"I think I may be done with dating for a while," I said.

Mom scoffed. "Don't say that. You still have time. You don't want to be alone at forty, do you? Can you imagine? Nothing to live for but work, work, work."

"Actually," I said, a glutton for punishment, "I might take some time off work. Three full weeks."

"Wonderful!" Mom clapped her hands. "More time for your beloved mother. You can help me sort out the mouse infestation. Ooh! And go through all my old tax documents. I have no eye for that sort of thing. We could even do lunch and shop for my mother-of-the-bride dress."

I could think of little I wanted to do less. The alternative was to be bossed around by Aidan while spending my free time helping the person who stole my job get acclimated, all for the privilege of losing three weeks' worth of pay. In my current state of mind, I couldn't determine which sounded worse.

I decided to test the waters. "I was thinking of going away for a while."

"What? Where?" Lily said.

Mom's mouth puckered. "Yes, where?"

"Well—"

"You should do a staycation," Iris said. "Stay at a hotel for a couple nights. Do a spa day. We could get massages together."

Mom ran her fingers through her hair, beaming now. I swallowed hard against my narrowing throat. "We could do a whole spa weekend!" she said. "Iris doesn't have to be back in the classroom for weeks, and, Lily, your summer session is almost done, right?" Mom looked at Iris. "I know you said no bachelorette party, but we could make it a wedding shower weekend. Ooh, I love this idea." She practically squealed.

Iris nodded. "Carmel?"

"Ojai," Lily responded. "Or Palm Springs."

"It'll be a million degrees."

"What about Mendocino?" Mom said.

I was used to them talking around me, but something felt different this time. Their excitement cut straight through. Like I wasn't invisible but completely absent. Yet, the whole conversation was centered on my constant, ever-reliable presence. They didn't think I'd go anywhere, and why would they?

I spoke before I meant to, before I even knew what I was going to say. "Wait." I cleared my throat, wrapped my paper napkin as tight as I could around my pinky finger. "Not a staycation. Something farther afield. Like Paris. Maybe."

"Paris? We can't up and take a weekend trip to Paris," Mom said, exasperated.

"No, I mean a trip to Paris by myself."

"Alone?" Mom's hands fell to the table. "You can't be serious. She's not serious, is she?"

"No way. It's not safe. You wouldn't go alone, would you?" Iris asked. "Not all that way."

"Yeah, right," Lily said. "Way too far outside your comfort zone. Remember when you went to sleepaway camp in the Sierra and had to come home early because of hives?"

"That was poison oak." I didn't remind her how jealous she'd been that I convinced Mom and Dad to let me go.

Iris stared at me wide-eyed. "You took me to your college orientation because you were too nervous to go alone."

"You begged to come with me." I didn't care to go into the fact that she'd been a comfort to me, too, my fourteen-year-old sister who already knew how to talk to people more easily than I did at eighteen.

I wasn't sure why I was bothering to protest at all. I hadn't really considered what traveling solo across the world would mean. Other than a couple of family road trips to Nevada and Oregon, I'd hardly spent time outside of California. *People travel alone all the time,* I wanted to say. But I wasn't "people." I was Rose Zadeh with the pristine passport and the pathological sense of responsibility. What did I know about traveling to Paris anyway?

"It's only an idea," I mumbled. "I haven't looked at flights or anything."

"Well, that's a relief," Mom said. "Can you imagine what your father would think? You know how he felt about travel. Anything could happen in another country. It's better to stay closer to home." Mostly, I found Mom's Dad reminders tiring, but today, the words chastened me as they were intended, his last words to me always reverberating in my head.

The twisted napkin tore apart in my hands, and I nearly spilled my water, catching the glass right before it fell.

Mom ignored the interruption and continued. "Iris needs your help with all that logistical stuff you do well. Less than two months to go, and we have the dress fitting coming up and all the details to finalize. I don't want the stress catching up with her." To Iris: "What if you have a flare-up right before the wedding?"

Lily jerked upright in her chair, her elbows colliding with the table. "Can we not talk about this anymore?"

Iris gave her a passing glance—we all knew how Lily freaked over any talk of illness—then reached over and clasped my hand. For a heart-thud of an instant, I thought she might encourage me to skip the wedding chores and go to Paris.

"Are you serious about the dating thing?"

I pulled my hand away, and she pinched her nose.

"Why? What did you do?"

"I gave him your number. And I sort of already said you'd go."

5

Eager to get the whole thing over with, I made plans to meet Iris's friend of a friend of a neighbor two days later. But despite my best efforts to navigate traffic, I was late, and the lapse seemed to set us off on the wrong foot, the evening quickly dissolving from awkward to excruciating in the dim retro lights of the trendy bar where Frank had suggested we go.

We bantered, the innuendos wearing on me. The same thoughts kept circling the drain. I didn't get the promotion. I didn't deserve to be promoted. I would never be enough. I was going to be forced to move in with Mom, and one day, I would die alone and be eaten by rodents. I gulped my drink, the mezcal burning all the way down.

When conversation lagged, I found myself overcompensating with excessive laughter. I had a bad habit of laughing extra hard when something wasn't funny, as if I could make up for someone's lack of cleverness by sheer force of amusement. I jabbered on to fill the blank moments that kept growing bigger like spilled drops of salad oil on the silk blouses I hated but wore anyway because someone once said they flattered me.

Frank needed to like me. It was the bare minimum to meet, the lowest bar of approval.

When he excused himself to go to the bathroom and didn't come back, I told myself there was a line. Or he was having best-not-to-imagine intestinal trouble. After fifteen minutes, I couldn't pretend anymore.

The bartender slid the bill toward me, and my hands shook as I pulled out my wallet.

"When did he leave?" I asked, not meeting his eyes.

"The minute he stood up. I knocked off one of the drinks."

I read the tab.

"I see five drinks."

"He had one before you got here." The bartender shrugged. "That's the one I comped. I'd wipe the whole thing, but my manager is here tonight."

"Don't be silly," I said, and left a stupidly big tip.

❦

I stormed the dark parking lot, lit by a single buzzing streetlamp, trying to remember where I'd left my car. Stupid Frank. Stupid me—I should never have agreed to the date in the first place.

This was it. I was done with dating. Done. What more did I need from the universe to know I should call it quits? I pulled my phone from my purse to inform Iris. I stumbled, and it plummeted to the pavement. I sank down, patting the ground at my feet.

The second drink may have been a bad idea.

I could not call Iris. She wouldn't understand. How could she? She'd known she wanted to be a teacher since she was a kid, she'd met Ben in high school, and her future came together precisely as she'd planned. Despite growling and turning grim-faced every time any of us so much as mentioned a boy's name, Dad took to Ben straightaway and all but blessed their marriage back when the shy couple ended their dates with a hug at the front door.

I found my phone and used my flashlight to navigate my way around the parking lot until I located my car and climbed in.

Should I drive? I let the AC chill me to the bone to clear my head. After a few minutes, I was wide awake, teeth chattering. I sat for another fifteen, sipping lukewarm water from a Swig bottle before I was sure I was okay.

I looked left, I swear I did, before I turned. The street was empty. Not a soul in sight. The lane was clear, and all of a sudden, it wasn't.

As I turned right from the parking lot onto the street, out of nowhere an SUV in the middle lane charged over the line toward me. Adrenaline shot my heart into overdrive. I slammed on my brakes and attempted to steer to the shoulder, but the SUV didn't stop fast enough, hitting me square in the driver's side.

The impact ricocheted in the spaces between my bones. The car jerked forward hard. My body went one way, my neck the other.

My life should have flashed before my eyes, but all I could think about was my blood alcohol level. *What if I hurt someone? What if I lose my license?* Somewhere in that split second, dying seemed a preferable alternative. And then, as if nothing had happened, the car came to a standstill.

My neck hurt. My ears buzzed. I'd bit my tongue and tasted iron. But I was fine.

I pushed the driver's-side door with my body weight, but the lock wouldn't budge. Giving up, I crawled over the console to the passenger side and made my way outside. I expected the SUV to be somewhere nearby, but there was no one around. I was alone, my car crunched on one side like a cheap toy. Shaking to my core, I waited for my reckoning. When none came, I crawled back into the car, plucked my phone from the floorboard, and dialed the one person who wouldn't judge me.

6

My car was totaled. Lily, who had sensed my panic on the phone, pulled up in a rideshare within minutes. She called the tow truck and my insurance company. "I was the one driving," she told me. "Got it?"

I'd fought the impulse to tell her no, this was my responsibility, and nodded my agreement, grateful for her willingness to lie.

She ordered another car to take us home, and she was decent enough not to say anything the whole drive. She tucked me into bed the way I used to do for her when we were little, with a kiss on top of the head and a pat of the blankets.

"Thank you," I said. "I'm sorry."

She turned out the light, shut the door with a quiet click, and I fell straight to sleep.

In the light of the morning, cold shame-sweats washed over me. The night before sat at the edge of my vision, hovering close but impossible to look at dead on.

Emotional cramps came in waves, every mistake I'd ever made replaying in my mind all at once. Why had I agreed to the stupid date? Why had I been dumb enough to believe Aidan would promote me? Why couldn't I say no to Mom? Each thought made me hate myself a thousand times over.

Rubbing my sore neck, I wished my body were a suit I could unzip and leave behind. Instead, I did the next best thing. Took my very first sick day. Like it mattered.

I mindlessly scrolled my phone while streaming *Midnight in Paris*, the one Woody Allen movie I made an exception for. Mom believed the right movie at the right time could cure almost anything, and since childhood, my sisters and I had relied on movie marathons for various emotional ailments. The last big one had been an ode to ugly ducklings—*My Fair Lady*, *Can't Buy Me Love*, *Clueless*—as planned by Lily to get me through my thirtieth birthday rut. I'd tried not to read into the theme too much.

Midnight in Paris worked for a little while, until I made the mistake of checking my email.

> To: Rose Zadeh
> From: Aidan McKensie
>
> Rose,
>
> I shouldn't have to tell you it's quite inconvenient for you to take your first PTO day two days before you're scheduled to be out of the office for three weeks. I do trust you'll complete your outstanding tasks before EOD Friday, despite your ill-timed day of rest.
>
> Best,
> Aidan

I resisted the urge to throw my phone against the wall and set it down on my bedside table while I stewed.

"Relax. Enjoy the break," Kara kept telling me. "Stay in bed all day drinking wine by the box. Whatever you need to do to get some headspace."

But work was my lifeline. The hours, the structure, the words for Genomix were the only real thing I had outside of family. The thought of being trapped in my apartment for three weeks with nothing but Lily's stuff and my mom calling hourly to ask for favors made my chest burn.

When Lily's indie dance music started rattling my walls, the bass shook something inside me loose.

I tore into the living room where I found her in my chair, bobbing her head to the beat and typing on her phone. I wanted to yell but the words caught in my mouth. Last night could have been so much worse, but she'd saved me, no questions asked. Lily put herself first, but she could be unexpectedly benevolent, too, revealing a spirit of generosity as rare and fleeting as a double rainbow.

No, I couldn't complain about the noise or the mess, not after what Lily had done for me. I would bite my tongue and give proper thanks, in the hope that a little gratitude might rub off on her.

Except I couldn't do that either. No sooner had I extinguished the burn of frustration than the flame rose again, fire licking at the back of my throat.

My notebook, my Paris notebook, sat splayed open on the coffee table, not at all where I'd left it, serving as a coaster for a venti Starbucks iced tea.

"You're awake," Lily said.

I picked up the notebook and slammed the dripping plastic cup down on an actual coaster.

"I am."

"You okay?"

"Fine!"

"Mom called. I told her you were sick and now she's freaking out because you never get sick." She squinted, considering me. "Can you call her back? Make it sound mild. Bad period cramps or whatever."

"Okay." I could imagine all the times Lily had used that as her excuse to get out of something. It probably worked like a charm. Life must be so much easier when you didn't care what other people might think, what effect your actions might have.

"Like soon, because otherwise she'll just start harassing me—"

"I said 'okay.'"

Lily raised her hands in surrender and made a face implying I was the difficult one.

In my bedroom, I propped the warped notebook on my lap, each page sopped with a cup-size ring. The prices, the dates, the words, blurred at the edges, running together into an indecipherable web. It wasn't so much the violation; it's not like this was a typical diary. Lily needed somewhere to set her drink and grabbed any old thing, her distorted way of being considerate. The black cover had already been dinged and the bottom corners bent. It didn't look special.

But it was the principle.

I was the notebook, a log of inaction, used as a coaster by Lily, and everyone. Everyone who didn't think I had it in me to surprise them. Well.

What was I waiting for?

I opened my laptop and searched for flights to Paris. In three days' time, I could travel for $2,000. This, I knew from my collating, was a terrible deal. It was no deal at all, a last-minute booking for suckers and the truly desperate. But I didn't need a deal. I had money saved. I had three weeks' paid vacation at my disposal. What I needed was an escape hatch, a parachute, an exit.

Enter Paris. *Au revoir*, San Jose.

Dear Gladys,

Say hello to Rose Zadeh, solo traveler and intrepid explorer.

I've gone and done it. I'm going to Paris. My dream trip. My fantasy city. It's really happening, and I can hardly believe it, but I have a plane ticket and the angry texts from my mom to prove it.

I'm happy, Gladys, or at least I would be if I weren't so worried. About hurting my family and sucking at my job, and, oh, you know, failing at the one chance I may ever have to be someone else. How can you tell the difference between anxiety and excitement? How do you know when you're doing something for yourself or just being selfish?

Yours,
Flight Bound with Baggage for Days Delilah

7

Weekdays during our childhood, Dad was a brick wall, unscalable and impassable. He worked late, rarely made it home for dinner except on Fridays, and once he was home, he didn't have the bandwidth for his daughters' big emotions and minor squabbles. He would tuck us into bed before he retreated to the couch, barely able to smile past the knot of tension between his eyes.

The weekends were different. That was when he hoisted Iris on his shoulders and chased Lily around the yard screeching like a T. rex. That was when I sought him out in the kitchen and he welcomed me with a cheerful, "What's cooking, Rose?" like that was some great joke.

When I was little, he set me on the counter to watch him, and later, he let me balance on the step stool. Eventually, I grew big enough to stand beside him, peering over his dark, hair-streaked arms to the stove.

He taught me how to grind saffron strands in the handheld mortar and pestle—not too hard or the precious threads would scatter—and the way dried fenugreek leaves looked just like dried parsley but smelled like maple syrup if you rubbed them between your fingertips. The dried whole limes he used had the faces of angry old men, and after I named them, he let me drop each into the *ghormeh sabzi* and stir until they softened.

Once—I couldn't have been more than seven or eight—I found him squatting on the kitchen's linoleum floor leaning over a broad cardboard box. It had arrived earlier in the week, carted into the entryway by Dad's longtime friend, Hamid, one of the other Persian guys he'd lived with when he first arrived in the US. Hamid had stopped to visit the Zadeh family during a recent trip to Tehran and generously carted the package back with him.

After he set down the heavy box, Hamid had pulled a handful of dried mulberries from a bag in his pocket and handed them to me with a wink.

"More treats in there," he'd said, and since then, the box had taunted my curiosity. It languished all through the week in the entry, until, finally, Saturday, Dad in the kitchen, plucking goodies from it like Mary Poppins with her carpetbag.

Dad opened a plastic-wrapped package that looked like a Fruit Roll-Up except it didn't come in the colorful box I recognized from the supermarket. "Try it." He tore me off a piece. "*Lavashak.*"

When I popped the leathery bite in my mouth, the flavors of salt and sour plum puckered my tongue. I went back for more while he kept digging. There was a baby blanket for Lily, and for Iris, a homemade doll with black eyes and hair, nestled in a woven purse.

Finally, from the bottom of the box, he pulled out a small leather pouch with a delicate gold bracelet inside.

"This is for you." He slipped the thin band over my hand, the overhead light shining in the metal as I swished my wrist back and forth, marveling at the feeling of the bangle against my skin. "Fourteen karat gold. Do you know what that means?" he asked.

"What?"

"It means this bracelet is precious, like you." He swept his arms out wide. "It came from very far away, across the whole world. It means your grandparents are proud of you and want you to have a good life."

I didn't know my grandparents except by a few photos and the cadence of their voices on the phone. They sounded so far away and were so impossible to understand they might as well have been calling from another planet. That they cared about me enough to send such a special present filled my scrawny frame with importance.

Dad continued. "You shouldn't take it off in case you might lose it. If you don't want to wear it, I'll hold on to it for you."

He put out his hand to take back the bracelet, and I snatched my wrist to my chest.

"I want to keep it," I said. "I won't lose it. I promise."

Dad patted my head with his dry paw. "I know you won't. I trust you."

With his hands on his thighs, he lifted himself from the floor. "Now, what should we cook today? Hmm? I feel like pasta. How about red sauce?"

We set to work opening heavy cans of whole tomatoes and plucking cloves of garlic from their skins. With each movement, my eyes returned to my glittering gift. I didn't take it off until my arm grew so big that the band began to dig into my skin and had to be cut by a jeweler from my wrist.

❦

The bracelet was on my mind as Iris drove me to the airport. I kept the cut piece in a box on my bookshelf, and I wished I'd thought to bring it with me before I left, like it might have been good luck to have it in my pocket as I traveled halfway around the globe. It took me a while to notice Iris was giving me the cold shoulder.

"Don't be mad," I said as Iris pulled up outside the international terminal.

She shook her head, refusing to look at me. "I'm not. I hate when people leave."

We both knew she was talking about Dad, but what could I do?

"It's a temporary goodbye."

"The timing feels weird. And you're missing my final dress fitting."

"I wish I could be there," I said. "But I've seen you in the dress, and I know you'll look beautiful."

She blinked rapidly and stared out the windshield, twisting her hands on the steering wheel. If she started crying, I wouldn't be able to get out of the car. "Iris," I pleaded.

"Move it along," a voice barked outside the window. "No idling." The officer flung his arm toward the road and glared at Iris.

"You gotta go before I get a ticket." She popped the trunk, and I leaned over the console to pull her in for a hug.

"I'll make it up to you," I said. "And we'll text."

I hauled my luggage to the curb and watched her drive away until I knew she was long gone. After I made it through security, my phone vibrated, and my heart lifted. Iris might be texting to tell me it was okay, let me off the guilt hook. Instead, the message was from Lily: Thanks for loaning me your apartment.

Well, at least someone was happy I was going.

No sooner had the thought cheered me, she followed with another text: Oh, also, big thanks for ditching me during my emotional crisis. Cool, cool.

I squinted at the words, trying to discern if she was joking. Possibly. Probably not.

I'm still here if you need me, I wrote. She didn't respond. Which was just as well. I needed space to calm the giddy, bouncing kid inside me. The last two days had been a frenzied push to get everything ready, including having my car declared totaled by my insurance company and leaving Lily with strict instructions not to burn down my apartment and to water FiFi every few days. I figured her continued stay was my penance for the car wreck, and I still hoped time away from Dev would do her some real good. Apparently, I'd forgotten to factor in her general neediness.

Oh well. Paris was happening! At-the-airport, flight-departing-in-two-hours happening.

There was no going back.

I choked down a dry turkey sandwich with the help of a tongue-curling Bloody Mary and thumbed the magazines at a newsstand kiosk until my flight was called.

I couldn't believe I was going through with this. I'd never so much as traveled out of state alone, and now, I was on my way to another country where I couldn't even attempt to speak the language without embarrassing myself. I would be on my own for more than two weeks. It was what I wanted, right? Nothing but myself and Google Maps to guide me.

A rush of cold sent goose bumps rising on my arms. Oh God. What was I thinking?

I should have settled for a spa day in San Francisco or a solo night somewhere boring and safe, like Sonoma or Solvang. Wait—I shook off the impending panic—boring and safe were not the point. I was in the market for adventure.

Once I was settled in my seat, I pulled out my phone, calmed by its solid weight in my hand, the promise of home right at my fingertips, and texted Mom an "I love you" and a quick farewell. Her response came in a string of lightning-fast texts.

Alice Zadeh:

I can't believe you've decided to go through with this . . . I still think it is a terrible idea. Your father would kill me if he knew I let you go . . .

I've forwarded Marco Dariano's information to your email . . . Reach out to him when you arrive. It would make me feel so much better to know there's someone there you can trust . . .

KEEP IN TOUCH! BE SAFE!

Be safe, as if it was all that safe in the US. Please. I should have known she wouldn't be a comfort. Even when we were little, she wouldn't let us go down the big slide except on her lap. She still reached out to grab our hands in a crowded parking lot. But the words "let you go" clawed at me. She still thought she got a say.

And whose fault is that?

With a rough jab, I switched my phone to airplane mode and stuffed it deep into the seat pocket in front of me. I fidgeted with my backpack, cracked my knuckles, clenched and unclenched my toes.

"Nervous flyer?" The voice was sweet, melodic with a gentle French accent. It came from a woman with a fierce black bob seated to my left. Her neck was long and thin, her collarbone pronounced and delicate beneath a soft white tee.

"A little," I said. "I've never been to France before." Or out of the country, for that matter, but I didn't want this chic woman to think me an uncultured American.

"Ah," she said, "here," and slipped into my palm a small candy wrapped in lavender paper. I popped it in my mouth, and a cool peppermint sensation spread across my tongue. The woman smiled.

"Keeping the mouth busy calms the heart."

"Are you from Paris?"

"Originally, yes. Now I live in the south of France in a little bitty village." She pinched her thumb and forefinger together. "My husband and I are flying into Paris to see our daughter before we take the train the rest of the way home."

"Mm-hmm." Enchanted by her voice, I half listened and half imagined all the pleasant conversations I'd have with the French in the future.

"Our daughter runs an art gallery in the Third. She has a big opening the night after tomorrow."

I perked up a little. "I'm staying in the Third. The Marais, right?"

"Yes, wonderful. Have you heard of Guy Laurent?"

I considered pretending I had but thought better of it and shook my head.

"I hadn't heard of him either. My daughter, Elise, she is a follower of avant-garde art. But not me. In general, my daughter and I are quite different. I respect her independence, but sometimes it veers on unpleasant. What is your name?"

"Rose Zadeh."

"I'm Marine Desjardins. My husband is Alain." She gestured toward the back of the plane.

"I could trade with him, if you wanted," I said, although I didn't want to lose my row near the front.

She raised her hand. "*Non.* That is not necessary. I prefer to miss him a little, you know?"

The plane sped up as we coursed down the runway. The heavy body lifting in the fabric of my being, a bird taking flight. I gripped the armrest.

"What are you doing in Paris?" Marine asked.

"I've wanted to go for ages." She passed me another mint. "The opportunity presented itself. Sort of."

"Ah." She tapped a trimmed red nail against the armrest between us. "Your first time in Paris is special." She frowned. "There is also the potential for dismay. Like making love, no? When expectations are so high, it is not a recipe for success. I always tell this to my clients when they fall in love. The endorphins are like a drug, but you must stay in touch with reality."

"Are you a therapist?" She seemed the part: wise, kind, intimidating.

"Research psychologist. My publisher says you Americans would refer to me as a love coach. I study physical communication. You know, body language."

"Oh." My body stiffened on command, and she laughed.

"See, it is obvious you are nervous, agitated, but the question is, why? Without yet having an answer, my suggestion to you is to embrace the body language you want. If you are sad, smile. Scared? Open yourself up. The real emotions often follow, and the world responds in kind."

I released my arms and tried to relax my shoulders.

"Much better." She patted my hand. "Now, tell me, is it fear of flying or something else weighing on you?"

"I need to have the trip of a lifetime," I blurted without thinking. "I have three weeks to do it."

Marine cocked her head. "That is a lot of pressure for a vacation."

I barked a nervous laugh. The plane vibrated against its ascent; my grip on the armrest tightened. "Well, if I'm going to upset my whole family, and I basically have, then it needs to be worth it." What was I doing? I had said more aloud to Marine than I'd even admitted to myself. The plane's engines churned, the cabin rattled, and the words kept coming. "One sister is hurt because I'm abandoning her before her wedding, the other sister is annoyed because I'm abandoning her during a so-called emotional crisis, my mom's panicking because I'm abandoning her, period. And my dad . . ."

The plane dipped and my stomach somersaulted. I closed my eyes.

"An air pocket, I think." Marine lifted my hand and placed another mint in my palm. "So you will have the best Paris holiday ever, and then what?"

"Then? Then, I go back home. But I'll always know I did this one kind of amazing thing that no one, including me, believed I would have the nerve to do. Even if my life is . . . even if nothing ever changes, I'll have this time to look back on. And maybe . . ."

"Yes?"

Maybe I'll figure out what I want to do with my life. Maybe I'll find a reason not to come home. The words flashed through my mind before I could stop them. As quickly as they came, I tossed them aside, like the handful of cringeworthy responses I'd composed to *Your Grrl, Gladys* letter writers when I didn't think she'd nailed the answer. Who did I think I was trying to solve other people's problems when I couldn't even fix my own?

I doubted Marine could understand any of this. She emanated confidence the way the men who worked at Genomix did. Like certainty was part of their DNA. Was it possible for someone like me to become more like Marine? I thought of *Gladys* again.

"Do you give advice, as a love coach?"

She squinted up at the air vents in thought. "I am able to name things many people feel but don't know how to express. Bodies speak the words of the heart. Most minds are not very engaged listeners. I write to help people translate the language of the body so they can listen better and speak what's inside more clearly."

"I write, too. Nothing like that, though. Nothing that matters."

"All words matter." Marine's purse inched out from the seat in front of her, and she reached down, fiddled with the contents, then nudged the bag back with the toe of her Hepburn-esque ballet flat.

During the lull in conversation, Genomix's new slogan reverberated in my mind: *Changing your life from the inside out.* I was proud of the words because I thought the slogan's success meant the new role would be mine, but the message didn't mean anything to me. It was marketing jargon to make people feel safe sharing their DNA. I explained as much to Marine without going into the enforced time off.

"You know, I was the same. In the beginning, I studied only biological topics, sleep, memory, because they seemed to carry more gravity—uh—no . . ." She shook her head, searching for the right word.

"Gravitas?"

"Yes! More gravitas. But I grew bored. I found language interesting, so I turned my attention there, and then to unspoken language. In the end, I realized my true passion is human connection. There is nothing more important, I believe. I wrote my first book, and I continue to study and learn." She paused. "To answer your question, I would not say I give advice. I've always found suggestion to be more powerful than advice. Do you agree?"

"Oh gosh, what do I know? I can hardly advise myself."

The seat belt light dinged, went dark. The plane had leveled out, the ride had smoothed. I released my hold on the seat rest, and my lungs filled.

"There are different kinds of knowing. I have known you less than one hour, and I am certain you are smart and thoughtful. Perhaps you know more than you think you do."

I shook my head, unsure what to say. I'd said too much already. The static that marked the loudspeaker coming to life sounded throughout the cabin and the captain informed us we'd reached cruising altitude.

"In that case"—Marine read her watch—"I have approximately eleven hours to convince you."

8

"A ride?" Alain said for the third time as we stood by the baggage carousel, his gray hair rumpled from the rough fabric seats of the plane. The sleep creases on his face made me smile, but I refused the offer.

I would do this myself.

I pocketed Marine's email and phone number and promised to let her know if I ever ventured to Provence.

"*Merci*," I said to her and Alain, and a memory of Dad's voice came back to me, his polite thank-you in Farsi each time I made him a cup of tea or fitted his slippers on his feet once he was too weak to bend over: "*Merci, Rose joon.*" A thorn poked my lung, and I waited for the hole to seal, the space to fill so I could take a breath and move again.

Wobbling along with my luggage, I searched for the train that would take me to the city's center. Less than an hour later, I was pleased to be settled on a seat hurtling toward my next stop, as if I'd passed some test I hadn't even needed to study for. I'd paid for international cellular service, and the moment I turned on my phone I was flooded with text notifications.

I wouldn't look. Not yet.

Dragging my suitcase off the RER B and into Gare du Nord station, I stumbled into a throng of people shifting from one direction and another, the frenetic pace leaving me breathless.

Other than a few school-sanctioned field trips by bus and one trolley ride while visiting San Francisco, I'd never taken public transportation. From the driver's seat of my Mazda (RIP), the notion had seemed, if not glamorous, at least convenient, even a little righteous. Amid the frenzied movement, the disturbing warmth drifting from the tracks, and the reproachful signs I couldn't read, I wouldn't have described the experience as exciting or even convenient.

I shoved my suitcase against a wall and attempted to orient myself. To reach rue du Vertbois in the Marais, I needed the 4 to Réaumur-Sébastopol station.

I followed the signs, jostled like a fallen leaf carried on a current, not a grown woman with a large bag, purse, and suitcase.

Things got worse at the next ticket kiosk thanks to my credit card, which refused to glide into the machine. Once I managed to force my card inside the slot, the machine wouldn't recognize it. I tried another kiosk, same thing. Heat flared beneath my clothes, nausea rolled over me. *Do not panic,* I told myself, hands vibrating as I attempted the final kiosk. When my card slid into the card reader, a current of relief rushed my limbs, strengthening my momentary success into fearlessness.

The feeling was fleeting.

My suitcase got stuck sideways in the turnstile, the backup earning me more than one angry comment and an incomprehensible but severe scolding from a man wearing the pointiest shoes I'd ever seen. On the other side, a small woman with a tuft of white hair attempted to speak to me. All I could do was shake my head like the clueless person I was. I didn't blame her when she threw up her hands and wandered away.

A grasp of French *really* would have come in handy, but I couldn't even speak the language of my ancestors. Dad had refused to teach us Farsi: he was becoming a real American, he had real American daughters, and real Americans spoke English. It wasn't until I got to high school and other kids with immigrant parents questioned my inability to speak my dad's native language that this omission morphed into something glaring, strange, and a little sad. If Mom had also been Iranian, it might have been different. As it was, by the time Dad recognized his mistake, we were too old to pick up anything more than a random word or phrase.

Out of my depth and bumbling around the Metro station, I would have given anything to be bilingual, as if the ability to speak another language, *any* other language, would prove me more sophisticated and worldly than I appeared. Stick me in cargo shorts, a Hard Rock Cafe T-shirt, and sandals with socks up to my calves, and I'd only look marginally lamer.

Happy, Dad? I'm an American, alright, the embarrassing, tourist kind.

But then, Dad had plenty of experience as a fish out of water, didn't he? He'd learned the hard way to have Mom check his important emails for embarrassing ESL typos. And to never raise his voice in public. After 9/11, he stuck an American flag outside the house like the rest of the neighborhood, only he never took ours down.

How exhausting for him, the constant cultural trial by fire with everything to lose, and here I was griping two hours into my travels. I rolled my shoulders back, held firm to the handle of my suitcase, and pushed myself forward, muttering a string of *Sorrys* as I puttered my way through the station, onto and off the next train.

Miraculously, I reached my stop, but the exertion of carrying my bags up the flights of stairs left me bent over and gasping. Rattled and exhausted by the time I made it to street level, my arms and legs had gone to pudding, and I was desperate for my apartment rental.

But I still had farther to go, and the last leg required a clunky walk down narrow, stained sidewalks dodging pedestrians and piles of dog crap, my back burning. My mood lifted when I found the oversize door and pushed my way into a cramped courtyard smelling cloyingly sweet, not of the pastries I imagined in my most vivid fantasies, but of overripe fruit. Flies buzzed around a collection of overfilled trash cans. I was too delirious to care.

I fumbled with the keypad to access the door keys and nothing happened. I tried again, but the code I punched did little except make me more panicked and frustrated.

"Okay. I'm okay."

I plucked my phone from my backpack and dialed the number of the apartment owner, Paulette. I couldn't pretend not to see the red notification bubble hovering over my Messages app, but I wasn't ready to think about home yet. Not when I hadn't even officially made it to my destination. Fortunately, I didn't have time to think about it for too long. Paulette answered on the second ring, and she was decent enough to not sound too put out when she told me she'd leave work to come let me in.

"The lockbox is not so reliable," she said. "Stay there."

I laid my suitcase down and made myself as comfortable as I could on top of it, until Paulette appeared, helping me to my feet. Together, we carried my luggage up the five circular flights of worn wooden stairs, our footsteps echoing against the stairwell.

The apartment's herringbone floors gleamed with light passing through three sets of tall windows in the living room, each bookended by ribbons of black curtain. Black-and-white prints sparsely dotted the white walls. Modern and stylish, not unlike its rightful owner, Paulette, who was compact with café-au-lait-colored hair knotted in a tight, round bun at the base of her neck. Her cheekbones flamed pink, from the walk up the stairs to the apartment I assumed, but otherwise her skin shone as pale and pristine as the marble coffee table we sat around. I, meanwhile, stayed sticky with sweat, still panting from the exertion.

"Be careful with the plumbing. It is ancient. Picky."

"Picky. Okay." I hardly listened, too jet-lagged to think straight, too busy tugging my shirt for a bit of air. "Do you have AC?"

She looked at me blankly.

"Air-conditioning?"

"Ah, no." She laughed through her nose, as if I'd told a silly joke. "It can help to close the shutters during the day. I leave them open because it is prettier this way, no?" Apparently, she was an evolved human impervious to heat. "Now, please tell me, would you like any recommendations?"

"Coffee," I said. "And croissants. I would like a lot of both."

She raised a finger, pulled a pen and notepad from her purse, and began to draw a map. "From the door, turn left until you hit the next street, then right, then left. Boulangerie Etienne. The best pastries and croissants, first thing in the morning."

She charted some more lines, squinting in concentration.

"Here"—she pointed to a small square—"the best coffee. Brass Key. American style, which I think you will prefer. In France, we drink milk in our coffee only with breakfast." She smiled. "As a reminder, I tell my guests to use proper greetings when you enter a shop or café. *Bonjour*, *bonsoir*, et cetera. Most Parisians speak some English, but they prefer you try a little French first."

"That's really helpful." I made a mental note. "Thank you."

"What else?" She tapped her pen against the table, her eyebrows inching up. "Ah, yes, *bien sûr*!" She lifted a pointer finger in realization. "You've heard about the art theft?" I gave her a blank stare, and she shooed my ignorance away with a shake of her head. "Some drawings were stolen a few days ago from a small museum in the Ninth. It's a great mystery because the night guard says the doors were locked and could not tell the cameras had stopped working."

"An inside job?" I muttered.

"The guard does not say so. But he wouldn't, would he?" She threw open her hands. "The city is captivated. It is the biggest art crime here in close to a decade."

"The sketches were valuable?"

"They are not famous works, but still, they are valuable enough. Even the smallest museums in Paris are full of treasures. That is not why everyone is so excited, because perhaps it is practice for something else. A bigger museum."

I nodded politely. All I wanted to do was kick off my shoes and pass out. How sweet to be horizontal, eyes closed, feet up.

Paulette must have sensed my waning interest. She quickly added, "I'm telling you because you will find extra security at the museums. This means lines will be longer. I assume you booked tickets in advance, but I suggest you visit early or late. Yes?"

"Oh, I haven't booked anything. I haven't actually planned anything." A quizzical look muddied Paulette's clear face. I sounded ridiculous. It was one thing to keep your plans open, entirely another not to have a single reservation.

How could I explain that after my many years dreaming of Paris, envisioning striped-awning-lined boulevards, river boats gliding along the Seine, the moody sound of accordions playing under lamplight, I hadn't thought in specifics or practicalities? What *had* I expected? The city to roll out a red carpet leading me from one place to the next? That wasn't quite right either. It was more like I imagined being bopped with a magic wand, one that would enchant me with the adventure of a Hollywood movie, the spirit of a plucky heroine, and the guts I lacked at home.

When I'd told Mom about booking my ticket, she'd given me an earful that ended with an annoying platitude: "Just so you know, wherever you go, there you are." And as she predicted, here I was, mauled by jet lag, disjointed by my bumpy arrival, and 100 percent me. Still waiting for something to happen, like I'd waited for a promotion, a boyfriend.

Perhaps sensing my uncertainty, Paulette said, "You know, I like to get to know the people who stay with me. Good to know people from everywhere, yes? It is one reason I rent my apartment, not only for money. Would it be nice for us to meet later this week?"

I sensed a pity offer and wasn't sure befriending my apartment host made much sense, but I nodded eagerly just the same. If I wanted things to be different, I'd have to do things differently. Paris wasn't going to happen to me. I had to seek it out.

"*Bon, je dois y aller.* I will email." She smoothed the stray hairs sneaking from her forehead and placed the pen and notepad back in her purse. "I will leave you to be settled. Do you have other questions?"

How do I make sure I do all the things? What are all the things I should do?

"No," I said. "I don't think so."

She paused, waiting for me to change my mind, perhaps. When I didn't say anything else, she stood.

At the door, she shoved her makeshift map into my sweaty palm. "I will stay with my parents, not too far away, so call if you need help." The space between her eyebrows wrinkled. "Will you be okay?" I could imagine how she saw me, disheveled, exhausted, confused. Clueless.

"Yes," I said. "I'll be fine." I hoped it was true.

9

I woke disoriented in a dark, sweltering bedroom to the urgent call of a siren rushing outside the building. I didn't recognize anything and confronted a heart-stopping split-second of terror before I remembered where I was.

What I was, was starving. I'd passed out as soon as Paulette left and now it was after eight. I last ate on the flight, a banana and a lead bagel purchased in the airport because I found airline food barely palatable. My stomach roared in protest. I dug through my bag in search of sustenance.

Protein bar in hand, I opened the window and let the summer night sweep over me. The city smelled like warm asphalt and exhaust, and a sweeter scent I couldn't put my finger on.

Scooters and cars sped down the street, voices rose from a café at the corner, somewhere nearby music beat into the night. I was used to traffic and noise and hot nights, but here the sounds, the sensations, enveloped me in a new way, as if I'd stepped into a parallel world.

A current of energy nipped my nerves.

I hadn't been in contact with home in almost a day. The realization made me giddy and a little nauseous, too. Mom would be beside herself, and I swore to Iris I'd check in the first moment I could.

Notifications lined my phone.

Alice Zadeh:

Why didn't you text me to let me know you'd landed safely?? I had to search your flight number. Now where are you? Text me all the time so I know you're okay.

I promised Sylvia you would email Marco. She's like me and worries a lot. It can't hurt to know someone in the city . . . Lily misses having you at home, but she said not to tell you, so don't tell her I said anything . . . Iris was in a mood at her dress fitting . . . I wish she wouldn't take on so much . . . The rodent infestation continues . . . It's possible I'll be eaten alive by rats in my sleep. Please let me know the moment you get this, so I don't worry to death.

Is your phone working?

Hello?

Iris Zadeh:

You're there! I'm so excited for you. But also devastated you're not here. I had the dress fitting today, and Mom and Lily were too busy enjoying the prosecco to care what I looked like.

What do I do without you?

Please send pics. And help.

Bisous 😘

From my seat in the window, I drank in the subtle breeze. It unnerved me how home could be so far away and so near. Their messages were arms pulling me back. If I let them reach me, they wouldn't let go. My trip still felt precarious, like a single wrong move might send me tumbling through a portal straight back to my apartment in San Jose. I sent them a quick group text: I've arrived safely. It's bedtime here. I'll send more updates soon ❤

Mom would find the lack of information infuriating, but at least it would allay their fears and give me more time.

Dad was on my mind again. Our situations couldn't have been more different. I mean, c'mon, how do you compare traveling to Paris at thirty-two on little more than a lark with fleeing a turbulent country amid political chaos? But alone, so far from California, my thoughts buckled under the weight of his reality: flying solo to a new country, barely an adult, where he had no family, little money, an unsteady grasp of the language and way of life, and the knowledge, wedged beside his passport and a black-and-white wallet-size picture of his parents, that he would never go home again.

Even though he hardly mentioned how he left Tehran and even though I couldn't remember hearing the whole story in a single sitting, his journey was family lore. Somehow, the facts were part of the Zadeh daughter DNA.

Fact: While other young men took to the streets of Tehran to protest the Shah of Iran in what would become known as the Iranian Revolution, Mohammad Zadeh stayed head down in a state of keen awareness. He had to get out and he had to get out now.

Fact: To procure a visa, he waited every day for a week in the line outside the hulking US Embassy building in Tehran. When it was clear he was running out of time, his brother created a diversion at the door, and with the security guards' broad backs turned, Dad rushed to the next free window.

Fact: In the first days of 1979, with opposition toward the Shah increasing, Dad gave what would be his final farewell to his parents and his brother and decamped to the airport, a few hundred borrowed dollars in his pocket, where he waited for four days as one flight after another was canceled. On the fifth day, he boarded what turned out to be the last flight from Tehran to London before the airport shut down.

Fact: After a brief stay in London while he secured his flight to the US, he finally landed in SFO a week later to stay with a friend of a cousin. He slept on a twin mattress on the floor of a ground-level room with four other Iranian guys, and even though it was winter, they kept the sliding glass doors open every night because the sounds from a nearby intersection reminded them of sleeping on the roof back home.

He was a dishwasher and a gas station attendant and a janitor at an orthodontist's office, and as his English improved, a busboy and a service associate at a Toyota dealership. He went to school one class at a time, struggling in everything except math, the numerical language both familiar and obedient, working toward a degree in computer science. And one day he walked into the Pins and Lanes Bowling Alley in Santa Clara where a young blonde woman, with a gold cross dangling around her neck and a penchant for talking too much to the customers, waited tables on the weekends.

Dad would say facts were like numbers: reliable, clear, all you needed to form an answer. But even with the few facts he'd shared, I sometimes feared I didn't really know him. I craved his words so I could inhabit his story, but his experiences, the building blocks of my entire existence, had been buried alongside him.

Once, a few months before he died, I'd gathered the courage to ask him what it was like when he got here. He described waiting outside the terminal at SFO for his ride to arrive, shaking with exhaustion and excitement. "My teeth were chattering. I looked around and couldn't recognize anything or anyone. People rushing around me, going wherever they needed without a care. I was no one to them, just another guy," he said. "I was so happy. I made it to US." After chemo, he'd begun to drop certain articles of speech, like "the," more and more frequently, his accent thickening as his hair disappeared. "It was an impossible dream. But I did it. Freedom."

"Weren't you scared?" I demanded.

"No," Dad said, a little sharply. "No. I wasn't thinking about that. You don't understand, Rose. I had to come to the US. I knew I belonged since I was a young boy. I didn't want to leave my family, but I *had* to. I wanted opportunity, freedom, democracy. I wanted a voice that counted."

The sounds of Paris rushed back to me, pushing me into the present. I looked out the window again, the streetlights creating a warm glow across my lap.

Paris.

I had made it, too.

I stood, shivering as a whiff of breeze caught my bare arms. *I made it all the way here. On my own.*

A growl sounded from my belly again. The bar had satiated me for a minute, but the portion didn't fool my ravenous hunger. I hadn't anticipated exploring the city streets tonight, but it was dinnertime, and I wanted to prove something to myself. To Dad. He was the bravest person I knew. Perhaps here in Paris I would discover he'd passed some of that down to me.

First, food. How hard could it be to find a table in a cozy neighborhood restaurant? After all, this was the land of butter and cream. Effortless dining was basically guaranteed with the purchase of your plane ticket.

The harsh scent of cigarette smoke tickled my nose as I crossed the street to Brasserie Colette. I'd done a quick search for classic French restaurants in my neighborhood and found one with the best *poulet rôti* this side of the Seine.

I came to the entrance at the same time as a couple not much older than myself. The man held open the door, his lip twitching toward a smile.

"*Bonsoir,*" he said, and I nodded. His partner and I passed through, and together we hovered by the door waiting for the maître d' to notice us.

The woman spoke to me in French. "Sorry?" I said, struggling to recall the few default phrases I'd tried to memorize.

"Ah, I thought you might be American," she said pleasantly.

"Is it that obvious?"

She glanced at her companion, then back at me. "Are you traveling alone?"

I squared my shoulders and straightened my posture, trying to match her height. "I am, actually. First night."

"Wow. Good for you. How daring you must be."

Before I could respond, the maître d' appeared, limping and unhurried. He placed a pair of reading glasses on his nose and ran a skinny finger down the pages of a heavy book set on a high table. Then he removed the glasses and said something to me. I recognized only a curt "bonsoir" at the beginning.

"*Bonsoir,*" I attempted. "Uh, *je ne parle pas francais.*" His head didn't so much as tilt with recognition. I was aware of the man and woman watching. "Um, *pardonnez-moi*. I mean, *parlez-vous anglais*?"

"Yes, of course." But his eyes said much more, something like, *You are an American moron and it pains me to waste my breath on the likes of you*. He cleared his throat. "I asked if you were next. Or . . . can I?" He gestured with a jerk of his wrist to the couple next to me.

"Oh, me? No, yeah, they were next." The heat from the nearby kitchen caught up to me, and I tugged my blouse for a burst of cold air.

"No, no," said the man with the twitchy smile, resting his hand on the woman's shoulder. "Please, go ahead."

"Thank you, but I really insist."

The maître d' huffed his impatience, and the woman looked at me, head cocked with pity. "Are you sure?"

Suddenly nauseous, I couldn't open my mouth but nodded, smiling. The couple was led away to a table, and I fled the restaurant as soon as I was out of their line of sight.

Outside, the sweat on my back left me cold and clammy. I stepped from the curb to cross the street and a loud honk startled me backward. A scooter zipped off into the night, the driver tossing out an angry shout as he passed. Everything was unfamiliar here, even the insults, the sound of a horn blaring on an empty street. I clutched my bag, resisting the urge to call home.

My vision blurred. I rubbed my eyes and blinked away the threat of tears.

I would not cry. I would not cry because I was on the trip of a lifetime. I had one chance to get this right, and I wasn't going to waste another minute.

Dad had looked out at the busy Arrivals terminal, every sign unreadable, every face unrecognizable, and he didn't say, "Gee, maybe this was a big mistake." I may not have been born with Dad's nerve, but I could channel his optimism. Tomorrow would be better. It had to be.

Dear Gladys,

I've dreamed of Paris for more than a decade. The trouble is that for all my dreaming, I never planned a single thing. It's barely been a day, and I'm starting to have my doubts.

All those ferociously upbeat travel articles I binged after booking my flight might have been written for a different sort of person. I was an idiot to think I could do something like this on my own, wasn't I?

I'm not brave, Gladys. When my mom said I shouldn't go, I should have listened. There's still time to turn things around, but how? How do I go home bearing tales, not a tail between my legs?

Sincerely,
One Part Regretful, Two Parts Panicked in Paris

10

The next morning, I stepped from the apartment building's courtyard back onto rue du Vertbois. The heavy doors clicked shut behind me. Bright shafts of sunlight snuck through the cloud cover; the air was muggy. I yanked off my sweater and stuck it into my little leather backpack. The sounds of construction—a jackhammer pummeling a patch of road, an electric saw whirring inside a building, metal clattering against metal—followed me as I walked in the direction of the Metro station.

First stop, the Eiffel Tower, of course. I'd memorized the route and which train to take before leaving the apartment but pulled out my phone anyway, more confident with it in hand. My body swayed as the train car trundled through the dark tunnel. A gray-haired man seated across from me shook out his newspaper, and I caught a brief glimpse of the cover image, a simple sketch of a figure in profile. I didn't have a chance to see the headline and wouldn't have recognized the words anyway, but I knew it was about the theft. A real-life Paris art heist. And here I was in the thick of the excitement.

I couldn't help grinning when I made it off the Metro and exited at La Motte-Picquet-Grenelle station, which left me tongue-tied just to think. The day had warmed in the time I'd been in transit, and back aboveground, I was uncomfortable even without my sweater. Still, my spirit was light each time *La Tour* came into view.

But like some sort of trick of the eyes, the closer I got, the less magic it held.

By the time I stood beneath its massive metal undercarriage, I felt only sweaty and tired and repelled by the swarm of tourists. The place was a hive of activity, and waiting in line, I flashed back to the one time my parents loaded us in the car and drove to Disneyland. Same lines. Same crowd. Same sense of anticipation pinned down with disappointment because everyone was experiencing the same brand of magic as you, and what's so magical about that?

I nestled into the elevator car. The gears whirred, carrying the car slowly up to the top, and I wanted to be excited. But even though the city view was neat, hazy as it was, I couldn't shake the sensation of expecting something more. Crossing the Golden Gate Bridge back home, whitewashed buildings rising above the fog, the bright-blue bay below, was grander, more picturesque.

Back on the ground, I wandered for a while, starving for lunch, too intimidated after my experience the night before to try one of the places busy with locals and too determined to avoid an overpriced tourist trap. I settled on a bakery with a glass case of small baguette sandwiches so perfect they looked molded from marzipan. I scarfed a salty *jambon-beurre* standing on the corner, and went back for another: prosciutto, arugula, and fig jam. I walked toward the Louvre with a third tucked in my backpack.

A purse thwacked my arm hard enough to leave my elbow aching. The body bumping into mine belonged to a woman who all but growled at me.

I rubbed at my elbow and dodged the next person headed in my direction. The number of people surrounding all sides of the place du Carrousel shocked me. I'd read online to avoid the Louvre's pyramid entrance, and instead walked to rue de Rivoli, but the crowds were intense.

To think, for a second, I'd found the prospect of an art heist thrilling. More like annoying. Another moment where the reality couldn't compete with my fantasy. Could it ever?

Besides the packs of people, security was fierce. Stone-faced men as solid and menacing as gargoyles stood with guns at the gates. Inside, people in stiff suits looked out of place, their eyes trained on the visitors, not the art.

The halls and galleries were, luckily, less busy than outside. I ambled without a destination and soon became disoriented, each canvas blurring with the next, until the artwork didn't seem remarkable but as commonplace as cheaply framed Van Gogh prints on a coffee shop wall.

Eventually, I found the *Mona Lisa*, and after wriggling my way through the mass of milling visitors angling for a close-up peek, I decided this was no way to experience art. Surrounded by some of the most beautiful works ever created, and my throbbing arches were the number one thing on my mind.

Maybe the museum was my problem. Everyone said you had to go to the Louvre, but I'd never heard anyone say they had the "best time ever" there.

What time was it, anyway?

I dug through my backpack in search of my phone, one pocket, another, but it was nowhere.

"No." This couldn't be happening. "No, no, no."

Blood rushed to my head. The space between my eyes throbbed.

I retraced my steps, but back at the entrance of the museum the reality of my situation began to sink in. With the knowledge came the terrifying recognition of how alone I was. There was no one to help me retrace my steps. No one to look one way while I searched the other direction.

Frantic, I ran to a hefty, angry-looking security guard. "*Excusez-moi?* I need help."

"Yes?"

"Where is the lost and found?"

"Information desk," he grunted, and pointed somewhere behind me. Before I could get far, a firm American voice literally stopped me in my tracks.

"Is this yours?"

The question came from a man dressed in pastel-green chinos and a light pink collared shirt unbuttoned at the neck. I averted my gaze from the sneak peek of velvet chest and took in his remarkable face. He was short, not even an inch on my five-five frame, but whatever he lost in height he made up for in a face so beautiful I momentarily forgot what I was doing. As far as I could tell he was unflawed and eerily symmetrical, except for the slightest snaggletooth of his left canine, an imperfection that only made him more appealing.

Was this gorgeous person really talking to me? I looped my hair behind my head, holding my backpack in front of me like a shield, and looked around to see if there was someone else he might be speaking to.

"I'm sorry?" I said when he didn't move.

He thrust a slim lady's wallet toward me. My wallet, in fact.

"Where did you find this?"

"It was on the ground."

It must have fallen while I was digging around for my phone. My phone. I had to find my phone. My internal mute button disengaged, and panic began to pierce through me again. Blood pumped through my legs, ready to race to the information desk. Even mid freak-out, I couldn't quell my awareness of the gorgeous man standing in front of me. I fumbled to wedge my wallet into my bag and attempted to swing the pack over my shoulder without revealing my sweat-compromised armpits. When that didn't work, I let the bag dangle from my hand and tried to look like someone who wasn't on the verge of jumping out of her skin.

"I lost my phone."

"You mean your wallet."

"No, I mean, I was going to the lost and found to find my phone when you stopped me."

"You lost your wallet *and* your phone?" He cocked his head, eyeing me closely, and a wave of queasiness rolled over me. I couldn't sound more clueless if I tried.

"I didn't know I'd lost my wallet. I couldn't find my phone, and God, what is wrong with me?" I put my hand to my forehead, woozy from the residual jet lag, the heat, the panic. There were people everywhere I looked, and I couldn't remember which way I'd come.

The man's perfect lips slipped into a worried frown. "Let me help you."

"Oh no, that's okay." That's the last thing this guy wanted to do. Men this good looking did not stop to help random women. Not women like me. "I'm sure it's waiting for me in the lost and found." My eyes scanned the large space, trying to determine exactly which way to the information desk. When I caught sight of the sign, I set off in its direction, calling over my shoulder to Gorgeous Guy, "Thank you so much for my wallet."

At the desk, too distraught to attempt a word of French, I launched into English, but even that came out jumbled.

"Your phone was stolen?" asked the bored-looking middle-aged woman behind the desk, trying to understand.

"No, lost, not stolen." Stolen. The word tipped me upside down. A stolen phone seemed so much worse than a lost one. I pressed my hands to the solid countertop. "Possibly stolen. But can I check here first?"

"You should alert the authorities." She spoke as if reciting off a checklist. She probably was.

"I want to see if it was turned in."

Her cheeks scrunched. "If the thief turned it in?"

Deep breaths. Stay calm.

I inhaled, and before I could try again, a familiar voice was speaking to the woman in French. I glanced behind me to find Gorgeous Guy. They exchanged a few more words and the woman stepped away from the desk.

With her gone, his blue eyes landed on me, and I felt like a wilting flower kissed by the sun.

"I know you don't want any help," he said, "but I caught a snippet of your conversation when I passed. I thought a translator might be useful. She's checking to see if anyone turned in a phone. I have to warn you, it's probably long gone."

"Stolen?"

He opened his hands apologetically just as the woman returned, hands empty. She shook her head, said something fast and sharp. I didn't need a translation to get the gist. I groaned.

"It's okay," Gorgeous Guy said. "Getting a phone is one of the few things to do here that's not needlessly complicated."

"Where do I do that?"

"I'll show you."

I grimaced, thinking of my email, my texts, my mom. "My family is going to freak out when they can't get ahold of me."

"You'll message them with your new number. You can download apps for everything you're missing. Your photos and contacts are all on the cloud, aren't they?"

I nodded. The cloud, that nebulous nowhere place, suddenly seemed as hallowed as the museum walls around us.

A man bumped me hard, knocking me into Gorgeous Guy's arms.

"Whoa there." His voice reverberated in his chest like a drum, and I jerked myself upright before he noticed my ear pressed against his shirt. "Let's sit," he said, ushering us toward the exit. "You need a minute."

"I shouldn't. I need to—"

"Where are you from?"

"California," I said, breathless.

"It's early there, right? You have time to get a phone and load up minutes before anyone back home is the wiser. If you let me, I can help," he said, his tone soft and calm. He ducked his head toward mine, his mouth close, his breath cool and minty. "It'll be okay. Trust me." And even though I had no real reason to do so, I decided to believe him. My heartbeat slowed.

At the exit doors, my handsome companion gave a quick nod to one of the guards who, without so much as a change in expression, lifted his meaty forearm in acknowledgment.

"Do you know him?" I asked.

"It's not my first trip to the Louvre. Or my twentieth, for that matter. I'm one of those expats who find the proximity of so much incredible art and history too much to resist."

"You picked a busy day to go."

"People-watching is half the fun."

Outside, the sun washed over us with fierce midday heat. Gorgeous Guy paused in the bright light, offered his hand to shake. "Kid."

"Kid?"

"My name. Kidridge, but I go by Kid." He smirked. "What's yours?"

"Rose."

"As lovely as your namesake."

Whether he was flirting or teasing, I couldn't be sure. I grinned despite myself. He reminded me of royalty, a distant cousin of William and Harry's, perhaps. It wasn't just how handsome and polished he was. He had an air of invincibility, one I wanted to cloak myself in.

"May I get you a drink while you get your bearings?" he asked.

"You must have something better to do."

He put a hand over his heart, his face faux-stricken with indignation. "I'm not going to abandon a fellow American in her time of need. What kind of gentleman do you take me for?"

The too-good-to-be-true kind, I could have said. But I gave a sheepish shrug, and he hitched his arm through mine, his warm biceps smooching my skin with each step. I melted a little closer, inhaling his spicy citrus scent, and let him lead me outside toward a café, where he pulled out one of the woven plastic chairs I'd been longing to sit in all day. All my life, really. I sank with relief into the seat. Warmed by the pleasure of his touch, I hoped I didn't look as pink as I felt when he sat down across from me.

"See." He gestured at us. "This is better."

I wasn't sure about that. In his grip, I'd been upright and held, and a little scared, but in a new way, a way that made me want more. Now he focused on me, studying my face. Suddenly exposed, I touched my neck, and when his gaze dropped there, I stuck my hands in my lap. I'd never had a man look at me like that before, like I was a treat.

To avoid his eyes, I looked at the ground, pretending to study the lace shadow drawn by the etched design in the metal table.

A young server approached, and they exchanged a slew of quick French.

"May I order something for the both of us?" Kid asked without bothering to glance at a menu.

"Please."

I was clearheaded enough to know alarm bells should have rung. I should have known better than to allow a stranger, a man, to all but accost me, then ply me with drinks. I had no way to call for help. But I didn't want to. There was nowhere else I wanted to be but sitting at a café in Paris acquainting myself with someone I'd never meet back home.

The server disappeared.

"Have you been here before?" I asked.

He cut me a curious look. "Why?"

"You didn't have to look at the menu to order."

He laughed and pointed his finger at me. "Someone's paying attention. I've lived here long enough. I know what to ask for. In this case, two glasses of something bright, light, but boozy enough to take the edge off a rough afternoon."

As if on command, the server set two sweating glasses in front of us, each fizzing and orange-brown, garnished with the curl of a fragrant lemon peel.

"Aperol spritz." Kid raised his glass and tapped it against mine. "Cheers."

The drink, almost too bitter, coated my tongue like medicine. Against my will, Dad in the last days of his life crossed my vision, how his mouth barely parted enough to place a tab of morphine under his tongue. How he smiled as his lips came together and the morphine dissolved. His broken last words . . . *No, not now.*

To wash away the memory, I drank more too quickly and searched for a way to keep the conversation going. I asked, "How long have you lived here?"

"In Paris? A few years. But I've been in Europe more than a decade."

"Where are you from originally?"

"East Coast," he said vaguely. "What about you?"

"California. San Jose."

"Ah, a techy then."

"Not really," I admitted. "I work for a medical tech company, but I'm a marketing writer. What do you do here? To live?"

He chuckled, swiped at a stray curl cascading down his forehead. "Living is quite easy if you make a point of it. It's enjoying life people struggle with. Well"—he swirled the ice in his glass—"not me. I find life to be quite delightful. For instance, here we are." He waved his hands toward the busy street, the steady stream of passing pedestrians. "You've lost your phone, and yet, we get to enjoy this moment together."

"My phone." Stress sloshed with the alcohol in my gut. "It's not like me to lose things."

"That happens, you know. When you travel far from home, a different part of yourself emerges."

"A worse part?"

"More like the stifled part. The part champing at the bit for some freedom, a chance to ditch your inhibitions."

Kid leaned back in his chair, hooked a foot over the other knee. "Don't worry. We'll sort out your phone situation, I promise. In the meantime, I'd love to hear what brings you to Paris."

"It's hard to explain."

"Try me," Kid said, a frisky grin drawn across his face, half in shadow. "I want to know."

Behind a stretch of clouds, the sun teetered toward the horizon, showering us in pale light through the flapping awning over our heads. The air smelled like the nutty scent of a nearby patisserie, and the faintest bit of Kid's cologne. I pushed my phone from my mind and settled in, mimicking Kid's easy posture, leaning back, one knee over the other. I could relax until my glass was empty. Then, I'd go.

A passing scooter stuttered loudly as it kicked into gear. I looked up to catch the scooter's driver, a woman in a sleek black helmet, a floral dress gathered at her thighs, blow a kiss to someone on the sidewalk.

"This needs to be my *Roman Holiday*."

"I haven't seen it, but I get it. I do. You're looking for a story. Something to write home about?" He tilted his head. "Proverbially speaking, I mean."

I sat up and tapped my hands on the table. "Yes! That's it exactly."

Conversations with the guys back home didn't go like this. It was all, *What do you do*, *what do* you *do*, back and forth all night long. Even when they deigned to toss a real question in my direction, I suspected they didn't listen, or heard only what they wanted to.

"But, hey"—Kid leaned forward, too, his voice softer now—"I know pop culture would have you believe Paris is the place for escape, mystery, adventure, romance, et cetera . . ."

"Right."

"Here's the dirty little secret." He waggled his finger at me. "If you stay long enough, it's like anywhere else. It's all in what you make of it."

"Okay, so how do I make it an escape, mystery, adventure, romance, et cetera?"

His eyes crinkled with amusement. "I can teach you."

I had no doubt he could. Everything about Kid screamed pleasure and fun. The same electric current of fear and excitement I'd experienced as we'd walked to the café zipped over me again.

"First," he said, "another drink." He raised his finger for the server.

"I can't."

"You can and you must. This is lesson number one. Embrace the moment."

"I'll fall asleep."

"An espresso, then. My treat."

"But my phone. I have to get a new one ASAP."

"I'll help you," Kid said. "On one condition. Swear you'll ditch the backpack. It's literally like walking around with a target on your back." He touched his fingers to his thick gold-blond curls, so soft looking you couldn't help but wish it was your fingers running through them. I clasped my hands around my backpack. "A crossbody bag is what you need. It'll suit you better, too."

Before I could protest further, the server returned. Her eyelashes fluttered as she talked to Kid, but he barely looked at her, his blue eyes lingering on me like he was reading my future.

At Orange, the Verizon of Paris it seemed, Kid negotiated with one of the employees in French while I waited. Goodness, his jawline, like something from the cover of a steamy supermarket romance novel. It was hard not to stare now that his attention was finally turned elsewhere.

I distracted myself by fiddling with the phones and tablets on display. Eventually, I was handed an iPhone and given a number with France's country code.

"The phone's refurbished and a bit old, but she'll do the trick," Kid said. "May I?" He palmed the phone and typed for a minute before giving it back to me.

"My number. I've got to meet someone, but text if you need anything. And call me when you're ready for lesson number two. I'd be happy to show you around my Paris." He tipped an invisible hat and gave me a coy smile. "It's been a pleasure, Rose. Until next time."

A minute later, I'd lost sight of his pastel-colored form in the crowd.

What a strange day. Kid? What kind of name was Kid anyway? Kidridge was worse. It sounded like a ski resort in Tahoe, not a grown man.

But there *was* something youthful about him. His short stature along with the sparkle in his eyes and impish expression made him feel otherworldly, a character from a fairy tale.

I was curious about him. Who wouldn't be? But I couldn't call him, could I? No. No, I wouldn't. After all, I wasn't here to meet anyone. Even ridiculously hot men with impeccable manners and great conversational skills. Especially them.

11

The evening light pierced through the low clouds outside the musée d'Orsay. The white-hot day was idly easing to an end. I'd strolled along the Seine on my way there, the water sparkling gold. My new crossbody bag hung light on my shoulder.

Over the last few days, I'd ventured from one attraction to another, up the endless steps to the Sacré-Cœur, where I'd slipped inside for shade and solitude to find the basilica stunning in gilt mosaics but as crowded and muggy as it was outside; to the marché Grenelle, where I bought two dozen chocolate bars for Iris; and the jardin du Luxembourg to rest my sore legs while mind-bogglingly well-behaved children brandished long sticks to launch boats into a tranquil pond. I crossed île de la Cité to see Notre-Dame, charred, towering beneath the scaffolding, howling with the noise of builders at work, and continued onto Shakespeare and Company, charmed by the creaking floors and book-cluttered rooms. It was exactly how I imagined it, only so much better because I was there, smelling the books, feeling their smooth covers beneath my fingertips.

A pocket-size notebook with an embossed image of the Eiffel Tower caught my eye, and I left the shop with the fabric-covered pages in my hands, alongside a bookmark decorated in a silhouette of Sylvia Beach's profile and the words "Citizen of the world."

But despite the miles logged and the perfunctory travel boxes checked, the true Paris, the one I'd imagined, eluded me. A Paris that would swallow me whole, the line between myself and the city blurring and becoming one.

I needed insider access, something different than what the guides recommended, what everyone told me I *had* to see. I couldn't stop thinking of Kid's farewell, the promise of *his* Paris. If he was the gatekeeper, then I wanted in.

"Go big or go home." That's what Aidan liked to say during our rebrand brainstorms.

I couldn't go back with nothing but a phone full of photos and ticket barcodes. I needed stories. The kind you could recall over and over again without them ever getting old.

So I'd done the only rational thing I could do. I'd called Kid.

"You need a reminder why you came all the way to Paris," he'd said on the phone after I explained my predicament. "I'm the guy to give it to you. Trust me."

I had, but where was he?

My heels scuffed against the inside of my oxfords, and I kicked myself for not wearing my sneakers. This was what I got for trying to dress like a sophisticated American with friends in Paris. A look that was becoming less realistic by the second as my meeting time with Kid came and went. He'd sounded happy to hear from me when I'd called, but I suspected he was the kind of person who sounded happy all the time.

The line continued to snake inside. A tour group gathered on the street corner, their guide waving a purple flag. A loud honk startled a flock of pigeons feasting on crumbs beside a metal trash bin.

I worked hard to appear as though I was people-watching rather than being stood up. I checked my phone. Nothing from Kid, but messages from home. Iris had taught Mom how to use WhatsApp, and now I was being inundated. I distracted myself by responding.

Alice Zadeh:

You need to send me updates. MOM.

Rose Zadeh to Alice Zadeh:

Don't worry. I'm having the best time.

Everything couldn't be better.

You don't have to sign your name, fyi.

Iris Zadeh:

Hello?! How is it so far?

We're all dying to know, but Lily is too stubborn to say so.

Btw, she's still on a "break." It doesn't seem to be going well. And she's done a number on your apt. What a slob. Sorry!

Rose Zadeh to Iris Zadeh:

The history! The art! The cheese! Ooh la la!

Did you know Parisians actually walk around with baguettes tucked in their totes?

You and Ben should cancel Hawaii and honeymoon here instead.

Six weeks to go! So excited for you guys!

Rose Zadeh to Kara Carmichael:

I don't miss work at all, not even a little bit.

But humor me, has Aidan hired the guy yet?

Is he skipping around my empty desk?

As soon as I messaged Kara, I regretted it. I shouldn't have asked about work, not here, not when I was about to be rejected for the third time in two weeks. I closed the app and checked the time. Twenty past. I decided to wait five more minutes and then go buy a bottle of wine and recover from my latest humiliation in the comfort of my pajamas. What had I expected with a guy like that?

I kicked at the pavement, leaving a scrape on the toe of my shoe. I crossed my arms and tried to blend into the stone wall at my back, wishing I could morph into a statue, someone stately and ancient, with discerning eyes and literal thick skin, completely impervious to rejection.

At twenty-four past, Kid appeared out of nowhere, a big grin on his perfect face. I smiled back despite my attempt to appear hardened.

"You didn't leave," he said.

"I mulled the idea over."

"I'm pleased you went against your better judgment. I always appreciate such an instinct in a companion." He didn't apologize, but back in his company again, I found I didn't care.

We made our way inside, where Kid threw his hands up toward the vaulted ceilings. "This place," he said, his voice awash in awe. The building, a former train station, *was* a marvel. Waning sunlight slipped through the glass rotunda, reaching to the heavens. The walls glimmered with gold, a trick of the light. My heels clicked against the polished floors.

"Now"—his eyes twinkled—"are you ready to see *my* Orsay?"

He was pretentious, without a care to pretend otherwise. Somehow, I couldn't manage to be troubled by the sort of entitlement I loathed in men like Aidan or Lily's Dev. If I wasn't careful, Kid could quickly become a bad habit, the kind that made you feel good enough to forget it wasn't good for you at all.

As he led me through the galleries, everything felt different than it did when I was on my own. It was as if through Kid's lens, the art became alive, each scene, person, statue, a real entity with a story to tell. When I was a kid, I loved to watch the scene in *Mary Poppins* when they jumped into the sidewalk-chalk drawings, and being with Kid was a lot like that.

"Did you know Gauguin was a stockbroker before he became an artist?" Naturally, Kid boasted Wikipedia-level knowledge of each artist's personal life. "He's making money hand over fist, doing what he was educated to do, and all the while this desire to create is building up inside him like a monsoon. Then, whoosh"—Kid's arms swept the room—"he started painting and didn't stop. Or so I imagine."

"Didn't Gauguin also take up with a thirteen-year-old girl in Tahiti or somewhere?"

Kid yelped in amusement. "Tough critic, eh?" He cocked his head to look at me. "You said you're a writer?"

"I write. But not prose. Newsletter copy, press releases."

Kid tapped his lip. "I expect you must harbor some grander authorial notions."

"I have no illusions about becoming a Pulitzer Prize winner, if that's what you mean."

"Is there somewhere in between mindless writer drone and award winner?"

Kid didn't wait for me to answer before leading me into the next gallery, his fragrant cologne of clove and lemon wafting as he moved. "I sketch on occasion. For my eyes only. Do you have a secret drawer of unfinished manuscripts?"

I thought of my Paris notebook. That didn't count. "I don't want to be a novelist, I swear."

"Ah. We're making progress. Now we know what you don't want. What is it you do want to do?"

"Something that matters."

His eyes darted dramatically around the room. "Thank God Hemingway isn't around to hear you say fiction doesn't matter."

I nudged him with my elbow. "That's not what I meant." He grabbed on to my wrist, looping his arm through mine, and my heart batted at my ribs. Was this a date? I didn't want it to be a date, but I didn't *not* want it to be one either.

"Your company—medical, you said?—helps people, no?"

"In theory. The lab techs might believe that, but it doesn't matter what kind of company you work for, marketing writing is about creating the right image, and the right image is the one that stands to make the most money. Capitalism 101."

"You're above making money?" The question was delivered without judgment, but I couldn't meet his eyes.

How privileged I must have sounded. Dad would have scoffed in disgust.

When I'd told him I was going to be an English major, he'd choked on the deep-brown walnut in his mouth. He ate them at breakfast, straight from a jar filled with water he kept in the fridge.

"How will you provide for yourself?" he'd sputtered, his mouth curling in distaste.

It was impossible to explain to him that I had no head for business, not beyond marketing jargon, but words came to me naturally, the way, I imagined, a visual artist saw the world in gradations of light and color. When I wrote I could be confident, as long as what I was writing was a clear assignment, something to be packaged and digested, bland as a piece of white bread.

Trying to write down my own thoughts was like attempting to translate the few letters from Dad's family, written in Farsi, I'd found tucked in an old shoebox in his closet. Each character was beautiful on its own and sometimes, rarely, but *sometimes*, possible to pinpoint with the help of a Farsi dictionary for English speakers I'd bought for the task. Together, the symbols looked like nothing more than an unintelligible mishmash of pen marks. Even my letters to Gladys were only imagined, safer in my head than on the page.

But English was basically Dad's third language, after Farsi and math, and I suspected I was as unknowable to him as those letters were to me.

That day in the kitchen, he'd made me vow to use my degree to find a stable job, and I had. Making Dad happy, earning a decent paycheck, and the occasional drip of approval from Aidan had been enough, for a while.

"I got it." Kid snapped his fingers and pointed at me like he'd landed on the answer. "A Paris guidebook for young, beautiful millennials trying to escape their sad lives."

I flushed while my mind stuttered over his words. Beautiful? Sad lives? He thought I was pathetic. He thought I was beautiful! I laughed to avoid an awkward silence.

"A guidebook? I don't think so."

"A writer with no authorial or journalistic aspirations. How fascinating." Kid considered me. Under his scrutiny, my eyes landed on the floor. "I don't think I've met your kind before."

I laughed again, a hollow sound in the cavernous gallery. *Me neither,* I could have said.

"I'll admit, writing a novel sounds pretty romantic after wandering the Orsay for an hour. I get how the city has that effect on people." I meant it. For the first time since arriving, I saw Paris how I'd envisioned the city from afar: a romantic, swirling mix of hedonism and architecture and art. The charged air made me want to sit down and write . . . something. But I was so used to writing pull quotes and fake PR mumbo jumbo, I wasn't sure where to begin.

"What perfect timing," Kid said, leading me toward a busy painting, a bustling city tableau I recognized as an old friend when the canvas came into focus. "Renoir. *Bal du moulin de la Galette*. Paris as it should be. Conversation, energy, community, affection. This is exactly what you're describing, the Paris that makes you want to create something from nothing. Or better yet, something enchanting from something broken."

"Yes," I said. "It's beautiful." I'd stared at the tiny print in my apartment for years, and here it was, up close and in person. The scene woke me, the hypothetical becoming real before my eyes. Anything seemed possible.

Kid turned to me, his piercing eyes wide and serious. "I have an idea."

12

A crowd gathered in front of an unassuming storefront. Light blazed from a picture window onto the sidewalk. When I'd told Kid where I was staying, we'd taken a car from the 7th arrondissement back to the Marais for dinner. He knew a place, he'd said. Him, along with everyone else in the neighborhood.

"We'll never get in." I slowed my pace as we neared the bright-red door. Kid nudged my shoulder affably as he zipped past me. "The place is a matchbox."

A single bar spanned the length of the room, fitted with stools, each one occupied. Red paper lanterns dangled from the ceiling.

"C'mon now. I wouldn't lead you astray."

I waited outside while he snaked his way through the door and past the throng. Was he planning to slip someone a few euros? If anyone could pull off a maneuver like that, Kid was the guy, and I half expected it to happen while I watched from the window. Instead, he reached over the bar and gripped hands with one of the chefs. Kid spoke, and the chef's head reared with laughter. A minute later, Kid pulled me inside.

"Two seats are about to open and they're all ours."

I gaped at him in wonder.

"Stick with me," he said, like someone out of a movie. I wouldn't have dared compare myself to Audrey Hepburn, but Kid could have been Gregory Peck, if Peck were a foot shorter and blond. "I know people. Speaking of." He pulled his phone from his pocket. "Mind if I?"

I shook my head, and he turned to take the call. He spoke in French, the lyrical language flying off his tongue, and I couldn't have understood a word if I tried. Instead, I checked out the room. Two cooks behind the counter tossed noodles and vegetables in blackened woks over licking blue flames. At the bar, heads bent over huge ceramic bowls. Pop music I recognized from home flowed from the speakers. A hip spot. Electricity zipped down my abdomen like downing a strong drink on an empty stomach.

At the counter, Kid ordered for the both of us after introducing me to his chef friend.

"How do you know him?"

He twirled chopsticks in his left hand and smiled. "I know loads of people." A non-answer. Was this how he maintained his mystique? I tried a different approach.

"How did you end up in Paris?"

"Same as you."

"I doubt that."

"Came to London for university. Spent a debaucherous year traveling after, followed by a year or so in Rome, before settling here. Otherwise, same story. I'm a dreamer. Paris sang to me."

"Not precisely the same."

"I avoid precision unless I have no other option. Even then."

I made a point to look him up and down: pale green pants cuffed in even folds, contrasting lemon-yellow argyle socks, a V-neck T-shirt, distressed to perfection, manicured fingernails, hair glossy with a well-conditioned sheen. He raised his hands as if I'd caught him.

"Fine. Precision has a time and a place. It's like art. First, you create, create, create, and only then can you refine."

Our bowls of noodles arrived. The taste of ginger coated my palate, and I smiled. It wasn't as mouthwatering as the triple-crème cheese I'd been devouring, but it made me happy all the same to be eating wok-tossed noodles in the middle of Paris with a practical stranger.

"It's good, isn't it?"

Mouth full, I nodded. I swallowed, wiped my lips. "You said you sketch. So you're an artist?"

"When I was younger, I hoped to be. Now I know better. The wisdom of age."

"You've traded art for . . . ?"

He took a bite, another.

"Tell me you like tiki drinks," he said. "Rum. You must love rum."

"You didn't answer my question."

"Do you or do you not like rum?"

Confused by his runaround, I shrugged. "Sure, I guess."

"Good enough for me." He stood from the bar and lifted my purse. "Coming?"

"Don't we need to pay?"

"Already settled." He gave an enthusiastic goodbye to the chef. But he didn't lead us to the door we'd come in. He pushed farther back toward the end of the bar, where a narrow opening led into a darkened stairwell.

We'd left the bright noodle shop and navigated a long hallway lined with dried bamboo. Kid ducked his head through the doorway so low the squat space made him look tall. I followed. On the other side was a room five or six times the size of the noodle shop with another bar, feathered in palm fronds, and a dozen small tables lit by glowing red votives. The hum of conversation and the incessant rattle of cocktail shakers drowned out the sound of the rolling bass rattling in my bones.

I sat at an open table while Kid went to the bar. He shook hands with the bartender. Figured he'd be friends with him, too. Kid somehow knew everyone, but who the hell was he?

He joined me at the table carrying a tall, frosted glass topped with a miniature pink plastic pirate's sword stabbed through a cherry.

He handed me the drink. "Yo ho ho and a bottle of rum."

I sipped it and let the taste roll around my tongue. It *was* rummy, also sweet, sour, and spicy all at once.

"You like," he said.

I did. It was my second drink of the night, and my nerves succumbed to my curiosity. I wanted to know more about this guy. "So, tell me, Kid, are you in the habit of befriending people off the street?"

"If I say yes, will you be disappointed?" His eyes were bright with humor, but I registered a drop of truth in the twitch of his jaw muscles. I plucked the cherry from the sword and popped it in my mouth, letting its sweet tang melt on my tongue. I decided to play his game and ignored the question.

"You gave up art and—"

"God, no." He threw his hands up in exasperation. "I could never give up art. Art is life. What I gave up were my delusions of becoming an artist. And I'm all the better for it."

"You walked away?"

"How old are you?"

"Thirty-two." The number barely meant anything to me. At any given moment, I felt younger or older than I was. The eldest sister and the inexperienced one, perpetual child and everyone's caretaker.

"Thirty-two years old, and you're only now following your dream."

"I guess." Without meaning to, I thought of my dad and the drumbeat that brought him to the US: opportunity, opportunity, opportunity. Still, he knew his immigrant story could have ended up differently. Tucked between the facts of his life, there was luck, always luck, on his side since day one, and by default, ours, too. He never let us forget it.

According to Dad's philosophy, you didn't squander luck; you worshipped her. Luck didn't want your attempts at creativity, only hard work and ritual personal sacrifice. In return, she might grant you freedom, to own a home, to vacation with your family, to pursue a passion project on the side. This was Dad's version of the American Dream, the bright light at the intersection of fortune and hardship, and it cast a pall over anything else. Other kinds of dreams, if you even dared to speak them aloud, were an embarrassing display of entitlement.

Before I could stop myself, I said, "My dad wanted me to have one kind of life, and I wanted to do right by him. After all he sacrificed for me. He worked himself to the grave to provide me and my sisters a better life than the one he had. A two-story house in a safe neighborhood. Private school. College tuition . . ." I trailed off, suddenly aware that I didn't know *exactly* what Dad had wanted. Freedom, he'd said, and I'd filled in the blanks over the years. It was another thing about him I'd never know for certain.

"And now?"

"Now, he's gone." I sighed. "I'm closer to middle age than childhood. Only I feel like I'm still on the verge of adulthood waiting for a real grown-up to tell me what the hell to do." I studied the dance of the candlelight to gather myself. "Sorry." I looked up at him. "We're getting too deep."

"Not possible. I live for intense conversation." He clocked an elbow onto the table and set his chin on his hand. "Tell me, do you think you're really waiting for someone to tell you *what* to do or to give you license to do it? Because I can give you the green light. I'm very encouraging."

A wink sparked across his face, and I examined his features, a feat of human engineering. Was that why I felt like a puppet on a string around him? He raised a finger, my mouth popped open, and out the words spilled. Catching myself staring, I blinked and looked away.

"Another drink?" I asked. "The next round's on me."

"I think not." He stood, and for one terrible second, I thought the night was over. "What'll you have?"

I tried to protest, but he cut me off. "No," he said, "it's nothing."

Two drinks later, we stumbled into the street, or I stumbled. Holding my arm, Kid maneuvered without a care. We walked toward my apartment, a quarter mile away, and my palms began to sweat. My nerves hiccupped. Was this when the other shoe dropped? When my stupidity caught up with me. First drinks, then a dark alley. I imagined my mom watching *60 Minutes*, crying to Iris and Lily, "I knew she shouldn't go. I told her not to. No one can ever say I didn't warn her."

But the night was so nice, Kid's hand so firm, his presence so warm and commanding, the worries I normally clung to slipped my mind.

He stopped in front of my door. I rubbed one dusty oxford against the other. I'd forgotten my aching arches. Kid placed his pointer finger beneath my chin and tilted my head. I held my breath, unsure of what I hoped would happen next. We locked eyes, and the street spun. It wasn't desire, but something similar, something sure to ruin me. I girded myself to pull away, step inside, lock the door between us, but before I could, he reached out and, well . . . he booped me on my nose.

I blinked in surprise, and my illusions dissolved.

"Drink two glasses of water before bed. Those drinks were sugary." The smile he gave me made me think of Rhys's face when he dumped me at Dad's memorial the summer between sophomore and junior year of college. A smile that said, "You're sweet but . . ." There was always a *but*.

A breath later, I stood alone on the street, the tip of my nose burning from his touch.

13

I relaxed on a bench in the place des Vosges, wearing the one dress I'd brought, flouncy at the knee, demure at the neckline. The clear cerulean sky released the day's humidity with an exhale of fresh air, and the city didn't feel like the inside of a stuffy terrarium. My bare legs basked in their freedom. On my walk over, I'd narrowly missed stepping into a pile of . . . something really gross, and even that near miss felt like a win.

Paulette had emailed suggesting we meet during her lunch break. The park was busy—a murmur of voices moved on the breeze, children's laughter rang out above the racket of city sounds, an amateur violinist played the same notes over and over. I struggled to enjoy it, too caught up in my thoughts. I'd been making my head spin checking my phone all day. With nothing to do but wait for Paulette, I couldn't resist looking again.

Not even an emoji from Kid—*womp, womp*—but notifications from Mom and Iris.

Alice Zadeh:

I'm going to keep worrying . . . All Dad wanted was his family to be safe and sound . . . TOGETHER . . . Can you blame him?

Imagine if you could never come home again. It's too frightening to think of . . . Also, I know you haven't emailed Marco yet . . . I promised his mother you would . . . Don't make me a liar!

P.S. Ben put out traps for the mice . . . it's been a BLOODBATH . . . I'm beside myself with guilt . . . He says I need to call a pest person . . . how do I know which is best? Vasilis, from the diner, says he has someone to recommend.

Oh, how I wish you could help!

Iris Zadeh:

Mom is obsessed with the Marco thing. His mom doesn't like his girlfriend, and they think you'd be a better match.

Don't tell her I told you that.

Can you please email him, so I don't have to hear about it?

JK.

I'm glad you're happy.

I'd be too terrified to travel by myself. But you're more independent than me.

Lily says Ben and I have a codependent relationship. She says high school sweethearts are destined to be codependent.

But I like being with Ben, and I've never met anyone I like more. So that says something, right?

I miss you. And the more I miss you, the more I miss Dad. Mom will walk me down the aisle. But it's not the same. I wish we could all be together. At least it'll be better once you're home.

"Rose. *Bonjour.*" Paulette swooped beside me wearing a stiff, oversize skirt and satin blouse in bright yellow, a walking statement piece. She sat down on the bench.

"*Bonjour.*" I stuffed my phone in my bag, along with the surge of guilt brought on by Iris's message, and smiled wide, a tactic I'd taken to using with shopkeepers and Metro attendants and anyone who might find my general blundering Americanness off-putting.

"How is your trip?"

"Good, mostly." I laughed a little. "Not exactly what I expected."

"I thought you said no plans, so no expectations, yes?" If only no plans meant no expectations. She ran a finger around her lips as if to remove an invisible line of lipstick and turned to face me. "I think my guests either love or hate Paris. It crawls beneath their skin. Is that how you say it?"

"Gets under their skin?"

"Yes, gets under their skin, or like this." She flung a hand over her head.

"Goes over their heads?" I said, trying to understand. "*Gets under their skin* means it's annoying, like an itch."

Her face brightened. "This is why I love when I have Americans to stay. I need to practice my English. Have you been to LA?"

"Of course. California is big, but everyone goes to LA at some point."

"I lived there." I heard the pride in her voice. "For one summer. I fell in love with an American old enough to be my father and decided I wanted to be an actress."

"What happened?"

"I did one audition, but I didn't care anymore. I wanted to come back home. The old guy was married. This is no surprise." She exhaled and her cheeks puffed. "I was tricked."

I wasn't sure whether she was referring to the guy or LA. I nodded. She scanned the park, blocked her eyes from the sun, and smiled.

"It is the perfect day." She stood and smoothed her skirt. "Come. We will go to the market."

While we walked, Paulette told me about her job, and I shared everything I'd seen of the city thus far. In the back of my mind, the same thoughts kept bumping into each other, vying for my attention. Work, Aidan. My sisters, Mom, Dad. I'd traveled across the world to release the hold my family had on me, but I couldn't stop channeling all the same worries I had at home. The set change didn't matter. Paris wasn't a genie in a bottle. Dad said if you wanted something you had to fight for it. "What are you willing to give up?" he wanted to know. It was an important question. What was I willing to give up? I was so stifled by everyone's expectations at home. Here, mine were the ones holding me back.

I followed Paulette through a metal archway between buildings. Inside the enclosed space, my eyes widened. A large courtyard held two dozen small, canopied kiosks, beneath each a variety of stacked green vegetables and lettuces, baskets of summer fruits as fragrant as flowers, round metal platters heaped with delicate pinnacles of ground spices, tables of cheese and bread.

I couldn't help myself and bought almost more than I could fit in my bag. Paulette purchased a heavy bag of plums. She handed one to me and took one for herself. The sweet-sour flesh puckered my mouth, and I swiped at a drop of juice sneaking past my lips.

"Delicious, no?" she asked. I agreed, but delicious wasn't the right word, not specific enough. The flavor tasted of being eight years old, filling a plastic container with plums from our tree. Standing on a step stool beside Dad to stir a vat of bubbling plum jam, the steam kissing our faces.

The next stand held bins of nuts, and Paulette helped me translate while I bought a paper cone of roasted, salt-crusted pistachios, laughing to myself as a memory lifted to the surface: Dad yelling at Lily for licking all the salt off the shells before putting the whole pistachios back in the bag.

The pistachios and the plums would have made a good galette. I could finely grind the pistachios and work them into the dough, roll it out and heap the center with sugared wedges of plum. Or make a tart shell with the nuts and layer thin slices of plum on top. I couldn't wait to get back to my own kitchen so I could try the combination out.

I paused for a fraction of a second, out of step with my own thoughts.

No, thank you, I did *not* want to go home. My trip had only begun, and both the plum and the pistachios tasted perfectly fine as they were.

Paulette interrupted my thoughts. "What's next for you?" We'd passed back onto the sidewalk, and she swatted a fly from her face. She probably meant next on my agenda, but it was a bigger question than she could imagine.

"I don't know." My mind abandoned the sliver of quiet street. I pictured myself zipping around the city on a scooter, holding on to Kid for dear life, my hair trailing behind me.

"You have a funny smile on your face," she said.

"I do? I'm glad, I guess."

Paulette laughed. "I was excited, too, in LA. For a little while. Like a movie, right?"

Like a movie was exactly what I wanted.

❦

While out with Paulette, and after, at the Picasso Museum and eating falafel on the sidewalk for lunch, tahini sauce dripping on my hands, I wondered if Kid would call.

My mood sank with the weather. By the time I was back at Paulette's apartment, the sky was stark white with cloud cover. I put on my comfy pants and settled in for the evening.

I wandered into the narrow kitchen and inspected my purchases. In addition to the pistachios, I'd bought a baguette, a round of soft, bloomy rind chèvre, a small bag of arugula, a perky shallot, a half dozen freckled eggs, and a miniature bouquet of fragrant chives.

Paulette's sparse kitchen and cabinets held an impressive collection of condiments and pantry staples. I sliced the shallot and soaked the thin, pink half moons in a mix of white wine vinegar and salt. Dad believed the best meals included onion, but my sisters and I couldn't stand them raw, so he'd taught me how to take the edge off their pungent heat with an ice-water bath or a quick pickle.

With no sign of Kid, I was in for the night, and my plan was to put together a kind of picnic dinner I could devour hand-to-mouth from the comfort of Paulette's couch. With Dad on my mind, the ingredients began to transform into something more toothsome.

On the nights I had to stay up late finishing homework, I would sometimes hear him moving around the kitchen. I'd sneak downstairs to find him hunched over a cutting board with only the dim light above the sink for company. Before him would be a palette of fixings. Shredded jack cheese, a mound of chopped red pepper, cherry tomatoes, feta, maybe some scallions or whatever else he could scrounge from the fridge. I'd sit down at the island and watch him begin his masterpiece.

"The key," he would say, as he cracked eggs single-handedly into a small bowl, "is a quick whisk, a splash of milk, and adding salt to the mix early."

He'd pour the mixture into a buttered pan, turning it this way and that like a TV host. "You have to coat the pan, but as soon as the eggs set, start to pull the edges toward the center like so."

After the cheese and vegetables were scattered and tossed, the eggs not quite cooked through, he'd turn off the stove and let the residual heat from the burner finish the job, a perfect soft scramble.

"Nooshe jan," he'd say, handing me a fork.

The only thing Dad liked more than Persian food was an American diner-style breakfast. It was part of the reason brunch at Village Diner had become our family thing. But I think he loved performing for me in the kitchen most of all, the final moment when his plate was piled high with a velvety scramble, toast with store-bought strawberry jam, a couple of steaming breakfast sausages he excavated from the freezer, and he would garnish his eggs with chopped parsley and a theatrical flourish.

We didn't share a first language, but we could always speak to one another with food. I found myself performing for him in Paulette's kitchen as I whisked the eggs and finely chopped the chives and broke the cheese into creamy bits. I didn't know how to make a proper French omelet, but I did my best, folding the edges over the melting cheese like a crepe, scattering the top with chives and a healthy grind of pepper. I dressed the arugula with the vinegar from the shallots and tossed the greens and onion together in a glug of olive oil. This I set on the side of my omelet, with a slice of baguette smeared with butter and a runny lavender honey I found in Paulette's cupboard, describing, in my head, the way the bright taste of the shallots and peppery arugula would mingle with the richness of the eggs and cheese.

It was nothing like the scrambles Dad threw together, too refined. Still, I recognized some part of him awaken in me with my first bites. Even if he'd hate for me to be so far away from the family, he wouldn't be able to resist these flavors.

"The eggs could use a touch more salt," he'd tell me. "And where is the meat?"

I smiled with my mouth full. He wasn't wrong, but it was good enough as it was.

❦

When my phone rang, I nearly dropped the dish I'd been washing. Of course, Kid would call when I least expected it.

Drying my hands on my pants, I picked up my phone and cleared my throat. I didn't recognize the number, but who else did I know in France? I would count to ten before answering. At least, five. One, two, three—

"Hey," I said. "I was wondering if you'd call."

"I'm sorry. Perhaps I have the wrong number." It was an American accent, but a voice I didn't recognize. "Is this Rose Zadeh?"

"Yes . . . Who's this?"

"Marco. Dariano."

"Oh." My excitement ran straight into a brick wall.

"Your mom gave my mom your number and asked me to reach out." He sounded as enthusiastic to call me as I was to hear from him.

"I thought you were someone else. You have a French phone number."

"So do you, and I, however, actually live here," he said, like his expat status should come with a title change.

I pushed the irritation from my voice. "You surprised me, that's all."

"Should we set up a meeting? To satisfy our moms."

"Or we could not and tell them we did."

The line went quiet, and when he responded, his voice was heavy and vexed. "I wouldn't do something like that."

"I was kidding." The guilt would eat me alive. Marco didn't know that. We hadn't spoken since we were kids, but surely, he didn't think I'd lie about something so silly.

"Okay . . ."

"Sorry. Let's meet."

"When would be a convenient time for you?"

So stuffy. This was going to be a chore. Whatever, it didn't matter to me. I needed to get the introduction over with, make Mom happy, and move on. Then I thought of Kid calling me while I was out with Marco, and that did seem rather convenient.

"Tonight?"

14

Marco suggested a natural wine bar in the crook of an L-shaped street in Les Halles. From a grungy patch of sidewalk, a handful of stone steps led to a small cellar with no more than four tables and the same number of seats at the bar, where a boisterous trio of men huddled, erupting in a burst of laughter as I passed. I had a flashback to my blind date with Frank, and my insides clenched.

This wasn't a date, but it felt like one.

Why had I let myself get pressured into this? Two minutes on the phone had told me Marco and I had nothing in common anymore. I couldn't remember if we ever did. We'd talked about books sometimes, and movies, homework assignments and other kids at school. We'd never bonded.

But I was here, and I might as well make the best of it. In a couple of hours, the evening would be behind me, and in the meantime, at least Marco was a distraction from thinking about Kid.

I sat at one of the empty tables, took a final, disappointing glance at my phone, and tried to decipher obscure French wines by the flickering glow of a tealight nestled within a tarnished brass wall sconce. The red-lipped woman behind the bar tossed me a glance, her messy ponytail bobbing as she wiped down the countertop. She set down her rag but didn't rush over.

A half minute later, at eight o'clock on the dot, Marco marched into the bar. I would have recognized him even without the navy button-down he told me he'd be wearing. The face of a boy I used to know grown into a man with amber eyes, sharp eyebrows that cut across his forehead, and high cheekbones. His broad shoulders filled out his blazer, but he hunched forward slightly the way a taller man might.

"Bonsoir," he called to the bartender. She smiled and they spoke for a minute before he came to the table. We exchanged a stiff half hug as familiar strangers do, and I attempted to relax into my seat despite the tightness in my belly.

Marco brushed invisible debris from his lap. More raucous laughter rose at the bar. Marco's head turned toward the sound and his eyes narrowed. An itchy silence descended on our dark corner.

"Come here often?" I said, attempting a joke.

"I live nearby. They have a good selection. I like the quiet." On second thought, he added, "I wouldn't say I come here more than a reasonable amount."

"I was joking." He gave me a blank stare, his jaw working behind his stubbled cheeks. "You know, 'come here often,' the pickup line." More blank staring. I squirmed a little in my seat. "It was a dumb thing to say." I caught myself tearing at the edges of the paper menu. I shoved it away before I ripped it into pieces and tucked my hand beneath my leg. "Sorry."

"Me too." He smoothed out the menu I'd mangled. "For not getting the joke. Again."

"So, um," I sputtered, going in for take two, "do you ever miss home?"

"I miss my favorite phở place. Have you been to Pho House 1 on West Santa Clara?"

"In the little strip mall across from the huge strip mall near the SAP Center?"

"That's the one," he said. A faraway look passed over his face. "And strip malls. I miss those, too, sometimes."

"Not possible."

"They're not pretty, but they serve a function, don't they? All those options right there. Cultural melting pots."

I made a skeptical face. I refused to get on board with glamorizing the rat maze of strip malls that encompassed San Jose.

Marco continued, "I find something kind of amazing in the mundane. Paris is exceptional. It wears its beauty for anyone to see. Think what a pop culture icon it is, *An American in Paris*, *Amélie*, *Casablanca*, which doesn't even take place in Paris."

"I love *Casablanca*."

"Me too," he said. "I've seen it fifty times."

Okay, fine. So we had at least one thing in common.

"My point is you admire the ornate buildings, not the cracks in the facades. But the cracks tell the story. For me, it's the same with art. The most mundane moments have always captured my attention. Strip malls are unremarkable until you see them as the embodiment of so many American dreams." He paused. "I didn't mean to go on. Occupational hazard."

His words released a memory inside me. My dad taking me to Costco as a kid. Iris was maybe two, and Lily not yet born or too young to even join us, so I must have been six or so. I held Iris by the hand, and we flitted about eating as many free samples as we could find, until Dad would call our names. He delighted in finding deals, pointing to shelves of products as if we were on some sort of magical Wonka-type tour, not in a big-box warehouse.

"Look there," Dad said, gesturing to a container the size of my torso crammed with bright-green pistachio halves. "What a deal. Shelled," he added with awe. "And there." He pointed to a massive jar of peanut butter. "Can you imagine the number of sandwiches?"

I tried to guess how many peanut-butter-and-jellys the jar could make, like how we tried to guess the number of beans in the jar on my teacher's desk. "Two hundred?" I ventured, but Dad was sifting through the sweatpants for sale. Later, he bought a VCR.

I didn't realize until I got older that Costco wasn't some special-occasion place, not an amusement park or a funhouse. To this day, I still got a little thrill when I stepped inside one.

Marco cleared his throat, and my mind jerked back to the present. The conversation had lagged while I'd been lost in thought, and it was Marco's turn to look strained by the silence. He tugged his shirtsleeves. "To answer your question, I don't miss San Jose much, but I think about the old neighborhood often. Growing up there was pretty good."

"It was. Kind of our own little Mayberry." I could see the neighborhood as it had been when we were kids. Flat as a painting, similar ranch houses with rectangular patches of dying lawn. In front of our house, an overgrown plum tree with shiny purple leaves and three rosebushes perfuming the walk to the front door in the spring. Dad tended them with a zeal reserved for family and work (not necessarily in that order), growing dark brown beneath his worn safari hat, discolored at the brow line. Sometimes he would cut a stem straight from the bush and snip each thorn before handing it to me.

"There was always somebody around ready to play," I said.

"I remember playing with you."

"Playing?"

Marco lowered his eyes, and even in the low light, I thought I could see his cheeks flush. "Not playing exactly. We were in the same pack. We roamed around together. You were always hiding from your sisters and writing in your diary."

A sound erupted from my throat somewhere between a cough and a laugh. I'd forgotten about my devotion to my diary with the little lock and key, filled with all the hopes and complaints and observations I couldn't say aloud. I kept it hidden inside my pillowcase, until my mom found it and told me we weren't allowed to have secrets in our house. Of course, *she* was allowed a normal private life, but not me, Iris, and Lily. I either had to leave the diary unlocked or ditch it. I'd torn out each scribbled page and tossed the scraps in a neighbor's trash can.

"I can't believe you remember that," I said. The notebook from Shakespeare and Company sat unused at the bottom of my bag, and I stifled a weird impulse to show it to Marco.

"I always wanted to know what you were writing about. I sort of hoped it had something to do with me."

"You did?" There was no mistaking Marco's pink cheeks now. I'd definitely made him blush. Maybe he wasn't as stodgy as he seemed. I hid a smirk behind my hand, but I couldn't help needling him a little. "Did you have a crush on me?"

He lifted the menu. "I suppose you could call it that. I was curious about you. You had an air of mystery."

Mystery? Self-conscious, preteen me? I bit back a laugh, dying to tell Iris. "That's really sweet," I managed. There was something undeniably endearing about admitting to a twenty-year-old crush.

Marco shook out the menu as if it were a newspaper. "Shall we order? A bottle to share?"

"Sure, you choose. I'll drink anything."

While he scanned the options, I tried to recall him as a boy, nothing specific coming to mind. He'd always just sort of been around, mostly quiet, especially among the other kids.

The voices at the bar rose again. Marco's head craned to watch, and I followed his gaze. I couldn't understand what was happening except that the bartender was involved, the sound of her voice drowned out against the men's.

Marco set down the menu and tugged his cuffs again. "Excuse me." He stood and took three long steps to reach the other end of the bar. I watched as he called to the bartender, pulling her from the men. They spoke briefly, the bartender nodded, and then she returned to her post at the back of the bar, plucking a bottle from the honeycomb rack on the wall.

I reached for my bag to check my phone again, but before I could, Marco approached the group of men. I gaped when he placed a hand on a brawny shoulder. What was he doing? Did he really want to start something with these guys? They looked like the type waiting to take offense. I imagined Marco getting punched in the face and a brawl breaking out.

He said something that caused another menacingly cheerful reaction from the group, and they glanced back at me. I braced myself for trouble, phone in hand, as if I knew who to call for help. A moment later, they all stood, patting Marco on the back as they tumbled out the door. The bartender set a bottle on the bar with two glasses. She leaned in to plant a kiss on Marco's cheek.

He came back to the table carrying the wine and the glasses, his flush traveling the length of his neck, the faintest red print of lips on his face I decided not to point out. He undid the top button of his collar.

I shook my head in amazement and dropped my phone in my bag. "What was that?"

"They were harassing Noelle." Marco tipped the bottle and began to fill our glasses. "I asked her if she wanted me to get rid of them."

"How did you get them to leave without a fight?"

"I told them I'd pay for their drinks if they moved along to their next stop." He set a glass of wine in front of me. "I might have added something about wanting a quiet evening with my girlfriend."

"Brilliant."

He raised his glass, and we toasted from across the table. The wine was vibrant red and smooth, sweeter than I expected. I watched Marco take a long drink, his eyes fixed on his glass. With his collar undone and the lip stain on his cheek, he looked different. Less stuffy. More approachable. Now I was the curious one. He wasn't exactly what I expected.

As he lowered his glass, a mask fell over his face, tightening his features. He didn't button up his collar, but he tugged the two halves together and sat up straighter.

"Let's see," he said, as if checking a list of discussion topics, "where have you visited thus far?"

I listed the places I'd seen, and we settled into a safe, surface-level talk about Paris and careers. Which was fine. Not everyone could be like Kid, carving out canyon-deep conversations. Had he texted? I couldn't help stealing a look at my phone while Marco poured the remainder of the wine into our glasses.

He raised an eyebrow. "Somewhere to be?"

I abandoned my phone back in my bag. "Nope." I hoped he didn't register the disappointment in my voice. "Nowhere but here."

❦

A short while later, Marco and I stepped from the wine cave onto the sidewalk, the street quiet except for the faraway rush of traffic. The bartender followed us to the door, locking us out. She waved at Marco as she joined a young man waiting for her down the block.

"We closed the place down," I said. My eyes blinked against the bright streetlight while Marco checked his phone. I took my own from my purse to request a car. "I guess we won't have to lie to our moms now." And mine would stop harassing me.

He looked up from his phone and cocked his head. "I try not to lie." His gentle gaze rested on my face. "I certainly wouldn't lie to my own mother."

"Right." I couldn't bother to explain, for the umpteenth time, that I was kidding. "Of course not."

"Can I call you a cab?"

"Thanks," I said, "but I already requested a ride."

"I'll wait."

"It's okay. I'm fine on my own."

He didn't move and we waited in silence, me glancing at my phone every ten seconds or so, him steadfast with his hands in his pockets. I'd begun to get used to his oddly formal manner and I should have appreciated his chivalry, but the gesture bugged me. He probably wanted to tell his mom he'd made sure I'd gotten home okay. I didn't need a babysitter. I felt more independent than I had, well, ever.

When my ride showed, Marco opened the door for me. I offered my hand for a shake. His fingers were hard and dry, rougher than I expected.

"Thank you for the wine," I said.

"Enjoy the rest of your trip."

"I will."

He hovered at the door a second longer than necessary. "Until next time, I guess."

The night hadn't been bad. In fact, the whole evening was far less terrible than I anticipated, but I didn't feel the need to see him again.

I nodded. "Goodbye, Marco Dariano."

The door clicked shut, and I left Marco standing on the empty sidewalk.

❦

The car left me outside Paulette's building. In the courtyard, I clawed through my purse for my keys. When I couldn't find them, I dumped my purse on the ground and ran my fingers along the empty lining. Nada.

This was not good.

I raced back to the street hoping I'd find my driver idling, but no such luck. The road was empty, the restaurant across the way dark and quiet. "Freaking A."

How could this be happening? My phone, my wallet, now my keys? I could be absent-minded, but I'd never been so careless.

I texted the driver first, and after thirty minutes when I hadn't heard back, I gave in and texted Paulette. First, an apology for texting so late—was after 10:00 p.m. considered late in Paris?—followed by a plea for help. She didn't respond. I huddled like a stray cat on the steps of the doorway, both disgusted with my general suckery and sorry for myself.

At eleven o'clock, I decided the time had come to find a hotel. But when I picked up my phone, I dialed Kid's number instead. As soon as it rang, I hung up, my hands tingling.

I tapped my phone against my forehead. What was wrong with me? It was one thing to count on him for some entertainment, but I couldn't expect to be rescued. Unless, calling him was, in effect, me rescuing myself. I shook my head. I felt as if I was arguing with Kara again. When he called back—*if* he called back—I'd ignore it. Or I'd tell him I'd butt-dialed. Maybe he was asleep. Maybe I didn't have to worry—

I answered the second it rang.

"Kid," I said. I racked my brain for an excuse to both explain my random call and get off the phone. He spoke before I could manage to come up with anything.

"You okay?"

"Yes, it's just . . ."

"What's happened?"

I sighed. Who was I kidding? I hadn't misdialed. I wanted Kid's attention. I wanted an excuse to call. "I've done it again. This time I've lost my keys, and I'm stranded outside my apartment considering taking up residence in a garbage can somewhere."

Kid snorted in amusement like I hoped he would. "You absolutely can't do that," he said. "The dumpster options are abysmal in the Marais." His words slurred at the edges. "You have to come here. You can stay with me. I'll text the address."

"No, I couldn't impose. I'll take a hotel recommendation."

"Hotel? Absolutely not. I wouldn't think of it. Please come."

Staying with Kid sounded like a terrible plan or a sensible option, depending on your perspective. Mom, for instance, would hate the idea, but I decided to embrace my optimistic side.

I wanted to do things differently. Here was my chance. San Jose Rose Zadeh would never stay with a man she barely knew. Paris Rose Zadeh, on the other hand, believed sometimes caution should be tossed with yesterday's trash.

15

I'd known I was headed somewhere nice when the car crossed the Seine into Saint-Germain, but the building I stood outside of, craning my neck to see the top, was more regal than I anticipated. If Kid lived here, I wasn't surprised. The old-world decadence of the building's mansard roof; the quaint, narrow street; the potted begonias adorning each window ledge, all dutifully touted Kid's bespoke sensibilities.

No, I wouldn't have been surprised—if it weren't for the frowning female face that greeted me when I knocked at the singular door on the seventh floor.

"Oh. I must have the wrong apartment." Her expression remained blank, but her narrow nose twitched, her tigerlike eyes pulled up at the corners. I tried French. "*Pardonnez-moi.* Uh . . ."

The woman crossed her arms over her narrow torso. "You're here to see Kid," she said in a thick French accent, her voice rough and low, as she turned to let me in.

"*Oui.*" I followed her inside. She was long and lithe. Despite her deep voice, her frame looked delicate enough to blow away. Who was she? Kid's girlfriend?

She padded across shiny, inlaid wood floors, down a short, dark hallway, and into an open room with a massive dining table and two forest green velvet couches centered around a grand, soot-free fireplace filled with stacks of magazines.

Kid sat at one of the couches, his bare feet settled on the coffee table.

"Kid," the woman said. He leaped up at the sound of her voice.

"You're here," he said to me. "Brilliant. And you met Regina. Regina, Rose. Rose, Regina."

He grinned and slugged back a glass of whatever he was holding. Regina disappeared without a word.

"Hello, you." He patted my head and his lower lip popped into a pout. "You poor thing."

"Is this your apartment?"

"God, no. It's Regina's, at least for the time being. But doesn't it feel like home?"

I had no idea what he meant, but I didn't let my face show it. Regina returned and handed me a full tumbler of red wine. In the other hand, a squat brown bottle, which she splashed into Kid's empty glass.

"We're two bottles in," Kid said. "You'll need to catch up."

Regina seemed sober, and I suspected it was Kid who had taken down the majority of the two bottles. He stumbled back toward the couches.

"What happened to the music?"

Regina tapped her phone, and a moment later, Tom Petty's croons filled the room. Kid flopped on the couch and sang along, his words a jumble.

Left with Regina, I didn't know what else to do but try to win her over.

"I didn't know this was your apartment," I said apologetically. "It's lovely." When she didn't respond, I said it again, raising my voice above the music.

"I can hear you," she said, her tone flat and unyielding. Her even teeth were big and vivid white, but she tucked them beneath pursed lips.

I would finish my wine and politely excuse myself. Kid must have made a mistake, asking me here. I had clearly stumbled into some kind of weird relationship. An open one? Oh no. Good for them, but that wasn't my thing. I could barely handle one person, let alone two.

I skirted Regina's sour gaze by roaming the room, feigning interest at the many pictures on the wall. They were professional photographs, some in black and white, all of Regina. Regina on a yacht in a gold bathing suit. Regina walking a catwalk in a drop-waist dress draped in feathers. Regina in a YSL ad. The pieces fell into place. My mouth dropped.

"You're a model," I said. "Like a real one." Not like the few friends I knew who modeled for catalogs back in high school. Or one girl from my freshman psych class who became an Instagram influencer and took half-naked photos on the beach for some surf brand. "Like Paris Fashion Week."

"Yes," Regina said, sounding bored.

"She's gorgeous, isn't she?" Kid offered from the couch.

The truth was I hadn't thought her model-like, not in the traditional way at least, but now I was a bit starstruck. And aware of my squat frame.

"She's quite successful."

"Congratulations." The wrong thing to say. Regina's face twisted, as if she'd caught a whiff of something awful. I downed the rest of my wine in two hearty gulps. Before I could stage my graceful exit, Kid was talking about a trip to the south he was taking over the weekend. He wanted me to come, he said, so he could show me more of France, his grin somehow contagious because I found myself smiling, and even caught Regina with an upturn in her lips a time or two.

I committed to leaving. After Kid's next story. After his next joke. After the next song, the next album, after we finished playing a botched hand of gin rummy that ended with Kid and me in hysterics and Regina clucking her tongue.

At two in the morning, Kid splayed across the length of one of the couches, his head in my lap, his feet in Regina's. Half-asleep, I twirled one of his curls between my pointer finger and thumb. With his eyes closed, he lifted my other hand from his cheek and pressed my fingertips to his lips. At first, the flirtation was nothing, the pleasant sensation of skin against skin, but before I understood anything had changed, the press of his lips was unmistakably a kiss. My eyes sprang open to find Regina watching us. I pulled away my hand and dropped my fingers from his hair.

"I should go," I said.

"No, no." Kid roused himself. "Regina has an extra bedroom, and I'll tuck myself in right here on the couch." Did the sleeping arrangements explain the nature of their relationship? Regina and I stood, and Kid laid back down and nuzzled his face into the cushions.

"I don't want to be a pest."

"It's far too late for us to send you off in the night," Kid said, his speech muffled against the fabric. "And where would you go? It's no trouble. Right, Regina?"

"Come," she said to me. She led me farther along the hallway we'd first walked down, to a moonlit room with a tall queen bed, a single bedside table, and a lamp shaped like a leopard ready to pounce, both eyes glowing red.

"Here." She handed me a pair of red silk pajamas and left the room.

The pajamas bunched at my feet and the sleeves hung past my hands, and I felt like a child wearing her mom's clothes.

I'd tucked myself in, ready to subdue the leopard, when Regina materialized in the doorway, wearing, of all things, a floor-length flannel nightgown. She leaned against the doorjamb and lifted her chin. Though she'd supposedly been drinking for hours and though it was closer to sunrise than sundown, she appeared in control, her unique features impervious to fatigue. Clearly, she wasn't in her thirties yet.

I couldn't hold her youth, wealth, and thin figure against her, not when I was lying in her bed wearing her clothes, ones she'd been decent enough not to warn me might be too small in the waist. And the night was so late, the bed so soft, her pajamas so smooth. My eyes slid shut and snapped open. Regina remained silhouetted in the doorway, her black outline immovable.

"Can't sleep?" I ventured. My eyelids burned with fatigue, but I had to say something.

"On the contrary," she said in her heavy-accented English. "I'm exhausted. Only when Kid visits do I ever stay up so late."

Here it was. I'd been caught in a long-game foreplay between them. I should have left the minute Regina answered the door.

"I swear I didn't know he was with you." I rubbed my stinging eyes. "I'm not trying to get in the way of anything."

"You cannot get in the way. We are not lovers. In general, I prefer the company of women." She blinked. "I am thinking of you."

"Me? I'm not looking for a relationship. Not with a man. Or a woman, I mean. Maybe with the city itself, which sounds ridiculous, I'm sure. You kind of have to understand what Paris means to a foreigner like me who grew up on all these movies and books . . . It's cultural, I guess." What was I going on about?

"This is a strange American thing?"

"It's hard to explain."

"I will explain then. Kid is handsome, like a movie star, but he is not a movie star. I am telling you to be safe. I can't say more." She lifted her hands and backed out of the room. Before I could ask what she meant, she disappeared, leaving the doorway a gaping black mouth.

"Regina?" I whispered into the dark, but there was no response, not so much as the sound of footsteps.

16

I left Regina's jammies folded on the bed and stepped into the hallway. The night before was like a tide coming in. The images surfaced and receded and surfaced again. Marco, lost keys, calling Kid, Kid's lips on my fingers, Regina in her flannel nightgown. A warning.

Ugh. I pressed my fingers into my temples and took a deep breath.

This wasn't like me. Waking up in a random bed wondering what I'd gotten myself into. I was the person who went home alone and regretted what I hadn't done, not what I had. Nothing really *had* happened last night—Kid and I hadn't made out, he and Regina weren't, apparently, an item—so why did I feel as if I'd raided my parents' liquor cabinet and woken up surrounded by the empty bottles? Something Lily had done, never me.

With a bang to my brain, I realized that's exactly why I'd called Kid the night before.

So long San Jose Rose, I'd promised, and sure enough, it was as if I'd jumped from my own story into someone else's. Good, right?

Needing a minute to collect my thoughts far away from the watchful eyes of Regina's leopard and Kid's impossible-to-resist smile, I tiptoed toward the front door. The wafting smell of breakfast sausages sent my stomach into a starvation tizzy and intensified my urgency to get out of there. Someone was awake.

I would text Kid later.

Or I wouldn't. Seeing him again might send me tumbling over an edge I wasn't sure I should cross. Then again, I wasn't sure I shouldn't cross it. And didn't I sorta wanna kinda cross it? My radar was off. Regina had told me to keep away, but why? How did I know I could trust her intentions either? So much thinking made my head throb.

As I reached the entryway, footsteps sounded. My name echoed down the long hallway.

I turned around to see Kid smiling and waving as if we'd run into each other on the street. I laughed to hide my discomfort.

"You're up early," I said.

"I'm terrible at sleeping in. Anyway, Regina's making breakfast," he said. "Crepes." He eyed the bag hooked over my arm and pouted. "Now, now, Rose, what kind of respectable houseguest leaves without a goodbye? Regina will have her feelings hurt."

He had a point. I couldn't be rude to a woman who'd let me sleep in her silk pj's.

I followed Kid to the kitchen where, sure enough, Regina stood over a small cast-iron pan.

"Look who I found trying to leave," Kid said. He pulled a barstool from beneath the counter and gestured for me to sit down, but I held my ground.

"I *am* leaving. I wanted to say thank you for letting me stay over."

Regina's spatula dangled midair. She kept her eyes on the crepe. "You're welcome."

"By the way," Kid said, "I wasn't joking about going to the south. I'll be devastated if you don't come. Totally wrecked."

"I'll think about it." I tried to recall the specifics of what I'd agreed to.

"To be honest, you'd be doing me a favor. My mate's bringing his wife, and we need another woman to round out the group." He hopped from the barstool. I tried to catch Regina's eye, but she was pouring batter from a ladle and didn't show any inclination to acknowledge I was standing in her kitchen.

Kid continued, changing course. "Don't say anything now. Think about it and I'll text you details."

A few minutes later, I was back on the streets of Paris. I still didn't have my keys.

❦

I decided to walk to Paulette's, and took my time, hoping I'd hear from her before I made it back to the building. It was early, the earliest I'd been out at least, and people roamed the streets but wordlessly, as if those of us awake were trying to keep the city asleep as long as possible.

When I made it back to the Marais without word from Paulette, I began to wander down roads I hadn't walked before. I'd come to know the neighborhood well enough to stray from the path, and I began to test myself. How far could I wander and find my way home?

Home.

I meant Paulette's, of course. Back at *home* home, the previous day's evening was over. Mom would be settled in bed with a TV series and a wedge of CBD mint chocolate. Iris and Ben would already have been asleep for an hour, tomorrow's workout clothes folded beside their bed. And Lily would . . . well, Lily might be up to anything.

I missed Lily, a little. She'd be fascinated by Kid. And she'd love Regina. She'd yell at me for not rifling through her drawers. For not stuffing the silk pajamas in my purse.

When I was a block away from rue du Vertbois and Paulette hadn't texted me back, I slipped into Brass Key for *un café noisette*. The coffee bar's decor screamed hipster-bland, something you'd expect in San Francisco's Mission District: bespoke pendant lights, spindly white chairs, succulents galore. As Paulette predicted, the familiar ambiance appealed to me.

Always eager to practice their English, the staff brightened when I walked through the door. It was the one place I could procure a croissant without having to butcher the French language or count coins from my palm like a child. I wasn't up for the level of humiliation required to order from somewhere old-school, like Paulette's other recommendation, Boulangerie Etienne, even for a flakier pastry.

I recognized the girl behind the counter but hadn't learned her name. She waved from behind the churning espresso machine.

"Bonjour," I said.

"Hey." A minute later, she was pulling a shot for me. "How are you?" she asked.

"I locked myself out of my apartment rental. I'm waiting to get back in."

"Oh no. I'm sorry. That's terrible."

"It's my own fault, but it sucks."

"Yes, it sucks," she said, the slang sounding a little funny with her accent. "Are you staying nearby?"

"Around the block."

"Why are you in Paris? Is it"—she paused, the espresso dripping into a small glass tumbler—"for work or fun?"

"Fun," I said, the word misshapen in my mouth. Was that why last night made me uncomfortable? The whole scenario had been weird, sure, but also sort of fun. Certainly exciting. And exciting wasn't really in my wheelhouse.

I'd been in Paris a week by myself. I'd shown I had it in me, whatever "it" was everyone back home assumed I didn't have. But that wasn't enough. I couldn't bear to fit back into the same worn grooves of my life so seamlessly.

When I returned to San Jose, I had to do so knowing I'd tasted enough of another life to make my bland one there palatable.

The second I sat down with my espresso, Kid's text arrived: You MUST come to Cassis. If you won't do it for me, think of lonely, estrogen-deprived Lois stuck with a bunch of brutes.

I chuckled.

Tell me more, I typed.

The house was huge, he wrote, and I could stay in my own suite. You won't regret it, he added, which, if this were a movie, all but guaranteed I would.

I could hear my mom's notorious sharp inhale. Traveling to an unknown city in a foreign country with a strange man. She'd be beside herself. If she knew. But the more days that passed, the further I felt from home. A week ago, I would have told Kara and Iris everything, asked them to analyze each moment for meaning, mine Kid's every word for information. But I was happy to have Kid to myself.

Fun, I'd told the barista, and fun I knew Kid could provide.

17

Paulette turned the key and let us both inside.

"I'm so sorry," I said. "I'll pay for a replacement."

"It's not necessary," she said, but she was more distant than the day prior in the park. "I will gather a few things while I am here."

In the bathroom, I heard her open the locked closet and dig around. I waited in the living room, equal parts guilty to have lost her keys and dragged her home, and eager to have the place to myself.

When Paulette came back, she hugged a small bundle of clothing beneath her arm, a tight frown on her face. My throat narrowed. My head had begun to throb.

"Paulette, I feel terrible. Please let me pay for the key."

She waved her free hand and slouched onto the couch. "No, no. It's not that. I'm staying with my parents, and they're making me so mad."

She went on to tell me a long story. She'd had a fight with her parents the night before. They didn't like her renting her apartment to strangers. They wanted her to go back and finish her degree so she could make enough money to afford her apartment without having to rent it out at all. They didn't like her friends, and the experimental theater and music venues she liked to frequent. She thought they were snobs.

"My parents are very traditional. Conservative. I am upset talking about it." She brushed her hair from her face. "I should not say all this to you. How is the rest of your trip shaping up?"

I rubbed the back of my neck, glad I'd brought a bottle of ibuprofen from home. "I'm going to Cassis for a few days. Have you been?"

I realized my mistake as soon as the words left my mouth and Paulette's sober face brightened.

"How long will you be gone?"

"Um . . . I mean, not long, just a couple of nights," I said, backtracking.

"This is perfect. I will stay here while you're gone." I opened my mouth to speak, but she cut me off. "I will refund you those nights, of course. *D'accord?*"

I couldn't say no, not after losing her keys and inconveniencing her again. What was the real harm? I wouldn't be here anyway.

"Sure. Why not? It's your apartment."

She jumped up, smiling, her palazzo pants swinging on her way to the door.

"Perfect, perfect, perfect. See, it's good luck you lost your key, otherwise, I'd never know."

Rose Zadeh to Iris Zadeh:

Did you know there is more than one of those bridges covered in "love locks"?

Sort of kills the romantic buzz. And no, I'm not jealous.

The man of my dreams (if only) will come bearing actual keys to my front door. I keep losing mine.

Btw, I met Marco. He's decent but with the sense of humor of a cardboard box.

Ironically, I think I may have bored him more than he bored me. It's as well SINCE I'M DONE DATING.

At least for the foreseeable future.

Convince Mom, okay?

Iris Zadeh:

Done with dating. Got it.

Related-ish . . .

Has Mom mentioned anything about texting Vasilis?

Vasilis as in the Village Diner owner?!

Yes! He gave her his number!

She says he's helping her sort out the mouse problem (or is it rats? I can't get a straight answer).

Either way, wtf?!

Love you.

Alice Zadeh:

How come you don't write more?

I need to know you are safe so I don't worry myself sick . . . Marco told his mom you met and he enjoyed your pleasant company.

Rose Zadeh to Alice Zadeh:

Calling someone pleasant company isn't a positive sign!

Sorry to dash your matchmaking dreams.

Kara Carmichael:

You're not missing anything here.

The new guy's name is Brent Pawson.

He used to work at the San Jose Mercury.

Yep, that's it.

No more experience than you—less, since, ya know, you've worked here for years.

But he is a cis white male, so yay! Glad he got a leg up.

I've been adding subtle typos to his copy just to keep him on his toes. I know, I know. But I can't help myself.

Eat a pound of butter for me, and please stop worrying about work.

I don't want to hear from you until you're home.

I mean it.

I can be scary when I have to be. But you know that.

Rose Zadeh to Lily Zadeh:

Hey. Iris says things with Dev haven't improved.

What you need is a clean break: no phone calls, texts, coffee dates. No contact.

Put some real distance between the two of you and see what happens. You might be surprised. Lots of hugs.

Dear Gladys,

I wanted the Paris trip to end all Paris trips. So naturally, I'm departing Paris for a beach getaway, French Riviera–style. Cassis is no Monte Carlo, but that's kind of the allure. I'm picturing bottomless bottles of rosé, vats of steamy mussels, and beautiful people in barely-there bathing suits. I'll fit right in.

That, for the record, is a joke.

I'm certain to be a fish out of water, turquoise-blue Mediterranean water, no less. I've never done anything like this before, but Kid talked me into it, and I'm pretty sure Kid could sell a Bordeaux Popsicle to a woman in a white dress. Who is this Kid fellow, you might ask? I have no clue! Do I like him? It's hard not to. But my real question is, do I let my guard down enough to find out how much?

Sincerely,
Side-Tripping and So Clueless Somewhere in France

18

The world flew by in a blur, an impressionist landscape visible from my window seat, remaking itself over and over again. Yellow fields, hills undulating in the distance, olive trees with arthritic branches, punctuated by occasional stops alongside station platforms where clusters of passengers disembarked and scattered like dropped coins.

I pulled out my Eiffel Tower notebook to write what I saw, but every time I brought pen to paper, the words wouldn't come. My thoughts somersaulted against the picturesque backdrop.

A mini trip with Kid and his friends. If this Lois was anything like Regina, I was in for an interesting time. Regina's warning flashed across my mind, and I batted it away. She was too strange to trust.

A more pressing concern loomed larger the farther I traveled from Paris: Did I want something to happen between me and Kid?

What I'd written to Iris about dating was true, but I was beginning to reconsider my hard no on romance. A heart-pumping fling didn't sound all bad. I sure didn't mind looking at Kid. He was most definitely out of my league, but I'd be lying if I said that wasn't part of his appeal.

So, fine, I had a crush. Crushes were safe, right? They could go either way. Even if being around Kid made me feel like I was teetering on the edge of a cliff.

As for whether he felt the same, I couldn't say. He had to feel something, right? Or why invite me along?

So I would borrow a page from Kid's book and become, at least for the time being, Super Chill Rose. Which meant less analyzing and more enjoying. If Kid was my ticket to adventure, I was climbing on board and ready to ride. Err . . . um, yeah, Chill Rose had no need to examine that Freudian slip.

I forced Kid from my mind and turned my attention back to the view. As fences gave way to expanses of fields and vineyards, I found myself remembering the woman I'd sat next to on the plane. Marine Desjardins, with her impeccable bob and stained lips. This was the France she'd described to me.

My throat fluttered a bit when we pulled into Avignon. Kid said he'd pick me up in Provence instead of the port city of Marseille, so we could drive the countryside together. It sounded romantic, didn't it?

All at once, I was itchy and too warm and—no. No. I wasn't going to psych myself out. He might not even show. I steeled myself against the outcome, but when I saw him in the parking lot, relief flooded my train-stiff muscles.

I made myself comfortable on the worn leather seats of the old silver Saab he drove, his friend's, he told me when I asked.

"You're here," he said.

"I am."

For the briefest slip of a second, I wished Iris and Lily were here, too, to see me as I was in that moment making my way alone in the world.

He gave my knee a squeeze, and a few minutes later, we were off, Kid navigating one roundabout after another as we snaked our way to the coast.

I sensed the sea before I saw the turquoise blue. Cool wind pushed through the open windows, whipping my hair. The scent wild and fresh, as if it'd traveled miles over every type of terrain. Fields gave way to knobby trees and outcroppings of rocks.

As we pulled down the hill into Cassis, I gasped and Kid laughed. The Mediterranean was like a jewel in the sun, glinting and bright. The village stretched down to the water, pulled toward the beach as if by magnet. That's how I felt, too, greater than myself, pulled by something more powerful than even my own desires, to wherever I was destined.

We drove down the hill toward the water. Before we reached the beach, Kid cut right, and the car climbed along a stretch of winding cliff, houses on both sides. Another right, and then left, and we pulled down a long driveway to a sprawling all-white home, square and simple, like stacking blocks. Blazing-pink bougainvillea surrounded the door and lavender bushes dotted the perimeter. Fat bees buzzed past my head. The entrance was pretty, if unremarkable. But who was I to complain? I'd been whisked away to the south of France. A dilapidated shack would have done the trick.

"After you." Kid held open the front door. "Mind the wedge."

"The what?"

Kid nodded toward the ground where a wooden doorstop sat propped against the doorjamb. The door slid mostly closed, catching on the wedge before it could latch in place.

"We keep the door open so we can come and go," Kid explained, nudging me forward. "It's easier than fiddling with the code. It's one of those keyless locks."

"Fancy."

"Only the finest."

Right then, we passed from the plain entryway into a sprawling living space. It was like I'd walked into a celebrity's home, one of those indoor-outdoor setups you only see on TV, with oversize floor-to-ceiling glass doors opening to a bright-white patio the size of my apartment back home and an infinity pool that seemed to cascade straight down the cliffside and into the sea. The other side of the room sported a shiny white kitchen and an island topped with a vein-riddled black stone slab.

"What do you think?" Kid grinned, clearly fishing for compliments.

"Wow."

"She's something, isn't she? I'll show you your room." He grabbed my bags and we headed down a hallway and up a flight of stairs. "On the left," he called from behind me, and I walked into a beautiful space with a plush white bed, tile floors, and sliding doors leading to a sunny terrace.

"Is this the best room in the house?"

"There are no bad rooms here." Kid set my bags down. "I'm down the hall."

"Is it yours?" I didn't know what Kid did or where he'd come from. The house made that clearer than ever. A wave of wooziness rolled over me, and I sat down on the bed.

"Temporarily." He sat down beside me, bounced a little, then lay down, hands behind his head. "It's on loan—ignore the random family photos. For now, think of it as yours. The others are down at the beach," he said. "I thought first we could grab a bite, you and me."

Did that mean he wanted time alone with me? I didn't let the question linger. For once, I refused to overthink things.

"A bite sounds nice. A glass of wine wouldn't hurt either."

Kid's mischievous grin. "One? You'll have to do better than that."

❦

Kid and I walked into town and ate lamb gyros in soft pitas from a stall near the beach. We sat on a cement retaining wall butted up against the sand, dipping our hands into a shared bag of greasy fries.

He pointed out his friends by the water but didn't call to them or suggest we walk over. Instead, he described them one by one: Henri, the rigid Frenchman; Diego, a flirt from Argentina; Lois and Emile,

Québécois here on semipermanent vacation. Emile's family owned a global boutique hotel brand based in Montreal, and they stayed free wherever they went.

"Emile's never done a real hard day's work in his life," Kid told me, his voice waffling between reverence and envy.

"How do you know them?"

"We all sort of found each other, I suppose." Another unsatisfying answer, but before I could press him, he reached over and dabbed a bit of hot sauce from the edge of my mouth. My lips parted, and I clamped them back together, heat rising through my body.

I dusted the dry sand from my bare legs. "Should we go say hello?"

"Not yet. Let me show you around first."

He hopped from the wall and offered his hand. Rather than jumping down, I traipsed along the wall like a tightrope walker, something I hadn't done since I was a girl and practiced balancing on every sidewalk curb I could, my sisters waddling clumsily behind me.

The town was small. Strolling, we saw most of it over forty-five minutes. There was Kid's favorite place for mussels; his favorite apartment building—baby-girl pastel pink like the colors he favored; the sidewalk where he'd broken his foot one ill-fated trip. We stopped at his favorite bar.

"A drink, *mademoiselle*?"

I followed him inside. We sat down at one of only a few tables and were greeted by a woman in a faded floral apron, who was probably a decade older than me judging by the lines on her tanned face but seemed somehow younger in the carefree way she walked on the balls of her feet and sashayed her hips. Kid began to banter with her, and soon they were both smiling and gesturing at me.

My eyes darted between them, unable to keep up.

"Congratulations," the woman said with a thick French accent, the syllables catching on her tongue.

I turned to Kid, but before I could question him, he threw his arm over my shoulders and pulled me close to his side. His lips grazed my cheek, and my skin flushed the same way it had the night at Regina's.

"My fiancée doesn't speak a word of French," he told the server. Fiancée? I put my hand to my face, the feel of his lips still pulsing on my skin, and tried to make sense of what was happening.

"You are a beautiful couple," the server said to me in her halting English.

Kid nudged my head with his. "Tell her how we got engaged."

I looked at him dumbfounded, and he laughed. The server joined him. "Don't worry. You don't have to speak in French," he said to me. "She says she understands English well."

The server gave me an encouraging nod. I wiped my palms against my lap and loosened my sweaty legs from the wooden seat. I had no idea what to do and my mouth hung limply open until Kid pressed a hand, miraculously cool and dry, against my knee.

"Fine, I'll start. We were outside the Louvre," he told the server. "We'd been in the museum for hours, and the whole time, the ring was burning a hole in my pocket. Finally, I told her, I said, 'Rose, I have to stop.' I dropped down on one knee right there. And before Rose knew what I was doing, the crowd was already clearing around us." He turned to me, practically glowing, like a man who'd actually popped the question to the woman he loved. "And you said . . . Well, go on, tell her what you said."

What the hell was he doing? I didn't know, but with the server's dancing eyes trained on me, I felt compelled to join him, even as I carefully hid my left hand under my leg.

"I said . . ." I paused, getting my bearings. "I said yes, of course." I put my right hand to my chest, feeling the excited bounce of my heart. "My heart was pounding, so all I could think to say was, 'Yes. Yes, I will,' over and over again. But it didn't matter because the cheers and the clapping all around us drowned out my voice, and I felt like we were in a movie, you know? We couldn't stop smiling, and people were coming up to shake our hands and hug us."

The server's hand mirrored mine as she clutched it to her chest, her lips and brow line scrunched in a puppy-dog look. "So romantic," she said.

I nodded, my head fuzzy.

"But then we figured out she'd lost her phone, and we spent the whole rest of the day dealing with that. We only arrived in Cassis a little while ago, and we haven't had time to celebrate properly."

Face lifting, the server raised a finger. She spoke rapidly in French to Kid and hurried away. Kid pushed a strand of hair behind my ear and leaned toward me. When he spoke, I could feel his breath slide down my neck.

"She's getting us a bottle of something good to celebrate."

When I turned my head, our eyes, and lips, were only inches apart. I could barely breathe but managed to squeak out a few words. "What are we doing?"

"You'll see," he whispered as the woman returned carrying a glistening bottle already sweating in the midday heat. A metal bucket was tucked beneath her other arm, with two champagne glasses dangling from her fingers.

She popped the cork, filled our glasses, and nestled the bottle in the bucket, the sound of ice rattling against the metal. The whole time she spoke to Kid, I sat dumbfounded, my body caught in the excitement, my head a swarm of confusion. She left us with parting wishes, and Kid stuck a glass in my hand.

"It's on the house," he said. "A gift for the happy couple." He examined the label on the bottle. "And a decent gift at that. Women can't resist a good love story."

"Kid," I whispered, "we can't just steal this. I mean, we can afford to pay for the bottle. I can pay for the bottle."

"It's not about the money, silly." Kid grinned. "She's happy to treat us. And you did good. Think of it as your reward."

He tapped his glass on mine. "To us."

We sipped, and I couldn't deny the way the bubbles sparkled across my tongue and gave my body a lovely rush.

"But why?" I asked, glancing back at the sweet woman behind the bar.

"I find sometimes it's better to ask, 'Why not?'" He leaned back, crossed one leg over the other. "You must admit it was sort of fun. Wasn't it?"

It had been, for reasons I couldn't explain or didn't want to consider too closely. Something about being in Kid's company, something about that kiss, made me feel a little reckless. What was the harm in a single bottle? I'd make sure to leave a big tip.

The bucket of ice soon melted, the bottle drained. I didn't plan to drink so much, but I wasn't about to waste a drop.

"Let's have a second." He waved to the server.

The alcohol spread like syrup through my legs. He must have read the uncertainty on my face because he said, "I'm not ready to get rowdy with the crew yet. I'm enjoying our alone time. Aren't you?"

Super Chill Rose nodded and agreed to another round. "As long as we pay for this one," I said, silently praising the powers that be for a full stomach to sop up the alcohol. "And not another bottle. Just a glass."

By the time we made it back to the beach, his friends were finishing off a case of lukewarm beer. Kid introduced me to the group, Lois squealing with joy and kissing my cheeks, so unlike aloof Regina. I liked her at once.

"Enchanté," Henri said, handing me a beer.

I grew warm and bright in their company.

19

I was floating in the pool with Lois. Her long blonde hair fanned out along the water like a paintbrush dipped in yellow. She was gorgeous but friendlier and somehow more human than Regina. I hadn't brought a bathing suit to Paris, but in my inebriated state, a pair of plain black underwear and a mismatched black bra made for a suitable alternative.

Lois wanted to know how I met Kid, and when I told her, she grazed her fingers against the water and said, "Ah, I see. What do you think of him?"

"What does anyone think of Kid?"

She waited for an answer, her fingers leaving gnome-size wakes in the water.

Finally, I said, "He's like no one I've ever met."

"Me neither."

"He makes me feel—"

"Special?"

I cocked my head. Was she mocking me? I couldn't tell. Her mouth stayed upturned in a placid smile. I decided to change the subject. "How did *you* meet him?"

She shot me a look beneath her starlet-size sunglasses.

"Did he say?"

"No."

"He's in the same business as my husband."

My forehead wrinkled. "I thought Kid said Emile's family are hoteliers."

"Emile works for his father, but he has his own business, too." She twirled her fingers some more before responding. "Acquisitions."

"What do they acquire?"

She waggled her hand back and forth as if to imply this and that. I chalked her indifference up to the fact she didn't have a head for business and moved on to questions about their travels, which she was all too happy to describe.

"We met Kid here on the Côte d'Azur. Saint-Tropez, I think." She smiled. "This is my favorite place on earth. One day I plan to come and stay forever."

"What about Montreal?"

"It's a pretty city, but it never felt like my home. There, I was boring Lois Leblanc. Here, I can be anybody." She slipped from her floating chaise into the water. "And we've met such fascinating people, people who've changed our lives. Like Kid."

"I think I can relate." She nodded knowingly but didn't prompt me to elaborate. She walked to the steps, and I wondered what her previous life looked like back in Canada before she'd ever met Emile. If she thought her life was boring, I could only guess what she'd think of mine, and yet, we were somehow here, together. I took a sip of my drink and leaned back onto my floating chaise, the reflection off the water almost too much for the lenses of my sunglasses.

"Once in Monte Carlo"—Lois stepped out of the water, stretched her dripping arms into the air—"Kid came to stay with us—at one of Emile's hotels, of course. We were celebrating some success of theirs, so we all got stupid drunk in the bar and before long, Kid was telling anyone who came in he'd buy them a drink. He'd shout the bartender their orders." Lois pretended to call over her shoulder to an invisible bar, "'A martini, very dirty, three olives. Whiskey, Blanton's.' When he didn't like their order, he'd change it for them, but in the way he does everything, so people didn't take offense but were flattered. 'A cosmopolitan? No, let's try a French 75' and so on. Emile and I thought he was something. It was incredible to watch. Probably thirty people came into the bar, and by the end of the night, Kid knew them all by name, and they him, of course."

She laughed and so did I. At the same time, something in the back of my head sputtered to life despite the alcohol coursing through my blood. A tiny cog turning. I ignored it; Lois kept talking.

"It's the end of the night and everyone's gone but us. The bartender says he's closing. He slides the bill toward Kid, and this absurd number stares up at him, and we couldn't stop laughing. I'm expecting Kid to pull a stack of bills from his pocket, which seems like something he would do, counting them one by one." She mimed someone counting out money. "Guess what happened?"

"What?"

"Nothing at all. Kid didn't move. He acted as if it were any other night, the bill a reasonable amount for three people having a few drinks. I realized he was waiting for Emile to offer to cover the cost, on the hotel. And he did. I still can't get over it." She walked toward the deep end, a shiny bronze statue in the sun, and flexed her toes against the lip of the pool. "Emile said to the bartender, 'Put it on my tab.' The bartender came and removed the check from the table. Kid got a big smile on his face and patted Emile on the back."

"What did Emile do?"

"Nothing out of the ordinary. He didn't reprimand him or show any displeasure whatsoever."

"But why? Why would he pay?"

"He said, 'It's the price of doing business with Kid.' Isn't that fantastic?" She dove into the water, leaving me struggling to make sense of what she'd shared.

She'd spoken with admiration, plainly impressed with Kid's prowess. I, on the other hand, didn't know what to think. Kid acted like he had all the money in the world, but then again, as far as I could tell, he was a professional couch surfer. Unless, he hadn't been using Emile for money but testing him. For what? Loyalty? In any case, the whole thing didn't make him sound redeemable, and for the first time, his entitlement made me uncomfortable.

And then there was the matter of the bottle we'd shared at the bar. The engagement story he'd spun so easily. Was it all in good fun?

I swallowed down the question along with the last of my drink. A moment later, Henri appeared with a tray of bright orange spritzes, and I found myself too content to worry.

20

We abandoned the pool for dinner, and I drifted through the passing conversation a happy observer. We dug into a platter of cheeses after the meal. I drank more to wash down the intense, funky flavors.

"Tell us, Rose, what's been your favorite part of Paris so far?" Across from me, Lois planted her elbows on the table. Wet strands of hair clung to her bare shoulders. I tucked my own behind my ear, self-conscious of my state of half undress. I'd thrown my dress over my makeshift bathing suit and the water soaked through, leaving a dark outline above each breast.

I cleared my throat. "The freedom for sure," I said. "At home, it was all commute, work, obligation, blah, blah, blah. The grind, you know?"

"That's the pleasure of vacation," Lois said. "Parisians probably think Paris is a grind."

"But what about the food?" Emile said, looping his arm over Lois's shoulders. "It's the best in the world. Has it blown your American fast-food mind?"

"The cheese, especially"—I gestured at the table—"but to be honest, I had a bad experience trying to visit Brasserie Colette. It's sort of tainted my point of view."

Henri clutched a fist over his heart as if he'd been punched. "You can't hold Brasserie Colette against the city. It is—how do you describe it?—stuffy, old. They care too much about rules. You must go somewhere young and fresh." He pointed to Kid beside me, at the head of the table. "You must take her to L'Incompetent."

Kid smiled, tossed his fork down. "Sure, I will."

"Hold him to it," Henri said to me. "He is . . ." He paused to find the word, snapping his fingers when it came to him. "Cagey."

"Tricky," Diego added, a twinkle in his eye.

"What are you ganging up on me for?" Kid tugged on my wet hair and leaned in close, his voice a whisper. "You won't listen to a word they say, will you?"

I didn't have time to respond before the others jumped up from the table and began pushing back the chairs. Someone turned on the music and we danced, our glasses trickling over the edges, our bare feet sticking to the floor.

Diego had moves, and he kept grabbing my wrists and pulling me toward him. I sensed Kid watching, so I moved closer to Diego. A rush of embarrassment, for playing the game, made me fumble about in his arms. His fingers grazed my lower back, his lips my ears, and each time, I waited for Kid's reaction. His expression never changed, but I sensed a rising tension in him. Or thought I did.

The alcohol muddied my thinking. Maybe I needed to let it, make way for my crush to become a sexy liaison. Other women did stuff like this all the time. Kara would encourage it, and Lily, too, for that matter. Though Lily probably wasn't the best example.

When the music changed and Diego went to get us water, Kid's chair was empty. My skin tingled and sweat collected at the nape of my neck. The night air poured through the windows, sluggish and warm. A new playlist started, but I didn't stick around to see what unfolded.

I found Kid in the study drinking from a tumbler. I expected him to be annoyed by my appearance, but he smiled when he saw me, the smile of a man whose guest arrived right on time. Had he planned for me to follow him? Expected me to? Did it matter? Didn't I want to be there? It was so easy to get my wants confused with someone else's. I shooed away these annoying thoughts and moved toward him.

He sat in the center of a huge leather chair and waved me over. I perched on the oversize arm cushion beside him, but not for long. Without thinking, I slipped down onto his lap and between his open arms. His free hand gripped my thigh, and he lifted his glass to his mouth.

"Careful," he said. Whether he wanted to avoid a spilled drink or was issuing a warning for something else, I couldn't tell. Whatever he meant—or didn't—I did the unthinkable next. Something Lily would describe, with compliments, as slutty.

I straddled him, my dress riding up to my hips.

"Do you think that's advisable?" he asked.

"I'm not thinking at all."

The music pulsed through the walls. Kid smelled like whiskey and ocean water.

"I've always believed thinking to be overrated." He stared straight into my eyes. "Action. Now that's when things get interesting."

"What sort of action did you have in mind?"

His lips spread into a wicked grin; his eyes narrowed. He set down his glass and reached for my waist. Was this happening? Did he want this, too? What was he hiding behind those pool-water eyes?

But there was no more time for questions. When he kissed me, I let go. My remaining inhibitions gave way to desire. I fell but in a wonderful way, like when you flop down on a soft bed and the edges rise around you. His mouth was gentle, and I pressed closer to him, longing for more of the feel-good want purring inside me.

He tasted sweet, his tongue flicking mine with care and practice. My hips sank lower, my thighs holding him tighter. He'd abandoned his drink at some point, and now his fingers played down the length of my body and back up again.

We stopped for a breath, and I couldn't help but pour over him, a vicious thrill humming between my legs. *This is what it's like to make out with someone drop-dead gorgeous, someone everyone else wants, too.* His eyes were quizzical at my stare, but he smiled and drew me back down toward him, this time more urgently. His hands tugged at the edges of my dress, hitching it up to my waist. His pelvis thrust into mine.

My adrenaline spiked, leaving my head clearer. I saw what was happening and clarity washed over me. *Not here, not now, not like this.* We had two days left together. I had almost two weeks left in Paris. There was time for more, when we were less drunk, when I felt more coherent, when I wasn't sticky with chlorine and sweat.

But once I decided, I didn't know how to extricate myself from his dry hands and warm body and searching mouth. I kept kissing him, wondering what I should do, waiting for things to advance to a point of no return, aware if he pushed me, I might not stop him.

Something Lily told me ages ago popped into my mind, one of her attempts to help me find a boyfriend or at least get laid. "Leave them wanting more. It always works. Always," she promised.

I reared back a little. When he followed, I pressed my hand to his chest.

"We should . . ."

"Do we have to?" His teeth grazed my neck. A chill ran down my spine.

"Tomorrow?" My voice was a whisper against his hair.

His fingers drifted down my back, stopping at my waist. "Tomorrow."

A few minutes later, I was stumbling in the dark toward my room, giddy from the turn of events but more so from my own gall.

21

The heat of the morning radiated from the french sliding glass doors across my pale bare feet. I caught my blurry reflection in the glass and grimaced. I ran my fingers through my tangled strands. That's what I got for going to bed without washing the chlorine from my hair. That, and another headache, more cotton mouth.

The house was still for the first time since we'd all come back from the beach the day before, and I knew I needed to enjoy the calm before another day began. I didn't think I'd ever be able to drink again.

I stepped outside and leaned against the railing. I'd never stood on a balcony overlooking anything but howling highways and stark buildings with reflective windows that left glare marks flashing before my eyes. I'd definitely never stood on a balcony big enough for a king-size bed and with a view of the sea. I turned my face to the sky and attempted to let the first rays of sunlight bleach away any stains of unease from the day before.

Yesterday fit together like a broken mirror, distorted and messy. Particulars were hazy, but I remembered in detail my kiss with Kid.

I kept thinking of what I'd said to him at the end of the night: "Tomorrow." So provocative, so confident. The embarrassment I expected to find didn't come. In its place, a swimmy uncertainty that ventured close to excitement.

I wanted to tell someone, Kara, my sisters, but it wasn't the sort of thing you called long distance over, and what would they have to say? I didn't want their opinion to ruin it for me. Better not to hear it at all. If only I could live in a bubble where I never had to know what anyone else thought, where nothing was ever needed from me.

I wanted to see Kid. To face him, clearheaded, after last night. Would he pull me into his arms or pretend it never happened? More importantly, what would I do? Super Chill Rose would play coy, flirt but not touch, let Kid come to her. I could do that. Couldn't I?

In the bathroom, I filled a glass with water from the faucet and chugged, mouth dripping, over the sink. Then I filled up another. I checked the clock. Seven a.m. It was way too early to go see him. I forced myself to close my eyes and empty my mind.

Two hours later, the hangover hovered unrelenting, but at least my headache had gone. I took a hot shower and dressed. My cheeks were pink and my eyes heavy, but otherwise, I looked functional.

Before I could step from the room, a slip of paper peeking underneath my door caught my eye. I plucked it from the floor. A handwritten note, from Kid:

Rose (by any other name would smell as sweet),

Work calls and I must head back to "gay Paree." Yesterday was a ball! I hope you think so, too. Please do enjoy the rest of your stay and make the most of it for poor, missing-out-on-everything me.

Yours,
Kid

I slumped onto the bed.

He'd left? He'd left me at *his* guesthouse with *his* friends, and a line from *Romeo and Juliet*? Did he want me to swoon? God, I felt dumb.

Was this a punishment for not sleeping with him? Or would he have left anyway, and I'd at least saved myself that particular off-brand humiliation? Did it matter? I was still humiliated. It was Genomix all over again. Aidan might as well have hopped on a plane to France and followed me to Cassis, I could so keenly see the edges of his lips curling while he asked me, "Do you think you *deserved* to have sex with a guy like Kid? In your heart of hearts, deserved it?" between sips of Chablis.

Was this proof I was in over my head?

Regina's warning rang loud as a bell, clanging to the rhythmic *tsk tsks* of Iris's and Mom's potential *I told you so*s. A wave of nausea forced me upright.

I gathered myself, swallowed down my queasiness.

Step one: pack clothes.

Stumbling, frantic and fallen, to my overnight bag, I found my resolve. No, I would not go home like more of a loser than I had when I left. No, I would not move into Mom's place on some godforsaken future date, when I was sixty or fifty or, please help me, forty, believing I'd squandered my one chance at living like a whole person instead of an ensemble cast member in a Zadeh family production.

Step two: leave, the sooner the better.

But I didn't know how to get from Kid's stupid-perfect villa all the way back to the train station. Or where I'd stay when I got back to Paris, seeing as how Paulette was squatting in her apartment. I wasn't even sure I wanted to go straight back.

I could get a room in town and hang out at the beach for a couple of days, but I'd risk an encounter with the group. I could head east to Cannes, but in truth, I wasn't all that keen on seeing more of the Côte d'Azur. An inn in Avignon?

Then it dawned on me. Marine, from the plane. She'd offered me a place to stay if I ever found myself in Provence. I wasn't quite in

Provence, and I was more lost than found, but I hoped that would count.

I called before I could convince myself not to. Desperate times.

"Allô?" Her familiar voice, a relief.

"Marine? *Je suis* Rose, uh, from the plane ride to Paris. The Paris virgin?"

"Rose," she said with recognition. My shoulders relaxed. "It's wonderful to hear from you."

"I'm here. Well, more accurately, in Cassis, it's a long story but I wondered—"

"Yes, you must come for a visit! Stay the night! Cassis is a drive. How will you get here? Do you have a car?"

"No—"

"It's no matter. My husband will come get you."

"I don't want to put him out."

"The timing is right. Alain is in Marseille this morning, and he can pick you up on his way home. It's fate! Can you text him your location? You will be so comfortable here. *Super!*"

Comfortable sounded like what I needed. A break from being a tourist, a break from feeling lost, a break from complications.

"Can't wait," I said.

22

A half an hour later, I'd gathered my things and inched my way downstairs. Alain and I had agreed to meet in town, and I wanted to avoid running into anyone on my way out. I would walk the half mile or so, get an espresso, and skip morning-after small talk with Kid's friends.

But the moment I stepped into the hall, Lois called my name. "Did you hear about Kid?"

I followed her voice to the kitchen island, where she sat plucking raspberries from a rough ceramic bowl.

"He's gone."

"I know." I caught myself before mentioning he'd left a note. "He told me."

"Emile with him."

"Oh, I'm sorry."

She popped a berry in her mouth and studied the stains on her fingers. Dark half moons eclipsed the soft skin beneath her eyes. She was hungover, too. The realization was a comfort somehow, though she wore it much better than I did.

I slung my bag over my shoulder. "I'm going to stay with a friend for the night."

"You won't wait for them to come back?"

"They're coming back?"

"Emile said tonight. What did Kid say?"

"He didn't." I wanted to check the note again, though I knew he hadn't said if he'd be back, had in fact implied he wouldn't, but I'd ripped it up and flushed it down the toilet. "I have other plans."

She cocked her head and studied my face. "You know? I like you. You're nice."

My ego could have used the compliment, but she'd said it as if it were both a surprise and an inconvenience, as if I were a reality TV show contestant she hated to vote off the island.

I slipped out the front door still held ajar with the wooden stop. How odd to leave the door open even through the night. Then again, everything about the last twenty-four hours had been a little odd, as if I'd been wandering through a fun house and finally found the exit. With a final glance behind me, I vowed to put the whole thing out of my mind.

After downing a double espresso from a café, I waited in the squat, sea-kissed town square until Alain appeared in a paint-stripped Citroën that screeched to a stop in front of me. He bounded from the driver's-side door and lifted my bag into the trunk with the courtesy of a chauffeur.

Inside the car, he lobbed a pile of books from the front seat onto the floor of the back, and as I settled, he patted the straw-like gray wisps on his head, then dipped his hands atop the dashboard and plucked from an unseen crevice a pair of plain black sunglasses. As he put them on, pleasant wrinkles webbed from under his eyes.

With a turn of the ignition, the car sputtered to life, French talk radio blaring from the speakers. Turning it down, he said, "My English is not so strong as Marine. May we sit quiet and listen as we go?" I nodded, happy to avoid lost-in-translation small talk.

Two hours later, we turned down a quiet dirt road, then a winding gravel driveway, the car's wheels kicking up a cloud of dust outside my window. Alain cleared his throat. *"Et voilà,"* he said. "We are here." I smoothed my pants, hoping I'd appear presentable to Marine.

Oak trees clawed at the sky, beneath them a big stone house with green shutters and a glassy wading pool.

We pulled in front of the house, and Marine popped out the door holding a fat tabby in her right arm, waving with her left, the loose sleeve of her white cotton blouse collecting at the elbow. When we stepped onto the driveway, Alain kissed her cheek, and she rounded the car and pulled me into a big hug. The tabby's soft fur tickled my nose, and Marine's eyes went round.

"You're not allergic?"

"I'm not. He's adorable."

"Candide." She lifted his paw for me to shake. "He is a lamb. Don't worry if he brings you a dead mouse. It's good luck."

I laughed, completely charmed, completely thrilled to be there. Completely over whatever was with Kid. I didn't need Kid to have an incredible trip. Look where I'd landed! All on my own! I could have thrown up my arms and twirled around like the GIF of Maria von Trapp from *The Sound of Music* that my sisters and I liked to share after emerging from an extra-long visit with Mom.

"Come, I'll show you around," she said.

The property stretched much farther than what I'd seen from the driveway, and every angle stunned like promo shots from a travel site. The olive grove, the bent metal chairs with worn wooden tables clustered beneath shady patches in the grass. Adirondack chairs stationed like friendly gatekeepers.

"Here is where I read." Marine relaxed into one of the chairs. I sank into another beside her and took in the view, my chest expanding.

"I can see you are settling in," Marine said. "Rest here. Later if you want, you can help me cook. I love a dinner party, don't you?"

After the madness of the past twenty-four hours, I was so relieved to have wound up in this beautiful place, beside Marine, so happy to have dodged a bullet with Kid, I believed she was referring to me, that I was the party. *How sweet,* I thought.

"In fact"—she eyed her wristwatch, shiny and gold—"I should get to the market. I want to be all done before they get back."

I didn't follow. "Who's getting back?"

Marine chuckled, and I forced my mouth to smile.

"Elise, of course. My daughter and her new boyfriend. They've been visiting Provence. A couples getaway."

I could see my peaceful evening fading away, but I put on a smile. I was grateful for Marine's generosity and glad to have a place to stay for the night. A memory from the plane, Marine venting about her daughter, came back to me, but I knew how mothers and daughters complained about each other, and it didn't mean anything except that they knew each other better than anyone.

"Sounds nice," I offered.

"Marco will be happy to have you here," Marine continued.

I did a double take. "Marco?"

"*Oui.* He is also an American. What fortune, no?"

But not the same Marco. It couldn't be.

23

Marine directed me to an unlabeled bottle while she chopped garlic at a massive butcher block in the center of the kitchen. "It's my friend's table wine," she said. "Great for cooking. And drinking while cooking."

I dropped the opener on my way to the bottle, and once I wedged the corkscrew into the cork, the metal claws kept scraping over the lip and down the bottle's smooth neck.

"Are you alright?" Marine asked.

"Fine." I knew she was watching, and I tried to relax despite the growing tension inside me. "Just terrible with these things."

I hadn't told her I happened to know a Marco. I hadn't asked any questions about Elise's Marco that might have led to confirmation one way or the other. I was hoping Elise would arrive with some other American Marco and the problem would resolve itself. But I was anxious. Something about Marco's connection to home, appearing so unexpectedly, left me out of sorts, like running into my gynecologist at the grocery store.

"Do you need help?" Marine asked.

"I got it."

I yanked the cork free and served Marine and myself each a tumblerful. The honeyed wine coated my throat, and I shook off my worries.

What did I care if Marco Dariano showed up? Anyway, what were the odds it was the same Marco?

"What else can I do?"

"Sit, sit." Marine gestured to a barstool. "Keep me company. I'm always alone in the kitchen. Alain works around the house every free minute and Elise was never interested." She tossed the garlic in a hot pan of oil; the scent lifted in the air. "Tell me, how has your trip been?"

I ran my finger along the rim of my glass, biding my time, not sure how much I should share. Marine sniffed out my indecision.

"No secrets," she reprimanded.

I looked up from my glass, and much to my surprise, found myself telling Marine all the thoughts collecting inside me. Not about Marco. But about Paris not living up to my expectations. About my embarrassing encounter with Kid. Even about my dad. How disappointed he'd be if he knew I abandoned my responsibilities for some whirlwind vacation. He'd surely believe I'd be better spending the three weeks off work looking for a new job, not gallivanting around France.

She listened without interruption, except now and then to ask for an ingredient.

Soon the kitchen was fragrant with a delicious savory smell, our glasses empty, and I hadn't shut up. Marine put down her spoon and stepped away from the pot she was stirring. She refilled our glasses and tapped mine.

"Chin-chin." She removed her apron and laid it on the barstool beside mine. "I will tell you what I think, okay?"

She watched me with sharp eyes, waiting for my consent, her usual happy expression replaced with something more sober, her jaw set, her lips straight.

"Okay."

"Your father worked hard to make a life in a new country and provide for his family. He believed that there is no place greater than the

United States. You say he did not like to travel, and it is understandable that the idea made him uncomfortable. He immigrated at an intense time, and Middle Eastern people are discriminated against in the US. Here in France, too, of course." She leaned onto the counter, her head tilting toward mine. "That doesn't mean he felt the same way for you. Parents, especially the ones who risk everything to move to a new country, want better for their children. Who's to say he would begrudge you a vacation?"

"I never thought about it like that before." I squinted, struggling to adjust my picture of Dad. "I don't know. I guess it's possible."

"See, you are thinking too much and experiencing too little. Your brain"—she tapped her head—"does not always know best. Your brain is a busy bee too practiced at filling your ear with *bzzz bzzz bzzz*, the thoughts of everyone else. Sometimes what is the right thing to do will be here." She placed her hand over her heart. "Your heart doesn't lie. It doesn't know how to mimic family. When you hear your heart speak, you can trust it is your true voice."

I opened my mouth to whine that I couldn't hear my heart over everyone else's opinion, but she stopped me.

"You must get quiet to hear it. When I say quiet, I mean quieting the noises up here." She gently thunked my head with her knuckles. "Because why does it really matter whether your father did or didn't want you to travel? You are here now, and I prescribe returning to Paris without expectations. Don't try to mold the city into what you think it should be. That's all fiction based on movies and books. Paris is a place like any other, which means it is messy and inconvenient and sometimes terribly lonely. But you can still have this . . . what do you call it? Life-changing vacation?"

"Trip of a lifetime."

"Yes, trip of your lifetime, if you open yourself up." She rested her hand atop mine. Her familiar lighthearted smile had returned.

"I do not mean steamy rendezvous with charming men, although there is nothing wrong with casual sex. But remember what it is you are looking for."

I stared into the ruby swirl of my wine.

She was right, of course. I was so used to thinking things over, considering angles and outcomes and alternative outcomes, I didn't know how to be any other way. My head could talk my heart out of anything.

"Merci," I said.

"D'accord." She turned back to the stove. "They will arrive any minute. You should take a shower. Elise will steal all the hot water when she comes. Go."

The dismissal was kind, but the reminder of mystery Marco's impending appearance left me unsteady as I navigated the way to my room.

❦

When I stepped into the living room, refreshed from a real, actual, glorious hot shower, not one of those bathtubs with a handheld head like at Paulette's, Alain waved and called toward the kitchen something which sounded like, "Rose's here for dinner," but in French.

"I'm sorry. Were you all waiting?"

I came down late on purpose, hoping to have some kind of imaginary upper hand when I encountered Elise and Marco.

"No, sorry, please," Alain said, offering me a glass of wine. I accepted the glass and followed him into the kitchen, where the aroma had only deepened since I'd gone. Despite my discomfort, my mouth watered with anticipation.

"Allô! Bonsoir," Marine said. She'd been working for hours but her hair held its sleek edges and her smooth face remained composed. Frenchwoman magic. "I'm finishing. Take your wine outside. They're on the terrace."

Alain directed me to a covered patio with a big stone table twinkling from the efforts of a dozen candles. I composed a smile on my face, lifted my shoulders, and sure enough, there was Marco Dariano in starchy jeans and a button-down talking to a thin woman with a '60s-era Mia Farrow pixie cut. The infamous Elise. "Cool as a cucumber," Mom would say. She was too cool for me, and way too cool for Marco. Yet, here they were. Her hand glued to his forearm, her eyes locked on his face.

"Bonsoir," I said reflexively.

"Très bien." Alain nudged me with his elbow and beamed like a proud French tutor.

Marco turned, his expression ping-ponging from surprise to concern to something unreadable. I'd caught him off guard. Clearly, Marine hadn't mentioned my name.

At my side, Alain began introductions, and I readied to interrupt him and explain how, in a truth-is-stranger-than-fiction moment, Marco and I actually went way back. Marco's nervous gaze darted among the group, and the words caught in my throat.

"How do you do?" he said. He reached out his hand, and I shook it as if we'd never met before.

"It's a pleasure to meet you," I offered in return, my mind spinning. I couldn't imagine why he'd pretend we didn't know each other. What was there to hide?

"*Two* Americans, what a treat. And a surprise," Elise said. "I asked *Maman* why she didn't tell us you were coming, and she said you appeared out of the blue, like a stray dog."

"Elise." Marine snapped at her daughter as she joined us at the table. "Rose is welcome."

"I was making a joke." To Marco she said, "My parents are always collecting animals out of nowhere."

"I *am* something of a stray. Your parents were kind enough to include me anyway."

"You were in Cassis?"

Marco's brow furrowed for a half second. "What were you doing down there?" A hint of judgment tinged his voice. I needed to be careful. Anything I said in front of him could get straight back to my mom.

"A friend invited me for a few days."

His brow cinched again. "What friend?"

Elise laughed and shoved his shoulder. "You sound like her father."

"She arrived in Paris recently." He cleared his throat. "I was curious if she knew anyone in the area."

"Actually, I do." I glared at Marco. What game were we playing here? And why was I going along with it?

24

I didn't out Marco to the group. I played along, uncomfortable lying to Marine and Alain but compelled to maintain the unspoken bargain I'd entered with Marco when we'd shaken hands as strangers. Fortunately, I didn't have to do much talking since Elise kept slipping into French and preferred to keep the conversation directed toward her. I was happy to savor the food, rustic and rich, the kind of long, drawn-out meal one imagines when one spends far too long dreaming of a trip to France.

"In English!" Marine said to Elise for the fifth time.

Elise finished her thought in French and said, "Sorry, Rose. I'm sharing with them—"

"Have you heard about the big art theft?" Marine asked me.

Elise crossed her arms.

"It happened a couple of weeks ago," Marine continued, ignoring Elise's obvious displeasure at being interrupted.

"I heard. I noticed the extra security at all the museums."

"Yes, it's an alarming situation."

"Paranoia," Elise said. "This is what I was saying. At the gallery, they've hired twenty-four-hour guards. It's too much."

"It's all modern art there anyway," Marco said.

Her head swiveled to him like a bird of prey. "So?"

"If the thieves wanted a contemporary work," he mumbled, "they would have stolen one."

"Thieves?" I asked. "How do you know there's more than one?"

"Just conjecture. One man to distract the guards, for instance, while another loops the camera feeds and grabs the art. It wouldn't be all that hard at a small museum."

"Marco has been following the news closely," Elise said.

He folded his napkin neatly and placed it beside his plate. "I'm curious, given my line of work."

"Marco teaches art history," she said to me with obvious pride. "At the American University of Paris."

"I know," I said. Elise cocked her head, Marco coughed, and I realized what I'd done. *Oh no. Backpedal.* "I know what Marco's talking about, I mean. My friend Kid said—"

"Kid?" Marco said. "Not Kidridge Sweet?"

I laughed. Marco knew Kid. My world was shrinking by the minute. I was more amused than surprised.

"Who is this Kid?" Elise asked.

"Such a strange name," Marine said, refilling our glasses. "It sounds like a cartoon character."

Marco scoffed. "Cartoon character is an apt description." I wasn't shocked that a stick-in-the-mud like Marco wouldn't be fond of Kid. His attention returned to me, his face pinched. "How do you know him?"

"How do *you* know him?"

"He's shown up at my office hours a few times. He tried to audit one of my classes."

"What's so wrong with wanting an education from a fine teacher?" Marine asked, smirking at Marco's clear distaste.

"Presumably, he's there for an education, but I know his type. And I don't trust him."

"Now *you* are being paranoid. My mother is right. You are good at what you do." Again, Elise turned to me. "Marco is an exceptional lecturer, like a motivational speaker or something. He makes it all so interesting." That seemed hard to believe. I nodded politely. Elise squeezed Marco's arm and redirected the conversation back to her job.

Soon she was speaking in French again, and my mind wandered. Hours had passed since I'd arrived, the evening sky glazing the property in shades of purple. A gust of wind sent goose bumps up my arms. I sensed Marco watching me, and when I looked, we locked eyes. I expected his gaze to dart away, but it didn't. For a few long seconds, we stared at each other. Was he trying to communicate something? If so, I didn't know what. My eyes, on the other hand, demanded to know what was up with the charade. But he blinked and pulled away.

His response to Kid intrigued me. Jealousy. That must be it. Kid was everything Marco wasn't, and something of an art expert himself.

A minute later, we stood to carry plates to the kitchen. I helped Alain do the dishes while the others settled in the living room. He washed and I dried, stacking the clean items on the lovingly nicked butcher-block countertop. My sandals glided across the smooth stone floors. Piano music sounded from the speakers, and Alain and I found a rhythm in sync with the melodic plinking of the keys and muffled voices from the other room.

Setting down a heavy platter, I rolled my shoulders, stretched my neck. I yawned into the back of my hand as Alain handed me a round serving bowl.

"Ah, ah, ah," he said. "No sleeping on feet."

I could have drifted off in that welcoming kitchen, comforted by Alain's quiet presence. To think twenty-four hours ago I was dancing with Diego to make Kid jealous, and now Marco and I were playing make believe as if we'd never met before. It was too similar to the afternoon I'd spent with Kid pretending to be engaged. A tremor of worry washed over me with the flush of water from the sink. I rubbed the dish towel over the bowl I held and nearly dropped it on the floor. Carefully stacking it with the others, I took another from Alain with both hands.

What was I doing? I'd traveled all the way to France to find myself, not become someone I wasn't at all.

As one of her cautionary tales, Mom liked to tell us about the time, on the cusp of womanhood—her words, not mine—she wound up, through no fault of her own, dating two men—"boys, really"—at the same time, without the other knowing.

"I was a flirt," she'd say. "But it backfired."

She found herself falling for one of the guys but didn't know how to break things off with the other.

"I put it off because I didn't want to hurt him. I didn't want him to think I was the sort of person to cheat on someone. Because, in my mind, I wasn't."

"Was this before Dad?" I asked one of the first times she told us the story. It might have been when Iris refused to invite all the girls in her class to her eighth birthday, or when Lily started spreading tall tales about random neighbors, or Mom might have shared it without cause, preparing to cue the moral of the story for the next time she needed it. She had anecdotes for every occasion and could adjust any one to suit her message. Who needed fables and fairy tales when you had Mom?

To my question, Mom said, "Well, it sure as heck wasn't after!" About the two boyfriends, she added, "The longer I pretended, the worse I made it. Eventually, the one found out, of course. Not from me. And do you know what he told everyone?" She paused for dramatic effect. "He said I was a two-timing tramp. And I was!" She wagged her finger. "The point is, think before you act because what you do is who you are."

Mom would warn me to think more; Marine wanted me to think less; and I didn't know what to think. Listen to my gut? How? Trying to hear your inner voice with a half dozen others in your head was like trying to stay in your lane with a back seat driver screaming in your ear and lunging for the wheel.

❦

The scene in the living room was like something out of *French Châteaux* magazine, if such a thing existed. Fluffy blankets scattered across upholstery, a fireplace filled with more flickering candles, a decanter of something gold and—judging by the bottle—expensive, beside a plate of bite-size chocolates.

Elise was speaking to her mother in French again, and it was time I roused myself from the chair by the window and said my good nights. The moment I stood, Marine interrupted Elise and beckoned me over.

"Thank you for a wonderful meal," I said. "I'm going to rest up before my train trip tomorrow."

"Non, non, non," Marine said. "Elise and Marco will drive you back." She tickled Elise's cheek. "Won't you?"

Marco's jaw dropped. Elise managed to appear both disinterested and disgusted.

Was I *that* bad? I'd thought some pretty lousy things about myself, but I wouldn't say I was terrible company. I didn't even want a ride. I could picture myself making uncomfortable small talk, overcompensating with unnecessary information as I was prone to do. But their response stung. First, Marco pretended he didn't know me, and now, Elise couldn't bear the thought of having me in her car for a few hours.

I looked back and forth between the two in disbelief. Marco managed to control his panic, his jaw clenched as if fighting to swallow something foul. I watched him share a private look with Elise, and it dawned on me: Marco must be embarrassed. He didn't want his French girlfriend to know he hobnobbed with American riffraff, and clearly, Elise wasn't a fan of mine. Fine. What did I care what some buttoned-up drag thought of me? I hadn't wanted to meet him in the first place.

I shook my head. "It's okay. The train is great. I'm looking forward to it."

"Absolutely not. It makes no sense. You will save the train fare, and they are driving straight there, yes?" Marine jabbed Elise in the shoulder and she shrugged. "*Bon.* It's settled. Now you go get rest." I could have protested further, but Marine was a force, and we all knew when we'd been overpowered.

I'd sleep the whole way in the back seat or pretend to sleep if I had to. No conversation necessary.

25

The next morning, we gathered around the rough wooden table in the kitchen, eating soft-boiled eggs and delicate croissants Alain had picked up from the bakery in town, and listened to Elise grumble about her terrible night's sleep.

"The bed is too soft, and all night the crickets, *ch-ch-ch-ch*, outside the window. The back room is much better." Her eyes flickered over me—the back-bedroom thief—before she poured her coffee.

"How did you sleep, Marco?" Marine asked. "I didn't know the bed was so awful."

"Fairly well. No complaints from me." Generous of him, given I caught him rubbing at his lower back while Elise jabbered on.

"He sleeps like a dead person. Is that how to say it?"

The idea of Marco and Elise sharing a bed made me squirmy. For some reason, despite seeing them right in front of me, I couldn't really picture them together, especially not in bed. I suppressed an uncomfortable smile.

"Like the dead?" I offered.

"What I said." She used her knife to crack the lid of her egg. I had tried the same maneuver and managed to mangle the thing.

"So," Elise went on, "Marco will drive, and I'll sit in the back seat to sleep. Okay?"

She couldn't have known how much I pined for the safety of the back seat, *my* back seat, the one I'd planned to have for myself, but I seethed nonetheless.

"Ah yes. Marco and Rose can discuss all things *américaines*. I'm sure there is plenty to talk about. Perhaps you have mutual friends! Six degrees of separation, or so they say."

Marco choked on his coffee. Alain patted him on the back.

"Maybe we do," I said, smiling at him with my teeth.

If looks could kill, Marco would have keeled over.

❦

An hour and a half later, the car zipped along the highway on our way back to Paris, and Marco and I had run out of talking points. Or I had. He hadn't contributed much. It was hard to make conversation under the guise of two people who'd just met when you'd spent an evening together a few days ago.

The longer we sat in silence, the more jittery I became.

"So, uh, Marine and Alain are great, aren't they?"

"Yes," Marco said.

"They'd make the best in-laws. You're lucky."

"Huh?" Marco's head pivoted to me and back to the road. He held the wheel at ten and two, his knuckles taut and bloodless. "In-laws?"

"If you and Elise . . ." The curl of his lips cut me off. He glanced in the rearview mirror. Elise snored softly.

Uh-oh. I'd stepped in something. Marco might be a Rhys-level commitment-phobe. Or it could be the opposite. He might be worried she'd think he was coming on too strong if he was too enthusiastic about their future.

"I'd say it's fairly premature to go down that road," he said. "We've only been together six months."

"Sorry, I meant hypothetically."

"Oh. Well, then, yes, hypothetically speaking, they would make excellent in-laws."

"Elise is the lucky one, I guess. To have them as parents."

"Your mom isn't . . . I mean, your parents—" He glanced in the rearview mirror again, before switching course. "I mean, you wouldn't describe your own parents as ideal in-laws?"

Wow, we were really committing to the act now. Studying his face, I could see his eyes were scrunched in concentration, his cheeks drawn and serious. I would go along with the ruse, but I wouldn't make it too easy for him.

"My dad's dead, so he's out," I said, and watched Marco's Adam's apple rise and fall. He twisted his hands against the steering wheel.

"I'm sorry to hear that."

"My mom, well, I think she'll be a nightmare mother-in-law, but that's Iris's problem. Not mine."

"Iris?"

"My sister."

He nodded, remembering.

I went on, "She's getting married next month. Which is great. Because she and her fiancé are ridiculously perfect for each other, and it takes the pressure off me to procreate."

His eyes dashed in my direction. "You don't want kids?"

"I'm ambivalent, I guess." Mom treated her daughters like we were parts of her body she let out into the world each day, phantom limbs she could not stop thinking about, our absence almost too much to bear, making the prospect of motherhood somewhat terrifying. Maybe I wanted kids, but at the moment, all I wanted was a life of my own. "What about you?"

"I'd like to get the chance to be the kind of father I didn't have."

The AC prickled my skin. I turned the vents away from me, rubbed my arms.

"Here." Marco fiddled with the controls.

"That's okay. If I'm the only one who's cold."

"No, really. I want you to be comfortable."

He put a hand in front of the vents to feel the air, then played with the controls again. The blast of cold air slowed, and I quickly warmed, but my skin stayed raised. I looked at the countryside out the window, trying to focus on the meadows covered in yellow straw, the nests of lush trees. Alongside the road, trimmed trees spiraled toward a frothy white sky. A field of electric lavender followed. I gasped and pointed. "Look!"

Marco glanced out my window, his eyes brightening. "Beautiful."

"Maybe sitting in the front seat isn't so bad," I said.

"What's that?"

I shook my head. "Nothing."

"You know, Marine and Alain certainly like you," Marco said. "Marine especially. I think she's quite impressed with the fact that you're traveling alone."

"She is?"

"She speaks highly of you, almost with pride, really."

"Shh." I pointed to the back seat. "We don't want Elise to get jealous."

He cracked a smile, conjuring the hint of a rather sweet dimple I hadn't noticed before. *Huh.* So he did have a sense of humor.

Quiet passed between us. This time, I let it linger, until Marco pulled the car into a gas station.

"Do we need gas?" I asked.

"I'm going to grab a water. Would you like something?"

I passed on the offer, and Marco stepped outside. He made every effort to close the door without a sound, but the minute it clicked into place, Elise shot up, glassy eyed.

"On est où?" She massaged the corners of her eyes. "Why did we stop?"

"Provisions." She cocked her head, suspicious of the word. Or me. I wasn't quite sure. "Marco needed something to drink."

Her eyes remained focused on me, and I shifted a little in my seat.

"Did he speak about me? While I slept?"

Warning alerts dinged in my head. If I lied and said he hadn't, she'd be miffed. If I said he had, she'd demand to know more. I decided to try a different tactic.

"Why? Is something wrong?"

She licked her lips and stretched like a cat basking in the sun.

"He's met my parents for the first time, so I'm curious. We haven't been dating long. It's new." She dabbed something from the tip of her tongue and began to dig through her bag. "He's a unique American, isn't he? Not loud or aggressive." She bobbed her head dreamily. "He is humble and kind. What do you think of him?"

It was a trap. It must be. Had she sniffed out our wine night?

"You don't care what I think," I said.

She watched the entrance of the convenience store and pulled herself between the two front seats, so our heads were almost side by side.

"You are an American, so you have better . . ."—she struggled to find the word—"information?"

"Insights?"

"Yes, what I said. Tell me, do you think he likes me much? His demeanor is sometimes unclear."

Elise, insecure? I couldn't believe it.

I made a serious face and went silent long enough to lend my words extra weight. "He's a reserved person. He would take meeting your parents as a big step, so he must like you a lot, right?"

Her lips pursed into something like a smile. "Right," she said. "Exactly. Now, let's switch." She shooed me from the front to the back.

As I walked around the car, one question I couldn't answer batted around my brain like a bug. Why was the guy who claimed he didn't lie lying to his girlfriend about me?

26

Elise and Marco spoke in French the rest of the way, leaving me in peace, alone, in the back seat. I couldn't wait to return to Paris and Paulette's pretty apartment. As countryside gave way to small towns gave way to suburbs, a burst of adrenaline left me tapping my toes against the car's floorboards. This time would be different. No expectations. No worrying about home. And no Kid.

Unless . . . my phone buzzed. A text: Where have you been?

The moment I thought about him, Kid appeared. How dare he ask *me* where I'd been. Wasn't he the one who pulled the Dear John?

He didn't deserve a response, but I deserved an apology. I typed: I've been staying with friends. Where have you been?

Lol, he wrote. Three little dots appeared, disappeared, and appeared again. I waited. Finally:

I know I shouldn't have left like that. I want to make it up to you. Where are you now?

On my way back into the city. But I'm not up for hanging out. I'm too

How long until you're back?

Prob 20 min. Why?

K

???

After that, nothing. No more texts. No more three little dots. I checked and checked and checked again. I didn't know why I'd responded in the first place. What had I expected?

By the time Marco pulled up in front of Paulette's building, I was desperate to be alone and wallow a little. A bath, a glass of wine, a plate of brie, all at once. Drown my sorrows. Baptize away my sins.

Marco hopped from the car to get my bag from the trunk. When he handed it to me, he didn't let go right away. His lips parted and he swallowed. I readied myself for an explanation. Instead, we both turned at the sound of my name from across the road.

"Kid," I said, shocked. I didn't have time to conjure the morning-after shyness I expected at the sight of him.

He crossed the street, waving as he walked toward us, as if we didn't see him coming. And see him we did. Even amid my surprise, I sensed the fury rising off Marco. He wasn't exaggerating. He *really* didn't like him. But Kid strode up to Marco with an outstretched palm. "I know you." Marco didn't take Kid's hand, but the smile never left Kid's face. He tapped his fingers against his lips. "*How* do I know you?"

Marco bristled like an angry cat. "Most recently, you crashed one of my classes."

"Right, right," Kid said. "The professor. Good to see you, pal."

Marco clenched his fists, his mouth crimped with disgust. Before things escalated, Elise slammed on the horn. "It's time to go," she hollered from the window.

"You're needed, driver." Kid grinned.

I yanked my bag from Marco's tight fist and pulled Kid toward me.

"Thanks for the ride. *Au revoir,*" I said.

When the ignition started, I demanded an explanation from Kid about what he thought he was doing showing up unannounced.

"I had no choice but to ambush you." He pulled a bouquet of miniature blush-pink roses from behind his back like a rabbit from a hat and gave me a sheepish smile. "You skipped town so fast down in Cassis, you didn't give me the chance to apologize. I never meant to abandon you."

"You didn't *abandon* me. But a word of warning would have been nice. Some context for why you'd up and leave after inviting me all the way down there."

"A work thing came up in the wee hours, and I had to bolt." I shook my head, and he flung open his arms, the flowers dangling by their necks. "Fine. You're right. It *was* work. But it was also that I overstepped with you, Rose."

He had the decency to look embarrassed, but I didn't want to talk about this right now. I didn't want to talk about this at all. I didn't need to be rejected all over again. My bag was growing heavier by the second, and I heaved it to the other shoulder.

"The other night—" he started.

"Let's just not rehash things, okay?"

"No, no. I need to apologize. I wasn't a gentleman. I let my physical interests get in the way of our friendship. I want to be friends. I really do."

Here was the miserable part of a crush. The humiliating "let's be friends" speech that left you feeling squashed, mashed, squeezed into nothing. Into a speck. Crushed.

"It's fine," I said, shifting my feet. "We both got carried away."

I looked back at the door and rubbed my shoulder beneath the bag's strap. I was so close to my home away from home, a quiet evening just around the corner, time to lick my wounds. If only Kid would take the hint.

"I'm going to make it up to you, I promise. I owe you more Paris lessons. But first, I want you to come to a party with me."

"Now? I'm exhausted."

He laughed and lifted the bag from my sore arm. "No, sweet. You can get your beauty sleep. Wednesday night."

I shook my head. I wasn't up for more of Kid's antics. A party? Hell no.

"Don't say no. Let me help you upstairs and talk you into it."

Before I could refuse, he glided away with my bag, leaving me standing agape in the street.

I wanted my night alone. I did. I wanted the bathtub and the cheese and the wine. I needed Kid to go away, and the sooner I let him in, the sooner he would.

I tried to explain this to him as we walked up the five flights of stairs, him lugging my bag, me lugging something, too. The remains of my dignity?

Flashes of the night in Cassis kept coming back to me. I was a fool, but at least I was a fool without witnesses. No one back home knew, which basically meant my silly dalliance never happened.

Once I got rid of Kid, I would never have to think of that one dumb, spritz-fueled mistake again. But he was impossible to say no to. He wouldn't take no for an answer, and he seemed so glad to see me, so eager to prove he really did want to be friends.

"You can't stay long," I said as we came to the fifth-floor landing. "I mean it. I'm tired, and I've been looking forward to getting home."

Music thumped from somewhere nearby. At Paulette's door, the sound grew louder. My heart fell in line with the beat.

Kid nudged me with his shoulder. "Are you throwing a party and forgot to invite me?"

I ignored him and opened the door expecting . . . I don't know what. Paulette had said she'd be gone by now. I told her I was getting back on Monday, and here it was, Monday evening. I imagined her and a boyfriend in flagrante delicto. I poked my head in, but the living room was empty except for French pop music blaring from the speakers.

I followed the sound of voices into the kitchen. Kid hung at my heels.

Sure enough, there was Paulette in an apron standing at the counter talking to someone hidden behind her. Her hands flashed up and down as she spoke in English, and I noted the disastrous state of the kitchen before interrupting her.

"Paulette," I said, unable to control the note of accusation in her name. She craned her neck toward me, her eyes bright with excitement.

"Rose! Guess who is here? Ta-da!" She drew back to reveal the last person I expected, had I been expecting anyone at all. I froze.

Lily.

In my Parisian apartment.

Uninvited.

"Lily." She couldn't be here, but she was.

"Who?" Kid said at my shoulder.

"My sister."

She gave me a half smile, a sheepish shrug, and a familiar flutter of her eyelashes that said, *Don't kill me, okay?*

I should have been mad enough to maim her, but I felt nothing except numb shock. It didn't make any sense.

"What are you doing here? Why—"

She stood. "Before you say anything—"

Kid stepped out from behind me, delighted by the turn of events. "Aren't you going to introduce me?"

A ping of energy passed between them, their bodies immobile for a millisecond.

It wasn't so strange. They were both extremely pretty. It would have been weird if there wasn't a spark of mutual attraction. Still, it stung a little given the last forty-eight hours.

What else could I do but introduce them? "Kid, this is Lily."

"What a pleasure. This is a thrill. You have to come, too. All three of you."

"I'd love to," Lily said. "Where are we going?"

"A party," Kid said. "Night after tomorrow."

I grabbed a glass from the cabinet and set the roses inside, avoiding Lily's wandering eyes.

"Should we sit?" he asked.

They gathered around the table, and reluctantly, I pulled out the chair next to him. The evening had drifted so far away from my earlier plans. There was nothing I could do but surrender.

"How did you two meet?" Lily asked. "I'm dying to know."

Kid reached out and squeezed my shoulder. "We met pursuing our shared love of great art."

I wiped my sweaty palms across my pants. An annoying smirk crossed Lily's face. "How romantic. I didn't know you were such an art lover, Rose."

I gave her a cloying smile. "Guess you don't know everything about me."

"Guess not," she said, returning the same smile.

"Anyway, Kid helped me get a new phone when I lost mine."

Lily looked at me dead-on across the table, a teasing glint in her eyes. "Your knight in shining armor."

I kicked her shin, and she reverted to an innocent doe-eyed stare.

"So who are you anyway?" Lily said to Kid. "What's your deal?"

A personal prompt was Kid's cue to deflect, but he surprised me when he opened his palms and said, "What do you want to know?"

Anything!

"Everything," Lily practically purred.

"There's not much to say. I've had a lucky life."

"Oh please," Lily said. "That's the best you can do?"

"You are trying to be a man of mystery," Paulette said.

Whether it was her deadpan French delivery, Lily's coy smiles, or because, for once, the question hadn't come from me, Kid started spilling his guts.

27

He grew up in Connecticut, some idyllic, bougie suburb near enough to Manhattan for a quick commute—although neither of his parents did. His father stayed at the pied-à-terre Monday through Friday, and most weekends, too. His mother was a mild agoraphobic who left the house under duress for obligatory social outings among her set—"keeping up with appearances," Kid said with a shrug—and only by town car driven by a man named, for real, Percy Butler.

On occasion, when his mother had to be in the city, on a Saturday night for instance, she would bring along Kid and his brother. Kid lived for these trips. He loved New York. The noise, the people, the freedom. During the week, he was your average upper-class private school kid, but when he was in New York, he could be anyone. His parents kept him on a long leash, which meant he and his brother could go wherever they wanted as long as Butler drove them.

As Kid spoke, however, it became obvious he wasn't at all your average upper-class kid. More like a 1 percenter. The pied-à-terre was a three-thousand-square-foot apartment on the Upper East Side overlooking the park, and his father was a third-generation commercial real estate mogul, owner of enough of the city to ensure Kid's kids' kids would never have to work a day in their lives.

The plan was Kid would follow in his father's footsteps. He'd be groomed to take over the business when his father retired, private school to boarding school to Harvard to a polished boardroom with views of the Hudson.

Kid had no head for the dry business of buildings. He didn't care what his father did, didn't care for the obscene wealth and comfort it brought—so he said. He wanted to draw.

He took his sketchbook to the Met as often as possible, copying the greats, studying them as best he could without a clue what he was doing. And he got better. Eventually, his mother arranged on certain days of the month for him to arrive at the Upper East Side's beloved Stryker Museum an hour before it opened and have the place to himself. She was a member of the board, naturally.

Kid's father, however, didn't care about his dedication, didn't even humor it, and for a time, Kid tried to please him. But the minute Kid started at Harvard—his father's alma mater and recipient of the family's generous donations—he knew he was doomed. First, he changed to premed, figuring he had a passing interest in the subject and being a doctor might at least curb his father's disappointment. He graduated, barely, but never applied to medical school. Instead, he enrolled at NYU as a fine art MFA. If he practiced his craft, his father might notice, might at least care, he said.

Kid tried. He did. He continued to take advantage of his ties at the Stryker. He practiced all the time. But he wasn't good enough.

"Good enough for what?" Paulette asked, interrupting his monologue. She'd been listening so dispassionately I didn't realize she'd been paying attention.

"Better question," Lily countered. "For who?"

"For whom," I said. Lily frowned but didn't take the bait.

"For me," Kid said, like it was the punch line to a bad joke. *Hyuck, hyuck.* None of us laughed. "And my parents and society at large. Here's the truth. I was a decent artist, but not good enough to make it. If you can't make it, what's the point?"

Paulette made a funny noise with her throat, a cross between a grunt and a sigh. "This is such an American thing." She raised her fingers in air quotes. "Not being enough. Always scared to upset your parents. It's a national obsession, no?"

I thought of Dad, how what he thought of me lurked under the surface like a monster, big, scary, and impossible to discern.

"Don't worry," Kid said. "Once I knew I wasn't going to be an artist, it was like pure freedom rained down on me. I moved to London as soon as I could."

"I thought you moved to London for school," I said as his story sank in.

He looked briefly taken aback, then shrugged. "*After* school. Unless you count an education in the school of life, then yes, London was absolutely my university experience. Way more valuable, by the way."

"What have you been doing since?" Lily asked, and we all knew the question she wasn't asking: Are you freeloading off your father? Lily had managed to get more out of Kid in thirty minutes than I had in over a week, and she had no qualms asking for more.

"Imports to the States. People will pay a fortune for specialty European products. It's boring. I despise discussing it for fear of being uninvited places."

"Antiques?" I asked.

"Sure. Antiques, alcohol. You name it. Which brings me to Wednesday's shindig. I have some potential investors coming, and I need interesting people to entice them."

I knew Kid didn't need us there. He knew more "interesting" people than most would encounter in a lifetime.

"We're the best you can do?" I said, only half-joking. Kid let out a laugh so big you'd think I'd delivered a real zinger.

"That, right there, is exactly why I want you to come. Say you will, please. Give a guy a thrill."

He was so determined, so endearing. And Lily was watching me so closely.

What the hell was she doing here? Following me? Reporting back to the home front? So much for getting away from everything. So much for the best trip ever. Now my sole goal would be accommodating Lily, making sure she didn't get into any trouble Mom could blame on me.

If I said no to Kid, she'd want to know why. She'd pick me apart until no piece of my trip would be mine, and mine alone. In her eyes, everything I'd done would become small. And everything I felt embarrassed about would become an amusing anecdote for her to share with Iris.

"What do you say, Lily?" I said. "Sounds like fun to me."

It was the lesser of two bold-faced lies I leveled at her that evening.

Iris Zadeh:

OMG.

Lily spent a small fortune on a ticket and hopped a plane. Backstory: she officially broke up with Dev. And got fired!

I didn't realize she hadn't told you until I went to Mom's yesterday!

Anyway, Mom hates you're both gone but says she sleeps easier knowing you're together. Do with that what you will.

I can't believe my two bridesmaids are gone. And left me alone with Mom. I swear to God, if she asks me how I'm feeling one more time, I'm gonna lose it.

Smack Lily upside the head when you see her.

Alice Zadeh:

Look at the trend you started . . . If Iris buys a ticket to Paris, I hold you responsible!

You must keep an eye out for your sister . . . she's in a delicate place between the breakup and getting fired . . . she needs your support.

Rose Zadeh to Alice Zadeh:

I always watch out for her, don't I?

Yes . . . and this is why I love you . . . you always do the right thing . . . I can't wait until you're both home!!

There was no reason to lie again.

But after Kid left, after I'd read the messages from Mom and Iris, I was a fallen power line sparking in a storm, looking for trouble. So when Lily asked if we were an item, I said yes, leaving out the failed make-out session and how I'd been warned to stay away from him. I was writing my own story now, the way I wanted to. In control.

"I knew it," she yelled, launching a pillow at my head as we turned down the blankets to crawl into bed.

"Quiet, please," Paulette called from the living room where she'd curled up on the couch, claiming she couldn't show up at her parents' home so late.

Lily laughed and clamped her hands over her mouth. In a half whisper, she said, "I knew it. I could totally tell. He's dashing, isn't he? Nice work."

"Please don't make it a thing."

"What would I do?"

"Because it's not a thing. It's a fling."

"Look at you," she said with mirth.

We crawled into bed, and I switched off the light. She could torture me with this in any number of ways, but I savored the awe in her voice.

"I guess Iris owes me twenty bucks."

"What?"

"You claimed you were done with love, and I bet Iris you'd hook up with someone the moment you got off the plane. Iris said you're too cautious for that sort of thing. I thought being here might make you better. Bolder, I mean."

"Thanks?"

I still didn't understand why she was here. Without copping to the breakup or losing her job, she'd given me some lame-ass excuses. She needed to stretch her wings. Now that summer session was over, she was going stir-crazy in my apartment. She wanted a vacation before classes started again. Or did she just need to make sure I didn't have this one thing to myself? My breath caught against my ribs. *I didn't invite you,* I wanted to say.

Instead, I said, "Mom is beside herself, having you here."

The room glowed orange from the lights outside bleeding through the gaps in the drapes.

"Duh. But what's new, you know?"

"What about work?" I said, needling her.

"I want something new anyway."

"And Dev?"

"I don't really care what he thinks."

"Okay." I took a breath. "How do I put this? It's not that I don't want you here. It's just I really wanted to prove I could do this trip on my own. The same way you need space from Dev, I need space from . . ." *Don't say* you. *Don't say* you. "Home."

Lily turned onto her side facing me and propped her head on an elbow. "I totally get it. But you *have* proven you could do it. I mean, holy shitballs, you should have heard Mom before you left going on and on about how you'd never go through with it. To be honest, I didn't think you would either. But you did! I'm only here because you did it first. You legitimately inspired me."

I would have been more flattered if it weren't for the utter shock on her face, the marvel of how someone as boring and reliable as her oldest sister could elicit real, "legitimate" inspiration. With Lily I had to take what I could get. Impressing her was a feat I didn't have much experience with.

"That's a really nice thing to say. I'm not sure—"

"I get it, Rose, I really do. But you're the one who told me I need distance, right?" She flopped down onto her back. "And I thought we could spend time together. Do sister stuff." Yawning, she said, "Remember how we used to explore the neighborhood like it was a magical village we'd stumbled upon and speak gibberish to each other like it was another language?"

"You mean you followed me and Iris around."

"Whatever," she said. "You know what I mean."

"We were pretending to speak Farsi."

"Exactly. We could explore this magical Parisian village together and speak gibberish but pretend it's French."

My viselike rib cage softened at the memory. I didn't want her there, but she'd traveled so far, I couldn't send her away. She had come for a reason, even if I wasn't sure exactly what it was, and my job was to be there for her, the pact of sisters I entered so long ago. Rolling my shoulders, I adjusted my pillow and tried to settle myself next to my new bedmate.

In time, her breathing grew heavy with sleep. Despite how tired I was, I couldn't drift off. Pressure continued to build in my chest, and each time I inhaled, the pressure got worse.

Lily's noisy breathing threatened to snore, and her leg inched over to my side of the bed. I might as well have been back in my tiny apartment, her space invading mine. I might as well have been a child again, cuddling Lily in my bed so she'd stop fussing. Pressing my face into her hair to hold back my own cries.

28

Iris had fallen ill out of nowhere. Or, at least, it seemed that way to me as an eight-year-old who'd only known my sister to be happy and playful and prone to fits of giggling that left all of us laughing.

Unlike Lily, who was already dedicated to living up to the cliché of the terrible twos, practicing and refining the use of the word "no" as if she knew how well this skill would serve her later, Iris, at four, rarely cried.

It was a Sunday afternoon. I remember because Dad was home, and he usually went into the office on Saturdays.

One minute, Iris and I were playing in our room, and the next minute she was howling in pain.

"What's wrong?" I patted her back and picked up her matted stuffed lamb. Her rigid arms wouldn't accept him, would do nothing except ball her hands into fists. Her wails brought Mom rushing into the room. She dropped Lily from her hip and demanded to know what happened.

"We were only playing," I said. "She didn't get hurt."

Mom glared at me. Tears pricked at my eyes, but Iris's cries tore Mom's attention away. She brushed the hair from Iris's forehead and wiped the wet splotches from her cheeks. Iris kept wailing, the sound mutating into something more like a moan.

Gripping Iris's shivering, delicate shoulders, Mom said, "What is it? You can tell me anything," as if innocent, impossibly sweet Iris weren't in pain but needed to confess some wrongdoing. Iris claims she couldn't express what she was feeling, that she was too young to find the words to explain the disturbing sensations brewing inside her. From the outside, it seemed she'd lost the ability to speak, and this only added to the fear.

Lily was all over Mom and Iris, still demanding to be the center of attention despite Iris's cries. I kept my back pressed against our bedroom wall, willing her to stop crying, sensing a rising swell of anxiety all around us.

"Mohammad," Mom yelled into the living room where the TV shared the details of the hushed golf matches Dad liked to watch on the weekends.

"She won't stop. She won't tell me what's wrong. She won't speak," Mom said as Dad entered the room, her words getting more frantic with each sentence.

Dad kneeled on the floor in front of Iris, and when Lily attempted to climb into his lap, he said, "Not now," and nudged her aside. Then, to me, "Come get your sister."

Lily squirmed as I pressed her to my bony body, my heart thudding against her dark curls. We watched as Dad began to examine Iris.

He rolled up her pants. "Here," he said. There was a red rash across her legs, not blistering but bright and angry. "Does this hurt?" he asked Iris. She whimpered in response. Mom stood and paced. She brought her fingers to her lips as if to bite her nails and then yanked them away.

"Should I call 911?"

"No," Dad said. "We'll drive her to the emergency room."

I followed them downstairs, Iris in Dad's strong brown arms, Lily gripping my sweaty palm. It was a flurry of movement to find the car keys, get Iris out the door, and into the car.

Lily and I stood on the threshold of the garage. No one had barked at us to put on our shoes or find our coats. Mom hadn't picked up Lily's diaper bag. Dad opened the garage door. "What about us?" I said. He looked at me and Lily, and there was surprise in his eyes as if he'd forgotten we were there.

"Wait here," he said. "Watch Lily."

I'd never stayed home alone before. I'd never babysat Lily without anyone else around. I clung to her chubby toddler body, inhaling her familiar candy-sweet scent. When Lily was a newborn, Iris and I would cup our hands over her soft spot, her pelt of black hair rising and falling with each heartbeat, feeling the miracle of our baby sister: another one of us, our own.

As our parents buckled Iris into her booster and Mom slid into the middle seat usually occupied by me, I squeezed Lily closer until I could feel the *tup-tup-tup* of her heart.

"Keep the door locked," Dad hollered. "We'll ask Mrs. Cruz to come check on you." Our next-door neighbor, Mrs. Cruz, a hundred years old, who smelled like dirty socks and made us eat her dirt-dry biscuits whenever she watched us on the weekends.

I wanted to beg them to take us, too. I would stay in the car. I would find a way to keep Lily quiet. It was too late; the garage door was already closing. After it squeaked shut, I pulled Lily into the house, checked the lock on the doors. *Iris is fine,* I told myself. *They'll be home soon.*

But Iris didn't come home. Neither did Mom. Only Dad, right before dinnertime, his face heavy, his furry brows stitched together. He fed us and put us to bed without more than a few words. I knew better than to ask the questions that burned my belly. *Where are Mom and Iris? What was wrong? Would it be okay?*

The week passed like this. Mom at the hospital with Iris, coming home only to shower and change her clothes, and Dad caring for us like a robot. He spent evenings rubbing at his forehead and muttering words into the phone like "leukemia" and "lupus," words I couldn't decipher but the sound of which made it hard for me to swallow.

He tucked us in and read to Lily each night, but he didn't really seem there at all. I tried to say as little as possible, asking for nothing, bribing Lily to keep quiet with the Hershey's Kisses Mom kept hidden in her underwear drawer.

In the mornings, we were chaperoned as usual, me to elementary school, Lily to daycare. Dad fed us breakfast, packed our lunches, and even picked us up, before heading back to work until dinnertime. Mrs. Cruz would stop by, offer to fix us a snack, but otherwise, Lily and I were on our own. She watched TV while I did my homework. Then we would play.

She wanted to sing together. She begged to ride on my back as if I were a pony. She liked when I pretended that she was my baby and rocked her in my arms. She screamed if I didn't give her what she wanted. She kicked her pudgy legs whenever I told her no. She would yank on my hair if I didn't respond to her fast enough. Her outbursts left my eyes pinching back tears, so I stopped saying no.

"Yes, here's another ice cream sandwich."

"Yes, you can play with my toys."

"Yes, we'll leave the TV on."

Please be happy, so it'll feel like a game and I can forget to be scared.

Iris came home exactly a week later, following a blood transfusion for a platelet disorder that seemed to retreat as quickly as it appeared. I learned more when I was older—how sick she'd been, how terrified Mom and Dad were waiting for a life-altering diagnosis, how lucky we all got in the end when she mostly got better—but that evening, what I saw was my little sister pale as a ghost and as tiny as the chickadees that pecked at the bird feeder outside our bedroom window.

She returned to her happy self but more tender, more susceptible to discomfort of any kind, migraines, tingling fingers, rashes, and all the other unexplained symptoms she would collect over the coming years. It was the same for our family's ecosystem. The scars weren't visible, but we'd slipped from stable footing to icy ground, aware the only thing between us and devastation could give any minute.

Dad propped Iris on my bed, Lily sandwiched between us, and we watched as he and Mom began to reorient our rooms.

"I want to stay with Rose," Iris said, her voice quiet and raspy. "I don't want to switch rooms." She'd said what I was thinking. I didn't want to share a room with Lily, and if any one of us should get the little single bedroom next to Mom and Dad's room we called Lily's nursery, it was me. Me. I was the oldest. And Iris and Lily were closer in age.

"This way you'll be near us in the night. Just in case," Mom said, catching her breath. "It's only temporary. As soon as you're one hundred percent, we'll move Lily back." Her voice was upbeat, but her mood was ripping hot, like she might burst into tears or screams any second. Iris and I knew not to argue.

They'd shoved Lily's crib into my room and placed it against the wall just as Iris's bed had been. I listened to her little exhales while I tried to fall asleep, tried not to move. Every time I switched sides, my stomach tumbled. I rubbed my belly in circular motions the way Mom would do when I had the stomach flu, but the flip-flop feeling stayed.

When Dad's shadow appeared in the doorway, I sat straight up.

"Go back to sleep," he whispered. "Iris needs her lamb." He began to sort through the pile of toys on the floor. Lily rolled over.

I didn't lie back down, waiting to see what would happen. Would he come to me? Sit on my bed? Push back my hair and kiss me good night? Would he thank me for watching Lily, for being brave? I wanted his reassurance so badly it took all my control not to leap from my covers and throw my arms around him.

When he gave up looking for the stuffed animal, he turned to find me still staring at him.

"What is it?"

I sniffed back the tears collecting in the corners of my eyes. Dad didn't like when we cried. I wanted to be strong for him, but even if I could hold back the tears, I couldn't seem to hold back the need bubbling up from inside.

I needed to tell him I was afraid I might get sick, too. I needed him to know I'd gotten an A on my spelling test. I needed him to sit beside me on the bed, smooth down the blankets, and hug me good night. But I didn't know how to say any of that, and I said the wrong thing.

"No one talked to me today. Everyone's ignoring me."

Dad ran his hand over his face and tugged at his jaw. "I don't have time for this," he muttered to himself, something he said when he was overwhelmed at his job and disappointed in colleagues who worked half as hard for twice the kudos. The tears were hot now, tiny fire ants trying to escape my eyelids. When he looked at me, he had a scowl so deep he could have been a bad guy from a Disney movie. "Don't be selfish, Rose. Not now. Please."

Three heavy footsteps later, he was gone, the door shut tight behind him, and Lily was stirring in her bed, beginning to snuffle. If she woke up Iris, it would be my fault. Dad would come back in with the same terrible look of disappointment on his face, and I'd have failed all over again.

I carried Lily into bed with me, her squishy body snuggling against my churning belly. Her thrashing limbs would keep me up, but at least everyone would sleep. I would stay awake all night if I had to, clinging to Lily like the dolls I told everyone I'd grown out of. I would do whatever it took to make Iris better. To make our family okay again. Pressing my cheek to the top of Lily's head, I felt for the long-gone soft spot through her thick, sweaty hair, and eventually, I slept.

❀

We'd traveled so far together, Lily and I, not to Paris, I mean. Through the current of life.

I didn't have a single concrete memory from before Iris was born, myself only beginning when I became a sister. First one, then the other, and me not so much rising to the top with each addition but sinking farther below the surface, becoming the foundation on which to build.

I was annoyed with Lily, for taking over my apartment and following me across the world, but I couldn't come out and say so. I'd never been able to, the same way I'd never been able to say no to her as a child. It wasn't just that I felt responsible for her. That was a big part of it, but not all. "Not the whole enchilada," as Mom would say.

We each had a part to play, a character we'd perfected over the years. If Lily was the lead actress, I played a supporting role. She was beautiful and I was basic. She required all the air in the room for a single breath, and I would rather suffocate. She asked, I offered.

If I didn't let Lily be Lily, then what would happen to me?

Tucked beside her, listening to the hum of another Paris night, feeling oh so silly for lying about Kid, I wondered if I never stood up to Lily so I wouldn't have to step into the spotlight. It was safer in the shadows, where no one could see you. Because if I found my voice, I would have to speak. I would have to say what I thought and ask for what I wanted.

Dear Gladys,

It's not exactly breaking news, I know, but I'm not always good at saying how I feel if what I feel might upset someone else. I'm not always good at asking for what I need. I thought away from home it would be different. And it was. At least, a little.

Until home came to me.

My little sister crashed my trip. She's not supposed to be here. I want her to leave, but I can't ask her to go. Not when she's clearly distressed. If I don't look out for her, who will?

I keep wondering, Gladys, who's looking out for me?

Kindly,
Stifling Her Screams Seraphina

29

I tugged at the ends of Lily's skintight dress, wiggling to draw the stretchy fabric farther down my leg. I let go and the hem sprang back up my thigh. "I'm not sure about this."

After sorting through my available wardrobe, Lily had demanded I come up with something more stylish to wear to Kid's party. "You need to step up your game," she'd said. In the two days we'd spent exploring the city together, we must have stopped in a dozen shops I could barely tell apart. Our efforts landed Lily the perfect clutch and nothing but sticker shock for me. In the end, Lily made me borrow something of hers.

From her perch on the toilet lid, she studied me, a strand of hair between her lips as I stood in front of the bathroom mirror.

Getting ready with Lily as spectator was nothing new. She liked to direct me before my dates, playing stylist and makeup artist, stepping in for whatever critical eye I lacked. There was a time, too, when I was the one watching her preen in front of the mirror, when she was a teenager, part young woman, part rare, untamed creature preparing to take flight.

The difference was I never cared how she dressed or what lipstick she wore. Standing in the bathroom doorway of our old house, I would pepper her with questions—*Where are you going? Who are you going with? Do you have your phone? When will you be home? Do you promise? Say, I promise.*

There was the first Persian New Year after Dad died, when Lily refused to stay in, despite Dad's request that we continue to celebrate Nowruz, keep alive his favorite traditions—boxes of *nan-e nokhodchi*, chickpea cookies dusted with ground pistachios; crystal bowls of chewy *gaz* nougat and dried mulberries; the *haft seen* table, a tableau of seven symbolic items beginning with the letter *S*, with its plucky dish of wheatgrass sprouts or *sabzeh*; and a dinner of *ash-e reshteh*, brothy noodle soup with beans, herbs, and wilted greens, alongside *sabzi polo ba mahi*, fish with herbed-flecked rice and its golden, crispy crust of *tahdig* I'd spent hours making, puzzling over Dad's stained *New Food of Life* cookbook and the notes he'd left in the margins.

It was my first attempt at cooking Persian food, my first time really cooking on my own, and I wanted everything to be just right. But how could it be without all of us there?

No matter what I said, Lily wouldn't budge. It was Saturday. She was going out with her friends.

I leaned on the doorjamb holding one of Dad's gold-etched glass cups, steaming with fragrant cardamom tea, and watched Lily brush her eyelashes with mascara, wondering if Mom would appear, knowing she wouldn't and hating her for it. Hating Lily, too. Even Iris, who was a broken faucet of pain and grief, leaking over us all the time. That day, she'd followed me to the bathroom, bleary-eyed, and said, "Why is she doing this to us?" To Lily's back, her swanlike neck, "You're so selfish sometimes."

Lily balked and pivoted to look at Iris straight-on, mascara wand dangling between her fingers. "Our entire childhood was all about you."

Iris's face twisted. "That is *such* an exaggeration. You think I like feeling sick?" A sob escaped her throat, and she retreated in tears.

Lily had turned back to the mirror, dabbing a pinkie at the corner of her lashes.

"You should stay," I said, one last appeal. "Because it's the right thing to do. For us and for Dad."

"He's dead. I'm pretty sure he doesn't give a rat's ass what I do."

"Lily." My eyes darted to the doorway, looking for signs of Iris or Mom. "Please don't say stuff like that. And by the way, you're still a minor. You can't just—"

"I can do whatever I want. You think you're gonna stop me? I dare you."

It took all my willpower not to heave the teacup at the mirror and watch the glass shatter, watch Lily's perfect face crumble. Because I was twenty-one and about to finish my junior year. I wasn't supposed to be living at home, playing house, caring for a teenager.

"If you leave, Lily"—I spoke through my teeth—"I swear, I'll—"

"You'll what? What will you do?" She cocked her head, perplexed, and my resolve faltered. When she was little, I knew how to appease her. I could convince her of anything with the right distraction. "Your pink dress is dirty but that's okay," I'd say, "because your purple one is magic," and her quivering lips would burst into a smile so wide I couldn't help but smile, too. Crisis averted. Happiness achieved. After she hit puberty and Dad died, she couldn't be softened, only scraped and sharpened and bent out of shape.

Before I had time to respond, she chucked her makeup on the counter, bounded from the bathroom and out of the house. That night she didn't come home, and she didn't answer her phone. Right before I decided we'd have to call all her friends' parents, she walked in the door, the crack of dawn washing the house in a foreboding glow.

Mom threw her arms around Lily, crying into her hair. "You can't do that ever again. Please say you won't. Please."

Over Mom's shoulder, Lily's eyes found mine, and beneath my relief, a tempest brewed inside me. I looked away.

"I won't," she said, and kissed Mom's cheeks. "Any leftovers? I'm starving."

With Lily's arrival in Paris, I sensed the same storm gathering strength. So much had changed since those first years after Dad died. I'd learned to stifle frustration when it thundered inside me. I'd learned to bite my tongue if I didn't want to make everything worse. Still, the feelings lingered, a dormant disease biding its time.

In Paulette's cramped bathroom, I smoothed the dress as best I could and said to Lily, "Well?"

She shrugged. "Halfway decent."

High praise coming from her and her itsy-bitsy silver camisole, slim black cigarette pants, and chunky blue heels.

She hopped from the toilet. "But you need the boots. Tell her, Paulette."

"They are good boots," Paulette said, riffling through her makeup bag. We were gathered in the narrow bathroom preparing to leave for the 8th arrondissement. I pulled again at the dress. It resisted my efforts, inching closer to my crotch with each failed attempt.

"I've never worn thigh-high boots in my life. I'm too short for thigh-high anything. And your feet are bigger than mine." I sank to the edge of the tub. "I think I should wear something I brought."

"Live a little," Lily said. "It won't kill you. And, for the record, my feet are barely a half size bigger than yours."

I pouted at her, then wedged my feet in the boots and yanked on the zipper. Standing on wobbly heels, I patted my hips. "I wish the dress had pockets."

"It's formfitting," Lily said.

"Where do I put my stuff? I don't want to have to drag my big bag around."

"Here. I'll take these." She slipped my ID and lipstick into her clutch. "Paulette has a key, and your phone will be in your hand all night. You'll be fine."

Famous last words. I should have known better than to take advice from Lily.

Ahead of me, Lily elbowed her way into the bar, a place called Just One More, decked out inexplicably like the front parlor of a San Francisco Victorian with high medallion ceilings and jewel-tone velvet sofas.

We ordered drinks and scanned the crowd for Kid.

"There he is." Lily pointed over the sea of heads. She moved toward him, and I grabbed her arm, catching my phone before the case slipped from my palm.

"He's busy. We should wait."

"He asked us to come. He wants you here. Stop being so lame."

In an instant, she dragged me across the room and planted me in front of Kid. I had an intense urge to smooth my dress, tug on its ends, but my hands held my phone and a drink. Kid took a long, dramatic gander at me and staggered backward as if he'd been shot.

"Where have you been all my life?"

"And what about us?" Lily said as she and Paulette came to stand beside me.

"You two clean up pretty well, too." He didn't look at Paulette. He practically had to peel his eyes off Lily.

He turned to the two well-dressed men at his side. I recognized Emile. To the other, he said, "This is the American girl I mentioned to you."

The statement caused an internal whiplash not unlike the car accident I'd been in back home.

He swung his arm over my shoulders. No. Absolutely not. I wasn't going to fall under his spell again. And what did he mean by "American girl" like I was sixteen? I slid out from beneath his hold.

"Enchanté," the man said, and introduced himself.

"Hello again," Emile said. "Lois will be happy to see you." He offered me his forearm. "May I?"

Unsure but too polite to demure, I gripped his biceps.

"Don't be gone too long," Kid said, flashing me a crooked grin.

Lily's laughter rang out behind me as we walked away.

When we finally found Lois, she jumped from her seat to greet me with a peck on each cheek.

"What a relief! I wasn't sure we would see you again. You left Cassis like a lightning bolt."

Emile roared. "You are so funny," he said, and kissed her temple. "I'll go say hello to others. *Excusez-moi.*"

Lois pulled me closer. "I didn't know if you would come tonight. Kid said you would but . . ." She tilted her head as if to imply she didn't need to fill in the blank. Before I could speak, she said, "Who is the tall woman who came with you?"

"My sister."

"My, my, my. What a beauty."

"Yes." I craned my neck to find Lily in the crowd. Lois jutted her chin toward the bar where Paulette, Lily, and Kid tossed back shots. Kid and Lily erupted into a fit of sputtering and laughter. Paulette dabbed her lips with a napkin.

"Do you need a drink?" I hoped my attempt to get over to the bar wasn't too obvious. Mercifully, Lois raised her empty glass.

In the minutes it took us to navigate to the sticky, black bar top, the others had vanished. I ordered a champagne and downed it in a few gulps.

"Good girl," Lois said. That word again, "girl," like I was a child.

I unlocked my phone and sent Lily a text: Where are you? Lois pattered on about the rest of their weekend in Cassis, and I tried to pay attention, but I couldn't stop looking for Lily. The champagne soured the back of my throat.

"I need to find my sister." Hugging Lois, I left her and pressed my way back into the crowd.

The room was dark and crowded, and I roamed aimlessly, my eyes straining to make out anyone recognizable. I couldn't leave without Lily, and Paulette had the key. Settling against a wall, I watched the bar in a way I hoped suggested aloof cool and not awkward wallflower with no friends.

I was fighting the hem of my dress when a familiar frown appeared in front of me.

"Regina."

She pursed her lips into something resembling a smile. "You are here with Kid?" Her words blurred together at the edges.

"I guess. I've barely spoken to him. Have you seen him?"

"I don't know why, but you are someone I like." Yep, a slur in her words and a slight droop in her eyelids. So she wasn't immune to the effects of alcohol, or whatever she was on.

"Thanks. I think."

She leaned near, and I caught the booze on her breath, and beneath, a layer of cloying perfume. My phone vibrated in my hand, but with Regina's eyes trained on me, I waited to check the text. "You are a nice girl—"

"Oh my God. Why do people keep calling me a girl? I'm probably ten years older than you."

She gawped, like she didn't know what I was talking about. My phone vibrated again, and I stifled the urge to look.

"What are you getting at?" I asked.

"Getting? I get nothing."

"It's a figure of speech. As in, what are you trying to tell me? About Kid."

"Kid?" Her eyes darted around as if he might be eavesdropping.

"Yes, Kid. What's so bad about him?" More vibrations. "I'm sorry," I said. "I need to check—"

She grabbed my wrist. "If he asks for a favor, tell him no, yes?"

"Yes?"

"No," she said. Her grip grew viselike. "Tell him no."

"Isn't he your friend?"

"*Oui, oui.* We are friends for years. He is a good friend. Who always gets what he wants." She wobbled and leaned onto my arm. Her languid expression broke into an awkward smile, and she cackled so hard she almost tipped us both over.

"What is it then? What are you trying to protect me from?" I demanded.

"Yourself," I thought she said, but the sound was garbled. She was too out of it to make any sense. I resisted the desire to abandon her, and instead dragged her to the bar, got her a glass of water from the bartender, and left her propped on a stool.

My head hummed like a wasp out for blood. I needed to find Lily and Paulette. I needed air.

Outside, the night was cool compared to the muggy bar. A string of motorbikes roared by, leaving the street empty. I breathed deeply, waiting for my head to clear. What was Regina's problem? Was she messing with me for some twisted form of entertainment? Was there more to her relationship with Kid despite what she said? Was she jealous and trying to keep me away from him? I wished Lily had been there. She would have known what to say. Where was she? I checked my phone.

Lily Zadeh:

Hey where r u?

Hello?

Paulette and I want to leave

T-minus 10, 9, 8 . . .

3

2

1

Srsly we going.

The last message was time-stamped ten minutes ago. They'd left. Without me. While I'd been cornered by Regina. I scanned the street. Of course, they weren't there. Their ride was probably pulling up to Paulette's right now. I texted back: Hello, I'm still here! Thanks for leaving me.

I considered finding Kid, but I didn't want to go back inside. I requested a car on my phone and while we drove, I stewed. About Lily. About Regina. About Kid. Mostly about me. Was I laughable? Easy to shrug off? My dress rode up against the car's leather seat, and when I tried to pull it down, I kicked the seat in front of me hard.

The driver turned around. "Hey."

"Sorry," I said, my dress glued around my upper thighs. I wasn't sorry. I wanted to throw a fit.

It was past midnight, and the lights of the city dimmed to a golden haze. I was on my way home from a party in Paris. I should have felt like a million bucks, but instead, it was more akin to having my dad pick me up from prom in the eleventh grade after my date ran off with Lindsay Whatshername because I wouldn't put out. Shame. White-hot shame. Not for something I did, but for who I wasn't.

I texted Lily during the drive, and again when the car dropped me off. No response. I didn't panic until I'd been standing outside for fifteen minutes ringing the buzzer.

I called and called again. After trying Paulette, my battery dipped to 10 percent.

A dial to Kid next that went straight to voice mail. If I went back to the party, I'd have to beg Kid, or God help me, Regina, for a place to stay, and what if they were gone by the time I got there? I'd be stranded with a dead phone and no wallet, and the stupid boots had begun to pinch my toes and make my heels ache.

How had I ended up trapped outside—again? Because my own sister didn't care enough to wait around for me. Because I'd agreed to go to a party I didn't want to go to against my better judgment.

I stood around a little while longer, willing Lily or Paulette to check their phones and watched my battery dwindle to 8 percent. It was time to make my last Hail Mary phone call.

30

Marco answered the door wearing a charcoal-gray robe, his sleepy face unreadable. His eyes flicked over my outfit. I pulled down my dress and rocked on my feet, my heels throbbing.

He opened the door wide enough to let me pass.

"I'm so sorry to wake you. Can you believe this is the second time I've been locked out? I've never locked myself out before. Back at home, I mean."

"It's fine."

He must hate me. But I couldn't care. Not right then, when I needed somewhere to sleep. Not to mention, he owed me one.

"Here." He led me to a bedroom. The dim light of a bedside lamp spilled over a made bed and a bedside table tidy but for a short stack of heavy books and a half glass of water. On top of a tall black dresser, a pair of sunglasses, a pile of change, and a faded brown leather wallet.

"This is your room," I said.

"I'd offer you a guest bed, but it's a one-bedroom."

"I can't take your room. I'm fine on the couch."

"I insist." He cleared his throat. "I left a T-shirt and shorts out for you to sleep in. If you want."

"This is really, really decent of you. Above and beyond."

"It's no trouble."

He hadn't followed me into the room, so we stood silent on the threshold for a long couple of seconds. I fought the desire to fiddle with my dress for the millionth time and snuggled my arms against my chest instead.

"Do you have a phone charger?"

"I left one on the nightstand."

Sure enough, a loop of white cord poked out from behind the lamp.

He shot out his hand toward me, a packaged toothbrush in his grip. "Here. There's a washcloth in the bathroom."

"Thank you—"

"Sleep well." Tightening his robe, he disappeared into the living room.

I brushed my teeth in the bathroom, marveling at how clean everything was, how the cubby-small space smelled like peppermint and sweet men's cologne. I splashed water on my face and plucked up the bright-white washcloth he'd left squared and sitting at the edge of the sink. Drying my face, I was reminded of something. A time I'd fallen from my bike, scraping my legs across the pavement, and Marco had pressed his sweatshirt sleeves against my bleeding skinned knees until my dad came to carry me home.

Maybe we'd been better friends than I had remembered. There was no pretending he hadn't put himself out for me tonight. I couldn't fathom why he'd bother for someone he pretended not to know, but I was grateful.

In the bedroom, I plugged in my phone, rolled off my boots, and peeled the dress from my body like a casing, the physical relief profound as I slid Marco's old T-shirt over my head, pulled the baggy shorts tight at the waist. The shirt was fragrant with fennel and detergent, and without meaning to, I found myself bringing the fabric to my nose for a deeper inhale.

Marco and I sat across from each other at a single wooden table tucked beneath one of the windows in his living room. A mug of coffee gave my hands something to fiddle with, the rich brew's scent tickling my nose. The *tick tick tick* of a wall clock somewhere punctuated the growing silence between us.

I felt like hell.

Not hungover, not from alcohol. The unforgiving morning light accentuated every one of my flaws, as though my clothes had been stripped and underneath were all my imperfections, real and imagined, written on my anatomy like a game of Operation. Except, I wasn't naked, obviously, but back in Lily's boots and dress, the latter somehow both tighter and baggier since we'd parted the night before.

My gaze wandered out the window. The view of the adjoining rooftops was quintessential Parisian, and the coffee was strong and hot. If it weren't for the company and the circumstances, in a parallel life, I might, at this moment, be living out the dreamy fantasy I once held so dear.

"Sorry," he said, interrupting my thoughts. "For waking you up so early."

"I'm the one that woke you up in the middle of the night." I stretched my legs from beneath the table. "Thigh-high boots? What was I thinking?"

"They're nice boots. I mean, I like them on you."

I looked up from my mug, but his eyes flitted away, leaving a neutral expression. Why had he acted like we didn't know each other in Provence? The question wouldn't roll off my tongue, which was thick and plastered to the roof of my mouth despite the caffeine. Maybe the answer didn't matter. After all, he'd been kind enough to let me stay the night. At the moment, I was too exhausted to care about much.

"Lily talked me into them." I gestured toward my legs. "The boots. She showed up here in Paris. Unannounced."

"Lily?" He cocked his head. "Your sister? That must have been a surprise."

"You could say that. She's the one who locked me out. Not intentionally. I think." I really should have been going, but I couldn't seem to summon the will to move. "She's good at the core, but she does whatever she wants. She's always been like that, and ever since Dad died her demons have taken over."

Marco nodded. "I've been meaning to say how sorry I was to hear about your dad."

I blinked hard and drank long and slow from my mug.

"I remember Mr. Zadeh so well. After my dad left, he would show up with vats of food."

That didn't make sense. "You mean my mom brought food," I corrected. I didn't remember Dad dropping off food for the neighbors. When he worked in the garden, he stopped to chat with people walking down the sidewalk, but otherwise, he kept to himself, let Mom do the socializing for them both.

"No, your dad. These huge pots of green stew and tubs of rice with the little sour berries."

"Barberries," I said, "and *ghormeh sabzi*." That was Dad's comfort food all right. How strange that I had no recollection of this gesture of goodwill. Maybe Mom didn't know either. He was private about so many things, especially his generosity. He'd regularly sent money to various relatives for years, including a niece who'd followed her husband to Singapore only to be divorced and left with their two children, and we didn't find out until culling through his accounts after he died.

"I think he thought we would starve without my dad around," Marco said. "Like my mom would forget to feed me."

A tired laugh escaped my lips. "My mom can't cook to save her life, so maybe he just assumed."

"There was another time—" He paused, started over. "I had this idea back then, without my dad around, that I needed to toughen up, be the man. Somehow, I thought this meant I needed to start fixing things around the house. Use tools, that sort of thing." He tapped his fingers on his mug. "The faucet leaked. Mom kept saying she'd hire a plumber, but we didn't have the money. I was going to surprise her by fixing the sink."

"Okay." I set my elbows on the table, leaned my chin onto my palm, my head suddenly heavy despite my interest.

"But I was too clueless to shut off the water beforehand. Water started pouring out of the open pipes, and I realized what I'd done but I couldn't get the shut-off valve to turn. I panicked and ran out of the house, dripping wet, panting, and there's your dad, calmly scooping dirt with a trowel. He took one look at me and came running. He shut off the water in a half second and spent another hour helping me sop up the mess, clean up the kitchen. He even walked me through how to wash and dry all the towels we'd used. When it was done, he looked me straight in the eye and said, 'What were you thinking?'"

The edges of his lips curved into a half smile.

"I said, 'I was trying to do something nice for my mom.' Your dad nodded as if he understood and left, leaving me shaking with relief that I hadn't caused actual damage. A few minutes later the doorbell rang, and there's your dad with his gardening gloves and his clippers holding a bunch of roses. 'Find a vase and put these in water, then leave it on the table,' he said. 'That's something nice you can do.'"

I inhaled, let his words wash over me. Marco didn't realize what his recollection meant. Sharing a story about Dad I'd never heard before was like bringing a sliver of him back to life. My throat tightened missing him, missing all the things I didn't know about him.

Marco cleared his throat, waiting for me to say something.

"He must have liked you—"

A knock at the door cut me off.

"Elise," Marco said.

I shot up, knocking into the table. My coffee splashed across Lily's white dress. I dabbed at the fabric, feigning nonchalance, like a mistress with nowhere to hide.

Marco handed me a towel and walked to the door. "Don't worry. I told her you were here."

She entered like a California cold front, skulking in dramatically as if to pretend she was afraid of interrupting something.

"Am I disturbing the sleepover?" Her mouth smiled but her voice didn't.

"Not at all. I was leaving."

"You are everywhere. At the home of my mother and father. Now my lover." Marco cleared his throat. The acid from the coffee creeped back up mine. "I didn't realize you'd grown so close on the drive."

"It helps to know a fellow American," Marco said. "I gave her my number."

"In case of emergencies," I offered.

The same slippery smile stayed on her face, but her nostrils flared as she looked me up and down. I crossed my arms and uncrossed them before she could tell how uncomfortable she made me.

"Your dress," she said.

The coffee had soaked through, the warmth spreading across my skin.

"I'm leaving." I was too hot and cold all at once, rocky with a rush of vertigo. I would have liked to crawl under the table, but my boots made it hard to bend down. I booked it straight to the door.

As I grabbed the doorknob, the strangest flitter passed over my vision, a blur of fluttering wings.

Then black.

❦

I came to in Marco's arms, staring into his eyes, lying on the floor in front of the door, while he knelt beside me cradling my head in his palms. He had dark hazel irises speckled with yellow I'd never appreciated before, and a square jawline, too, and a brow knit tight. Past his nape of brown hair, Elise stood cross-armed and unamused. I pushed myself up, head swimming.

"She's okay," Elise said. "See."

"I think you'd better stay on the floor." Marco pressed the back of his dry hand to my forehead. "You're a little warm."

"No, Elise is right. I'm great. *Super!* As the French say. Must have been low blood sugar. My body's gotten used to a certain amount of carbs in the morning, and if I don't get them, down I go." My brain was too scrambled to think of anything cleverer. "I need a croissant. That's all, I swear."

Marco looked skeptical, Elise disdainful.

"Perhaps you should go to a doctor," he said.

Elise scoffed. "He was thinking he would be a doctor once."

Marco blushed so hard his earlobes went salmon pink.

"I dabbled with the idea for a short time. Art called." The line sounded rehearsed. And familiar. Too busy trying to extricate myself from the situation, I didn't bother to ask any follow-up questions.

I got to my feet, Marco at my elbow.

"I guess you'll see my mom when she is here later this week," Elise said.

"Marine? She didn't tell me she was visiting."

"It is last minute, a meeting with her agent, but she said she will call you." She moved closer to the door. "She is devoted to her strays." She laughed. "I'm kidding, of course."

I laughed, too, though I didn't find Elise funny. To Marco, I said, "Thank you for the hospitality."

"Are you sure you're okay?"

The pain in my heels had moved up my legs, and now my whole body hurt. All I wanted to do was get back to Paulette's and take off these terrible clothes.

"All good," I said, but things were about to get very bad.

31

I stripped the minute I stepped into the apartment, Lily and Paulette spewing questions about where I'd been.

"We figured you'd stayed with Kid, until we saw your texts this morning." Lily had a towel around her hair and one held tight to her torso, her skin blotchy from the bath. "Where were you?"

"Kid. With Kid," I stammered. It was one thing to explain I'd stayed with Marco but another to admit Kid hadn't answered my call, that I didn't even know where he lived. Lily would have a field day with that, and you'd better believe she'd be all too happy to blab to Mom about my overnight with Marco. "I wanted to stay here. With you. Why didn't you answer? I rang the bell a hundred times."

Lily looked at me like I'd asked her to tell me the name of the big metal tower jutting from the skyline. "We passed out. I literally almost puked in the cab on the way home. Oh, and Paulette gave me these cute little earplugs, to block out the street noise." She meandered into the bedroom. "I'm so hungover."

"So hungover," Paulette said. She was lying across the living room couch with an ice pack over her eyes. "I never drink so much." She grunted. "Your Kid is a bad influence."

Lily came out of the bedroom wearing a thin black robe. She adjusted the towel on her head. I couldn't meet her eyes. I thought

I would choke on the anger rising in my throat. I shut the bathroom door and sat on the edge of the tub in my bra and underwear, goose bumps rising across my thighs. My body shook like a pot about to boil over, my lungs thick with cement. I took as many long deep breaths as I could until Lily started knocking.

"I should have waited for you, okay? Will you forgive me?" Her voice sounded distant through the door. I pictured her putting her cheek to the wood, her palms pressed flat. She'd swing between remorseful and righteous until I gave in. I took another deep breath, tapped the hollow at my throat, and turned on the bath faucet as hot as I could stand.

"Hello?"

"It's okay." All she wanted was absolution. She didn't care if I meant it.

"Rose?"

"You're forgiven," I called over the rush of the water smacking the porcelain. The knocking stopped, and I assumed she'd left until I heard another more tentative tap.

"You know Kid's going to be here in fifteen minutes?"

I wrapped a towel around my body. Wisps of steam followed me to the door, which I cracked open.

"What?"

"He's taking us to Versailles." Her face lit up. "He must have told you."

"Of course, he told me. I came home to get ready." The words came even as my body retreated, my cells begging me to lie down. I was so tired.

"I need to use the bathroom," she said.

The heaviness sunk deeper in my chest, but no way was I going to let Lily strut around Versailles with Kid while I missed out. "I'll be quick."

"Please do not waste water," Paulette shouted from the other room.

On the train, Lily and Kid chatted while I focused on containing the intermittent shivers quaking my body. I couldn't be getting sick. I refused to let Kid and Lily play tourists without me. This was *my* trip, not hers.

As we neared gare de Versailles-Chantiers, I choked down a couple of ibuprofens against my dry throat and stood to prove I could, white knuckling the bar by the door.

"We're here," I said.

"It's a short walk to the palace. Are you up for it?" Kid studied my face. I probably looked pale as a ghost. I rubbed my cheeks for color. "Or shall we hop on a bus?"

"Let's walk. Can we?" Lily said. "I want to take it all in."

"Rose?" Kid asked.

I tightened my grip on the bar. "You know me, up for anything."

Twenty minutes later, Versailles stood before us, a gilt fortress populated with the masses wagging selfie sticks and using full-size iPads as cameras.

Struggling to balance on the cobblestones, I checked my footing with each step, Lily and Kid always ahead of me. Great. I'd become the reluctant chaperone.

Kid had a friend who sold tickets, so we didn't have to wait in line. He ushered us into the gardens first. "Before it gets too hot," he said, though I was bone cold and would have loved to lie down on a warm patch of sun-drenched grass.

We trudged for ages through a wonderland manicured beyond reality. I'd wanted to take the little train but had been outvoted. Another Disneyland moment, when Iris and Lily got to choose all the rides.

And here it was, Fantasyland before me, like I'd willed it with my thoughts: Marie Antoinette's hamlet. Moss-covered, gabled roofs capped stone houses with arched doorways and dormer windows. Ivy climbed weathered brick walls. A tower watched over a quiet pond, green trees reflecting in the water. In my strange state, the sight of a wand-wielding fairy or a horse-drawn carriage with a talking rabbit wouldn't have fazed me.

I sat on a bench in a courtyard while Lily and Kid explored. A chill ran up my spine from the cold cement beneath me, pebbly under my fingertips.

"Rose?" Lily shook my shoulder and my eyes popped open. "Did you fall asleep? What is with you?"

"I was resting my eyes. Can't I enjoy myself?"

"You don't *look* like you're enjoying yourself." She gave me a pointed glare as if to imply I might be purposefully ruining her time.

"Well, I am."

She glowered, but Kid said, "Sure, of course. We're all enjoying ourselves." He hooked an arm around each of us and led us from the hamlet.

❦

If I could close my eyes for a few minutes. That's all I needed. The impulse to shut them, to lie down on the ground, was so intense, I had to will myself upright.

I leaned into the dense crowd inside the palace, letting the mass of people carry me from room to room like a caravan. I was smooshed but buoyed, a sensation somewhere between crowd-surfing and being trampled by a herd of cats.

I tried to follow Lily above the bobbing heads around me, but soon, floating adrift in a sea of bodies, I lost sight of her. When she grabbed my wrist, I yelped at the touch, my skin as tender as an unbaked baguette.

She hauled me into the next room. "Are you crying?"

I shook my head, but when I touched my face, my cheeks were wet.

She slouched on one hip. "Why are you being so weird?"

"Am I? I don't feel weird. I'm fine. Just tired."

We had come to the Hall of Mirrors. It was beyond opulent, decked in gold and glass chandeliers, blistering with the yellow light that blasted through towering windows. But where were the mirrors?

"Why are you yelling?" Lily hissed. Had I? Who could tell above the din? I couldn't hear myself think.

She dragged me to the other side of the room, abandoning me by a roped-off doorway. After a second, I realized I was looking at myself. "I found them!"

I pressed as close to the mirrored wall as possible until I couldn't see anything but my own face. I had a strange close-lipped smile I didn't recognize. I touched my forehead. It was hot and clammy. An oily strand of hair lay plastered to my temple. Did I look gray? I pushed myself closer. The moment my nose smacked against the glass I came undone and stumbled backward, clocking my heels on something, or someone.

"Sorry," I said. "So sorry," I repeated as I tumbled toward the ground, landing across one of the red ropes.

Embarrassment rubbed at the backs of my eyes, but only abstractly, because I knew I should be embarrassed, not because I cared. Hands found my armpits, and I was vertical. A guard admonished me. I couldn't understand a word. "Thank you for the lift."

"Kid!" Lily's voice rose above the clamor of pounding feet and talking heads. "She's over here."

Upright again, I knew I needed to lie down. The hard arms of the security person held me in place until Lily and Kid arrived. Kid spoke in French, and soon, the hard arms released me into Lily's custody while security escorted us outside.

"That was wild," Kid said. "I've never been kicked out of a palace before. Very rock 'n' roll."

"Very French Revolution," I said.

Kid laughed but Lily fumed. "I've never been so embarrassed in my life. What were you thinking?" She sounded like Mom. "Are you on something?"

Kid lifted my hair and pressed his hand to the back of my neck. The cold sent a shock straight down my spine. My lips trembled as my body began to shiver.

"Fever," Kid said. "She's definitely sick."

The words triggered a Rube Goldberg machine in my mind, one piece releasing another until I remembered why what Elise had said at Marco's, about him wanting to be a doctor, sounded so familiar. "You wanted to be a doctor," I said to Kid.

What a strange coincidence. But the thought vanished as the chills quaked through me.

32

The next few days were a fever-induced montage, flashes of passing time, moments of clarity, and vivid dreams coming to me like hallucinations.

My body ached as if I'd been pummeled with a sock full of quarters and shaken out like an old rug. Every moment cloaked in pain: clutching the comforter to my face, sirens outside the windows screeching in time to the throbbing in my head, cold and hot, hot and cold. Paulette placing a damp rag beneath my chin and telling me to breathe, the smell of eucalyptus and menthol so thick, I squirmed away, burrowing as deep into the covers as I could.

I dreamed I was by Dad's sickbed again, his mouth moving but the words too soundless to hear. I dreamed I was there in Paris starting my trip all over, but the city was empty, and the streets were mazes I couldn't find my way out of. In another dream, Marco came to me, considering me with his kind eyes and serious face, and set his palm against my forehead the same way he did the day I fainted in his apartment. This time, he held it there. He wiped my clammy forehead and put a straw to my lips, the water sweet and soft down my throat. Pure relief.

I came to, queasy and tired, my insides stretched and limp beneath my bones, but the pain was gone, my headache lifted. I picked up the glass of water someone had left by the bed and chugged what was there. I needed more.

I fumbled to get up from the bed and out the door of the dark room. A light was on in the living room and beneath it, Paulette on her computer, a sheen of blue reflecting off a pair of reading glasses. She pulled off the glasses and hopped up at the sight of me.

"Thank God. You are alive. But you shouldn't stand."

"I'm thirsty."

She took my glass and shooed me to the couch.

"How are you feeling?" She handed me a fresh water. I drank before answering her and wiped my lips with my sleeve.

"Tired," I said. "But okay." The windows were dark, leaving me with the disconcerting vertigo you get when you go into a matinee showing during the bright light of day and come out after the sun's set, like I'd lost a chunk of my life. "What time is it?"

"Almost ten. You have been sick for three days."

I let this sink in, trying to process the time passing without my awareness. The number of days left in my trip had dwindled.

"I thought you should go to a doctor. I cannot let something terrible happen to a guest, yes?" She shook her head as if to dislodge the disturbing thought from her mind. "Lily said no, you were strong."

Lily. "Where is she?"

"She has left again with your friend, Kid. She is with him all the time these past days, you know? She checks on you, but she doesn't stay. I'm sorry to tell you."

"Sorry for what?"

"Because it is tragic to have this kind of sister, yes?"

My first impulse was to defend Lily as not *that* kind of sister. The urge fizzled as quickly as it came. I knew what Paulette meant, but tragic wasn't the word. Maddening, maybe? Unfair? What I did know: I deserved better.

I took slow, deep breaths, drank the rest of the water, and took in the state of the living room. It was neat, like it hadn't been since my first days in Paris.

"Have you been staying here?"

Nonplussed by my question, Paulette pointed to her suitcase tucked away in the corner. "I would not leave you alone."

"You cleaned?"

"No, no. Not me. Your friend came, a man, another American. I trusted him at once. Not like my American ex, the scoundrel."

"Marco?" My dream flashed before me. Was that why his touch felt so real? "No one says 'scoundrel.' Try dick or asshole or prick."

"Asshole, yes, right. Anyway, this Marco worried for you. He said he emailed your mother for the address. He cleaned and brought soup."

"My mother?" Adrenaline pounded in my veins. She would be on the next flight if she knew I was sick. She would never believe I could do anything on my own. The urge to run cut straight through me. I waited for the panic to pass. "Soup?"

Paulette jumped up again and disappeared into the kitchen, calling, "I am told to heat it for you when you wake."

My throat tightened at the thought of food, but when Paulette placed a bowl in front of me, the soup brothy and steaming, my stomach softened with hunger and soon enough, I was tipping the last dregs straight into my mouth.

"More?" Paulette asked.

"Yes, more." What I was thinking was, *Marco, huh?* Marco.

❦

Marco Dariano:

Are you okay? I've been worried about you.

I hope you're okay.

I left soup.

Let me know if you need anything else.

Iris Zadeh:

Mom is going off about Marco.

I guess he emailed asking for your address there?! What the what!

Need info asap.

I have descended a wedding details rabbit hole. Napkin colors don't matter, do they? Help!

Oh, and Mom and Vasilis are definitely texting on the regular.

I sort of snooped in her phone. Messages are mundane but borderline flirtatious for sure.

He came over with the pest guy . . . and stayed for dinner afterward! Holy shite.

Mom says it wasn't a date, but if not, what was it?

Alice Zadeh:

Marco Dariano emailed me . . . he wanted the address of your apartment in Paris . . . he had a gift to drop off . . . what was it? Tell me asap . . . No chemistry my butt.

My home is rodent free!

Still waiting for an update . . . two days later . . .

Respond!

Lily told me not to worry . . . she says you're having too much fun to check your phone . . . I'm glad one of you could bother to respond before I panicked . . . I still want a response about Marco's gift . . . When you find the time . . .

Rose Zadeh to Alice Zadeh:

Sorry for not getting back to you.

I can't keep the days straight.

As for Marco, the gift was just extra tickets to a museum exhibition, for me and Lily.

Some sort of freebie through his university he couldn't use.

Lily never came home that night, and I didn't text her. I imagined her asleep in Regina's nightgown, cozy as a lamb, because I didn't know where Kid lived and couldn't picture a home that would suit him.

In the morning, I sat in bed listening to the rush of cars down the road. I half expected the illness to pull me back under, but although my muscles felt weak, I was refreshed. Three days of fever equaled one exceptional yoga class. There was something else, too. A heady sort of discomfort it took me a while to put my finger on.

The dream I'd had about Marco wasn't a dream at all.

He'd come to check on me, going so far as to email my mom. Some measure of concern seemed reasonable given I'd passed out in his apartment. But he'd also made me soup and stayed to clean up the apartment, sat beside me on the bed. Remembering his hand against my skin raised the hair on my arms.

I reread the texts Marco sent.

Thanks for the soup, I wrote. And thanks for not telling my mom.

The typing bubble appeared and disappeared, appeared again, and I found my heart quickening. Sure. I assumed you wouldn't want to worry her. Are you feeling better?

I considered typing something pithy, like, *I'd feel much better knowing why you're pretending you don't know me in public.* But I didn't have pith in me. I wrote, Much better. Thank you. 😊

Marco Dariano:

👍

That was the end of that. Why did I care? The question bumped around my mind, but I didn't dwell.

My spirits were low because I'd been trapped in bed for days while my little sister pilfered my vacation. Doing what, exactly, with my pretend boyfriend? I kicked away the thought and threw off the bedcovers.

The roar of city life down the street called to me. With my recent luck, I might fall down a manhole, or be hit by a scooter, or trip over a small dog. I would have to take my chances. Marine said no more expectations. I couldn't start from scratch, not anymore, not after everything that happened, but I'd woken from the flu or whatever it was as if from the dead. If that wasn't the time for a new beginning, then what was?

I didn't text Lily to let her know I was alive. She wanted to go off on her own, so be it. I'd just pretend she wasn't there.

I left without so much as a note on the bed. I left when Paulette's back was turned.

33

The city was how I left her, except—could I be imagining things?—less crowded, less frenetic. August was ending, and the energy had shifted. It was the first time I had ventured out on my own in days, and the streets seemed different, the air slightly less stifling.

Even the excitement of the art heist seemed to have cooled. At a newsstand beside the stairs to the Metro, I noticed the story had slipped farther down the front page of the daily papers, a print of one of the drawings barely visible below the fold.

I hadn't been into the musée de l'Orangerie, so I went there first, waiting in the stale Metro tunnel for the train to arrive. When Lily texted asking me how I was and where I was, I ignored her. In a dramatic gesture, I tucked my phone into the bottom of my bag and vowed to keep it there. I knew which stop I needed, and I knew how to get back to Paulette's from the station.

The sudden approach of a young woman startled me. She lugged a heavy canvas book bag on her shoulder and started speaking rapidly in French, pointing to her phone. All at once, she stopped, her round hazelnut eyes imploring me for an answer.

She looked normal, but who could say?

It could have been a scheme, a way to take advantage of naive Americans. How clever to use an innocent-looking girl. I wasn't falling for it. I kept my purse close and turned away, rather smug.

The young woman mumbled something behind my back before ambling farther down the platform where she approached someone else.

A low chuckle came from behind me. A bald man with a hefty belly waggled his finger in amusement.

"She was not trying to rob you, *mademoiselle*. She asked if you knew which stop she needed."

"I don't speak French."

"No, of course not. I can tell you are an American, but how was she to know? She is a young student from the countryside. She has little experience with tourists."

"I wasn't trying to be rude."

"She doesn't think you are rude. She thinks you are Parisian." He laughed so hard his belly jiggled. "Maybe these are the same."

I fought the urge to chase her down and apologize. I would explain to her how many times this city had got me. But she wouldn't understand a word, and also, she thought I was French. Me, French!

I savored her mistake all the way to Concorde station and into the museum, where Monet's water lilies made me feel neither Parisian nor American but wholly human. A collection of tissue and bone knit together with joy and sorrow and shellacked with shame.

Those flowers, a blur up close, unwound something within me.

Dad, who had traveled across the globe when he was barely a man, would never have found himself in front of these pinks and greens, blues and reds, even if he had lived longer. He would have made a point of it, not coming all this way. If he had, I knew he couldn't have helped but succumb to the beauty in these oval rooms. Nothing impressed him quite like man-made glory.

The plaques on the wall shared the story of Monet's cantankerous relationship with his father, a businessman who wanted more from his son than a career as an artist. Were we all trying to make our fathers proud, pleading for forgiveness when we couldn't? Monet had proved his father wrong, and Kid decided to do the same. What about me? I only ever wanted to prove my father right. That I could be the perfect person he wanted me to be, despite knowing I was someone else entirely. That I was insecure and sometimes careless, never for lack of trying.

Dad hadn't always been a father. He'd once been young and lost and flown across the world to change his life, and even though the circumstances were different, I sensed him in the wonder I experienced when I looked at those dreamy compositions.

He'd been with me the whole time, on my mind, and even though I couldn't know him any better than I had before I left San Jose, I felt as though I did, as if we'd been walking parallel to one another in two different lives.

Despite my best efforts, I couldn't ignore Lily's texts.

Even while they sat unanswered at the bottom of my bag, the impulse to respond to her needs stayed rooted in the back of my mind like an addiction I couldn't shake. Soon enough, I headed back in the direction of Paulette's.

When I arrived, the apartment was quiet. Lily lay on the bed in the dark. Her eyes popped open the moment I walked into the room.

She sat up and crossed her arms. "Did your phone die?"

"No."

"Why have you been ignoring me? I was worried."

Her lips were pinched, her jaw tight. She didn't look worried so much as irritated.

I chucked my bag on the floor and opened the drapes. Lily blinked against the glare, and I remembered the way she used to blink back tears as a child when she didn't get her way.

"Where were you last night?" I said.

"What's your point?"

"I'm trying to understand how far your worry extended."

"Um, okay. I've been checking in on you, checking with Paulette. It's my vacation, too. What am I supposed to do? Come all the way to Paris and spoon soup into your mouth?"

It was *my* vacation, for the record. And, yes, soup would have been a sweet touch. Anything other than gallivanting with my love interest (as far as she was concerned). Why did she have to come? Why did she have to make my trip about her? The fury and frustration rose in me.

She reached out and ran her fingers over the knobs of my knuckles. I didn't realize I was clutching the duvet. "Hey," she said. "I really was worried. You know anytime anyone gets sick, I freak out. Like it could be what happened with Iris all over again. Or Dad."

On the surface, Lily was all ferocity and willfulness, but beneath that was a deep well of fear. When Iris got sick, it shook our lives. Even though she was okay in the end, everything we understood about the safety of the world, the reliability of our parents, had seismically shifted. When Dad got sick? Well, the shift was familiar, but no less profound. No one knew that better than me.

"I'm fine," I told her.

"Don't be mad. If I took you to the hospital, I'd have to tell Mom, so I figured it was better to let you, like, literally, sweat it out."

"You didn't tell Mom."

"Hell no. She'd freak. I wouldn't rain that down on you."

I thought of my totaled car, Lily's firm proclamation, "I was the one driving." The anger retreated, slinking back the way it came, collecting in the pit of my gut. I sagged onto the bed.

"There was nothing you could have done," I said.

"That's what I told Kid." Her eyelashes fluttered when she said his name. I sensed they'd talked plenty about me behind my back. I didn't press for details. I didn't want to know.

"What did you two do without me?"

She flopped back against the pillow, her defiance gone.

"Tourist things."

I watched her closely, but her face was serene, her body relaxed. "Do you have plans with him tonight?"

"No," she snapped, sitting up. "Why?"

Changing course, I said, "I thought we could hang out."

"I came to see you, didn't I?"

"We could pick up some cheeses and charcuterie and watch something on Netflix."

"No, no, no, no. Let's *do* something."

I was worn out from being sick and walking around the city, but I didn't want to miss another night of my trip.

"What should we do?"

She raised her eyebrows and smiled. "I have an idea."

34

Lily and I had transformed into teenagers, something we'd never experienced in real life with six years between us, not when I was always setting an example. We gulped Lillet from the bottle, wandering around the parc des Buttes-Chaumont in the blue haze of twilight.

We explored for a while, daring each other to walk into shadowy thickets, until the thrill wore off and we tucked ourselves on a swath of damp grass beside a tree trunk wide enough for both of us to lean against.

"Remember how Dad used to do our hair?" she asked. "Those high pigtails. They were so tight they'd leave sore spots on the top of my head."

"That was you and Iris."

"You and Dad had your own things, too. You were always in the kitchen with him. I caught you guys that one time eating raw cookie dough from the mixing bowl, and he told me it wasn't safe for kids under twelve. That doesn't even make sense."

I chuckled at the memory. "He was overprotective."

"But you're lucky. He talked to you. You knew him."

"Um, so did you."

"Not the way you did."

I'd been in college when he died and still felt like a kid. Lily had actually been one. It was a six-year difference I took for granted, the time I got with Dad that she didn't.

"Braid my hair." Lily plucked a leaf from the ground and began to tear it into little pieces. She didn't lean her head toward me, but I knew she was waiting for my fingers to comb through her thick strands. I'd done this a few hundred times, a thousand, although not in ages.

When she was little, she used to demand to have her hair braided. If I was in the middle of homework or on the phone, she'd whine until I gave in. After I finished braiding her hair, she'd yank out the tie, pull apart the braid, and say, "Again. Do it again." She didn't care about the braid, only the fact of being attended to.

The ground was cold where we huddled, and I moved closer to reach her hair and her body heat. The feel of her soft hair wrapped around my fingers, its melon-y scent tickling my nose. It reminded me of all those other times when it was just the two of us, when, on occasion, the circumstances were inexplicably right, her mood just so, Lily would crack open the safe inside her and share: something that mattered to her; something that scared her; all the vulnerable bits she secreted away even from herself.

"Will you tell me why you broke up with Dev?" I probed, as gently as I could.

A quiet minute passed. I waited, braiding without another word, certain if I moved too fast, I'd frighten her away.

She sighed dramatically, a battle inside her waged and lost. "I wasn't the one who did the breaking. Dev dumped me."

"Why didn't you say so?"

"He said I was feckless and ruthless. He said I was a lot of quote-unquote less, and he wanted more." She turned to me. "Is that true?"

"No," I said without thinking. It was a force of habit to defend her.

"So I said, fine, and I sat down and wrote him a list of all the things I do for him, and do you know what he said?" Her voice was scratchy from the alcohol, her vowels drawn out. "He said I'd proved his point. I was so self-involved, I didn't know how not to be. He's the one who refuses to apologize for anything. How can *he* call *me* selfish?"

"You came here as an ultimatum for Dev? To run away?"

"If you can, so can I," she said. What did that even mean? She couldn't let me have something she didn't? "I already feel different."

I didn't like my own desires echoed in Lily's words. They sounded silly, crass, coming from her. You couldn't go to a new place and become a different person. Lily hadn't changed. If anything, by coming here, she was peak Lily.

As if she'd read my mind, she said, "Don't you think I've changed? Dev will think so. Right?"

"I still don't understand why you came here."

"I just needed space to stretch my wings and whatever."

She was such an emotional lockbox, the key long since misplaced or abandoned. Even here in Paris, with the guts to appear out of nowhere, without explanation, she would give nothing away. Tearing one fallen leaf after another, she clutched the bits in her palm, then tossed them all at once. They scattered, disappearing on the dark ground. At the same moment, something broke free inside of me. My head hurt with each breath. I wanted to find all the pieces Lily had thrown and put them back together into something completely new.

I swallowed over a lump. My throat contracted as I summoned the words. "I wish you'd try to be honest for once. At least with yourself."

"Are you kidding me?" She snatched her hair from my hand. "You always think the worst of me. Everyone does."

She pushed to her feet.

"That's not true," I said, scrambling in the dark to stand.

"And if we're talking about dishonesty, let's talk about you. Always pretending everything's fine. Always playing nice. You're so fake, you know that? Like with Kid. He says . . ." She looked away from me.

"What?"

"Never mind."

I'd been trying to avoid this conversation. With a wrenching twist of my gut, I knew I couldn't anymore. "Tell me."

She turned on her heel, and I followed, plodding along the grass, watching each step. Lily was faster than me, more agile, and I stumbled over gopher holes trying to keep up with her, suddenly afraid to turn around. The low-lit path out of the park felt sinister in the dark. Even when we reached the street, the tranquil neighborhood unnerved me. Without the cars and the people, my ferocious heartbeat could have echoed off the buildings.

I could see Lily and Kid laughing about the night in Cassis, how pathetic I was. I wanted to say it meant nothing, it was all a lot of fun, but the lump in my throat made it hard to speak.

She stopped in the middle of the sidewalk and gave me an anguished look before her eyes flicked to the street.

"We slept together," she said.

"You slept together." The broken piece inside me began to rattle.

"I had sex with him." She spread out her arms. "Are you happy? Now you know."

"You had sex with him."

"Stop repeating everything I say." She bit her lip and closed her eyes. When she opened them, a fat tear slid down her cheek. She wiped it with her sleeve. "He wasn't your boyfriend. He said you were just friends. He hadn't meant to lead you on."

She might have said these things to hurt me, that was the sort of thing Lily would do, but I could see she was telling the truth in the tight clamp of her jaw. Her beautiful eyes blinking with heavy lids.

"But you didn't know what I felt for him."

"I'm sorry, okay? What else do you want?"

This was my own fault. I should have known better. I *did* know better. I knew Lily better than anyone. I was the one who lied about me and Kid, because I couldn't admit he'd rejected me, because I'd wanted, for even a second, Lily's admiration, to be the older sister with her life together. With a life at all.

Now Kid thought I was desperate, and Lily was giving me a look of pity that stung so badly I would have been better off stepping on the hornets' nests Dad was always raging against in the yard.

I wanted to shrug her confession off. Go ahead, sleep together. See if I care. See how easygoing I was.

But Super Chill Rose didn't exist. I wasn't easygoing. I did care.

And the caring was what hurt. Caring what people thought of me. Caring what they felt and whether I could fix it, help it, make it better. Caring that they knew I cared.

All this raced through my head as Lily sniffled into her sleeve, somehow prettier with a pink nose. Deeper down, past the maze of thoughts, my insides trembled and sputtered, something hot and fierce coming to life. I steadied myself on a moss-covered stone wall abutting the sidewalk.

"I'm tired," Lily said. "I want to go home."

So go. Go away.

The words teetered on the tip of my tongue. Instead of delivering them, I skulked all the way back to the Marais and decided I would be out of the apartment the next day, and as far away from Lily as possible.

Dear Gladys,

I admit, I wanted Paris to be for me what America had been for my dad, if you skipped the parts about escaping the violent end of a corrupt government, avoiding the oppressive fundamentalist rule that followed, and leaving your loved ones behind forever. I know that's a lot to skip, but you get what I mean: I wanted a chance for reinvention.

I sound sickeningly white and privileged when I say that, don't I?

Because it's not like it was easy to build a life in the US as a brown-skinned man with a Middle Eastern accent. Nothing I've experienced could ever come close to that. And yet, if you'd asked Dad, he would have told you he hadn't been running away from anything but toward something.

The decision to leave, to do whatever he had to do to get on a plane, was made from hope, not fear, forged from an otherwise insatiable desire to be an American. He succeeded, and he expected from his daughters the same level of capital-S success. The good life had been handed to us. All we had to do was make it great.

Is that why I never believed I was enough as I was? Because I knew I would never live up to his expectations. What I could do was make myself as agreeable as possible, a shape-shifting cloud, an exhale slipping between words. If I was unremarkable, then I couldn't disappoint them. If everyone liked me, I could like myself. So what if I was the one disappointed?

Mohammad Zadeh came to a new country because he believed everyone, even him, a nobody from Tehran, deserved a shot at a better life. I came to Paris because even if I was a nobody, the magic of the city might rub off on me, like an eau de parfum that clings to your clothes.

But a strong fragrance is only a cover-up for whatever's underneath, your day-old underwear and unwashed hair and the trash you talk to yourself every day. That's me. A muddle of should-haves and would-haves and could-haves misted with rose water.

I know Paris won't change me. Only I can do that. I want to be able to say what I mean and ask for what I want, but I'm afraid the words will get lost in translation and leave me holding my beating heart in my bare hands in a world full of jagged angles and sharp corners. I'm scared, but what's new?

My real question: If I'm ready to start living out loud, where do I begin?

Kindly yours,
Majorly in Need of a Backbone in the Marais

35

Marine's perfume layered the air with the delicate fragrance of honeysuckle. We huddled in the corner of a nondescript café near île de la Cité, a place Marine appeared to know well as she greeted the staff. A minute later, a waitress set two small ceramic cups on the table.

"Elise said you locked yourself out and stayed with Marco. She was not happy."

I cringed as the hot espresso met my tongue. "I know. I'm sorry."

"You rub Elise the wrong way. She is threatened by you, I think."

"By me?" If Elise was threatened, it was a lion irked by a meerkat. But Marine didn't explain what she meant before moving on.

"Your sister has come, no?"

Marco must have told Elise, maybe to explain my appearance at his apartment. I wondered if Elise had told her mom how I'd fainted. Did Marine know Marco had come to see me? I guessed she didn't, and the thought made me surprisingly glad.

"Lily, yes. I wasn't expecting her. She showed up out of nowhere."

"Lily and Rose. You are both blossoms."

I ran my finger around the rim of my cup. "Sure. But we couldn't be more different."

"You didn't want her to come?"

"Lily does whatever she wants."

"You don't want her here."

"It's just . . ." Why was I trying to sugarcoat this, for Marine of all people? "No, I don't."

Marine tapped her lips again, lost in thought.

"Elise is a person who takes. Because I am her *maman*, it was always my job to provide for her. So I let her take all she needed from me. You know what? She took more!" She shook her head. "Finally, I said no. That's enough. She is still angry with me. She is whenever I say no, that hasn't changed, but for me, it's much better."

Elise must take from Marco, too. The image of him at my bedside popped into my head. How kind he'd been to me. How I'd misjudged him. Marine's thoughts somehow followed my own.

"Poor Marco," she said. "Elise says he comes from a mega-rich family, but this is not how he seems to me. He is humble. He is no match for my daughter." She tipped the last of her noisette into her mouth and dabbed the corner of her lips with a napkin.

"Marco is wealthy?" This was news to me, seeing as how I knew the middle-class, three-bedroom house he'd grown up in. By your average American standards, he may have been fortunate, but there was no way he'd qualify as "mega rich."

"His family owns buildings in New York." She raised a hand above her head. "Skyscrapers."

"Oh," I said, trying to make sense of this discrepancy in Marco's life. I knew what I remembered from childhood and what my mom had told me, which wasn't much, but enough to know when something didn't add up. I racked my mind to recall the specifics of what Mom had shared.

His father had left his mother for another woman when Marco was in middle school and bailed to LA or San Diego or some SoCal city. Marco only ended up at the chichi boarding school because Sylvia's brother worked there. If his father had been rich—New York real estate!—we'd have known. It would have been all the neighborhood ever talked about. My mother alone could have gossiped on the topic for months, years. She'd still be talking about it.

Marine continued while my mind raced to catch up. Something caught my ear. "What did you say?"

"He couldn't live up to his father's expectations. He knew he loved art, but he thought he could be a doctor instead, to please his father. But he failed at medical school, and he failed at being an artist, and no matter what he did, he was the big disappointment. Awful, I think."

Now, I was sure. That was Kid's story. Not Marco's.

Which meant? Marco had passed off Kid's past in place of his own? Or was Kid's past fabricated, too? I'd seen how he played with the truth. But Marco? How? Why? It didn't make sense.

"It's sad, no? The way parents always try to turn children into little"—she searched for the word—"zombies. Without their own brains. People should be encouraged to be themselves even if it's not always pretty. Being yourself is not selfish, and neither is knowing what you want. It's bad only if you don't let other people be who they are." She threw up her hands. "Forgive me. I could talk this way all day. Marco is good, but he's soft and Elise is sharp. A knife through butter."

I didn't know whether to agree or not. Nothing about Marco added up. But Marine had already moved on.

She lifted her bag. "Come. I want to show you something."

36

"I've walked the streets of Paris," I said, not protesting but wanting to prove my merit. "I've seen plenty by foot."

"You walk to go, to do, to see, not to observe. To *flâner*," Marine said, "is a Parisian art."

We'd come to the Seine after a stroll from the café. I leaned over the wall's edge toward the water. The faintest hint of breeze skipped off the opaque surface; it cooled my walk-warmed cheeks and helped to soothe the angst bouncing around inside me. Marine squeezed my wrist.

"This is how I know what I know. Walking Paris and noticing. Just noticing. It is an important skill. You will be surprised what happens when you stop doing and seeing and going. That is the head at work. This is the heart," she said, gesturing to the street in front of us. "Where are you staying?"

"Rue du Vertbois, in the Third."

"Bon," she said. "The gallery is on the way. You can walk me there, and we can practice our powers of observation."

Marine hooked her arm through mine, and we strolled the mile to Elise's gallery in quiet conversation. Marine did most of the talking. I knew to shut up and soak in her wisdom, not just what she taught but how she walked through the world.

She pointed out a young girl in yellow pigtails and a knit blue sweater a size too big twirling in front of an *épicerie* while her mother chatted with another woman.

"She is so free and light," Marine spoke in a whisper. "Do you see how she moves?" Whenever the girl spun, her mother would grab her shoulder and set her straight. A half-second later, the girl would spin again. "Her mother is saying, 'Now, now, you'll make yourself sick,' and the daughter says, 'But it's fun!'"

We both laughed, and something heavy unshackled itself from my limbs.

"On the plane you said you give suggestions, not advice, but all you've done is shower me in advice."

"Ah, see, now that is the power of suggestion. You listen to my words and your heart is open to them, so they sound like advice. For someone who didn't care what I had to say, it would all sound like conjecture."

"How do you do that? How do you say what you think is right without offending anyone?"

"Rose." She came to a stop in the middle of the sidewalk. "I offend people all the time. My work makes people very uncomfortable, and they find this upsetting. I can't control other people's reactions, can I? Like Elise. She feels how she feels. It doesn't change what I believe. You have to do what is best for you."

It made perfect sense when Marine said it. Yet I couldn't get the formula right. Even here in Paris, so far from home.

"All my life I've done what other people wanted. I've been the person they expected me to be. I don't want to live like that anymore, but I don't know how to stop. It's like you're telling me there's another path, but it's a thousand miles between me and there, and oh, by the way, you'll need to take a thirty-foot flying leap across a pit of alligators."

Marine chuckled. "You should write this down, Rose. What you're questioning, what you wonder about, many people, women especially, struggle with these same feelings. They're seeking the same answers you are."

"Write my questions down?" I thought of the questions I composed to *Gladys* in my head, the notebook I'd purchased from Shakespeare and Company waiting, empty and unused, the same way my passport had languished for years. I had bought the notebook for a reason. There was something I wanted to say even if I didn't know how to say it. "But it's all a muddle. I don't need more questions. I need answers."

"You must write through the mess first." She looked at me intently. "I don't mean to make it sound easy. You don't need to know what to say, only be willing to start. Learning is hard. But what's the point if we don't grow? Take me, for instance. The US edition of my book is about to publish. I must learn how to reach an entirely new audience. Different values. Different expectations. It's terrifying and exhilarating. There is a phrase, '*On ne fait pas d'omelette sans casser des œufs.*'" She paused, wrinkled her nose in concentration. "In English, I think it is, 'You cannot cook omelet without breaking eggs.' Do you know it?"

I nodded, smiling at the idiom on her tongue.

She continued as we walked on. "I would add to it and say, only one egg at a time. Keeps the mess manageable, right?"

One egg at a time. Sure, I could do that. I could try.

We neared Elise's gallery, and each step beside Marine made me lighter, a rock turning into a feather, a cobblestone into a croissant.

❦

The hollow, white room was empty except for the aggressive art lining the walls. Graffiti covered the back wall, a jagged crisscrossing of colorful lines. In the middle of the gallery, Elise and Marco stood like some kind of post-Modern exhibition, both glum, their hushed voices stern. I half expected Marine to stop and tell me what she saw in the hunch of

Marco's shoulders or Elise's arms slicing through the air. Marco bolted toward us and Marine gasped.

The sight of him reminded me all over again that he was lying, not just about me but about his past as well. Why?

"Pardon," he said to us, and darted from the gallery.

Elise and Marine began speaking in French, their voices tight and clipped. It was clear by Elise's dagger glances and angry gestures she didn't want me there. I didn't require Marine's expert interpretation to understand Elise would soon blow.

"I'll leave you two. Thank you for the lesson today." Before Marine could respond, I rushed to the door, offering a forced "*au revoir*" as I stepped outside.

I pivoted in the direction of Paulette's apartment and almost collided with Marco, who hadn't made it farther than the sidewalk.

He was fumbling with an unlit cigarette, and out of my mouth popped the first thing that came to mind, not at all the question weighing on me. "You smoke?"

He jerked his head up, and his eyes went big. Tucking the cigarette into his pocket, he glanced back toward the door.

"Don't worry, she's not coming," I said. "I mean, unless you hoped she would, in which case, I'm sorry, but she's not."

He cocked his head, like he was realizing something for the first time. "Do you have plans?"

37

Fighting with his girlfriend unleashed a side of Marco I didn't expect, unhurried and loose. An arm draped over a chair. Feet tapping at the ground. Indulgent swipes of crispy, golden *frites* through aioli. He joked with the server.

It was hard to reconcile the man who'd walked out of the gallery with the same one I'd met at the wine bar less than two weeks ago. The one who seemed about as fun as getting stuck in rush-hour traffic. The one who was thoughtful, sure, also aloof, tense, and cold as a summer evening in San Francisco.

The one who claimed not to lie.

We made polite small talk, Marco rambling about the difference between aioli and American mayo, until he suddenly changed course and said, "To answer your question, I don't smoke. Haven't for years. Unless things are"—he struggled for the words—"particularly challenging."

Um, not exactly the explanation I was hoping for, or the one he owed me.

I looked at my hands, my plate, the street, anywhere but at Marco. "So, look," I began, "we should talk because—this is awkward—but . . ." I trailed off, hoping he could somehow intuit my line of thinking, save me the trouble of having to ask. When he didn't, I tried to start over. "I have to ask—"

His face fell. "Let's talk about anything else. The weather? Isn't today beautiful? I love this time of year. The first hints of fall, the locals are rushing back to reality, and I'll be in a lecture hall soon and thinking straight again."

He made a show of taking the last bite of his steak, wiping his lips, and folding his napkin in an even square before setting it onto the table, and I waited, unsure what would come next.

"Okay, fine." He cleared his throat. "Elise and I are done. The fight you saw was the end of things. I saw it coming but even still." His cheeks sagged as he picked at a fry.

"Oh." I wasn't sure how to call him out now, not when he looked so dejected. I'd bide my time. Wait for another opportunity to push him. "Elise and you. Right. I figured as much when you stormed out. Did she give you the whole it's-not-you-it's-me excuse?"

"What? No." He rubbed at a splotch of aioli settling into his shirt. "*I'm* the one who ended things."

I couldn't bother to hide the shock on my face. I had the impression Elise oversaw the terms of their relationship.

He dipped his napkin in his water glass and returned to scrubbing, until he gave up and tossed the napkin aside. He drummed his fingers on the table. "Of course you'd think she'd broken up with me. Why wouldn't you?"

"I didn't mean it to seem like that. But she's so . . . and you're . . ."

"Weak?"

"No, no. That's not what I meant."

"What?"

I scrambled to think. Marine's phrase, "A knife through butter," popped into my head.

"What's so funny?" I asked.

"You. Your face. Trying to come up with something." He laughed, and his dimple crept onto his face. At the sight of it, I smiled, too. A little happiness gave serious Marco a rather irresistible mug. A ruffle of attraction flicked across my vision. I bit my lip to curb this realization from playing across my visage.

"You were saying something about my face?"

"I'm sorry." I waited while he composed himself. "It's just, usually I'm the one struggling to say the right thing after I've put my foot into it. It's great to see someone else try for once." He pushed back his seat. "I feel like walking. Care to join?"

Even with the crowded sidewalks and people darting between us, I sensed where Marco was in relation to me, the space filled by his body. Without understanding what it meant, I was sure it was the same for him. Like when my sisters and I used to try to talk to each other from our bedrooms using two empty kidney bean cans and kitchen twine. You couldn't hear anyone, but you knew they were there, at the other end of the line, trying to hear you.

"These crowds are killing me. Come this way."

He grabbed my hand, his palm papery and warm, and pulled me down the next street until we walked under green metal arches and into a park, quiet compared to the sidewalk and lush with bright grass and full trees and a thick hedgerow that surrounded its borders.

"One of my favorite places to hide out," he said.

"Do you have a lot of those? Hiding spots?"

His dimple made an appearance again. "The plight of the introvert, I guess."

I wished I could lie down for a minute, thanks to the frites, and I said so, yawning into my hand. We settled on an empty bench.

"Rest against me." He lifted his arm, and I set my head on his firm chest. I wiggled, trying to get comfortable. "Here." He sat us up, pulling off his fitted blazer to reveal a plain black T-shirt and a wedge of flat abdomen. I brought my hands to the edges of my face, casually shielding my eyes.

"Now you can lean back."

He'd folded his blazer into a makeshift pillow for my head, and I smelled laundry detergent, felt the warmth of his body through his thin shirt. Before I could relax into him, I shoved myself away. This wasn't good. I couldn't be attracted to Marco. First of all, Mom wanted me to like Marco, and I was not about to give her an excuse to say "I told you so." Second, I didn't need to set myself up for another inevitable disappointment. No, thank you.

"You okay?" he said.

I rolled my shoulders. "I'm good."

"You sure?"

Why did he have to be so damn thoughtful? I needed a distraction, quick.

"Why did you break up with Elise?" I asked. "What happened between meeting her parents and today?"

He didn't fidget or anything, but I sensed an aura of discomfort. He tilted his head back and stared up at the sky. The sun was enjoying its lazy summer dip. The park was active but hushed. The workday had ended, and people were mostly passing through on their way home. A lone white-haired woman wearing a lush fur bolero despite the heat nibbled a pastry and tossed the crumbs to the pigeons.

"We liked the idea of each other, not so much the reality. I knew we were on a time limit."

"Why today?"

"I'm not sure. I mean, well, it might have had something to do with you."

"Me?"

"Indirectly. Seeing you here, talking about home, it's got me thinking about why I came here in the first place. It's hard to explain." He puffed out his cheeks with a sigh. "Anyway, I told her I'd meet her at the studio. I arrived early, and she was annoyed. She wasn't done for the day. She didn't want me hanging around like a child she had to babysit." I cringed at the expression. "I told her I'd wait at the café down the street, but this bothered her more. I couldn't do anything right, and if I couldn't do anything right, why not do what I wanted to do? Which happened to be telling her I was done being bullied."

"Good for you."

"She didn't take it well."

"No, she wouldn't."

"She said some pretty mean things I can't bear to repeat. The kind of things that'll play on a loop when I can't sleep."

"That sounds awful." What did Elise think was so terrible about Marco? Whatever her complaints, they were probably the exact things I'd appreciate in a person. Of course, she didn't know he'd lied to her. Only I knew that. In his company, it was impossible to reconcile the lies with the guy sitting next to me. I kept my eyes trained on passersby, but my attention was on him.

"It's how it goes, isn't it?" He shifted to lean forward on his knees.

Out of the corner of my eye, I took in his long back, his nest of loopy brown hair. Reaching out to him felt like the most natural thing in the world, but I held myself back.

"I remember every mean thing anyone has ever said to me. Compliments go in one ear and out the other," he said. "Do you know what I mean?"

He tilted his head up at me, and I couldn't help but take him in. His easy, sweet smile sent my guard tumbling. I turned toward him with my whole body.

"At my job . . ." I hesitated. I'd finally managed to put Genomix out of my mind, but I wanted Marco to know I understood. "At my job, the only things that matter are all the things I do wrong. The successes, the extra effort, they all count for nothing. I tally my mistakes, and the rest I forget, until I believe what my miserable boss thinks about me. Why do I believe him when I know it's not true?"

"Your mind plays tricks on you," he said. "To keep you safe, I think. The problem is it keeps you small, too."

I'd never put the pieces together like that. Now that he had, it was as clear as the sky above our heads. As easy to see as the connection we shared.

38

We stayed in the park while the sun set, swapping stories from all the years we'd missed, making up for lost time.

When boarding school came up, he got cagey. It was an opportunity to push him for an answer about his made-up past, but whatever was happening between us felt too tender to press. That, and I was too chicken to make an accusation that might upset him, turn him away from me. So I listened and let myself forget there was anything unsaid.

"I changed," he said, "after all the time away from home. I didn't think I could go back once I graduated college. I'd taken four years of French in high school. I spoke it well enough to get by."

"What about your mom? Didn't she guilt you?" I thought of the phantom guilt hovering around me, the constant reminder I wasn't living up to expectations.

"Oh, sure she did. Properly. But she had her parents, and she'd remarried and had my little brother at home. Don't forget, she'd been the one to send me away."

"She was scared. You were getting into trouble."

He drew his head back in surprise. "How do you know that?"

"I've heard things. From my mom. Who heard them from your mom. Sorry."

"Don't be." He slouched. "Mom's always been an open book. But to think everyone talked about me. I was a kid."

"I know."

"I was thirteen and embarrassed all the time and my dad left without warning. That stings when you're young and believe no one on earth understands how you feel. All these huge emotions, and even if you have the vocabulary, you have no practice putting the words together to convey an ounce of what's rolling around inside you." He paused. "Wow, I'm an idiot. I can't believe I'm complaining about my dad moving a few hundred miles away to you of all people. It's nothing compared to your loss."

"It's not nothing. It's just different."

My dad was gone forever, except he hadn't left me. I'd never considered the nuance before, but there was a difference. Dad would never have chosen to leave. I'd watched him fight to hold on, even as the life slipped out of him. The memories of those endless last days took hold of me, and I couldn't shake them off. I didn't want to. There was something I wanted to tell Marco, something I knew intuitively he would understand. The words hovered on my tongue, but my mouth stayed clamped shut. I watched the pigeons pecking at the dirt.

A silence stuttered between us.

"I'm sorry," Marco said. "I shouldn't have said anything—"

"No. It's not that."

Another beat passed, and another, but Marco waited while I gathered my courage. "I was the last person who heard his voice," I finally said. "He stopped speaking a few days before he died."

It took me a moment to go on. I'd never told anyone this before, and though Marco couldn't know how much I was holding, he made room for the opening between us.

"He had a hospital bed at home in the living room, a hospice nurse coming every day. By then, we were all there all the time, me, Mom, Iris, Lily. Lily was only fourteen."

I could still see Lily just as she was, on the precipice of adolescence, still so childlike. One day, I'd caught her smoking a joint outside the garage, and when I confronted her, horrified, she stormed away. I found her lying in bed, tears collecting on the matted fur of an old stuffed bear.

I shook my head, remembering, trying not to remember, and went on.

"The hospice nurse said it would be soon when he stopped speaking. Mom and Lily filled the silence by talking, all the time. Iris read aloud to him. Sometimes I propped my homework on his bed. Mostly, I sat there without saying a word.

"The day before he died, I was alone with him for a few hours. I couldn't believe it when his eyes fluttered open and fixed on me. I didn't have time to call anyone else into the room. I went to him and grabbed his hand." I took a breath, my eyes burning with memory.

"He said my name. I'm sure of that at least. But then, he couldn't quite get out what he needed to. Every word was between raspy breaths. 'I need you' or 'I need to tell you.' And 'Don't leave' or 'Don't leave me.'" I shook my head against the uncertainty.

A sharp inhale caught in my throat. Every time I thought of that moment, it was like having the metal cage I lived in shrink an inch from all sides, but saying the words aloud gave me room to breathe. "His last words, and I can't recite them. I can't make sense of them half the time."

"But you've filled in the blanks over the years."

I looked at Marco, only to find he was looking at me. We held the other's gaze, until I blinked.

"He got really, really sick so fast. Four months between hearing he had pancreatic cancer and the hospice bed. Before his diagnosis—back when we were happy and dumb enough to think it was a stomach ulcer or gallstones or something else benign—I told him I was thinking about a semester abroad. He didn't yell or get upset, really, he just shut the possibility down. The conversation was over, and I felt humiliated for humoring the idea. This was right after I'd switched my major from business to English, and he was upset about that. He didn't like my boyfriend. Lily was acting out, and he thought I spent too much time with my college friends, not enough at home, even though I lived at home. He was always harping on me to set an example for my sisters, help my mother. His last words could have meant so many things."

"Or nothing at all," Marco said.

"What do you mean?"

"He was drugged, he was actively dying. You don't know what he was trying to say. *He* might not have known what he was trying to say."

"That's why I hedge. Cover all my bases."

"Oh, Rose." He said my name with such genuine compassion, my heart clenched. "You're a good person."

"So are you." *So why are you lying?* I wanted to know, and I didn't. Mostly, though, I didn't want the night to end. "I'm wide awake now. Should we keep going?"

Marco nodded. The white-haired woman stood, scattering the pigeons in a puff of twilit dust.

We walked the city side by side, inhaling her lusty night smells. Fresh-pressed waffle cones beckoned us to the open window of a *glacier*, where we ordered sticky scoops of vanilla bean.

"It's my favorite," Marco said with a sheepish shrug.

"Mine too." The sweet ice cream dissolved against my tongue and the flavor was a burst of joy. Perfect and fragrant. "You know, we all say vanilla is boring, but it's not. It's this incredibly complex flavor made with the seeds from the pod of this special flower, like saffron. Think of that. How something so small can be so much greater than it appears. Flowers and spices and butter. It's all there in one bite."

Marco stopped and cocked his head. "Are you eating the same vanilla I'm eating?"

"Ha ha. Funny. I'm just saying there's more to it than people think."

"I couldn't agree more. But let me try yours just to be sure." Before I could reply, he tilted his head, tucked his chin next to mine, and while I got myself worked up for a kiss, he snuck a bite from just above the neck of my cone. "No, now I'm sure of it. Yours is better than mine. Let's trade."

I gave him a playful shove, and we walked for blocks in silence, all the time my head swimming.

When he leaned in to speak, I had to remember to breathe.

"I love this city. Don't you?"

"Well. I mean . . ."

"Oh, don't say it. Don't say you don't like it because if you say it, we can't be friends."

"I do like it. I do." I tossed the remainder of my cone in a trash bin. "So much has been different than I imagined."

"Any new place has to chew you up and spit you out a few times before you belong. You wouldn't meet someone new and expect to fall in love overnight, would you?"

"No," I said. My parents claimed they'd fallen in love at first sight. I'd never believed them. Now, I wasn't so sure. Loud laughter carried from an apartment window above us. I looked up to follow the sound, hoping Marco couldn't see my face while I worked through my discomfort.

He went on, "These things take time. To build. There's so much to love here. Whenever I see the Eiffel Tower sparkling at night, I feel lighter. I can't believe my luck to be here."

"I haven't seen the Eiffel Tower at night."

He gaped. "You're kidding, right?"

"I haven't been out late much." I considered all the dinners I intended to take myself out to but never had. "And when I have been out, I guess I wasn't paying enough attention." Kid was as distracting as a magician, so unlike Marco. If Kid was all smooth moves, then Marco was false starts. But there was nothing fake about the safety of his presence, the comfort of his conversation.

He pulled out his phone and began to type. Was it a text to Elise?

"If you need to go, you can." I could barely hide the hurt from my voice.

"No, you need to go. But you have to keep your eyes closed the whole time."

I shook my head, uncertain where he was going with this. A second later, a car pulled up beside us.

"Our ride," he said. "Here." He opened the door and slid in after me. "Eyes shut."

39

I'd kept my eyes closed on the drive. After the car dropped us off, Marco cupped his hands over my face and nudged me forward. We walked pressed together, and when we stopped, I felt the bounce of his heart against my back.

"Voilà." He lifted his hands.

I gasped when I saw her, and hadn't been able to tear my gaze away.

We sat close together on the cool ground, our legs tucked side by side, staring up at the Eiffel Tower from the lawn near the base. She glittered gold in her evening dress, a million yellow lights. Around us, boisterous groups shared wine and food, couples cuddled in the glow.

The sounds of the city surrounded us like white noise, creating a bubble of our own.

"She's something else," I said.

"Didn't I tell you? And you might have left Paris without seeing this up close."

"That would have been a terrible mistake."

He shifted, resting back on his hands, and his shoulder touched mine. Without thinking, I fell into him, his arm scooping around my waist, the strength of him supporting me. To think a few hours ago Marine had been schooling me on body language, and now, I was a living tutorial.

"Want to play a kind of game?" I asked. "It'll be like old times."

"Will it involve me following you around on a bicycle hoping you'll talk to me?"

I shoved his shoulder with mine. "Funny."

"I can be."

I glanced up at him, the reflection of the Eiffel Tower's lights sparkling in his eyes. "I'm learning that about you. Here I thought you were a big bore."

"Did you? Well, I teach art history. I'm fairly certain 'big bore' was one of the job requirements."

"Two jokes in a row. Are you showing off?" He didn't look down at me, but his cheekbones lifted, giving away a wide smile. He squeezed me closer to him, and I stuck like Velcro. The breeze picked up, tickling our skin, sweeping my hair past my face. A sweet scent grazed my nose, and I inhaled.

"Chocolate." Marco pointed to a nearby trio of American women passing a flat box among each other, shouting the flavors in delight: "Salted caramel lavender! Honey mint!"

"Okay, in all seriousness, what game did you have in mind?" he asked.

I explained what Marine had taught me about reading people. The mention of other people's bodies naturally called to mind our own, and my skin buzzed with pleasure at all the places where we touched.

"So, those two, there." Marco nodded to a young man and woman who had the vibe of tired travelers, worn jeans, sturdy shoes, Patagonia jackets in bright orange and purple. They peered up at the Eiffel Tower, fingers pointing to the top. "Long-term couple. Been together since early college, recently graduated, and off to see the world together."

"You're cheating. That's basically written all over them. Marine's talking about subtleties, the interplay between one person's body and another's," I explained, pretending to ignore our own subtext as his fingers caressed my side.

"In that case, they both look like they're hankering for a long, hot shower."

"Together or separately, is the question." My cheeks warmed at my own words.

Just then, the couple turned and embraced, the woman discreetly squeezing a handful of her partner's backside.

"Together," Marco and I said in unison, and laughed.

The Patagonia couple wandered away, and the American girls gathered their things to leave. The park was emptying, and with the shift, I suddenly flew back into my brain. I'd forgotten how unexpected this was, me and Marco. How impossible. And yet.

I shivered against him, my nerve endings smoldering. I didn't care why he'd lied. Whatever the reason didn't seem important anymore.

"You're cold," he said.

"I'm not."

He draped his blazer over my shoulders, raising the collar to ward off the chill. His fingers grazed the hairs on the back of my neck, and I shivered again. He wrapped both of his arms around me, and I breathed in the smell of him and the clear evening air, letting my thoughts quiet.

"All things considered, today should have been a bad day," he said. "And I know it takes me a while to warm up. I know I'm not exactly an open book. But I just need to say that today was, is, one of the best I've ever spent in Paris. Or anywhere." He paused, cleared his throat. "Remember how I told you I was curious about you? When we were kids? If only I could go back and tell myself we'd be sitting here, like this."

"Me too."

"Yeah?"

"Yeah."

His words filled me to the brim, but I was light as air. If he wasn't holding me so tightly, I would have floated off the ground.

Pressed beside each other, we talked about more mundane things while the night grew colder. After most of the other people on the grass drifted away, he grabbed my arm, and I found myself staring into his bright eyes.

I longed for the kiss that, by now, I knew wouldn't come. Marco was not the type to kiss a woman on the same day he'd dumped another. We needed to go our own ways and sleep on whatever this was or might be.

"Can I take you to dinner?" he asked. "A real dinner? I'm on campus all day tomorrow and have a faculty dinner in the evening, but the next day."

"My last day."

"Your last day. Let me help you celebrate."

He waited for my ride to arrive and tucked me carefully into the car. My heart puttered happily the whole way back to Paulette's.

It was past midnight when I walked in the door. Eight hours since I'd left Marine. Eight hours with Marco. Eight hours and everything had changed. Paris had changed.

My face hurt from smiling. People say that, and you think it's another figure of speech, but I could attest it was true. I rubbed at my cheeks and inched the door open. Paulette snored faintly in the living room, but it was Lily I wanted to avoid. She'd texted me a half dozen times over the course of the night. Where was I? When was I coming home? Was I avoiding her? I kept my answers as vague as possible, which riled her. She hit me with a fleet of emojis— —then stopped texting. I hoped she'd worn herself out and fallen asleep.

No light shone under the closed bedroom door. Good. I turned the handle with a light touch, but as soon as I stepped inside, Lily rolled over and the whites of her eyes flashed from the bed. I pretended not to see her and changed into my pajamas.

She flopped a few more times before settling. Her voice startled me. "I'm awake. As if you couldn't tell."

I climbed in beside her, desperate to avoid a conversation. All I wanted to do was recount the night from the quiet of my own head.

"Where have you been?"

"I told you, out with Marine."

"Until one in the morning?"

"We had a late dinner." The lies caught in my throat, but the truth was all mine for once, and I didn't want to share with Lily.

She huffed. I had to give her something or she'd keep pushing and picking. "I said I wasn't mad about you and Kid, and I'm not mad. I needed a night to clear my head."

"You should have told me." With her assumption confirmed, she relaxed into the bed. "I talked to Mom. She called a couple of hours ago. She asked where you were. She wanted to hear your voice."

"What did you tell her?"

"The truth. That you were out with a respectable French lady, and I expected you home any minute."

"What did she say?"

"She wondered why I wasn't with you." A pause. I waited for more, staring into the dark of the bedroom. "I told her I felt like staying in."

"Oh." A trickle of guilt slithered through my body as familiar as the blood moving through my veins. I should be looking out for Lily. That's what Mom would say. But Lily was an adult, and for that matter, so was I. "Thanks."

"Iris was with her. She said you got something from your landlord."

"About what?" After Lily showed up in Paris, I'd tasked Iris with checking my mail, watering FiFi. The last I heard from my landlord, he said he'd be getting back to me about when someone would come to fix the light in my kitchen. He'd probably gotten around to doing it.

"She took a pic and emailed it to you." Lily turned away from me and soon I heard her breathing grow heavy with sleep.

I checked my phone to see whatever Iris had sent, but a text notification from Marco distracted me.

Can't wait for dinner 😊

I couldn't wait either, and the thought scared me. Me too, I typed back, but my simple response didn't hint at what bubbled beneath the surface.

What was happening?

A week ago, Marco was a pill I had to swallow to prevent my mom from hounding me, and now I wanted nothing more than to drink him down. Could love be like this? A bang out of nowhere? Love! What was I thinking? I had lost my mind, and it was wonderful and terrible all at once.

Our dinner was the day after tomorrow. In the meantime, I had two days left in Paris. Three weeks had been an eternity when I left San Jose, and now it was almost all behind me. I was going home, but I couldn't waste time thinking about that now.

Two more days.

Two whole days to do as I pleased. It was all I could think of during a blur of sleepless hours with Lily tossing beside me, and so I forgot about Iris's message.

Dear Gladys,

Something wholly unexpected happened. Remember that guy, Kid, I told you about? Forget about him. Let me introduce you instead to Marco Dariano, former boy next door.

Look, I know, for someone who swore off dating, I sure am making the rounds, but this, this, is different.

Marco is serious and staid and a little stuffy. He's also kind and thoughtful, and he has a way of saying the last thing I expect but exactly what I need to hear. He makes me feel safe and seen. As ridiculous as it sounds, I think he may be my Mr. Darcy.

I know so little of love and relationships. Add to that the fact he lives in Paris and I don't, and things get complicated. There's something else, too. He's been lying about his past, and I still don't know why. Okay, fine, I may be too afraid to ask. Only because I want what's between us to be real. Paris has proven to me I can't count on my imagination. How do I know what's the truth and what's fantasy?

Yours,
Fat on Pheromones and Mille Feuilles Felicity

40

My eyes stung with fatigue, but my body burned with energy as I ambled down rue du Vertbois away from Paulette's. I'd hurried out of bed and slipped from the apartment when Lily got up to shower, and Paulette was rousing herself from the couch. After the events of the previous day, I needed a few more minutes to myself.

It was cooler than previous mornings, and Marco's talk of the changing seasons came back to me. I'd like to see Paris in fall. *One day*, I thought, before I could stop myself.

At the end of the street, I turned left and came to a tiny shop coated in peeling brown paint with a green awning that said, without fanfare, BOULANGERIE. Behind the scuffed-up doors was Boulangerie Etienne, the bakery Paulette had recommended on my first day. When I'd passed in previous days, a line stretched beyond the threshold and along the sidewalk, the sweet smell of bread wafting outside whenever anyone went in or out. It was a century old and the best spot for croissants in the Third (the internet said). But the women who worked the counter, the hunched octogenarian owner and her silver-haired daughter, were notoriously unfriendly (also according to the internet).

The early-morning rush had come and gone, no one stood out front, though heads bobbed inside. I opened the door and a gust of warmth wrapped around me, a nutty scent tickling my nose. I inhaled.

Heaven. No one bothered with me, and for a few minutes, I lingered at the pastry case, telling myself I could leave anytime I wanted to.

But adrenaline from last night made me determined. And the smell was Pavlovian. When one of the women behind the counter, the mother, judging by her deep-set wrinkles and shrunken shoulders, caught me in her crosshairs, I willed my feet in place.

"Bonjour."

Her expression didn't change, and she didn't bother to raise her head.

"Trois croissants, s'il vous plait."

Her small eyes jumped to my face and bored into the center of my being. I rubbed the coins in my pocket together. For a painful half second, I debated how much worse it would make things if I repeated myself. Before I could try, she grunted and bagged three croissants from the case. I handed her exact change, which she counted before handing over the bag.

"Merci beaucoup," I said.

The bag was light as air. I might have been carrying a cloud, a hope, a dream. I lifted one of the croissants to my mouth. It shattered into a thousand pieces on the first bite, broken in the best way possible.

I zipped up the circular staircase in Paulette's building, bag of goodies in hand.

When my phone vibrated, I remembered the email from Iris I still hadn't read. But it was Marco at the top of my mind, and I stopped at once on the second-floor landing to check the message, too impatient to wait until I was back in the apartment. A twinge of disappointment when I saw it was from Marine, followed by a quick reality check. What did I expect? Marco and I had been together less than twelve hours ago. He was probably still asleep.

I read Marine's texts, and as I did, wire wound itself around my sternum, my head filled with static.

Marine Desjardins:

Such fun to see you yesterday afternoon. You are a delight!

I apologize again for Elise's attitude. She and Marco had a big argument.

Now they are working through it, which is for the best.

She'd written more, telling me she would send the English translation of her book as soon as she could, but I didn't process the information.

Working through it?

My weight flopped against the staircase balustrade. I wanted to crawl into the bag of croissants, burrow myself into their soft insides. Instead, I buried my head in my hands. Tears didn't come, but my whole being was sore with loss.

I'd let my imagination run wild. I'd fallen for a guy who'd broken up with his girlfriend minutes before. It wasn't unthinkable they'd get back together. Logic didn't make it hurt any less.

I replayed the night in my head. There'd been moments. Now I wasn't sure what they meant. We'd never kissed. And dinner? Dinner could be a kind gesture on my last night, not a date.

But no. I knew better by now.

I'd spent yesterday people-watching with Marine, learning how to sense things people couldn't admit to themselves in the way their shoulders slumped, their foreheads wrinkled, or one body met another. I didn't need a PhD in body language to recognize the way Marco's arm hooked around me, the way he leaned in and didn't move away, the way he looked at me as if he were seeing beyond my thirty-two years to the twelve-year-old he recognized beneath.

I knew enough to trust myself this time.

There *had* been something there. I was certain he felt so, too. Getting back with Elise didn't prove otherwise. But it hurt. I'd let someone in, let hope in, and nothing had changed. Marco had seen me and chose Elise.

The barbed wire inside me caught the soft tissue of my heart, flayed me wide open, and what spilled out wasn't more sadness but anger. Molten-hot anger. Volcanic anger. What an idiot. For once I wasn't just thinking of me. How could he? How dare he!

How could I let him? I gripped the bag of croissants with a tight fist and barged my way up the final three flights of stairs.

❦

Lily opened the door before I could get my key out of the lock.

"You disappeared again," she said.

"I went for provisions." Unable to relax my set jaw, I held up the wrinkled bag in front of my face.

"You're officially avoiding me. Stop pretending you're not."

I was so not in the mood for this conversation.

She followed me to the kitchen. The air was steamy, blue eggs tap-danced inside a pot of bubbling water.

"Bonjour," I said automatically to Paulette, who stood at the counter wearing a pair of men's sweatpants and a lace bralette.

"Morning. How's it going?" She'd taken to our English slang. I hadn't heard her utter a word of French in days.

"Croissants." I tossed the bag onto the table. She didn't budge but placed a hand on her stomach.

"No, thanks. I'm looking after my weight."

"You're *watching* your weight," Lily corrected.

"You're in a bad mood," Paulette said.

My eyes widened, thinking she was talking to me, that she could somehow feel the heat of anger burning through me, but she was turned toward Lily, who said, "No, I'm not."

"Is it because your mother called last night?"

Lily yawned into her palm and shook her head. Mention of Mom's phone call triggered my memory again. I pulled out my phone, swiping quickly away from my messages, and checked my email. There was the latest from Iris. I opened the attachment as Paulette said, "Is it because Kid did not call?"

I stopped what I was doing to watch Lily's reaction, hoping to see her squirm. "Oh my God, no." She crossed her arms defiantly. She stared at the place where her forearms met as if her chin was too heavy to lift.

So, there. I was glad he hadn't called. She could have a taste of her own medicine, as Mom would say any time one sister turned on another. I scanned the document while the two blabbed on around me.

"But you are mad, right?" Paulette asked.

"I'm annoyed that my sister has basically resorted to ignoring me, yes."

"Maybe she has a reason."

"Maybe she should just talk to me like a grown-up."

I finished reading the letter from my landlord and blinked in disbelief. Just when I thought things couldn't get more craptastic. "You've got to be kidding me."

"See," Lily said to Paulette. "See how she is."

"No, not you," I snapped. "My landlord is raising my rent. Twelve percent. Is that possible? That's like . . ." Numbers weren't my forte, and I scrambled my brain trying to do the math in my head. "At least, a few hundred dollars."

"You can afford it, can't you?" Lily asked.

I could, barely. Without the raise that was due to me, I wouldn't be saving money anymore, which meant I'd be that much closer to living with Mom one day. I threw my phone onto the table, knocking the pastries from the mouth of the bag. I could practically hear the croissants deflating like balloons, their perfect, crackling shells going soft in the humid air.

"Hello?" Lily said. "Earth to Rose. Can we talk, please?"

I didn't want to talk to Lily. I didn't want one of my last mornings in Paris to involve hard-boiled eggs and crappy news from home. I didn't want to smile and say to Paulette, "No, no, it's fine. I'll clean up, you use the bathroom first." I didn't want to respond to Marine as if her words hadn't punctured me open. I didn't want Lily pestering me until I assured her she'd done nothing wrong, it was fine she'd followed me to Paris and slept with my fling. Totally fine!

It wasn't fine.

And it was my apartment, mine, at least for two more days according to my rental agreement—if you could still trust something as tenuous as an agreement; I was beginning to wonder. And I'd had one of the best nights of my life, and now everything was ruined.

"Are you even listening? You can't ignore me forever." Lily waved a hand in front of my face like she used to do as a kid. I'd always hated that.

I grabbed her hand, gripping it tight. "You're right."

Her eyebrows arched, giving an impression of smug satisfaction I knew so well. The pastry dough turned to paste in my stomach and the space between my eyes throbbed, but her expression smoothed the way for what I needed to say. "I want you to leave."

"Excuse me?" Laughter crammed behind the faint curl of her lips, ready to spill over the edge at any moment. "Where would you like me to go?"

"Home? A hotel? Kid's bed? Someone's couch?" I pivoted toward Paulette, who I knew was watching, the perfect excuse to practice her English, a great story to tell her friends. "Speaking of couches, I want you to leave, too. This arrangement is no longer working for me, and you're not supposed to be here."

Paulette nodded as if leaving were her idea. She turned off the burner, abandoned the eggs in their water bath, and walked into the living room to pack her things. That, at least, was easier than I thought.

I stared at the steaming pot on the stove. "One egg at a time," Marine had said. I turned to Lily who hadn't so much as moved. Even her expression was the same. I had the urge to slap it right off her face.

"You're so jealous," she said. "You've always been jealous of me, and it's sad. But I can't help the fact that people are drawn to me."

I rolled my eyes. "Do you hear yourself?"

"Sorry for not basing my entire existence on what other people think. Sorry for having *actual* self-confidence. You might want to try it sometime."

"This is me confidently telling you I don't want you here, I never wanted you here, and it's time for you to go. You've crashed my trip and my apartment rental."

"Your imaginary boyfriend, too, right?"

The pounding in my forehead had gone straight up to *Psycho*-level intense, a knife jabbing between my eyes. Exhaustion overcame me. Rolling over and taking it would be so easy. I would apologize, and Lily would gloat for a while, and the fight would be over. Giving up and giving in was like magic, all conflict disappeared. But every time, it broke me a little. At this rate, someday soon, there would be nothing left to give.

I doubled down.

"This has nothing to do with Kid. What this *is* about is you're a selfish, entitled brat. I have two days left here, and I want to do what I want to do."

"Now who's selfish? If Dad could see you . . ." It was the verbal equivalent of both wagging her finger at me and holding my arm until I said "uncle." I thought of all the times I'd asked Lily to do something and she hadn't, all the times I'd done something for her when I hadn't wanted to, all the times she hadn't thanked me, all the times I'd pretended it was okay when it wasn't, all the times I'd bit my tongue when I wanted to yell, all the times I hadn't said what I wanted. If I had to go back home to my life, if it turned out I was destined to be poor Rat Lady Rachel, then I wasn't going to let Lily ruin the forty-eight hours of freedom I had left.

I scrunched my eyes against the pain in my head and waited until my heart fell from my throat. Then I said, with all the strength I could muster, "Get out. Now."

Anger cut through my voice, and Lily's demeanor changed. Her bottom lip trembled, her hands went to her face, and her shoulders slumped.

"I can't leave," she said. "We're in Paris!"

"You got here all on your own, didn't you?"

She sneered, wild eyed. "You're such a bitch."

"Good." For once, I'd out-bitched the bitch. She stomped to the bedroom, and I heard her throwing things around the room. I sat alone in the kitchen until Paulette, unfazed by the turn of events, came to find me.

"I'll head out now. Cool?" she said. Her American affectations had grown on me, and I figured I'd miss her in the singular way you can miss someone you'll never really get to know but wish you had.

"Cool. Thank you again."

"For the record," she said, walking away, "I think it is positive that you are making us go. I waited for you to figure it out."

"Figure what out?" But she was halfway out the front door. "Don't lose the keys!" she shouted behind her. A few minutes later, I followed noise in the entryway and found Lily wedging her legs into her thigh-high boots.

"Why—"

"I couldn't fit them in my bag." She stood, towering over me, her eyes bloodshot. "I can't believe you're doing this."

Neither could I, but despite her red-rimmed eyes, I didn't budge.

41

As soon as Lily left, I went into mild panic mode. I refused to believe the kind of rent increase my landlord expected was legal.

I searched online, my head pulsing with each new realization: my building wasn't subject to San Jose's rent ordinance or California's pending rent-control law, and I was basically at my landlord's mercy, and lucky, I guess, that he wasn't charging me more, since, as he pointed out, my apartment *was* undermarket, which was precisely what made living there doable. Now I'd have to find a new job or a new place to live, and I wasn't sure which would be harder.

The living room seemed hollow without Paulette or her scattered things, but the empty space gave me room to pace. Back and forth, I stomped, furious. If Aidan had given me the promotion, none of this would matter. He and his stupid "new blood is better for everyone" made me want to scream.

The time until my return flight was shrinking. I couldn't let this derail what little time I had left, especially knowing the shit show I was about to go home to. I needed to calm down.

Before I could think myself out of it, I grabbed my new notebook and excavated a pen from the junk drawer in the kitchen. Shoving aside the bag of croissants, I sat down at the kitchen table, hand hovering above the blank page. I glanced at the pot of eggs growing cold on the stove, and heard not Marine's voice, but my own: *Just begin, one word at a time.*

The words came slowly at first, my hand awkward and heavy as I recounted the events of the past twenty-four hours the same way I'd written in my diary as a kid, plodding along with facts: this happened, then that. Soon, the pen spirited across the page, my letters growing looser, loopier, my cramping hand barely able to keep up. Everything I left unsaid to Lily, how I wanted her gone but ached to think of her on her own; and to Marco, my desire for him like a candle lighting in a dark room on a cold night, the flame snuffed by the whiplash of betrayal; and what I couldn't tell my dad, and what I wished I'd said to him before he died, that I loved him, that somehow we would be okay, it all bled with the ink onto the paper.

I wrote every fear, contradiction, hope I could think of, and I wrote it all for me. Just me. For the sheer act of doing it, to see my feelings, all that pent-up analysis and longing, take shape, take up space. As the pages filled, what I wrote seemed to come from someplace otherwise unknowable in me. "The heart," Marine might say, but it felt more like soul, my truest self, distilled into something tangible. The more I wrote, the more I found I had to say, my own words leading me from doubt to knowing, from question to answer.

I wrote until my mind was wrung free of madness, and my headache lifted, my anxious thoughts cleared.

It was past lunch, and my phone showed two voice mails, fourteen texts, and the email from Iris, which I decided I would erase from my mind until I got home.

Surprise, surprise, the voice mails were from my mom, along with a few texts. Another handful from Iris. I didn't bother to listen to the voice mails. It was a pretty sure thing Mom would be livid, demanding I fix the situation with Lily, with a measure of *how dare I abandon my baby sister* thrown in. Her messages followed a similar line of thought. Apparently, Lily was already at the airport, alone and distraught. Was I really going to let her leave like that? Mom wanted to know. Iris's texts read more understandingly—she'd had plenty of her own run-ins with Lily's ugly side—but I didn't want to talk to her either. I wrote back, She'll be fine. See you in a couple of days.

My phone started blowing up on the spot. More from Iris. A call from Mom. Not ignored but politely declined. She would be furious. For once, I didn't care.

Was this how Lily felt all the time? Or had the thrill of defiance worn off for her ages ago?

On to the next texts.

Nothing from Marco, of course. Good. Good riddance.

Kid had reached out, twice. The nerve. First: Can we talk? An hour later: Please. I didn't bother to respond.

I flopped around the apartment in a state of spent emotion before decamping for the tub, where I ate stale croissants and pushed around the bloated crumbs until the water went cold and my fingers turned into prunes. I dressed in the same worn pajama pants and T-shirt I'd been wearing for weeks.

When my phone rang, I answered without thinking.

Kid.

"Doll, you're alive. I've left texts. Where have you been?"

"Nowhere." My head was pain-free but the emotional hangover left my brain stuffed with cotton so thick I had to turn up the volume on my phone. "I'm home. I mean, here, at Paulette's."

"Perfect." Half a second later the doorbell rang.

"Hang on, someone's at the door." I walked into the hallway and pressed the buzzer, my phone dangling in my palm. I heard heavy, quick footsteps on the stairs, like someone was running, and when I peered through the peephole, there was Kid, chest heaving, hair tousled. He might as well have hopped off a stallion or something.

I should have known it was him. If anyone, I thought it might be Lily with a dramatic mea culpa. In my defense, I was groggy. Butter and heartbreak saddled my post-headache brain.

If I'd had one of those accordion screens glamorous women in old movies used to change, I would have ducked behind it to throw on something—anything—else. But all I had were my arms, which I tucked across my braless chest.

"Don't fret." He kissed my cheek. "You're gorgeous." It was the gentlemanly thing to say but a blatant lie. I look disheveled at best, on-the-edge-of-a-breakdown at worst.

"What are you doing here?"

"I told you. You wouldn't respond to my texts."

"I've had a headache." My brain was starting to come to. "Did Lily call?"

"No. Well." He grimaced. "I didn't come because of Lily."

Sure.

"What did she say?"

"Not much. She said you kicked her out. She wouldn't say why."

Which meant he didn't know I'd learned of their little dalliance.

"I don't want to talk about Lily. I've missed you," he said. "Can we sit?"

He gestured toward the living room, and I led him to the couch. He carried a brown-paper-wrapped package the size of a laptop.

"I wanted to give you this." He handed me the package with both hands, carefully, like it was a stick of dynamite. As soon as it was in my hands, he brushed it off, hopping to his feet, cruising the room. "It's nothing, a parting gift, to commemorate our time together."

It didn't seem at all like Kid, but something told me this, whatever *this* was, meant something significant to him.

"Thank you," I said, taken aback.

Kid raised his palm before I could begin tearing the paper. "Not now. Later, when you're alone." His tone was somber, and I stared at the package beneath my fingers, trying to imagine what could have such an extreme effect on Kid. Whatever it was didn't last long. A moment later, he was fussing with his hair again, his smile fixed in place. "I want to take you out to dinner." He took a long look at me and glanced at his watch. "Don't worry. You have plenty of time to shower."

Kid would whisk me off to somewhere amazing. If I let him, he would overwhelm me with attention, his appeal irresistible. He was a charmsicle dipped in a thick coating of charisma. But I couldn't stomach dessert for dinner.

"I can't. Thank you for the gift. You didn't have to."

It wasn't in Kid's nature to take no for an answer. The calculations ran across his face, the effort to convince me minus the value of getting me out of the apartment. In the end, all he said was, "Are you sure?"

"One hundred percent. I need a night in *avec moi*."

"If you change your mind."

"You'll be the first to know."

A minute later, I was alone again. This wasn't how I had intended to spend my second-to-last night in Paris, but *c'est la vie*.

42

The minute Kid was out the door, I tore into the package.

Inside was a sturdy cardboard box no thicker than a bubble-wrapped envelope. I pulled back one of the end flaps to find a picture. A map of Paris, hand-drawn, meticulously detailed. Streets and monuments in black pen, except where the artist took license and broke out a location in color, the scale bigger and more playful. Each rendering gorgeous, a miniature piece of art unto itself: musée d'Orsay, the Louvre, the speakeasy in the Marais with the rum cocktails where Kid and I—could it be? I gasped. There, in the right-hand corner, a funny jagged signature, three letters: Kid.

He'd drawn me a map of Paris, our Paris. I didn't know what to think. The same guy who had the nerve to sleep with my sister had made me one of the nicest gifts I'd ever received.

I was touched. I was flattered. I was confused.

The thing was, for how much the drawing wowed me, how much care Kid had taken, something wasn't right. The gesture was too much. And yes, Kid was over the top, but this was different, like he was overcompensating somehow. Why? Was this an apology? Or something else? I'd seen how he operated. I'd watched how he wooed people.

When he needed something.

So that was it—he needed something from me. Was he after my admiration and compliments? He had them in abundance from anyone who knew him. What then?

My phone vibrated, and I slid the map back into the box.

It was Marco.

Does 8 p.m. work for dinner tomorrow? I'll come round to you.

I couldn't bear to reply. I wanted this day to end. For the first time since arriving in Paris, I just wanted to go home.

❦

I tried to sleep, but I couldn't get comfortable. I was too warm. The bed was too soft, the pillow too thick, the moonlight leaking through the drapes too bright. I flopped and flung myself across the bed. Fatigue pulled at my eyelids, but my thoughts spun.

I gave up on sleep and turned the light back on, pulling the box from Kid into the bed with me so I could ponder the drawing some more, as if it weren't simply a map of Paris but the route to find my way back to the beginning when I'd first arrived, when anything was possible.

He'd drawn the Louvre's glass pyramid like a diamond glinting in the sun, the place where we met marked with the *X* of a treasure map. He'd drawn a hundred teeny-tiny people milling around the place du Carrousel, and I remembered the crowds, the security, the intrigue around the art theft.

I'm not sure what made me look more closely at the box, a gut instinct or my inner workings putting the pieces together. I didn't expect to find anything. If I'd been able to fall asleep, I wouldn't have bothered at all.

There was nothing else inside the slot the map had come out of, but the walls running the length of the box were oddly thick. Using my finger, I found a seam. Each wall wasn't a single piece of cardboard, but two separate pieces pressed together like one. I began to pry one of the two sides apart with my fingernails. Though busting it open with scissors or a kitchen knife would have been easier, something told me to move slowly, gently.

The tiniest off-white edge of paper appeared once I'd made it a half inch down the seam. As I continued to pry, I saw more. It took me forever to open the cardboard enough to pull the paper out. When I did, my breath caught.

A single loose sheet. A sketch, in light, quick scrawl, on thick paper yellowed with age. I didn't need to be an art historian to know I held something old and valuable. I would have guessed, even if I didn't recognize the charcoal drawing; it'd been all over the newspapers. One of the stolen pieces of artwork. I moved with care, setting the delicate paper on the bedside table, my breath a scared bird fluttering in the hollow at the base of my neck. I dug into the cardboard panel supporting the other side of the box, and there, too, I found the seam, and within that seam, two more papers. These I didn't dare remove.

Shock didn't come, but a strange, internal disquiet left me numb.

Was there such a crime as accessory to grand theft? The best thing to do would be to go straight to the police, but I didn't know how to explain any of this. I'd seen enough movies to know things got lost in translation. I could call the museum, but I would encounter the same problem. An anonymous drop-off? But they had security and cameras.

What if I didn't go to the police? What if I didn't go to anyone? What if I put the sketch, Kid's drawing, the box, back the way I found them, packed my bag, and went home? I won't say the idea didn't tempt me, the path of least resistance, play dumb and no one's the wiser. I guessed my bag would be conveniently stolen at the airport on arrival or Kid planned to have someone break into my house after I got back. Either way, knowing Kid, it would be tidy and fairly painless. I'd be his hero.

Only I wouldn't, of course. Kid saw me as naive and weak, the perfect sort of prey. How convenient he found me that day blundering around the Louvre; he must have been on the hunt and thrilled. A wave of nausea clutched my throat. He'd stolen my wallet so he could be the one to give it back to me. He might have taken my phone, too, leaving me completely disoriented so I'd need to rely on him for help. Then he'd charmed me, like he knew he would. And he'd had the gall to sleep with my sister.

Did Lily know?

I banished the thought from my mind. She'd been manipulated, too, in her own way. He'd found both our weak spots and had his way with them. Almost. I suspected she'd been an unexpected diversion for him. A little fun along the way. He hadn't anticipated our falling-out. No wonder he'd come racing to the apartment to set things straight with me.

I thought of all the ways I'd been warned, all the times I knew something wasn't right, and how I went along anyway, anything to keep the status quo. *Don't make a fuss, Rose. Don't have any feelings of your own, you wouldn't want to make someone else uncomfortable.* A tremor rolled over my body because the sad fact was, I still didn't want to get Kid in trouble. It would be so easy not to, if I was willing to risk jail time. If I could live with being a criminal.

I was too panicked to move. The box sat like an accusation in my lap. The sketch I'd removed—I had no idea how much each might be worth, but Paulette had described them as "valuable" with a wide, open stare—sat on the bedside table, exposed to the touch of my greasy fingertips, my middle-of-the-night breath. I weighed my options over and over again. I talked myself into them and out of them one at a time until the churn of morning traffic started past my window.

I watched the sunrise on my last morning in Paris, and I knew what I would do.

43

Marco gave a jolt when he saw me but smiled. He wore running clothes, his brow lined with sweat. "You're a little early, aren't you?" he asked with a grin. I scrambled to my feet.

I'd been waiting in front of his apartment door for an hour with a priceless cardboard box hidden in my bag. I'd come far earlier than appropriate, hoping to catch him off guard. And in case Kid was keeping tabs on me, I figured the earlier the better. The lock on the building door was broken, so when someone came out, I'd slunk up the stairs and posted myself in the hallway until Marco returned.

He reached over me to unlock his door, grazing my shoulder. I flinched. He was so casual, so indifferent to the fact he'd led me on. I hadn't come to confront him. Now I couldn't think of anything else. I wanted him to feel as stupid as I did.

"Coffee?" He walked into the kitchen. The electric kettle churned to life. "You never responded to my text. I was a little worried I might be stood up."

"I don't want coffee," I said. "But you're right, I'm not going to dinner."

A second later, the teapot quieted, and Marco stepped back into the living room.

"Okay. Can I ask why?"

"You said you don't lie. Remember? You said those words to me."

"I know."

"Then why have you been lying to everyone?"

I expected an immediate denial or a litany of petty excuses, but the question left him speechless. He dropped onto the couch and ran his hand through his hair, shaken.

"I've been wondering when you'd ask," he managed. "I'm sorry for pretending I didn't know you, for not explaining sooner. It's complicated."

"Complicated because you've been pretending to be someone you're not, too?"

His face plummeted with the weight of getting caught.

"How did you know?"

"Does it matter? Didn't you know someone would figure it out eventually?"

"I didn't know I'd be running into you. I thought we'd have a glass of wine and never see each other again. Then, out of nowhere, you're at Marine and Alain's. All I could think to do was pretend I didn't know you. I didn't think it would matter. I didn't think we'd—"

"Why lie at all? Why Kid? You meet some random guy auditing your class and decide to steal his life story?"

He stood, wandered over to the room's single window, and leaned against the little table where we'd drank coffee together the last time I'd come here uninvited.

"I didn't meet Kid auditing my class. We've known each other since eighth grade when I started at boarding school. We weren't friends at first, but we weren't not friends. To be honest, I was a bit of a loner." He rolled his shoulders, rubbed his neck. "I'm kidding myself. 'Loser' is a better word. The other boys could sniff out my insecurities from a mile away. They all knew my uncle was the groundskeeper. Unlike the rest of them, I didn't have a family name, a family fortune."

He pulled out one of the chairs and took a seat. Discomfort splintered off him with every breath, but I wouldn't smooth the edges.

"Kid wasn't like the others. He didn't give a toss where I came from. All he cared about was himself and what others thought of him. In other words, how he is today, only less polished. He's picked that up over the years, the master manipulator act." He looked straight into my eyes, then down at his hands. As he fiddled with his fingers, my own clamped together. "Kid was beyond rich. The rumors surrounding his family were endless. How his dad was a megalomaniac with ties to some Russian oligarch, but also the mob, and various super PACs. It doesn't matter, the point is we all knew his dad was scary and powerful. Kid wasn't either of those things. He was small and weak, and a terrible student. The other boys picked on him."

"I can't picture it. Kid as some clueless teenager ridiculed by his peers?"

"Well, it's true. Prince Charming was not always so popular." Bitterness coated his voice, and I wanted to call him out, remind him this wasn't about Kid. He went on before I could.

"We got to know each other in freshman art class. No one cared about the class, except for us. It gave us life. I did pretty well in my other classes, but I was lonely beyond belief. Kid was failing every subject, so art was like the ego boost he needed. I wasn't a standout artist, but I didn't care. I loved getting lost in the technique, a break from my pathetic life. Kid, he was talented, irritatingly so. We spent hours together each week in the studio. Most of the time we didn't talk, it was more like shared camaraderie, and I started to feel less lonely, like I might have a friend. And then . . ." He sighed, lost in thought.

Marco and Kid friends? The idea was almost too absurd to imagine. I tried to picture them, two sad, creative teenage boys searching for something, and it started to sound plausible.

The silence dragged on. "And then, what?" I prompted.

"Then the real bullying began."

"What did they do to you?"

"Not me," he said, a barb in his voice. "At least, not then. I was under the radar enough to escape too much interest, but not Kid. They were cruel. They called him Daddy's Little Big Disappointment, you know, because of his size. They teased him for being gay, even though he wasn't. They put dead animals in his bed, mice and birds. They took turns pissing into his water glass, his shoes."

I swallowed past the bile in my throat. I could tell whatever had happened was worse than he made it out to be. "The teachers didn't do anything?"

"Hazing, they said." He waved a hand in front of his face. "Boys being boys. The thing is, Kid was smarter than those boys. Not academically. People smart. He figured out how to win them over. By the time sophomore year began, he'd started to create his persona, so to speak. He wasn't any better at school, art remained his only academic interest, but now art was part of his shtick. The rich kid bad boy rebelling against the family business. He'll be a doctor, sure, why not? And when med school didn't work, he'd move to Europe to dabble in art and women and whatever else he liked."

Nausea rose from my belly to my throat, where it collected tight as a knot. "What did he do? To win them over?" I asked, though I already had a guess.

"He turned on me. Classic, right? Asserting his dominance by finding the one person weaker than he was. And boy, he made a show of it. He wasn't as obvious as they'd been with him; his cruelty was more insidious. Thank God once he hit alpha male status the harassment stopped. They ignored me after that. Being invisible was better than . . . being the object of Kid's attention."

I came to the table, my bag clutched in my hands, and sat down across from him. He had such a gentle way about him, for one long moment, I wanted to reach out and cup his face. But I remembered Elise and the lies, and I was mad all over again.

"I didn't see him again until he showed up in my class one day, a stupid grin plastered on his face. He stayed after the lecture and I thought, *It's a miracle, he's come to apologize.* I imagined how magnanimous I'd be, but instead, he pretended he didn't know me. Can you believe that? How coincidental he'd show up in *my* class. He asked all these questions about specific artists, their processes, the value of their early sketches, and stared at me dead on, smiling the whole time, as if it was all one big joke to him. He did it just to torture me. I had to stand there and act as if I took him seriously in front of all my students. More of his standard humiliation tactics."

The cardboard box was heavy at my feet. Marco had also been tricked by Kid. I didn't want to tell him, but he'd figure it out for himself soon enough.

"Why tell people you were the guy with the scary, rich dad, and the failed art career?"

He leaned back in his chair. His fidgeting hands had gone still. "I met Elise right before Kid showed up. A couple weeks later, we were talking about our childhoods, getting to know each other, you know?"

In fact, I did know since he and I had done the same thing less than forty-eight hours earlier. I steadied myself for whatever came next.

"It all came tumbling out."

"You wanted to impress her."

His face contorted in anguish. "You have to understand, no one like Elise had ever been interested in me before. I just wanted to be the guy she wanted me to be."

"Oh please." Because Elise was so exceptional. I wanted to rush from the room, but I remained glued to my chair, waiting for the ugly details to purge the lingering feelings I had for him. Marco got to his feet and paced to the kitchen and back again.

"It's pathetic, I know, and I regretted it at once, but she was so taken by the story, I didn't know how to backtrack and admit I'd lied. I figured she'd break up with me soon enough and the problem would go away on its own, but she didn't. Elise is . . . she's complicated."

"Everything's complicated with you."

"Not everything." He shrugged and looked at me. Did he mean us? How he felt about me? "Elise might seem quite hard and cold, but she has another side."

This was too much. I didn't want to hear any more. I'd been such an idiot. Hands trembling, I fumbled with the zipper of my bag.

Marco paused his frantic pacing.

"You're upset," he said. "Let me take you to dinner tonight. I can explain. I can make it up to you."

"You can," I said, placing Kid's gift on the table. "But I don't want dinner."

44

I had less than twenty-four hours to go in Paris when I left Marco's house, my bag a little lighter, my heart that much heavier. After two strange nights of sleep, I walked the streets in a fog, almost like I was living my first day in the city over again. If those first days had been a blur of jet lag and the thrill of a new beginning, now it was all behind me.

I ended up back at Paulette's packing my suitcase as the afternoon faded into evening. I folded and rolled and crammed until my bag, bulging at the seams, zipped shut. When I finished, I was sweating from the work and starving. It was past seven o'clock, close to when I would have been meeting Marco.

Even if I didn't have a date, I refused to sit tonight out. I was hungry, for so much more than dinner, but dinner would have to do.

Before I could talk myself out of it, I opened my bag and riffled through my organized piles until I found my little black dress, wrinkled but who cared? A scalding shower, a swipe of eyeliner, and a dab of lipstick later, I was ready. A gander in the mirror revealed a decent-looking human being, and out I went for my last night on the town.

I had a restaurant in mind. L'Incompetent. The place Diego had recommended back in Cassis, the place no one could get into without a reservation, unless you wanted to wait two hours or more. But hey, I had nowhere to be until my 11:00 a.m. flight home the next day.

My heart pounded while I navigated my way through the Marais. I told myself it was from the effort of hurrying in low heels, but when I arrived in front of L'Incompetent, which from the outside looked like no more than a squat doorway and two narrow, open windows, the urge to turn around washed over me. It would be easy enough to find a falafel shop somewhere. A quick order at the counter and I'd be back out the door.

But I'd made it this far on my own. I wasn't going to give up now. If I humiliated myself, fine. I was allowed to be who I was, even if who I was happened to be a poorly shod American who knew little French.

A dozen or so people milled outside, talking beneath the halo of streetlamps. I'd be waiting awhile. No matter. I smoothed my dress, twisted my hair behind my shoulders, and walked inside.

A step down brought me into a candlelit stone room stuffed with people, a standing-only bar, and two high-top tables that sat eight. In the next room, double the number of seats. It was more cramped cellar than fine-dining restaurant. No doubt its size added to its popularity.

The host had a thin black mustache and clear eyeglass frames. As he scurried between the bar and the kitchen, he thumbed a pair of red tartan suspenders, pausing only to glance at an iPad mounted on the wall. Marine told me sometimes you had to use your body to trick your mind, so I squared my shoulders, lifted my chin, and did my best impression of a confident person.

After a minute, the host acknowledged me and dashed toward the doorway where I stood. *Here goes nothing.* I smiled and clasped my hands together.

"Bonsoir," I said.

"Bonsoir, mademoiselle."

"Je voudrais une table pour une personne, s'il vous plait."

He squinted his left eye and tapped his hands together. I prayed he'd say something I could understand, like "one minute" or "please wait," nothing too lengthy or complex.

He kept squinting and tapping, and I wondered if my basic French phrases were still too terrible to understand. His eyes brightened. "Ah," he said. "You are too lovely to eat alone or wait outside by yourself, so I am deciding what to do with you. But I know. I will seat you there, right now."

His clear words so caught me off guard, it took me a second to realize where he was pointing.

My anxiety grew tenfold.

"There? How?"

A single empty stool stood tucked into the corner against the window at the farthest high-top table surrounded on all sides. At least four people would have to stand midmeal and exit the table in order for me to reach the seat.

"You can crawl under the table or climb through the window." He said this without a hint of irony, and I couldn't hide the shock from creeping onto my face. He chuckled, and I found myself laughing, too. Of all the ways to embarrass myself, this I hadn't imagined.

I supposed I had to pick my poison.

Somehow the window appeared to be more respectable. I stepped back outside and began the awkward process by launching my purse through the window and onto my designated stool. This move attracted the attention of the table, and heads swiveled to watch me maneuver my way inside.

I moved with care, placing one foot onto the window ledge. Next, I'd need to step down and straddle the thing before lifting my other leg over. One of the women at the table recognized my dilemma and offered me her hand. I held her cool palm and brought my other foot onto the ledge so all I had to do was hop down to the boule-size space on the floor where I could stand upright.

A second later, I was on my stool, huffing from the exertion, not much worse for the wear. The table erupted in applause. My eyes darted to my lap, but I couldn't stop smiling.

The host passed down a fizzing glass of crémant blanc, and my tablemates raised their glasses to me.

"Santé," they said, toasting my feat, though they didn't know the half of it.

It was the best glass of bubbles I ever had.

I stayed longer than necessary, lingering over a dessert wine from a chateau I couldn't pronounce and a cheese plate with the gooiest triple-cream of my life, but the host didn't complain, nor the rotating cast of Paris locals and tourists who joined me at the table.

Mom had told me, "Wherever you go, there you are," the phrase delivered like a curse. Now, repeating it to myself, it sounded more like a blessing, that no matter where you went, you could find yourself, if you were willing to look. I meandered home tipsy, proud, and for the first time, truly and madly in love with Paris.

45

My high lasted the walk back to Paulette's.

I knew I'd left the keys before I turned onto rue du Vertbois. I could see them sitting in the little metal dish on the scuffed wooden table by the front door. The impossibly bulky front door with the automatic lock.

"No." This was not how the night was going to end. This was *not* how my trip was going to end.

It was after 10:00 p.m., dark and hushed except for the occasional rush of a passing car. So caught up in my internal suckery spiral, I didn't see the figure heading toward me. I reached the front of the apartment and dumped my purse out onto the sidewalk as one does when they want to look nuts, and then he pounced, *er*, rather, kneeled, right in front of me.

Blood rushed into my limbs, and I jumped back, landing on my tailbone, which had the added effect of me releasing a deep-throated grunt.

"Rose," Marco said, "it's me. Are you hurt?"

"Only my ego."

He clasped my hand to lift me off the ground. Back on my feet, I dusted myself off and attempted to put my purse back together. Adrenaline coursed through me.

"I didn't mean to frighten you. I thought you'd fallen or your bag broke or something. I'm sorry."

"You should be. You can't walk up to a woman alone at night without warning."

He planted his hand on his forehead. "You're right. I didn't think. Forgive me."

I softened a touch. "What are you—"

"Where were you—" he said, speaking over me. "You go first."

"I didn't expect to see you." I pawed through my bag again in search of the keys I knew I wouldn't find. I would have to figure out how to get inside the apartment without letting Paulette know I'd locked myself out again. I needed a miracle.

"I didn't think you'd answer if I called."

"Probably not."

"Were you at dinner?"

"I took myself out."

"Ah." Chastened, his mouth drooped. "I guess no company is better than bad company."

"I *had* company."

With a jerk of his head, he said, "You did?"

"I mean, me. Myself."

"Right. Of course." He bit his bottom lip and blinked hard. He had a kind face for being such a two-timer. "I did the thing we talked about."

My gut churned. Before I'd left his apartment, we'd discussed what Marco would do with the stolen art. We knew it needed to happen fast, before Kid realized I didn't have the package anymore. I hadn't anticipated I'd be seeing Marco so soon. I thought I'd be long gone, stumbling across a link online after the fact. We'd decided I shouldn't know the details.

"Did you . . . ?" I wasn't sure how to ask what I most wanted to know.

When I'd gone to Marco for help returning the sketches, I'd told him he could do what he liked with Kid, it was no matter to me. Now that I knew it'd been done, a bud of worry bloomed within me. I'd given Marco the perfect excuse to enact a kind of bittersweet revenge on Kid. What did it say about him if he'd gone through with it?

"I wanted to. But I didn't know how to do it without implicating you. I figured out another plan. I think it'll be okay. You don't have to worry."

He studied something in his hands.

"What's that?"

His face broke into a lopsided grin. That dimple again, shoot me.

"Your keys. At least, I hope they're yours. I stopped at the wine bar, where we met, after, well, you know, I needed something to take the edge off, and Noelle behind the bar said the girl I was with left them there. I've never been there with Elise, so they must be yours, right?"

He dangled a set of keys in front of me, the first set of keys to Paulette's I'd lost, and before I could stop myself, I launched myself into him, nearly knocking him off his feet. He laughed. "Whoa, there."

Catching myself, I dropped my arms and stepped out of his embrace. He set the keys into my palm.

"Thank you."

He walked a few feet before turning back. "Did you hear my mom is moving south? To the Central Coast."

I hadn't, and the news swept through me like a cold breeze on a wet day. If his mom moved, he and I wouldn't be running into each other, and while I had no plans to see him again, no reason to see him again, it disturbed me that I wouldn't.

The whole thing was too final.

"That's too bad," I said, which wasn't the right thing to say. The words didn't come close to conveying what I felt. Not at all.

He kicked at the ground and flashed me his dimple. "What about us?" he said.

It took me a moment to get the reference, a nod to our conversation at the wine bar, *Casablanca.*

"We'll always have Paris," I responded, happy to be the one playing Bogey, but my heart was a kink in a fragile chain I couldn't unravel. Some things weren't meant to be.

"*Au revoir*, Rose."

"*Au revoir*, Marco."

Alone in the street, I listened to the taps of his feet as he headed down the block. I waited until he turned the corner before I put the key in the lock and passed through the door to Paulette's for the final time.

Dear Gladys,

Home isn't a place. It's a feeling. And it feels like dread.

Everything was supposed to be different by now. The truth? My trip did change me, but not enough to unravel myself from the tethers of my life.

No question this time, Gladys, only a pagan prayer:

Let me remember I will never settle for being somebody's art mule over their muse. Let me keep faith that, sometimes, when it matters, I can say exactly what I mean. Let me never forget Paris.

Love,
Paris School Dropout at the CDG Departures Gate

46

It took me less than forty-eight hours in San Jose to accept I couldn't live without a car.

At the dealership, I missed Dad fiercely, a man who'd never paid full price for anything when he could negotiate for less, who had a shopper's scowl capable of making grown men grovel. So I used everything he taught me about haggling to purchase a gently worn sedan for a price I could manage. I'd nearly given in when the salesman tried to worm me out of an extra $500, but I held my ground, and the car was mine.

Under normal circumstances, a win like that would have been a shot of satisfaction straight to my ego. I'd even managed to wiggle my way out of Sunday brunch that week by blaming jet lag and an imaginary tickle in my throat. I should have been thrilled, but since my arrival back home, I'd lost my bearings. All the things I normally cared about didn't matter. Like my apartment, which Iris had commandeered as wedding central in my absence. I couldn't even muster the indignation to care about my return to Genomix.

All I could do, apparently, was think about Marco. I wanted to shove him from my mind, but his presence had grown roots. Everything reminded me of him. Strip malls and ads for a new exhibition at the Legion of Honor, the exit for our old neighborhood, and the lost-and-found key I'd stolen from Paulette and hung by my own front door.

Not a souvenir so much as a talisman to prove I'd done the thing I never thought I would.

I'd experienced the most beautiful city in the world, fallen for the last guy I expected, and had my heart crushed. It wasn't the trip of a lifetime I'd had in mind, but it was beyond my wildest imagination—and now I was back to work as if none of it had happened.

"Look what the cat dragged in," Aidan said. "Someone decided to grace us with her presence."

He caught me as soon as I reached my desk, before I had a chance to turn on my computer. "You *made* me go on vacation."

"Testy, testy, I see. The French have been rubbing off on you."

I couldn't humor Aidan today. I couldn't. "That's actually a blatant stereotype, like saying all men are misogynists."

Aidan balked. "Well, then." An all-legs blond guy with an Adam's apple the size of a baby's fat fist approached us. "She's back," Aidan said to him. Behind his hand, he stage-whispered, "It appears she's been influenced by the French. She's grumpy." The blond laughed. My jaw tightened.

"Brent, meet your second-in-command, Rose Zadeh," Aidan said. "Rose is your genie in a bottle. Ask and ye shall receive."

"Good to meet you." Brent smiled with all his teeth, aggressively friendly. "Should we plan a little tête-à-tête later today? I'll catch you up on what you've missed."

"Great," I said. "I can catch *you* up on what you've missed the past few years."

Brent's smile vanished. I made it a point to keep mine plastered on my face. Was I joking or not? Even I wasn't sure.

"In the meantime"—Aidan cleared his throat—"I need a thousand words for the newsletter by the end of the day. 'Kay?"

When they left, I settled into my chair and opened my computer. A second later a message from Kara popped up: OMG, Aidan is right for once. You are channeling a snooty Frenchman, and I'm here for it.

Rose: Not snooty. Blunt.

Kara: Whatever. It's a legit look on you. PS: Glad you're back.

Rose: I can't say the same, but I'm happy to see you. I missed you!

Kara: K, tone it down.

Rose: You know you have intimacy issues, don't you?

Kara: Your point?

Rose: nm

I *had* missed Kara, but the second I stepped back into the office, I didn't want to be there. It wasn't the post-vacation blues. It was too much like old times. I was tired of playing nice. I was tired of men making decisions for me. Not just at work, but it was especially blatant here.

I had hundreds of emails in my inbox, dozens from Aidan and Brent. I deleted them all, and a rush of freedom lifted me.

Next, I set to work on Aidan's thousand words. Interrupting me, Kara leaned her hip against my desk, nursing her same to-go mug with the stickers curling at the corners I could draw from memory. Everything about this place was painfully familiar, as if what I recognized wasn't just part of the office but a reflection of me I'd been avoiding.

"I keep waiting for you to spill," Kara said, "but I guess I'll have to bully it out of you. How did it go?"

"Fine. He's okay, I guess. In Aidan's graces already." I didn't bother to check my bitterness.

"Who? Brent?" Kara brushed him aside. "He's a dope. I mean your dream vacation."

"It was . . . weird."

"Weird? I'm gonna need more adjectives."

"Um . . ." Where to begin. Part of me wanted to tell her everything, and another part wanted to say it had all been perfect. Like what Marco had done, fabricating a story that had suited him. Or protected him. Truth was stranger than fiction, but fiction was almost always safer than the truth.

"Okay, fine, let's do it this way," Kara said. "What was your highlight and your lowlight?"

I glanced around to make sure no one was nearby and lowered my voice. "Can you keep a secret? Like to the grave?"

Kara's eyes narrowed, her red lips bled into a wicked grin. "Only one way to find out."

Our conversation started in the stairwell, but eventually, we had to move out of the building where we did a dozen laps around the parking lot. I told Kara everything I could remember about France, starting with the plane ride and Marine. Other than a few understandable exclamations—"That selfish little B!" when I told her Lily slept with Kid, and "Holy shit!" about the hidden artwork—she listened without interruption. In the end, it was Marco she was most hung up on.

"But you really, really like him," she said, trying to understand how I could stand him up for dinner and all but tell him to leave me alone.

"Under false pretenses."

"It sounds like the girlfriend is a controlling, capital-A asshat." Kara's bad language took a sharper dive the farther she went from the office. "She could have manipulated him into a reconciliation he didn't want."

"Whether he wants it or not, I can't date a guy with a girlfriend." This stumped Kara into silence. I continued, not sure whether I was trying to convince her or comfort me. "And he lives in Paris, which is very far away from here."

We stopped by the regular fleet of Priuses and Teslas plugged into the charging stations at the building's entrance. The sight usually sent Kara on a rage tear about privilege begetting more privilege. For once, she was too distracted to care.

"If you can't afford your rent, you'll have to move anyway. Right?"

"I meant to a studio or something, not back to Paris."

"Why not?"

"Because I live here. My family—"

"Oh, do not start with how much they need you because I will cut a bitch."

"Okay, fine. My job," I said, talking over her. "Kind of need one of those."

"Not this one." She swished her hand toward the building.

She wasn't wrong, but . . . I put my hands on her slender shoulders. "Kara, my protective friend, I am not moving to Paris. Anyway, it's a city like any other, you know? I'm not going to be a different person there than I am here. I've learned that the hard way. But you're right, I'm maxed on family. I need boundaries, I get that now, trust me, I do, but I don't know how to"—I mimed building something with my hands—"make them."

Kara tucked her hair behind her ears and shrugged. It was a simple gesture I'd seen her do a hundred times. Just then, it made me realize how grateful I was to be talking with a friend again. A sister could be a friend, but a friend could never be a sister, and this was a wonderful thing about friends. They were chosen and earned.

"Boundaries are simple," Kara said. "Just say no."

I'd said no to Kid and Marco, not in so many words, but still, I could say no here, too. I could try.

"Yes," I said.

After our huddle, Kara and I scurried back into the office, grateful to avoid Aidan's sight. I tried to work on my newsletter piece, struggling with the structure. I didn't know where to start or how to end.

My talk with Kara left me spiraling. I shook my leg beneath my desk, agitated and inexplicably excited all at once. The document sitting open on my computer was still blank, my cursor blinking. I needed to focus.

Dear Gladys, I typed, I hate my job—but I cut myself short.

All these times I'd imagined asking Gladys for help, I was actually asking myself, and I was the only one who could answer. Not Gladys. Not Crazy Rat Lady Aunt Rachel. But me, Rose. The question all along was, *What would Rose do?*

The realization knocked down a barrier deep inside, one I didn't know I'd still been holding up. The light shone in. The newsletter story suddenly came to me. The words assembled themselves on the page, and when the day came to a close, I had a solid article. I typed the kicker, and then, in an act of defiance I didn't know I was capable of until that moment, I deleted the whole thing.

In its place, I wrote, "I quit."

I sent the document to Aidan and cc'd Brent. Effective immediately, I wrote as the subject line.

❦

Kara released an uncharacteristic squeal when I told her about the email I sent to Aidan and Brent.

"Now what?" she demanded as we lingered beside our cars in the office parking lot. "What exactly is phase two of your plan?"

I didn't have a plan. Yet.

I'd bought a car, my rent was going up, and I'd quit my job. My life had never been more adrift, but the experience was more like floating than falling. I needed to act before gravity caught up to me, but I didn't know how.

I scanned the horizon, searching for a sign. The September sky was a slice of ripe plum layered in purple, red, and deep pink. I caught myself admiring the view, wishing Marco could see it, too. He was right. San Jose could be pretty in its own way.

Echoing my thoughts, Kara said, "About this Marco."

I opened my trunk and set down the Genomix-branded canvas tote I'd filled with the contents of my office desk, so she couldn't see the anguish cross my face.

"Have you considered reaching out to him?"

"Again, he has a girlfriend. A very sophisticated, very dainty girlfriend."

An image of Elise gave way to one of Marco. He had such kind, soft eyes, completely wasted on someone like Elise. I wanted to see his face again—I'd debated Google image–searching him—but I wasn't going to humor the possibility. I would not spend any more time recalling the comfort of my head pressed against his shoulder, his warm body tucked next to mine.

I slammed the trunk and crossed to the driver's-side door. "Marco and I aren't happening. Please let it go. I have."

"You didn't really have closure. You didn't get to ask him what the deal was with Fancy French Girlfriend. There might be more to the story. You deserve an explanation. Don't you care what he has to say?"

"Of course I do. I care too much, so I'd rather not know why he chose her over me. If I don't know what happened, then I can pretend it never did."

"That makes no sense," she said, exasperated. "Not knowing something doesn't make it cease to exist."

"Can we not have an existential debate right now?"

"Fine." She raised her hands and backed away. "I get it. And look, for whatever it's worth, I'm proud of you."

I rolled my eyes, but I couldn't help smiling, too.

"Let's get together this weekend and celebrate. We can do something wild. Which for you is like updating your résumé, right?" An amused twinkle danced in her eyes.

"You're not clever." I climbed into my car. "But sure. Saturday, maybe. I have brunch Sunday." I waved and pulled my door shut.

"You can quit brunch, too, you know," Kara hollered through the closed window as I popped my car in reverse.

47

A week without work and already I was ping-ponging off the walls of my crowded, but suddenly lonely, apartment.

I'd cooked my way through every pot and pan in my little kitchen and successfully made an Iranian-American mash-up dessert: a honey-walnut tart crust topped with a layer of sweet saffron cream and end-of-summer stone fruit. I'd even taken care to arrange the plum and apricot slices in perfect concentric rings and glaze the whole thing with fig jelly, so it glistened like gemstones set in a ring. It was pretty enough to sit in the window of a Parisian bakery, but I had no one to share it with. I ate it all myself so I wouldn't have to look at it anymore.

I missed Marco. Which was ridiculous and indulgent and silly and, without a doubt, a terrible use of my time. I didn't know him; we hadn't really begun. I didn't miss *him* but the possibility of us.

I'd tucked away my water-warped Moleskine with its dates and fares, replacing it with my new Paris notebook, finally, a real journal. Numbers had become words. I poured myself into each one, just like Marine had suggested, finding my voice in the runoff. The notebook was almost full.

With my left hand, I held the gold bracelet from my childhood, the gift from Dad's parents. I'd unearthed the cut band from the keepsake box on my bookshelf and kept it by my notebook, my fingers grazing the smooth metal and sharp edge as if it were a lucky charm. If I'd taken it with me, things might have turned out differently. Now it was a reminder of where I'd come from.

I sat writing, dreading my inevitable return to sister-mom brunch, when the buzzer rang, a delivery. It was a thick envelope with Marine's recognizable scrawl on the front. The first flutters of happiness since getting home kicked up within me.

Inside, an advanced reader's copy of her book's English translation, as promised, *Loose Hips Don't Lie: Body Language in Translation*. I clutched the book in my arms while I carried it back to my chair, and a bit of Marine's magic took hold of me again.

She'd stuck a note inside:

> Rose,
> I hope you enjoy my book. It is an honor to share it with you. You are welcome when you return to France. More lessons await!
> Marine

She was certain I'd go back to France, but the longer I was home, Paris drifted further away from my reality as if my trip was nothing but a vivid dream.

Yet, here in my hands, proof.

I checked the clock. Marine's words would have to wait. Anyway, I already knew what she'd deduce about the way I dragged my butt out of the chair and groaned as I stepped out the door.

❦

I was the last to arrive at the diner, and I paused halfway to our table, wondering if Kara was right. Could I walk away? They hadn't noticed me. All three of their heads were bent toward each other, studying something on the table I couldn't see, hands flapping about as they spoke. They reminded me of a kettle of pecking vultures.

That wasn't fair, was it? If they'd picked away at me, it was because I'd let them.

Before I could make up my mind about whether to stay or go, Mom looked up and caught my eye. She roused the others, and each of their faces trained on me as I managed the last few feet to join them.

"There she is," Mom said, her painted lips stretched to their limits. Iris squeezed my hand. Mom raised her arms, and I bent over to embrace her. Beside her, Lily ignored me, her topknot poking from the crown of her head like an apple stem. That's how she was going to be. Okay, fine. I was happy to ignore her, too.

Settling in the empty chair across from her, I made a point not to make eye contact. I hadn't seen Lily since I'd kicked her out of Paulette's. When she got back from Paris, she had enough decency not to go back to my apartment, so Mom's house it was.

I had no desire to speak to her. Not until she apologized.

"We were looking over the seating arrangements." Mom shoved a thick piece of paper toward me. "Guess who got her plus-one." She fiddled with her hair, proud as a peacock.

"Sylvia's coming?" I asked.

"A last hurrah before she moves to Paso Robles. I'm devastated she's going. It's the Central Coast without the coastline. What's the point?" Mom pouted, then her face broke into the mischievous look she got whenever she sniffed a rare piece of fresh gossip. "Now, we really have to discuss Marco . . ."

His name was a blast of freezing air to my heart. I couldn't speak. I sensed Iris's eyes on me. I hadn't told her much. Nevertheless, she'd gleaned some intel from everything I hadn't said, the way sisters do.

"He lives in Paris, and he doesn't appear to have any plans of returning. What's there to discuss?"

"That's not—"

"No, Mom. Stop, please. Whatever you're going to say, I don't want to know."

"Fine. Be that way."

A waiter deposited a glass of water in front of me and promised to return to take our orders. An unhappy fog descended over the table. Lily shook her leg, rattling her chair. Iris pinched her nose. Mom scanned the restaurant as if she were looking for someone. Eventually, she seemed to give up and turned her attention back to us.

She nudged Lily with her arm. "Did you tell Rose about you and Dev?"

Lily scowled at the table and shook her head, bun bobbing.

Mom ignored her clear displeasure and said to me, "They're getting back together."

I wasn't sure how to react. The news was disappointing, but it made sense Lily would go back to him. She'd traipsed across the globe, but nothing had changed. She probably couldn't stand to stay with Mom another minute, and without Dev, she didn't have access to her creature comforts.

"It's great news, isn't it?" Mom said.

"What do you mean?"

Mom was inexplicably pro-Dev. Dev would take care of Lily, and Dad would have liked him, she claimed, as if that mattered or was even true. As if that was enough for someone as strong as Lily languishing on a keg of potential.

"Now I have room for you, silly. How long do you think you'll manage to stay in your place with the rent going up?"

Reeling, I couldn't think of how to respond. I hadn't yet confessed to quitting my job, and I knew when I did, she'd have another reason to guilt me into living with her. A legitimate reason. I'd been so sure when I walked out of Genomix, but surrounded by my family and the familiar sounds of the diner, the world swayed.

What had I done?

I stared beyond Mom and Iris into the parking lot where my shiny new ride glinted in the sunlight. I could get in and go. But where? I'd had all these same thoughts before. Now I knew I couldn't escape my life—and I didn't want to. I wanted to live it, on my terms.

The waiter's reappearance saved me from responding to Mom's question. She haggled over the details of her order. Egg whites only, scrambled soft. Three pieces of bacon, not two, at no extra charge, to make up for the missing yolks. No toast, extra fruit, but skip the melon and banana. She was trying to lose weight for the wedding.

I ordered the french toast, and when the waitress left, Mom said, "I see your travels have given you a real sweet tooth."

I didn't take the bait, adding a hefty lump of sugar to my coffee so I could watch her cringe. When I brought the cup to my mouth, I couldn't drink. I couldn't believe no one had bothered to ask me how my trip had been.

"No Vasilis here today?" I said, more sharply than necessary.

Mom plucked at her hair again. "How would I know?"

"Didn't you mention lunch with him yesterday?" Iris asked.

"I wouldn't call it lunch. He brought salads from here, and we sat at the kitchen counter. We went for a walk."

For the first time, it dawned on me Vasilis might be more than a lighthearted crush or an excuse to pester her the way she did us. Dad loved to walk. He and Mom took miles of laps around the neighborhood after dinner and every Sunday morning. When he died, the habit stopped. If one of us so much as suggested a post-meal constitutional, she feigned a stomachache and retreated to the couch.

I wasn't hurt Mom might move on. I was relieved. If she had a life of her own, maybe she'd give me back mine. Maybe she'd stop using Dad against me. The thought caught me by surprise.

All this time I'd been letting Mom speak for Dad. I'd been trying to prove myself to him—through her.

Mom fluffed her hair and glanced around the room again. She twisted an invisible ring on her wedding finger. "Did you ask Rose about the thing yet?" she said to Iris, clearly trying to change the subject.

My hackles went up. "What thing?"

"Just a wedding favor. I thought you could step in as my day-of coordinator. I trust you more than anyone."

"No." I shook my head, swished my arms as if I could wipe away the request. "No, no. I can't do that."

Iris swiped a hand over her face and her expression transformed into something pinched and hard. "Seriously?" she said. "You won't even consider it?"

Mom's eyes narrowed. "You came back from Paris so high-minded, didn't you? This isn't like you. All this resistance." She leaned back, arms crossed. "Your father never saw his brother after he left Iran. He'd be so devastated by you all here right now. You and Lily fighting. Not supporting Iris during the biggest milestone of her life. She had a migraine for a week while you were traipsing across France."

I looked at Iris, wide-eyed, heart tipping toward my stomach. Before I could speak, she turned on me, too, her lips curling. "I'm fine, so don't worry. You don't have to feel guilty for bailing on me."

"What's that supposed to mean?"

Of course, I was worried about Iris. I'd been trained to study her, making scrupulous mental notes of her ailments should they need to be cross-referenced later for clues. *No, no, last time she had a headache for three days, she was fine for six months before the joint pain came back and only in her fingers.* I'd spent so much of my life looking out for her, occasionally annoyed with her. I could never remember being mad at her, until now. Of all of them, Iris was supposed to be my ally. She was supposed to be the reasonable one.

A thousand conversations flickered inside me, all the things I'd never said. My throat burned.

"My point is," Mom said, unnecessarily loudly, "what did Dad always tell us? Hmm? What did he say?"

"We're all we have," Iris and Lily intoned in unison, sullen as the teenagers they'd once been. We'd heard variations of this speech for a decade.

"All he wanted was for you girls to stay close and stay together."

I could see Iris nod in agreement; Lily still wouldn't look at me. I couldn't take this anymore. If I stayed another minute, I would burst from my skin. I slammed my hands down on the table, jostling the water glasses and silverware, and leaving Mom reaching for her heart.

"The thing is," I said, matching Mom's volume, the fire inside me rushing out, "we don't know what Dad would have wanted. We don't *know* what he would want at all, for us or for him. We don't know how being sick might have changed him. We don't need to live our lives as if . . ." What was I trying to say? "As if his is the one opinion that counts because he's not here to give it."

Mom's mouth fell open. I gasped at my own words. I hadn't planned to say what I did, but now that it was hovering over the table like Dad's specter, I knew it was the truth. Because Dad *was* gone. We could miss him and honor him, without deferring to his life philosophy. *Dad was gone.* It hurt, and I would have changed it if I could, but the fact was, I didn't have to worry about his approval or seek out his permission, and nothing I could do, no extreme example of model behavior, would bring him back.

"It's one thing to insult me," Mom said, "but I can't believe you'd talk about your father that way. He gave up everything for you to have the life you have."

"I'm grateful. You know I am. But my life isn't a bargaining chip. I don't owe it to him."

"You owe him everything."

Tears collected in Mom's eyes. When the dam broke, they trickled down her face, carving rivulets through her makeup.

I could have pushed back. Part of me wanted to leap from the table and scream "No!" at the top of my lungs. *No! No, I do not owe him everything.* Every father gave his child life, and if he could, opportunities, too, but what you made of it was up to you. Dad left Iran against his own parents' wishes to have a better kind of life *for himself.* The freedom to choose and speak up *for himself.* He talked often of family, and yet, he had left his and built another one. Maybe that was his only real option, but what was the point of his sacrifice if not for the next generation to have more options, better ones?

I had spent too long choosing my family over myself, others' expectations over what I wanted, and I was done.

So I could have screamed. Or I could have explained this whirl of revelation with the patience of a preschool teacher, but I knew no matter how I said it, Mom would never really get it, and I didn't need her to. It was enough that I did.

I stood and shoved in my chair.

"Where are you going?" Mom said, aghast. "The food hasn't come yet."

"I've lost my appetite. I don't even like french toast."

I calmly walked out the door of the restaurant and into the parking lot, blood rushing in my head, my heart knocking against my ribs. I didn't look back until I was safely at my car, and when I did, it was Lily's face I saw peering from the window, mouth lifted in a grin, eyebrows raised.

❦

After storming from brunch, I drove straight back to my apartment to stew.

Day-of coordinator? How could they ask for something so huge without a hint of humility? Like I was hired help and not a member of the wedding—a member of the family! I would expect no less from

Mom, but Iris, too? I clenched my hands and stomped past the living room and down the hallway. Iris's wedding supplies taunted me, and I kicked one of the boxes, satisfied to see my foot leave a dent.

In my bedroom, Marine's book waited for me, and the sight of it soothed my blistered soul. I took it to bed to read for an hour, tried to nap, and read for another. Eventually, I abandoned my bed and went to cobble the remaining contents of my fridge into dinner. Afterward, I wound up horizontal on the couch watching *Roman Holiday* for the hundredth time, but right then, I couldn't take the bittersweet ending and had to turn the movie off early. I settled for *Charade* instead. I watched it until my mind was pleasantly blank and my eyes burned with fatigue.

I crawled into bed ready to put the day behind me, but I couldn't resist cracking open Marine's book again. One more chapter would put me to sleep. One more chapter and . . . oh my God.

Working Through It Is the New Breaking Up

My heart soared to my throat. I jolted straight up. *Working through it.* The phrase was etched into my brain.

Marine had texted me exactly that about Marco and Elise after their fight. I thought she meant they were getting back together. What if she'd meant something else? What if she'd meant the complete opposite?

My eyes zipped over the chapter, searching for clarity.

We like to believe when something is over, it's behind us. Finished. Done. A neat package we can tuck into our closet or toss with the trash. But everything we do, everyone we love, stays with us in one form or another. Feelings fade, yes, while experience changes us. And thank goodness. Experience is how we learn. It's how we love better the next time.

I've seen hundreds of clients amid a so-called breakup or divorce. Many mourn the end of a relationship years after the fact. Grief, pain, or general discomfort following the loss of love—even if you initiated its end—is inevitable. I've found if we can reframe this end point into something else, a gain, a path forward, we lessen our struggle. When we stop resisting, grief and pain become momentum propelling you into the next phase of your life. They signify not a closed door but a long hallway with many paths.

When I ask my clients to swap the defeatist terminology of "breaking up" or "divorce" for "working through the end of our relationship," at first, they almost always resist.

"It's so awkward," they tell me. "Forced."

To which I reply, "Yes, and we know change is uncomfortable. Stay with it and see what comes. It's an experiment, nothing more."

Soon, they might begin to talk of their "breakup," catch themselves, and start again using new words. Instead of saying, "It's so hard. I'm so miserable," they say, "It hurts, but we're continuing to work through it." Aha! Now we can begin to focus not on the loss but what is gained.

48

So Marco and Elise hadn't been getting back together? Which meant Marco wasn't in fact a dirtbag?

Merde! I stood up, my insides sloshing like a shaky pour of wine. What had I done?

Walked away from something for no real reason? Or not for the right reason, at least. I could still see Marco in his apartment, the disappointment reddening his cheeks. Or was his face blushing from the shame of his confession?

But I'd lied, too.

I'd been lying for as long as I could remember, pretending I was someone I wasn't. That I wanted things I didn't. Weren't Marco's lies more of the same? If I was wrong about Marco, maybe I was wrong about myself, too. What if my life wasn't destined for a single adventure? What if I gave myself another option?

But what could I do? I was here, and Marco was there. I couldn't go back to Paris.

Could I?

I wasn't thinking straight. Something gnawed at me, a feeling I couldn't shake.

I grabbed my phone from the bedside table and ran the Google search I'd been wanting to do since getting home. The page loaded. I sucked in my breath.

There were few results, but I stared at a black-and-white headshot. I hadn't appreciated how attractive he was, how his chin cleft so perfectly, how his lips were a symmetrical bow. I'd forgotten the way his dark eyebrows lifted with the barest nudge of his forehead, how his eyes smiled when I said something clever, even if his mouth didn't. And that dimple—oof. I had it all wrong. Kid wasn't Gregory Peck. Marco was.

That was beside the point. I needed to know what had happened with the plan I'd set in motion. I'd spent all this time avoiding it, but I couldn't anymore.

I deleted Marco's name and searched for the art theft instead. The page reloaded and the screen filled with articles and pictures of the drawing I'd held in my hands. Farther down the search results, a headline caught my eye: "American Questioned in Theft of Returned Stolen Art from Paris Museum."

The naive part of me wanted to believe the American in question was Kid, but it couldn't be. Itchy with worry, I read through the story.

They hadn't named Marco, thank God, except to describe him as a professor at the American University of Paris. According to the article, the sketches turning up had aroused suspicions: "The professor, described as well respected and mild mannered by colleagues, has unexplained knowledge regarding the reappearance of the works of art. Without further evidence of a direct link to the crime, he has been released from police custody. The investigation remains ongoing."

Marco had said returning the art wouldn't be a problem. That I shouldn't worry. Now I realized how ridiculous that sounded. He'd been trying to protect me. He'd given Kid, his least favorite person in the world, a get-out-of-jail-free card to divert attention from me, and instead, he'd taken the heat.

I began to pace at the foot of my bed.

This was so clearly my fault I could barely breathe. I had to do something. I could turn myself in—tell them all about Kid. But that might make things worse for Marco. I needed to talk to him.

I dialed his number, though it wasn't eight in the morning Paris time. The phone rang and my whole body was a bass drum, one beat after another. One ring, and the line died. I tried again, and once more. I fired off an email, begging him to call me, but who knew when he'd check or if he'd respond. I couldn't have this conversation over email anyway. He had to hear my voice. I had to see him.

I was dizzy as if I'd spun myself in circles like my sisters and I did as kids, arms out, heads back, until we were sick. *Calm down. Breathe.* I sat back on the bed. I tried his number again and again and again, before launching my phone across the room. It landed with a thud on the carpet, and I dipped my head into my hands. I'd made such a mess of things.

It wasn't enough to say what you didn't want. According to Marine, you had to say what you did want. "Your 'why' can be anything. There's no wrong answer. There's only your answer," wrote Gladys.

The answer, *my* answer, felt like it was on the tip of my tongue, if only I could make sense of all the questions swirling in my head.

As soon as I'd seen Marine's text about "working through it," I'd been so desperate not to be taken advantage of, to prove I'd learned to stand up for myself, that I'd put Marco in a terrible position and completely bungled an opportunity to be honest about how I felt.

Marco was only part of it. I'd quit my job, sure, but I was as lost as ever—more so, if you counted the fact that I wouldn't have anywhere to live soon and was on the outs with my entire family. I moaned into my hands.

All this time, I'd been acting as if I were at the mercy of everyone else's desires and opinions, that I didn't get a say in my own life, but that was the excuse I needed to never put myself out there.

I'd been scared forever. Scared to disappoint anyone, scared to be disliked, scared to say no. Scared to say yes. I didn't know how to stop being scared, but I could still be brave. I'd been learning how since the moment I sat down on my flight.

So, fine, what did I want? What was my "why"?

I claimed I wanted my writing to help people. How about starting with myself?

I jerked up, hands falling to the bed. Suddenly, my head was clear, the room had stilled. But I wasn't met with a sense of peace. A great, engulfing urgency rose around me, and my breath came quick and hot.

All at once I knew what I had to do.

I dialed Marine's number.

"Allô?"

"*Bonjour*, Marine."

"Rose, is that you?"

"It's me. I'm sorry to call so early." I tried hard to hide the shake in my voice, but Marine was too attuned.

"Are you okay? It's late in California, yes?"

"I need to ask you something."

An idea had been brewing inside me since my last day at Genomix, before that even, the day Marine and I had our Paris *flânerie*, the details collecting like condensation, one drop then another.

On the phone with Marine, it all spilled out of me. I tripped over my words, still reeling from the news about Marco, but more determined than I'd ever been.

"Sorry. I'm not making any sense. Let me start over. Phew." Deep breath. "Okay, when your book is released, you'll need marketing, won't you?"

"Well—"

"You probably already have something planned. I'm talking about something bigger, more cohesive. Think about an on-the-ground American voice running your social media, communicating with readers, ghostwriting articles for publication in US-based magazines. Your book is just one of your platforms. Why not let them all thrive here the way they do there."

"You're saying . . ." I could tell she was processing my words, but I was too impatient to wait for whatever came next.

"I would be your voice in the US!" The line went quiet. I paced into the living room. I couldn't bear another second. "Marine?"

"Ah, sorry. I am here, thinking." She clucked her tongue. I pictured a trimmed nail tapping her upper lip. "I like your ingenuity."

My heart sank. I girded myself for a rejection, but no—I wouldn't give up so easily. Not this time. It wasn't about the job. I would find another one eventually. Whatever Marine's answer, I deserved this chance, and I wasn't going to pretend I didn't want it.

"I can do this," I said. "My experience is applicable, but more importantly, I care about your work and your message. I've been writing for myself, and I feel like I'm tapping into something that will resonate with your audience. I know if you give me a shot—"

"No, no, no, no, no, no. It's not that. I trust you, but it's a huge undertaking, Rose. There is not much time before the release date, and we would have so much to discuss."

"I'll come there. This would be easier to brainstorm in person, wouldn't it?"

"You just arrived home. I can't ask you to turn around and come back."

"I want to." I did. "That's how much this means to me." Also true. Not the whole story, but true, nonetheless. I opened my laptop. "I'm searching for flights now."

"Are you certain?"

My eyes flicked around my apartment. My chair, my bookshelf, FiFi, all the mismatched things I'd collected to make a nest for myself. But nests were impermanent. Nests were built and rebuilt with each new clutch of eggs, and after birds hatched, they flew.

"I'm sure."

"I will need a few days to speak with my team here, too."

"Perfect. I need time to get things together."

Actually, what I needed to do was disassemble my life.

Dear ~~Gladys~~ Rose,

What the fudge ~~am I~~ are you doing?

Sincerely,
~~Really Out of Her Element Rose~~ Me

Dear Me,

You got this.

Love,
Rose

49

After a brutal full day of travel with a lengthy stopover in New York, I arrived at Charles de Gaulle sick with jet lag. I trawled the newspapers, but it appeared news of the artworks' recovery had faded. For a second, relief calmed my anxiety-spiked heart. No news was good news.

I raced to Marco's, hardly aware of my surroundings. I tried to buzz until remembering the buzzer in his unit wasn't working. I sagged onto the sidewalk, too worn out to care what I looked like, disheveled and bag laden.

When I stopped moving, the reality of what I'd done crashed over me with a smack, and I dropped my face to my knees.

In the week since my conversation with Marine, I'd packed my apartment and put everything I owned in storage, leaving FiFi and my car in Kara's care.

I couldn't stand to explain myself to Mom, so I'd called Iris the day of my flight. We hadn't spoken since brunch, and she'd answered the phone with hesitancy in her voice, shifting quickly into an apology.

"Oh, Rose, I'm so glad you called. I kept wanting to reach out and then panicking you might not want to hear from me. Ben said I should, but I wasn't sure. I know I was a bit of a bridezilla at brunch. You know that isn't me. I'm just stressed out, and Dad's not here. I should never have brought up the coordinator thing. Mom convinced me—" She cut herself off. "I'm not blaming her, it's just sometimes I find myself going along with her because it's easier, you know, than resisting. I kept telling her I was fine, and she just would. Not. Listen. To the point I thought she might make me sick again. From the stress. Here I am getting married, and sometimes I still feel like I'm waiting to grow up, you know?"

"I do."

"Are you still mad? I wouldn't blame you, but I'm sorry."

I heard her hold her exhale over the line, waiting. I closed my eyes and let her apology sink in, searching for the words to respond.

A second passed before I could speak. "I'm not mad. You're not a bridezilla. You're just . . . the middle sister."

We both laughed, and a heap of worry lifted from me. "Look," I said, already peeling back the next layer. "I have to tell you something. I know the timing is bad."

I told her about my impending flight to Paris, the job I'd proposed to Marine. And Marco. How I couldn't reach him, even though I'd kept trying, and how I wanted to track him down and apologize properly.

Iris listened intently. When I was done, she cleared her throat. "You're going all that way to say you're sorry?"

There was a decent chance Marco might want nothing to do with me after the position I'd put him in, but I owed it to myself to tell him how I felt. Whatever he said, I could live with it. I wasn't worried about a happy ending anymore. I wanted a new beginning.

"I'm not trying to win him back," I told Iris.

She sighed. "I support you. But if you so much as miss a minute of the wedding weekend, I will fly to Paris myself and strangle you in your sleep with one of those pretty French-lady neck scarves."

"They don't really wear those, like not any more than the average woman does."

"You know what I mean."

"I'll be back for the rehearsal dinner on Friday. Cross my heart."

"And listen, a few of the out-of-staters replied no, so if you decide . . . I mean, if the opportunity presents itself for you . . . If you want to bring someone, you have my okay."

"Snagging a plus-one for your wedding isn't really part of the grand plan."

But sitting in front of the impenetrable wooden door outside his building, the minutes passing by, my plan didn't seem like much of a plan at all. Showing up on his doorstep? That was the best I could do? What if he wasn't there? He could refuse to see me.

Before I could catastrophize too much, the door opened, an older man barging outside.

"I'm visiting a friend," I blurted, picking up my bags.

I rushed up the stairs, sweat gathering at the base of my neck. I paused at Marco's door, trying to catch my breath. When I stopped panting, I brushed frizzing baby strands from my hairline and knocked, lightly at first, but before long, resorting to the club of my fist.

While I was at it, another nearby door opened and out stepped a towering woman with thick tortoiseshell eyeglasses jabbering at me in French. She punctuated whatever she was saying with thrusts of her pointer finger.

I interrupted her. *"Je ne parle pas français. Anglais?"*

She sized me up, and her nostrils flared as if she should have known better.

"You people don't stop, do you? Leave the poor man alone." She wasn't French, but British. "Anyway, he's not here."

"You know Marco?" I said, before she could slam the door in my face.

"Oh, don't start with me. I've been harassed enough, and I have nothing else to say, except he's a good person and deserves to be left alone."

She stepped back into her apartment.

"Wait. I'm his friend. I've been trying to get ahold of him, but his phone's stopped working. He's not responding to my emails. I just want to know if he's okay."

She squinted and studied me again, but relented with a shake of her head.

"You're not a journalist? You need to tell me if you are."

"I'm not. I swear. I've flown in from California." I pointed to my suitcase.

"I'm sorry to tell you, he's long gone from here. With the amount of badgering he's had to stand, he's changed his phone number. I suspect he's not bothering to check his email."

"Badgering?"

"The journalists. Scores of them. And that's after being questioned—and for the record, released—by the police."

"The robbery," I said, catching up.

"The drawings. They were returned, to him, at his office. It's hardly his fault, is it? The museum is riddled with guards. The criminals would be absolute idiots to go back there."

She was talking to herself more than me.

"Marco wouldn't hurt anyone. He certainly wouldn't *steal* anything. Now he's left his job, his reputation tarnished." Her eyes flickered to the ceiling while she spoke, before landing on mine. "If you're his friend, I don't have to explain to you how ridiculous this whole thing is. It's a miscarriage of justice." Despite her griping, I had the sense she'd fed some choice quotes to the press.

She removed her glasses, wiped them with the hem of her blouse. "It's been a zoo around here. Or had been. The last week has been quieter. The vultures all caught wind he's gone and given up."

"Do you know when he'll be back?"

"Not anytime soon. He moved out."

"Can you give me his contact information?"

She eyed me warily. "I better not," she said, and slammed the door.

Jet lag scratched at the backs of my eyes. My legs jellied beneath me. I forced myself to stay calm and used the last of my waning energy to pull out my phone, call Marine, and drag myself back to the Metro. I had a train to catch.

❦

I collapsed into my seat, pretending not to see the strange stain on the worn fabric cushion. The train was busier than I anticipated, and I was glad to sit on the aisle. I couldn't ogle the countryside from the window, but I didn't care. I had other things on my mind.

There was one person who would undoubtedly know how to reach Marco.

His mother.

But that required asking something of my own mother. The one who I stormed out on a week ago. The one I hadn't called since. The one who would be waiting impatiently for an apology of her own.

I pulled out my phone, checked the time, and unlocked my screen. It was late, very late, but Mom was a night owl. I pictured her propped in her big, all-white bed, her neon-pink eye mask pinned atop her head, rubbing lotion on her legs, a cheesy dating show playing in the background.

As soon as I dialed, the wheels would be set in motion. There would be no going back. Mom would know there was something more between Marco and me than I'd let on. The potential *I told you so*s left me exhausted. But Mom's words were just words. "Sticks and stones may break your bones," she used to tell us.

My screen had gone dark. I tapped it back to life, my finger hovering over Mom's number. It was the only way to reach him. I had to try.

I closed my eyes and pressed to call.

She answered on the second ring. "Rose? What's happened? Are you okay?"

"I'm fine."

"Oh, praise be. My heart is going a million miles an hour. You're not actually back in France, are you? I can't believe you'd leave without telling me."

"I'm about to leave Paris for Provence"—I lowered my voice, aware of the other passengers around me—"but I don't really have time to talk right now. I have a favor—"

"One minute you abandon us at brunch, the next, you fly off to another country . . ."

If there were a better way, I would have hung up right then, pretended the call dropped. If only there were a button to press when you needed more patience, like a morphine drip but instead of pain relief, a sense of not wanting to kill your mother.

"I've never been so shocked and disappointed . . ."

She wouldn't quit. Mom was never going to stop being Mom. I couldn't change her, even if I dared to try. I didn't want to change her. I just wanted her to stop talking and let me speak.

What would Lily do? She wouldn't think twice. She'd shut Mom down in a snap. With a single word.

"Mom." I raised my voice over hers, ignoring the looks tossed in my direction by my neighboring train passengers. "Mom!" I shouted into the phone, drowning out her diatribe. When the line quieted, I spoke again. "I'm calling because I need your help. I need you to be my mother and please help me."

"Be your mother—"

"Will you or will you not help me? Yes or no?"

I heard the rustle of bedding on her end of the line, and I imagined her huffing and puffing in a throne of blankets. When she spoke, her tone had cooled. "I'm listening."

"Thank you." I exhaled. "It's sort of a weird request, or not weird. Unexpected." *Just say it. Spit it out.* "Can you ask Sylvia for Marco's contact info?"

"What was that? I can hardly hear you."

"I said, can you please ask Sylvia—"

"That's what I thought you said. Did you hear what happened then?" Her voice rose a pitch. "How scandalous!"

"I can't talk about this right now. I'm on a train. Will you ask her?"

"Fine. I'll text her first thing in the morning. But you better believe you're going to fill me in."

A voice came over the speaker above me. The train began to rattle.

"Message me as soon as you can." She wouldn't quit, but I could. "Love you." I hung up and turned off my phone.

My head settled against the seat, and I closed my eyes as the train jerked to life.

50

Alain met me in Avignon, smiling and waving from his neglected Citroën.

"Bon," he said, jovial as usual. "You are back. I am glad to see you." He pronounced each word as if there were marbles in his mouth, but his toothy grin spoke loud and clear. I settled in the leather seat and leaned my head back. Despite my train nap, my limbs were made of lead.

Alain turned on the ignition. "Here we go."

By the time we were bouncing along the gravel driveway leading to Marine and Alain's Provençal home, I'd begun to come back to life. Thoughts of Marco hummed at low frequency in my mind, but I wouldn't get information back from Mom for hours. I needed to focus on the main reason I'd returned to France. I sat up straight and stared ahead as if I could finally see my future.

Marine came through the kitchen door waving a thick wooden spoon.

"*Bonjour*, Rose! *Comment vas-tu?*"

"Très bien."

The property enchanted me all over again. I'd been here a few weeks ago, and yet the straw-colored grass and rolling hills of grapevines turning gold and red in the distance told me summer had transformed into fall. The season had changed and so had I. "Oh, Marine," I said, overcome with excitement. "I'm better than good."

"Super!" Marine said, and led me inside.

❦

I showered and joined Marine in the kitchen, where she attended to a wooden cutting board mapped in regions of cheese, terrine, and nuts. The quiet stone room smelled like cinnamon. A deep brown Bundt cake crowned a glass cake stand. My mouth salivated. I'd barely eaten in the past twenty-four hours.

"Are you sure you don't want to rest?" Marine said. "You must be exhausted."

"I slept on the train. And I'm too excited to sleep. I'm overflowing with ideas. There's so much to talk about."

Marine laughed. "*Oui.* But first you must eat. Here." She handed me a baguette so fragrant it tickled my nose, walked me to the table, and placed the cheese board in front of me.

Marine was the wisest woman I knew, the most objective, and I wanted to tell her about Marco. Could she be objective about her daughter's ex-boyfriend when so little time had passed? And what if there was nothing to tell? He'd made a sacrifice for me, and the results had been disastrous. I couldn't blame him if his opinion of me had changed.

I checked the clock above the table. It was four o'clock, only seven in the morning Pacific time. Mom wouldn't get back to me for hours.

Marine chuckled. "You can't wait another minute, can you?" she joked. Nothing got past Marine, not even a glance at the clock.

It was accurate, even if that's not why I was keeping an eye on the time. I nodded, my mouth full of Fourme d'Ambert.

When I could speak, I said, "I'm ready. Beyond ready."

"Then we will get started, but"—she held up her pointer finger—"first, I need to tell you something. I've had time to think since we spoke."

I swallowed hard, and a sharp bite of baguette scraped down my throat. She couldn't be turning down my offer, not when I'd come so far.

"The job you presented to me was not quite right," she continued, the words bringing me back to Aidan's office.

I jumped in before she could go on. "I know you're taking a risk with me. I'm unproven in your domain. But, Marine, I swear to you, I'm all in. I'm going to show both of us I can do this."

"You've misunderstood me." She leaned toward me and placed her hand on mine just as she'd done on the plane when we met. My breathing slowed. "I'm not firing you. I'm promoting you. You see, I realized after we spoke on the phone, we need to have your voice as well. I am proposing we start a digital suggestion box for my readers where they can leave their pressing questions. We will not give advice. We will offer our suggestions. Or rather, you will. This will be your opportunity"—she shrugged—"and I can weigh in. Ah! We can do video conversations on the juiciest ones. Yes, I love this!"

I was completely swept up in her enthusiasm, but the confidence I'd tapped into slowed to a trickle, fighting against a familiar fear. "I've never written anything like that . . ." I trailed off, rejecting the first words that came to mind, that I was unqualified, that I wasn't good enough. I couldn't solve someone else's problems when I'd barely scratched the surface of my own. Gladys's words sprang to mind: *There's no right answer.*

"But I can learn," I nearly shouted.

"Exactly," Marine said with a chuckle. "This is what the best of us do, no? We learn. We empathize. We step falsely and try again."

Alain walked into the room from the patio door, washed his hands at the sink, and stood behind Marine, his hands on her shoulders.

"Mon cœur," she said to him. "I was about to share with Rose my little surprise."

Alain smiled and bobbed his head.

"I—we"—she looked up at Alain—"would love for you to stay here in France."

My mouth fell open. We'd discussed where I would live over the phone and left it that I would work back in the States. Writing articles and running social media didn't require many in-person meetings. Video calls would do. "Marine—"

"If you later move, for instance, to Paris, okay. Until then, please stay with us."

"It's such a kind offer. Too kind." Marine and Alain's level of generosity was new to me. I wasn't used to being on the receiving end of help like this. Gratitude overwhelmed me. I squeezed my toes against my socks to resist refusing at once.

"No such thing," Alain said.

Marine squeezed Alain's palm. "You are quite right." She turned back to me. "It would mean so much to us, and if you are here, we can more easily talk business. Don't you agree?"

"It would be easier without the time difference, but I—"

"Need to think about it. Yes, please do," Marine said. "In the meantime, we have so much to keep us busy for the next few days. Let's finish talking on the terrace."

We abandoned the cheese platter, and I followed her outside where we settled on an outdoor couch, the cushions snug and cool in the shade, and began to brainstorm. Alain brought us each a slice of cake and the spices danced across my palate. *I could get used to this.*

Could I? For real?

The sky was bright and clear. My head was in the clouds. Fat, puffy, cartoon clouds.

After all my fantasizing, all my outlandish dreams about Paris, I didn't know if I could leave my family to move here. But I needed to get out of San Jose. I needed a reason to start over, and it would be so much easier away from home.

51

Our throats dry and scratchy from talking, Marine stood, cake crumbs falling from her pants.

"We'll talk tomorrow," she said. "We must pace ourselves."

The sun dipped low in the sky. A breeze rustled the trees. Evening already. Morning back home. I resisted the urge to run to my room and check my phone until Marine sent me to rest before dinner.

As soon as I was out of her sight, I hurried upstairs, taking the steps two at a time. Sure enough, I had messages from Mom waiting:

Sylvia says he's interviewing for a job on the coast somewhere . . . He's also interviewing at a school in the US!

Will you call him? See the picture with his number.

I KNEW you'd hit it off, didn't I?

Ignoring her self-congratulations, I fumbled to get Marco's number into my phone. My fingers buzzed with anticipation, but before I could send the call, self-doubt grabbed me by the throat and began to squeeze.

I didn't have to call him. I couldn't convince him to like me, and I didn't want to. But I needed to be honest. I wanted us to at least have that if nothing else. No more lies.

A quick thumbprint to my phone and it began to ring.

Prepared to meet his voice mail, my goal was to play it cool, nonchalant—*I'm here in France, let's talk when you can.* So when he answered, the deep timbre of his voice stole mine. A moment of silence passed until he said, "Rose? Is that you?"

"Yes, it's me." A clamor of activity arose in the background, the clanging of dishes. "Is this a bad time? I can call back."

"My mother called to tell me you were looking for me. What are you doing back here?"

News traveled fast in the mother network. I should have known Sylvia would tell him. I couldn't feign casual indifference now, and as the phone warmed my cheek—or was it vice versa?—I didn't want to.

"I came to see you. You weren't at your apartment and your neighbor said—"

"I'm staying with friends in Marseille. Where are you now?"

"In Provence. I'm at Marine and Alain's."

"Oh." Notes of confusion and discomfort contained in a single syllable.

"I can explain. I want to explain."

The line between us buzzed, our shallow breaths the only sound. The background clatter behind Marco had vanished, and I imagined he must have slipped away somewhere more private. If my appearance in France was too much for him, he would politely excuse himself. I couldn't wait for him to say so.

"I want to see you. I need to talk to you in person. Please," I said.

"I can't leave right now. I fly out of Marseille. I'll leave early, and I can meet you on my way to the airport."

This was a shabby compromise, but I couldn't exactly ask Alain for a ride. My heart plunked against my ribs like a metronome while I waited for him to respond.

"No," Marco said. "No. That won't do."

The metronome kicked up a notch. My ear hurt from the pressure of the phone.

"I'll come to you."

His words rushed through me, and I inhaled everything they meant. He wanted to see me.

"Here?" I said. "You can't. What am I supposed to say? 'Hey, Marine, Alain, set an extra plate for dinner. I've invited Elise's ex.' It's one thing to see you. It's another to bring you into their home unannounced."

"After dinner then, late. Meet me at the end of the driveway. I'll text you with my ETA."

The call ended, and I sat frozen, staring at my trembling hands.

52

The branches hanging over the driveway blocked the moonlight. I used my phone's dim flashlight to guide me and tiptoed past the dark house as I made my way to where the long winding driveway met the main road.

At the end of the driveway, the trees thinned, revealing a dome of stars reaching to the heavens, a trillion bursts of light blending like brushstrokes.

The countryside was eerily quiet, not at all like home, and in the silence, I had nothing to do but listen to my own thoughts. I felt as if I was sneaking out of the house to meet the high school boyfriend I never had, as if at any moment Dad would shout my name and drag me back home. Except, unlike in high school, there were no rules I was breaking, just a choice I was making, and the difference was liberating. I shivered with nervous energy.

Right on time, headlights brightened the road and a small blue car stopped beside me. Marco stepped out, wearing a dark sweater over dark, cuffed slacks, and a somber expression I couldn't read in the dim light.

"Hello," he said.

"Hi." He passed next to me, and I thought he might be about to pull me into his arms. Instead, he moved around the other side of the car and opened the passenger door.

"I have the heat on."

He joined me inside a moment later, the door clicking shut behind him.

I'd been such a bundle of nerves to get to this moment, I expected to be shuddering with anxiety. Now that we were beside each other, the licorice smell of Marco's spicy cologne surrounding me, his presence alighting my senses, I was too excited to be scared.

Without thinking, I grabbed his hand from the gear stick. His eyes met mine.

"I didn't realize what would happen when I gave you the artwork to return. I should have, but I was so caught up in how mad I was, at you and Kid and my sister, and all the ways I felt walked on."

He tried to speak, but I interrupted him before he could get a word out. I couldn't stop talking. It was like Mom had invaded my vocal cords.

"But, God, Marco, your reputation, your job. I'm so sorry. 'Sorry' isn't big enough of a word to describe how awful I feel. If I could go back in time—"

He lifted my hand to his mouth and kissed my knuckles, the soft spring of his lips igniting a fire inside me. I could measure the space between us in inches, the windows fogged with our warm exhales.

"I would do it all again," he said, his lips hovering on my skin. "And I owe you an apology for roping you into lying to Marine, for not giving you a proper warning about Kid. I was trying to save my own skin."

Even the word "skin," with his mouth so near, made my body tremble. With some trouble, I pulled my fingers from his grasp and got ahold of myself.

"This is a serious conversation."

"Of course. I'm being very serious." He was still turned toward me, and when I glanced at his face, I could see his eyes searching mine.

"I'm trying to say sorry for all of it," I said. "Not just for what's happened with the artwork, but for misunderstanding. I thought after the day we spent together you had gotten back together with Elise.

Marine said you guys were 'working through it,' and I didn't understand what that meant. It didn't make any sense, to think you didn't feel what I did . . ."

"I felt it."

"You—" Words caught in my throat as his mouth pressed against mine.

Fireworks. Butterflies. A double rainbow. It was all there, in a single kiss, one that didn't end until a flashlight shone down against the driver's-side window.

Marco and I jerked apart as if we'd been splashed with a bucket of ice water. Three short taps on the glass followed. We exchanged a wide-eyed glance, and Marco rolled down the window. He blinked in the light, raising his hand to block the glare.

"Marco?" Marine said, incredulous. "Is that you?"

The light lowered and I could see the outline of Marine's figure, her eyes shining against the night. She moved closer.

"Rose?" Despite the dark, I could see her gaze hop between us. She read us like a cheesy romance novel. Stepping back, she waved the light as a message to step out of the car. I licked my lips, wiping away the taste of Marco, and swallowed a giggle collecting in my throat. I'd never been caught in the act before, any act, and my emotions were as knotted as a soap opera. Embarrassment. Excitement. Electricity. But not guilt. And definitely not regret.

Did Marco feel the same? I couldn't see his face, but his body stiffened like a marionette pulled taut. He opened his car door, and I did, too.

After the warmth of the heater, the air outside nipped at my cheeks and fingers. I rubbed my hands together.

We all began to speak at once, but it was Marco's voice that carried.

"Marine," he said. "I owe you an explanation."

My breath quickened. For him, not me. I knew what he was going to do.

"I lied to you, and Elise. I've known Rose since we were children. We grew up on the same street. Our moms are friends. We hadn't seen each other in years when we came here, but I knew who she was."

Marine's weight shifted to the other hip so she could give me a proper once-over, her thoughts clearly churning. Marco must have sensed this, too, because he said, "I put Rose in a bad position. I pretended I didn't know her, and she was tolerant enough to go along with it."

"I do not understand," Marine said, exasperated. "Why would you do this?"

"Because I'd already lied about my past. I said I was rich, that my dad had disowned me. None of it was true. I was ashamed of who I was. But that's neither here nor there. I pretended I was something I wasn't to impress Elise. It was disrespectful and foolish."

When he finished speaking, Marine was speechless, though from the tilt of her head, I guessed her mind was hard at work. My eyes caught Marco's, and I smiled with all the encouragement I could gather until his face relaxed and his mouth softened. I would have liked to plead for his forgiveness or fill the awkward space with laughter, anything to defuse the tension. But it wasn't for me to decide what Marine felt about Marco. Whatever breach of trust he caused her wasn't mine to patch. I had my own explanations to give.

Marine looked up at the heavens and sighed. "Aye," she said. "Elise will be very upset to learn this."

Marco's shoulders sagged. "As she should. I'll tell her myself. I should never have lied to her. I should have told her sooner."

Marine shook her hand, and the flashlight skipped off the black branches of the trees. "No, no, *this*." She waved the light between me and Marco. "You two together." She clucked her tongue. "She was not so enthusiastic to learn Rose would be working with me. I suspect this news will be harder for her."

I couldn't read the specifics of her face in the dark.

"I shouldn't have gone along with Marco," I said. "It's not who I am."

"I know that, of course, or I wouldn't have hired you. People make mistakes. They do things all the time that don't make sense. Like this, sneaking around my house in the night when you could have brought Marco to the front door."

A thousand caged birds battered their wings inside me, and I waited for her to tell me how disappointed she was. I waited for her mild tone to turn to anger, for her to tell me I was selfish and immature and a disappointment. I steadied myself for the fallout, steeled myself against whatever came next. I would pack my things, get in Marco's car, and we would go I didn't know where. The point was, it would be okay. I would be okay.

But Marine's voice never changed. She only made a curious "humph."

"Does this mean you have decided to stay in France?" she asked.

"Stay?" Marco jerked back as if he'd been pushed. "You wouldn't move, would you?"

He'd been so quiet while Marine spoke, the sound of his voice echoed inside me. In the dark with Marine watching, I couldn't decipher his curiosity. Did he hope I would stay or go?

"I'm not sure."

"Your whole life's in San Jose."

"Only because I haven't had a chance to live anywhere else."

"One must explore before settling down," Marine offered, before commanding us both back to the house.

❦

Marine left us on the landing between the guest rooms.

If this were a movie, if we were teenagers, she might have said something like "no funny business," or tapped her nose conspiratorially. Ever the consummate hostess, even when an uninvited guest arrived in the middle of the night, she simply wished us a good night.

Marco and I stared at each other as she walked away. His eyes were as probing as mine, each of us clearly wondering what the other was thinking. *What now?* The moment she was out of earshot, we both began to splutter awkward pleasantries.

"It's late," Marco said.

"We should get to bed," I said, speaking over him. "Sorry."

"You must be jet-lagged."

My body was a hive of anticipation. My nerves giddy with hope. My skin prickled with desire. "Well, no, actually. I'm wide awake. I don't think I could sleep if I tried."

"Me neither," he confessed.

I gestured to my door. "We could just talk."

"We'd better not." He tugged at the ends of his sleeves. His Adam's apple lifted and fell. "I wouldn't want to . . ."

"Right, definitely not."

"We shouldn't . . ."

"No," I said as I stepped toward him.

"Oh, what the hell," he muttered as our bodies pressed together. His hands gripped my cheeks and ran through my hair, my fingertips mapped the muscles of his back. The heat of him was dizzying, and I could not kiss him hard or deep enough. I had to be closer, skin to skin. I slipped my hands beneath his sweater and he moaned into my mouth.

He pushed me back toward my room, our bodies and lips still searching. When his heavy foot landed on mine, I yelped, and he put his hand over my mouth to quiet me. We giggled as he simultaneously tried to yank his sweater over his head and open the door behind me. The moment was like a scene from a rom-com, but there was nothing pretend—or funny—about the desire burning through me.

When the door opened, we all but fell into the room. Inside, there was no more time for laughter, only to kiss and touch and discover the hidden parts of ourselves.

❦

We hardly slept. Time felt too precious, our need too great. In the wee hours, he kissed me and tiptoed back to the other guest room. I didn't expect to sleep, but I did. Not long, enough to put some distance between myself and the events of the night.

I dressed and slipped outside, the sky crackling and gray. The land rippled behind the house for acres, a tangle of oak and olive trees, high grass and patches of dirt. The morning air was cool. At the pool, I slipped off my shoes and dipped my feet into the tepid water.

I had yearned for Paris to leave her mark on me, make me better, less afraid, but the city didn't change me. The experience had, leaving home. Dad's journey crossed my mind, and I realized with a trickle of discomfort that I hadn't thought of him in days. I hadn't heard his voice when I'd quit my job or booked my ticket back to France or tracked down Marco. Maybe I'd been avoiding him.

Marine wrote that when it comes to love and loss, grief is inevitable. That working through it is the way forward, the momentum you need for whatever comes next. She'd been talking about romantic relationships, but it was true of all kinds of love. It was one thing to say to Mom that I had to let Dad's vision for my life go. It was another to admit it to him, the part of him I carried deep inside me.

The sound of footsteps interrupted my thoughts. My head swiveled to find Marco approaching, painfully handsome as he squinted against the early glare.

Despite last night, or maybe because of last night, we were shy with each other. I watched as he examined his hands, hands that had caressed every inch of my body. Heat rose in my cheeks, and I looked down at the pool, my reflection shimmering.

A few seconds later, he bent over and untied his shoes, pulled his socks from his feet, cuffed his pants, and came to sit by me. Our pale toes danced together in the water.

What a surprise he was to me. What a treat. And to think he'd been there all along.

"You have a big decision to make," he said. "To stay or go."

We hadn't talked last night. It wasn't a time for talking. Now my heart was a rubber band pulled taut between two wants.

"What about you? My mom mentioned something about a school back in the States."

"The moms get around, don't they." He smiled. "It's USF, the University of San Francisco. I haven't interviewed in person yet. Soon. I have more conversations to have here first."

"The university in Marseilles?"

"It's a miracle any school in France would consider me." He leaned back on his hands. "My contacts there think an offer is likely. I would be lucky to get it. I have to go back this morning."

I was *this* close to asking where he thought he'd land, when he'd know. I could delay my answer to Marine, let the direction of Marco's compass guide me. It would be so much easier, so much like a fairy-tale ending, but I'd come too far to let someone else write the next chapter for me. If I wanted my life to be mine, then this is where it began.

"Don't tell me," I found the nerve to say. "Whatever you decide to do, don't tell me until it's a done deal."

He gave me a wounded frown and dropped his hand to his lap. I nudged his foot with mine, the first time we'd touched since last night, and the sensation of his skin against mine sent hairline shocks from the bones in my legs to the top of my head.

"It's just that whatever you say might influence my decision, and I've spent my whole life doing things because it saves me from disappointing someone. I don't want to pretend anymore. Not with you or anyone, especially myself."

"So we each decide for ourselves, and then what? You here and me there?"

The thought left me a little panicky, but the morning light, and the faintly warm breeze, and the water between my toes made me optimistic.

"Maybe," I said. "Maybe not."

A beat passed, but the space didn't require filler. Plenty was there in the moment, a current humming between us. He shielded his face from the sun to see me better. I wanted to trace the lines beside his eyes. Instead, I clutched his free hand in mine and pulled him toward me until our mouths met.

My thighs were pulsing, my lips bruised when we pulled apart. Marco's hands lingered on my face. "I have to be back in Marseilles," he said apologetically.

I nodded.

"All this time, I wondered about you." His hands dropped to mine, but he didn't take his eyes from my face. "I never thought I'd find you on the other side of the world when I was running away from everything I knew."

"You were running away?"

"I thought I was. For a minute. But you can't, can you? Not really. Not when you're running from yourself." His thick eyelashes blinked. "Where do you go from here?"

"Home." I had a wedding to attend.

53

Home. Mom's vanilla-scented apartment twenty minutes from my own. It wasn't where I'd grown up—I'd spent a handful of nights there over the years—and it wasn't where Dad had taken his last breath. Still. Funny how that happened, how home became a feeling, not a place.

Normally, every free space Mom had she covered in knickknacks and found items, birds' nests and seashells, chipped teacups filled with cinnamon sticks, books on tarot cards and herbal remedies. For the rehearsal dinner, we'd carefully tucked these items away and dusted the surfaces, wiped the windows with vinegar and newspaper. All that was left were our family photos on display, and these I washed with a damp rag, lingering over Dad's thirty-year-old face in one. I was older now than he was then, and yet, I remembered him so clearly, how solid he seemed. One day, I would be older than he'd ever had the chance to be. Disoriented with the passing of time, I left the framed pictures and joined Mom in the kitchen where two staff members from Dad's favorite Persian restaurant, Scheherazade, mounded barberry rice and skewers of ground meat *kabab koobideh* on white platters.

"Tables," Mom ordered, handing over two baskets of lavash. It wasn't much, but at least she was speaking to me.

Mom and I had called a truce for the wedding. Not in words, of course. Mom would never admit wrongdoing. For the first time ever, I wasn't about to apologize. We'd come to an unspoken agreement that we would exist harmoniously, at least for the weekend. No digs from her. No pushback from me. Even her cool demeanor toward me warmed once I told her about seeing Marco again.

In the living area, I tucked the baskets onto the two tables and checked the place settings. Laughter came from the patio where Iris and Ben stood hand in hand talking to Ben's parents and their mini wedding party, a single friend for each. The wedding would be big with Ben's extended family and their many mutual friends, but they wanted tonight small. Iris caught my eye and came through the sliding glass doors.

"Is everything ready?" She couldn't wipe the smile off her face, and my own mouth returned in kind.

"As soon as Lily arrives." I shrugged. "All that matters is she's on time tomorrow, I guess."

"I told her the bridal party is gathering an hour earlier than we actually are."

Laughing, I threw my arm around her neck and let my head rest on her shoulder. "You always were the clever sister."

"You're the best of us, Rose," she whispered. She looked at me, her eyes bright and nervous. "Do you think he'd like it?"

"He'd love it. He'd be so happy for you."

"I always knew he wouldn't be here, but it's still weird."

"He's here," I said, and hugged her close.

Lily's voice cut through the moment. "Where my bride bitch at?" she hollered from the entryway. Mom rushed from the kitchen. "Language," she said through gritted teeth, glancing back toward the patio. Iris and I exchanged a smirk.

"What's so funny? What'd I miss?" Lily said, coming to find us. "Are you teasing me?" When we began to laugh and didn't respond, she said, "Seriously. Whatever," and stomped away.

With the meal, we drank cardamom tea from Dad's set of delicate gold-etched glass cups. Mom set out the matching bowl filled with sugar cubes, and we made a show of sucking one between our teeth, like Dad used to most weekend evenings, legs crossed on the floor, holding court with his friends, a ragtag assortment of Russian, Indian, and Pakistani fellow immigrants, coworkers he'd befriended over the years.

In hindsight, it was a marvel, Dad's ability to straddle such a devastating line, the naturalized US citizen begrudgingly accepted into a world made for white men and the displaced person yearning for shared experiences.

I would never know how that felt, all the ways in which that experience shaped someone—the gift he gave me was I didn't have to. But I knew something about having one thing and longing for another. We shared that, Dad and me, and for once, I believed he would understand if I could tell him that I needed to go my own way now.

I considered us gathered in Mom's living room, Lily and Iris fighting over the *tahdig*, Mom forcing another heaping scoop of *ghormeh sabzi* on Ben's father's plate, Ben's mother marveling at the unexpected flavors, and I ached for Dad.

Forgive me, I thought. And I knew he would. Because my body was there, but my heart was one foot out the door. I deserved my own story. I couldn't have made it this far without him, but I had to do this next part, wherever it might lead, by myself.

I could spend the rest of my life fighting against the familiar tide of guilt. But I didn't want to anymore. Because I wasn't guilty; I was curious. I wanted to talk to him, share a conversation like two adults. I wanted to tell him everything I'd learned. Mostly, I wanted him to see me as I was. To know me, adult me. I wanted to hear his words, not imagine what they might be. But I didn't have his words, only mine, and that would have to be enough.

"Rose." Ben's voice pulled me back to the moment. "You have to read my vows and make sure they're good enough."

Lily laughed. "Um, they're supposed to be from *your* heart."

"My heart isn't so hot with words," he said.

More laughter. I saw Ben and Iris exchange a look, one revealing a bone-deep love that unfolded in me like grief and hope all at once. I wanted that, too.

Mom's neat chignon had come loose, and wisps of hair floated as she moved. She grinned, revealing her crooked bottom row, something she didn't do often.

"Isn't it perfect?" She swept her arm across the scene before us. A wide meadow with long tables covered in paper flowers and discarded wineglasses, and a makeshift dance floor beneath a canopy of twinkling lights and paper garlands. Music pumped through the speakers, a DJ's head bobbed against a pair of huge headphones, each of his picks prompting a vocal accompaniment by the guests moving on the dance floor. Iris wriggled in the middle of the crowd, yanking at her strapless dress, throwing her head back in laughter.

"It is," I said.

Mom caught herself and her smile faded. "Besides your father not being here, of course."

"Besides that."

The day had been cool, which, in wine country, meant the evening should have been cold, too cold, but it was like the earth had released its pent-up warmth for the occasion. I hadn't bothered with the sweater I brought, the night air coaxing faint goose bumps from my arms. I wore a pale lemon floor-length Grecian dress, the same as Lily. We were twins, while Iris stunned in ivory. You say these things, "she stunned," but sometimes they're true. This was one of those times. For once, Lily's beauty seemed subdued in comparison.

Mom looked at me closely, then back to the dance floor, returning a free strand of hair to its proper position with the others. *Here we go.* I prepared myself for a verbal flaying. I would turn and walk away. I would—

"We didn't have a reception, your father and me. Only a single person at our ceremony, besides the judge. An old friend of mine. She stood as witness, handed me a bottle of champagne, kissed me on the cheeks, and left us to ourselves."

That wasn't what I'd been expecting. I stayed beside her, waiting to see where this was going.

"Your father didn't have any family around, and my own had cut me off the minute I decided to marry him. I don't like to relive it, but I was so, so lonely. Your father worked two jobs and went to school at night. When I wasn't waitressing, I'd help him with his homework, write his papers. You know, I'd dropped out of school right after we married."

I nodded. I'd known she never finished her degree, but I'd never understood why. It was the early '80s, not the 1950s.

"I thought, what was the point? Even then, your father was so driven, so capable, I knew he was destined for success. I wanted to help people. And my first job was to support Mohammad, at school and at home."

She spoke with pride, and I remembered how she used to bring her energy-healing clients to the house and serve them tea in the kitchen, listening to their life stories, before she brought them into the den, where her massage table sat, and shut the door.

A faraway look passed over her face. "But the loneliness was like poison. I was sick with it. I'm not kidding. I fell asleep at night with my muscles aching. Regret can be like that. You hold it in your body."

She clenched her fists so tight her knuckles bulged, and I thought of everything I'd learned from Marine. What was I still holding on to?

"I didn't know that then, and I kept thinking, *What have I done to my life?*" she continued. "My parents wanted a neat and tidy life for me, and I'd ruined it by falling in love with a brown foreigner, a Muslim one at that." She swished her hand in front of her, as if to brush away an unpleasant thought. "His family wasn't devout, and even back then, he didn't identify as Muslim, but my parents didn't give two hoots about that. They didn't care that I loved him. Your grandparents were real hard you-know-whats.

"Sometimes, in the early days, I wondered if I'd done the right thing, choosing him over them. When he died"—she inhaled sharply—"I knew there would never have been enough time. Even if we'd died minutes apart at ninety-nine, it wouldn't have been enough time."

She paused and I didn't move, didn't so much as raise my glass of water to my lips for fear the tap of the ice against the glass would break her trance. The sounds of the wedding pulsed around us, but Mom and I were on another plane. She was still facing the dance floor, but I knew what she said was meant for me. She never talked about her parents, and she'd never shared these early parts of herself. But it was her longing for her husband I heard clear as the bass beating from the dance floor, and I understood all those comments about what would Dad say, what would Dad do, what would Dad think, were her attempt to keep him alive, give them more time together.

"Oh, Mom."

"You know something else your father used to say? 'Life goes on.'" She paused, and together we watched Iris move across the dance floor. We'd made it through this day, this monumental day, just another day without Dad. "Anyway, when the nausea started, I really thought I was dying. Punishment for disobeying my parents, leaving the church. When I figured out I was pregnant, it was like the sweetest kind of relief. I wasn't dying, and I wasn't lonely anymore." She finally looked at me, and her face was soft, her eyes wet but not teary. "I had you, Rose, and the love was so profound, I knew I'd never be alone again. And you were so pure of heart, such a loving sister and a good girl. Just like I'd been."

She grabbed my hand and held it above her heart, against her warm breast. I squeezed her fingers, her skin and joints as recognizable to me as my own hand.

"I love you no matter what. You know that. But . . ." Of course there was a *but*. I couldn't help laughing. She pursed her lips, and when she spoke again, it was same-old Mom. "It's just this letting fate decide thing with Marco. I can't stand it."

"Not fate. We're deciding, each of us, me and him."

"You know what I think of you living in France. God forbid."

"Your thoughts on the matter are clear, yes."

"Well." Mom tapped at her hair with her fingers, wiped lipstick from the corners of her lips. "I can tell when my opinion isn't appreciated."

I wanted to say that for as long as I lived, I was sure I could guess her opinion without ever having to hear it again. Her thoughts were as intrinsic to me as my own fingerprints.

"I better go find Sylvia," she said, releasing my hand. "Have you seen Lily?"

❀

I combed the dance floor and the dinner tables and the ceremony site, even the parking lot, but I didn't find Lily, or Dev, anywhere. A piece of my hair flew into my face, and I tucked it behind my ear as I changed course, seeking the solitude of the bridal party bathroom to refresh my look. Not that I had anyone to impress. Not without Marco there. Even though I knew it was impossible, I pictured him asleep in the same bed I'd slept in when I'd stayed in his Paris apartment.

For a moment, I wished I could rewind to that night, try again. Or further back, to the night we met in the wine bar. Even if the outcome was the same, I'd give anything to relive the time together knowing what I did now.

I missed him all over again. I might be missing him for a long time. I rested my hands on the bathroom door, wishing the night would end and I could be alone. Whatever the future held for Marco and me was on my terms, but that didn't make the possibility of losing him easier to bear. In some ways, it made it harder.

Flicking on the light in the bathroom, my heart jumped at the sight of Lily perched on the counter between the sink and the wall, her heels abandoned on the floor, phone glowing in her hand. Seeing her all sandwiched against her limbs snagged the softest part inside me. I wanted to hug her, but only nodded hello and went straight to the sink, pulling a tube of lipstick from the hidden pocket in my dress. If Mom and I had come to a truce, Lily and I were at an impasse. I'd crack first, I knew I would, but I wanted something from her. Not an apology, but a sign. A sign that she saw me.

I ran the lipstick along my lips, smacked them together, and looked at her. "What are you doing in here?"

Her body didn't move, but her eyes lifted in my direction. "Hiding."

"From?"

Her eyes drifted back to her phone and a rush of disappointment passed through me. Fine. I guess we'd keep this going awhile longer. Shoving the lipstick back in my pocket, I made to leave, but she reached for me. "Wait." She tapped her mouth. "You have lipstick on your teeth."

Baring my teeth at the mirror, I swiped at the stain. "Thanks."

She leaned back against the mirror and crossed her arms, let her legs dangle. "I'm hiding from Dev."

"Oh?"

"I told him about Kid, and do you know what he said? Nothing. Not a word. He wasn't even jealous."

Now I saw the red lining her wide eyes, the smudge of eyeliner at the corners where it'd been wiped away, the pink tip of her nose. She released a rattled sigh and shook the next round of tears away. "Kid was an asshole, by the way. He never even called me back after I left Paulette's. He ghosted me."

I didn't want to talk about Kid, but I wondered what had become of him. I assumed he was lying low, enjoying the fruits of someone else's labor. But he was nothing to me. Just someone who'd passed through my life. A bystander inadvertently caught in the background of a travel snapshot. "Ghosted" was the right word.

"Kid's not worth crying over."

Her lips curled. "I'm not crying about Kid."

"For the record, I also don't think Dev is worth it."

"I'm not crying about him either."

I cocked my head. "So what, then?"

"The patriarchy."

"Um, okay . . ."

"Because he didn't get to walk her down the aisle, and I shouldn't feel sad about something as stupid as that. Who cares, right? It's an empty, antiquated gesture." She sniffled and her brave face broke. "Except I care. Because of the stupid patriarchy."

"Aw, Lil." I took her free hand in mine and pulled her into me.

She shuddered a bit on my shoulder, then pulled away, dabbing at her eyes. "Does this mean you forgive me?"

"You're really dramatic, you know that?"

She barked a laugh, and I handed her a tissue.

"Can I?" She gestured at my hair, and I nodded. Fussing with the loose strands, she repositioned a pair of bobby pins.

"Don't bother."

"It's for you," she said. "To feel pretty."

After preening me, she leaped down from the counter, pulled a pink rose from a bud vase sitting on a shelf, broke the stem, and nestled the flower in my hair. She smiled. "Our fair Rose."

❦

It was close to ten, and the dance floor was packed. Lily had gone to find Dev. I couldn't see Mom and Sylvia, but Iris and Ben were hand in hand, speaking with some guests from Ben's side, probably starting their farewells. In an hour, the night would be over, and I wasn't sure what would come next, only that it wouldn't look like the life I recognized as my own.

Funny how someone else's wedding could feel like a punctuation mark in your own story. At my dinner seat, I checked my phone, and my heart lit up to see a text from Marco time-stamped five minutes ago: How was the wedding?

Beautiful. What are you doing awake?

Thinking about you, obviously.

😇❤

How's the party?

The night is warm, dancing is happening. Haha.

Nice.

The DJ sounds good.

From what I can hear.

???

Find me.

My eyes searched the venue. Was he really here? My skin tingled with anticipation. I plunged onto the dance floor.

"There you are!" Gleefully, Mom grabbed my arm and dragged me toward her.

"I have to go."

"What do you mean you have to go?"

I wrenched myself from her hold and ignored the sound of my name that followed.

He wasn't on the dance floor. He wasn't on the grass that surrounded the dance floor. He wasn't by the dinner tables. My phone buzzed in my hand: Still waiting.

Quelling a giggle, I bit my lip, afraid I might erupt with excitement. "Where the hell are you, Dariano?" I dashed into the parking lot, and there he was, standing beneath the moonlight. I stopped in my tracks, too overwhelmed to get closer. When he saw me, he drew back his shoulders and smiled. His dark hair was mussed and shining, his shirt unbuttoned at the collar. I liked him best this way, slightly disheveled.

"You look beautiful. Like a woman in a painting."

"What are you doing here? Did you have your interview already?" Last we spoke, he'd told me he would be scheduling his USF interview soon.

He shook his head. "Next week."

In a half dozen strides, he shortened the distance between us. He was close enough to touch, but I didn't reach out. Not until I knew what was happening. Or maybe I was waiting for him to reach for me first.

"You said you were tired of doing things to make everyone else happy. You said you couldn't make a decision based on me."

I nodded, trying hard to sustain my resolve with the anticipation of his touch.

He went on. "I could respect your decision, but I couldn't stop wanting you. And I thought, if she can decide for herself, why can't I?"

He took my hand and brought me close to him. "Because I want to be with you. That's what I choose. You and me."

I let myself be enveloped by him, burrowing my face in his broad chest and the sweet smell of his end-of-day skin. I wanted this so badly. I wanted *him* so badly. Here he was, giving me exactly what I needed.

I pulled my head back so I could look at him. I touched the rough stubble on his face. He hadn't had time to shave today.

"You came all the way here to tell me that?"

"My mom told me where the wedding was."

"Marco Dariano, did you crash a wedding to be with me?"

"I stayed in the parking lot, didn't I?"

I laughed, and we held each other, swaying to the electronic beat of Whitney Houston's "I Wanna Dance with Somebody (Who Loves Me)." His pulse thumped hard and fast against my ear, and my body felt like a cup spilling over. I'd pondered love in Paris, but now I knew. It certainly had been a life-changing trip.

"So"—Marco pulled back to look at me—"what did you decide?"

EPILOGUE

Tucked off rue de Beauce in the Marais, near a hidden parklet, there's a café without a single sign, not so much as an awning. If you peer past the wide windows, you'll see plain brown tables and a wooden chalkboard embellished with curlicue French handwriting nailed against a stone wall.

Beneath the chalkboard, beside the window, sits a table with two chairs, each dusted in a fine coating of chalk, where you can order a tender slice of asparagus quiche and a glass of luscious house white and watch the street as if watching a movie. You can see everyone, but no one can see you.

From this delectable vantage point, I scribbled furious notes into a brand-new Moleskine. Anything that caught my eye, I wrote down. The flick of a wrist as a bicycle messenger passed an envelope at an open door. Cheek pecks between friends, right then left. I was studying, just like Marine had taught me, and everything seemed relevant. Especially the confident approach of a handsome, dark-haired man with a grin just for me.

Marco entered the café and strode to our table, kissing my forehead before he sat down in the chair beside me.

"Working again," he said. "And on our honeymoon. Your mother would be very disappointed."

He nuzzled my neck, kissing my hairline. My Mr. Uptight was far more than meets the eye, his stiff demeanor hiding a physical passion I hadn't tired of. I squirmed playfully against his touch. He'd begun to grow a sort of scraggly beard during our three-week-long honeymoon, and I liked the way it tickled my face.

We'd gone to Sicily and Rome with a stop in Provence to see Marine and Alain, then on to Paris for a few nights so we could have the city to ourselves for the first time. We'd gotten lunch with Paulette the day before, and even Elise had invited us to join her at the gallery to see its latest opening. She was curt, as always, and made a backhanded compliment about how fortunate I was to have sat next to her mom on the plane those years ago, but otherwise, she was decent in her way. I still didn't understand why Marco had fallen for her. As he reminded me, "Sometimes you learn the hard way what you want and who you are."

Despite how great our trip had been, and how much I didn't want to leave Paris, I couldn't wait to get back to San Francisco.

I missed our potted plants and our cramped apartment where we fought over whose turn it was to cook. I missed my baby nephew, Iris and Ben's son, Moh, short for Mohammad after Dad—and I sort of, but would never admit under oath, missed Lily's unannounced visits to our home. But I especially missed work.

My and Marine's Suggestion Box had become a huge success back home, and now *Real Simple* wanted us to write a monthly column. Marine had tasked me with the job, and my first article was due in a week.

"Did you finish?" he asked.

"Actually, I've just begun."

He cocked his head and gave me a curious look. I didn't bother to explain what I meant, that I was at the start of something big, the rest of my life. Instead, I said, "I'm ready."

Marco gave me his left hand, his gold wedding ring smooth between my fingers. Except for the line of small diamonds that dotted mine, our wedding bands were identical. We'd repurposed my childhood bracelet, the gold melted down and crafted into matching rings, the shine no less brilliant for the passing years, the miles the precious metal had traveled. When I looked down at my finger, I heard Dad's voice, "I trust you," and it rang through me like a song.

Fin

ACKNOWLEDGMENTS

I began this book in secret during the throes of postpartum loneliness. As I write this note, I find I'm surrounded by support and encouragement, which goes to show, Marine is right: open yourself up, and the world responds in kind.

Speaking of, readers make the world a more beautiful place. Thank you, dear reader, for taking a chance on a debut novel. It means everything to me.

Sincerest gratitude to my lovely agent, Nephele Tempest, and the Knight Agency. Nephele, your publishing experience, editorial wisdom, and constant patience have made all the difference. Thank you for seeing something in Rose—and me—worth representing.

Melissa Valentine, thank you for making this book a reality and for making me an author. I'll forever be grateful. Tegan Tigani, you are equal parts compassionate and insightful. Thank you for helping me take Rose's story that much deeper. To the rest of the Lake Union crew—production manager Jen Bentham, cover designer Kimberly Glyder, editorial team members Heather Rodino, Tara Whitaker, and Sarah Vostok—without you this book wouldn't exist or look nearly so good. Your behind-the-scenes support is invaluable.

To my imitable writing group, Hadley Leggett, Amy Neff, and Erin Quinn-Kong, I'm still writing because of you and so lucky not to go it alone.

Lidija Hilje, you were the ideal first editor for Rose and her story. Your thoughtful feedback made my vision stronger in every way. Thank you for believing in the power of a "quiet" protagonist.

Thomas Juin saved me from some embarrassing French faux pas and helped add veracity to the section of the book that takes place in France. (Any outstanding mistakes are entirely my own.)

The Women's Fiction Writers Association provided an abundance of resources, support, and community during the entire writing process and beyond.

Molly Colbert, I'm glad we're on this journey together. We've sure come a long way since our query writing class!

And to my coven of incredible IRL women friends, some of you read draft pages of this book or my first attempt at a novel-length work, while others always encouraged my love of reading and writing. But all of you let me talk about this book ad nauseum and believed me when I said I would be a published author one day. Extra-special thanks to Melissa Buron, Melissa Butcher, Rachael Cardoza, Heather Sarge, and Abbey Teague.

My family has provided immeasurable support—as well as ample fodder for future books. Just kidding! (Or am I?) My dad, Yousef, not only graciously lent some of the true facts of his life to Rose's dad but he also answered every little question I lobbed his way. My mom, Sharon, reminded me time and again how stubborn (read: tenacious) I am and provided countless hours of childcare to let me finish a first draft during my first year of motherhood. Thank you to my stepparents, siblings, and in-laws as well. I love you all. And endless gratitude to my auntie Diana and grandma Joan, who nurtured my love of books and storytelling when I was a little girl.

Finally, my husband, Mike: none of this would be possible without your love and unwavering faith in me. Remember twenty years ago when you told me I'd be better off with someone else? Boy, were you wrong! Thanks for our beautiful life together and the realization of so many dreams. Yours forever.

BOOK CLUB QUESTIONS

For your book club meeting, might we suggest sampling some Persian food and/or champagne? *In lieu of the typical cheese board, consider a more Persian-inspired spread: Place a square of feta on a serving platter surrounded by walnuts, halved radishes, flatbread, and whole sprigs of parsley, dill, and mint.*

Discussion starters for LA VIE, ACCORDING TO ROSE

1. Which character did you identify with most? Were any of the Zadeh family dynamics familiar?
2. In chapter 2, Rose has been planning to watch *Roman Holiday* to celebrate finishing the rebranding. Have you seen the movie? How do its themes of duty, escape, and romance relate to the book? Do you think Marco is the Gregory Peck to Rose's Audrey Hepburn?
3. Rose and her family often think of what Rose's dad would have said or how he might have reacted. How does this keep him alive through memory, and how might they be misinterpreting or misunderstanding what he might have wanted?

4. Did you find Rose's disillusionment with Paris surprising or relatable? How does her relationship to the city change throughout the book?
5. About Gladys's advice, Rose says, "Reading her answers was like putting on a pair of prescription glasses you didn't know you needed. In the moment, everything in front of you became clear and sharp, and you wondered how you'd ever managed without them." Have you found a source of self-help advice or a mentor that makes you feel this way?
6. In her letter, Gladys writes, "It's not too late. Full stop. I'll repeat that: It's. Not. Too. Late. It's never too late." How does Rose show this? Have you ever created self-imposed deadlines or internalized societal ones? Is this a message you needed to hear?
7. Have you found your "why"? If not, are you searching? If so, what is it?
8. When Rose learns the truth about Kid, she describes herself as "the perfect sort of prey." What qualities do you think made Rose particularly vulnerable to Kid's nefarious intentions? In what ways do you think Kid tested Rose's loyalty? Is he a villain in this story? Why or why not?
9. During their last meeting in Provence, Marco admits to Rose that, like her, he was also running away from himself when he came to Paris. In what ways do Marco's and Rose's journeys run parallel? In what ways do they differ?
10. In chapter 12, Rose tries to articulate her father's version of the American Dream. Do you have a version of it? Did your parents?
11. After her evening at the Eiffel Tower with Marco, Rose writes to Gladys: "How do I know what's the truth and what's fantasy?" How do you think Rose figures this out? How do you?

ABOUT THE AUTHOR

Photo © 2022 Nazaneen Ganji

Lauren Parvizi worked for more than a decade as a digital editor and writer, including a stint as a love and relationship columnist, and earned an MFA from San Francisco State University. She lives in the San Francisco Bay Area with her husband and son. Find her online at https://laurenparvizi.com.